FUTURE SHOCK

The doorway of the control room slid open again, and Napoleon entered. He stood for a moment, as if expecting a fanfare of greeting, and then approached the forward screen, gazing intently at it.

"It's a sun, contained within an artificially made hollow ball, several million kilometers across," Oishi said, looking over at the emperor. Oishi could understand the confusion; he had stood dumbstruck as well when the reality of what the future was had settled into his heart and his mind.

"This it is hundreds of times bigger than our Earth," Napoleon whispered.

Aldin looked over at him and smiled. "Billions of times. Made long before us by an unknown race we call the First Travelers. Everything of Human hands is insignificant to what they created."

"Go straight into it," Vush the Overseer said, pointing toward the open section . . .

By William R. Forstchen
Published by Ballantine Books:

The Ice Prophet Trilogy:
ICE PROPHET
THE FLAME UPON THE ICE
A DARKNESS UPON THE ICE

INTO THE SEA OF STARS

The Gamester Wars:
Book One: THE ALEXANDRIAN RING
Book Two: THE ASSASSIN GAMBIT
Book Three: THE NAPOLEON WAGER

Book Three of
THE GAMESTER WARS

The Napoleon Wager

William R. Forstchen

DEL REY

A Del Rey Book
BALLANTINE BOOKS • NEW YORK

For Professor Gunther Rothenberg and Rick Schneid, Napoleonic Historians, who hopefully just might be amused that their hero was finally given a second chance.

A Del Rey Book
Published by Ballantine Books

Copyright © 1993 by William R. Forstchen

All rights reserved under International and Pan-American Copyright Conventions. Published in the United States of America by Ballantine Books, a division of Random House, Inc., New York, and simultaneously in Canada by Random House of Canada Limited, Toronto.

Library of Congress Catalog Card Number: 92-97249

ISBN 0-345-33584-8

Manufactured in the United States of America

First Edition: April 1993

PROLOGUE

To: Retuna and the Third Circle of Overseers
From: Vush of the Fourth Circle of Overseers
Subject: THE GAME!

The companions of my circle agree to your wager as stated. Results from the first "hit" as the lesser beings call it shall be in shortly. We accept your bid in support of the Larice circle against that of the Gablona circle. Odds of 3.7 to 1 for success by Gablona for the first attack agreed.

Actually, I'm rather hoping that the intended strike is unsuccessful, since failure will mean an extended "war game" that will certainly prove to be most entertaining. Retuna, do remember, my brother, that things like this on the commlink or in writing could be most embarrassing. As Overseers we do have our reputations to think of, so in the future I suggest that all such transactions be, as the lesser creatures say, "face-to-face." Peace be with all of you.

Island of St. Helena, Longwood Estate, midnight, June 18, 1820.

It had been a bad day. Today of all days always was a bad

day. Memories of other dates, though now bittersweet in their recollection, did not hold quite the same poignancy. How different it all would have been if that damnable Grouchy had only marched to the sound of the guns. It was all so clear now. He should have put Ney in charge of covering the Prussian advance. Ney would have come; Ney never would have lost the Prussians the way Grouchy did. And Grouchy in Ney's place. Grouchy never would have charged so recklessly and thus wasted his cavalry.

Five years ago today—Waterloo.

The thought stirred him from a restless half sleep, the thought, and the intermittent pain. He listened to the night noises. He could hear the sentry in the small garden outside the window. A pause in the footsteps, a muffled conversation—damned English, just the sound of the words grated. There was a soft laugh—a girl's. Of course, she was resisting slightly, honor demanded it. Not much could happen, the sergeant of the guard would be by soon, but the rendezvous would be arranged for later.

He smiled a bit, he could not begrudge a soldier that, even if he was a damned Englander.

He lay still on the sweat-soaked sheets. This day was hard; it was always hard to remember, especially when there were so many others. They marched in order through his still so well-organized mind—June 14, 1800 . . . Marengo. The legend of Marengo. The victory march composed to commemorate it, he could hear it again, the slow steady beat, then the wild flourish of trumpets. His fingers tapped out the beat, his eyes shining with pleasure and with tears.

Austerlitz, December 2, 1805. The crown jewel of his score of triumphs. The victory march of Marengo playing as the Imperial Guard advanced, storming the central heights. The thundering cannonade. And the cheers.

They echoed even here. How they had thundered in the cold winter air, how they echoed now in the stillness of the night. And only he could hear.

Prometheus.

Someone had called him that. "They will chain him to a rock, where the memories of his glory will gnaw and torment him."

It will never come again.

He closed his eyes, as if to hide himself from his own tears.

"I lost the battle of Marengo at five o'clock, and I won it back again at seven."

He remembered that, shouting it once when his staff started to panic. But when? Borodino, Leipzig, Waterloo? It must have been Waterloo.

He couldn't remember. It was true; he had heard it whispered and he knew it to be true. He was slipping away. He had already felt the first faint tugging of mortality even in the glory of Austerlitz. A flash memory of what he had learned in school, how when a Roman general was given a triumph an old man would stand behind him on a chariot and whisper, "Remember, all glory is fleeting."

As the sun set upon Austerlitz he remembered that, knowing somehow there would never be a moment like that ever again.

And then knowing that the body was betraying him. The weight coming to his slender frame, the eyes failing, and now the pain in his stomach, the ghastly pain.

"All glory is fleeting."

Is it really ending like this? he wondered. A shabby little room, chained to this rock. He listened in the silence as if half expecting a voice to reply with a denial, a warrior angel to appear to take him from this. And again to be arrayed, to walk the field late at night, to sit with his old grumblers about the fire and speak of the coming victory that he had dreamed and they would now create. Was this the final fate?

The victory march of Marengo. He could hear it again, and the cheering, the guard cheering on the fields of so many victories, *vive l'empereur, vive l'empereur*. Oh, but one more time, he prayed weakly, grant me just one more time, one final chance to know it all yet again, and he wept in lonely bitter silence.

CHAPTER 1

"COME, COME, MY FRIEND, THERE'S NOTHING TO WORRY ABOUT out here," Bukha Taug said expansively, while pouring himself another round of sparkling peach wine.

Leaning back in his floating pleasure couch, the richest Gaf of the entire Magellanic Cloud glided back over to Aldin Larice's side.

"This pleasure world of yours is on the far side of the Cloud," Bukha continued. "Why, hell, it's not even on the charts."

Lifting his feeding tube out of his meal trough, the Xsarn politely wiped off the last traces of excrement, a Xsarn's primary diet, before leaning over Aldin.

"Bukha's right you know," the Xsarn stated, his fetid breath washing over Aldin in a nauseating wave. "Corbin Gablona is most likely dead by now if those reports we heard are true. Anyone crazy enough to go back down to the Al'Shiga Hole most likely would be killed on sight. Those bastards are still in a frenzy over what you and your friends did . . ."

Aldin Larice, former gaming vasba, and now the richest Human in all the Cloud, held his hand up for the Xsarn to stop.

4

The insectoid was almost as bad as his old friend Yaroslav when it came to talking about the last game.

Aldin looked around at his companions.

Mari—he really didn't even want to think of her—was off in the forward section. It amazed him how adversity could throw two people together, maybe even make a couple out of them for a while. But once affluence came, it would all hit the old legendary fan. He suspected that down deep she was far happier as a barmaid in that godforsaken watering place back on the Hole, where knocking a customer out to roll them, or—though he did not like to think about it, either—to drag him upstairs for some entertainment, was considered high sport. Now, as his wife, the second one that is, she was the richest Human female in history and her tastes had run amok. Before going into hiding for health reasons, she had actually gone so far as to buy an entire planet, because she felt it looked kind of pretty. The damn place was absolutely worthless, but the real estate dealer still convinced her to sign on the dotted line.

It's not that I really don't like her, he thought dryly, at least as far as a wife goes. The first one, a blood relative of Corbin Gablona's, had been a raging nightmare. It's just that Mari's nagging tone sounded at times like screeching chalk on slate. They had stayed loyal to each other, though; he felt anything else was rather tasteless. In some ways she was still a rather good friend, but as for the rest, he would rather not.

A muffled sob sounded in the far corner of the room. Zergh, his partner of nearly thirty years of gaming, was mindlessly watching an old holo of a Gavarnian operatic romance, *Trag and Vula* for what he guessed must be the fifteenth or twentieth time. Twenty hours of nonstop Gavarnian singing, chest thumping, and the obligatory death arias while committing double suicide at the end was enough to turn any non-Gaf stomach. The more sentimental, the more gaudy, the better for a Gaf. Their love of incredibly bad wine, polka-dotted and striped polyesters, and gooey operas made him wonder how such a race had ever had the reputation of also being some of the most fearless warriors that had ever lived.

Zergh, as if sensing that he was being watched, looked over his shoulder at Aldin, motioning him to come over. The Gaf's facial hair was soaked with tears. Aldin smiled, waving his hand in refusal. The last thing he wanted was for the seven-foot-tall Gaf to use his shoulder as a sobbing towel. At least he wasn't as overblown in his sentimentality as some Gafs. There'd been a craze a generation or so back to hang oneself at the end of the thirty hour epic *The Return of Trag and Vula*. Zergh had threatened to do so on several occasions but had never seriously followed through on it, always arranging for someone to stop him at the last minute.

"Damn opera," the Xsarn snapped. "Zergh, they really aren't killing themselves. The poison turns out to be a bad batch sent by the matchmaker to fake their deaths so he won't get sued. That way we can endure that damned sequel."

Zergh looked over darkly at the Xsarn, who thought better than to continue.

Thirty years with Zergh; where had it gone? Aldin wondered. In their younger days they had climbed to the top as the best damn vasbas—arrangers of staged battles on primitive worlds and holo simulations for the wealthy class of Kohs. He figured he'd retire on that, getting at least a reasonable annuity from his old employer, Corbin Gablona. Damned time travel had changed all of that. Before, all he had to do was design computer simulations of famous ancient battles, or occasionally sneak down to a primitive planet, evaluate a war, calculate the odds, and then arrange the betting on results. But no, Corbin and the others, when they first realized time travel was possible, immediately latched onto the idea of going back into history to retrieve famous generals and bring them forward for entertainment and high-stakes bets on the results.

Gaming on warfare had been the one true passion of the ruling class, the Kohs. It had helped them to relieve the tedium of the unrelenting peace that the Overseers had imposed upon all who lived in the Magellanic Cloud. Everyone, down deep, had to admit that the Overseers were right, when several millennia back they had suddenly appeared and stopped a bitter three-way war between Gafs, Xsarns, and Humans who were locked in a deadly struggle for control of the Magellanic Cloud. The instantaneous and total destruction of half a dozen planets by the Overseers had convinced everyone that the mysterious beings held the upper hand and were not to be trifled with.

Gradually, a certain camaraderie had developed between the oligarchy of barons of the three species; they were linked together by education, class, good breeding, and their mutual love for gambling on nearly anything, especially warfare, either simulated or real conflicts that were occurring on primitive planets not observed by the Overseers. Occasionally, the Overseers would get word of a "little wager" and break the affair up, hauling a couple of the miscreants caught in their net into a reeducation school for peaceful coexistence.

A good vasba, a true gaming master, knew how to arrange a damn good simulation, or pick out a primitive war under a tight security net beyond the paternalistic eyes of the peaceful-coexistence police. Such an individual had to have a gutter-breed cunning and an instinct for survival mixed with a superb historical education and a certain panache that would enable him to float in the erudite world of the richest beings in history. It had been a comfortable living, until they all started breaking the rules that had kept their little sporting ventures lucrative and entertaining for thousands of years.

Alexander the Great had started all of this. Honor had prevented Aldin from screwing over the legendary Macedonian when Corbin and some others wanted to fix the game and see Alexander take the fall. The fact that Aldin had cleaned up with a couple of side bets, which was rather illegal for vasbas, really wasn't all that serious. But when the extent of his game fixing, and Corbin's cheating, had become apparent, he had suddenly found himself on the legendary Hole, fighting for his life.

He looked over at Bukha Taug, who was lounging on a hover chair, consuming yet another bottle of sickly sweet peach-flavored champagne. Bukha's plan had been beautiful, and he had at least been honest. They had cleaned everyone's clocks, coming out of the Hole game as the two richest beings who had ever lived, owning damn near 53 percent of all the corporate assets of the entire Greater Magellanic Cloud.

And for what?

Frankly, he was bored silly. The problem with living on the edge was that you got rather used to the view. It made life exciting, it made a goal. But when you finally achieved the goal, then what?

Aldin Larice sighed almost melodramatically and looked around at his companions. They were good company to be sure, true friends who had been close to him when he was nothing but a vasba. But was this the end of it all? he wondered. I'm rich, I can buy anything I want—and I'm sick to death with boredom. I no longer have any dreams, he realized sadly, no dreams but uselessly spinning out whatever time I've got left, indulging myself, and doing absolutely nothing that can offer a challenge. He remembered childhood, when for months he had anticipated a gift for his birthday. The gift, which must have cost his mother most of a week's wages, was beautiful—but even at nine he had come to learn that the anticipation was far better than the owning.

And besides, though he found it hard to believe, he was now one of the most hated men who ever lived. Just because he and Bukha had legal title to all those assets didn't really mean that they actually controlled them. The other Kohs had worked on every stratagem possible to tie things up, and in the process had triggered the worst economic depression in centuries, worse even than when the Bank of Hovde had announced that a ship bearing nearly all the precious specie of the Cloud had had a little accident—and run into a sun. It was a hoax, a little attempt to manipulate the precious-metals market, but it still had upset things for twenty years or so, until the ship was finally found in the bank president's private hangar.

This was far worse. The other Kohs had used their commlink systems and holo news stations, with their damnable "we're on the people's side" reporters, to paint him as a greedy exploiter of the common folk. The assassination attempts had finally gotten outright monotonous.

As for Corbin? Frankly, Aldin couldn't care less at this point. His old, obese employer had, of course, welshed on the 1.1 billion katars owed in payment for freeing him from the Al'Shiga's impaling stick. He expected that, and anyhow it was kind of hard to collect on a deal made under such duress. But there was vengeance in the old man's heart, of that he was sure. The reports that Corbin had actually gone back to the Hole were disturbing. The damned fool was too shrewd to go there just for the fun of it.

"If he's playing with Shiga," the Xsarn said, looking over at Aldin as if he had read his thoughts, "they'll cut his heart out and use it for a game of catch."

"My dear bloated cousin isn't that stupid."

Aldin looked up as Tia, his niece, came into the room, Oishi Kurosawa by her side. The young woman came around and playfully mussed Aldin's thinning hair.

Aldin took her hand and looked up at her. She at least had gained something out of all their adventures. After three years with Oishi, the transformation from spoiled little rich girl to charming lady with a regal bearing had been remarkable. Oishi looked down at Aldin and tried to force a smile of agreement.

"We've got a new security report," Oishi said quietly.

The others groaned. The old leader of the forty-seven ronin was now one of Aldin's most trusted friends and in charge of all security. The samurai had adjusted and mastered with glee all the changes from eighteenth-century Japan to life in the Cloud a millennium later.

"About what this time?" Bukha asked.

"A 'we are there for you' news report. Corbin Gablona's body is a seedbed for a Shiga rotting-man mushroom," the Xsarn said lazily, while motioning for a servobot to bring in his dessert.

"It's about Corbin Gablona, at least in that you are right," Oishi said, his features now fixed with purposeful intent.

The Xsarn shook his head. Oishi of late was considered by some as a bit too cautious, ready to see a plot behind every flutter of a window curtain.

"This was supposed to be a vacation, a chance to relax," Aldin Larice said quietly, attempting to suppress a retch as the Xsarn slipped his feeding tube back into his foul dinner and slurped up the rest of his meal.

To relax, simply to relax, was something Aldin found to be completely impossible.

Trying to stabilize the crisis had been a nonstop job for Aldin, consuming every moment from wake-up to collapse eighteen hours later.

Yet each effort seemed to disappear into a myriad of Byzantine laws governing trade, unyielding bureaucracies, and what he knew was outright obstruction. It never ceased to amaze him that some low-level government or corporate servant, who simply could not be fired, could derail desperately needed reform simply because a form wasn't filled out in just the proper way.

Dozens of planets that had once been major hubs of trade were now ghost worlds, visited only by an occasional tramp cruiser. Billions were out of work, tens of billions more living on the edge waiting for the good times of corporate expansion and trade to return.

He was the richest Human in the Cloud, yet he didn't dare show his face anywhere in public for fear it would be shot off. So this was living, he thought sadly, pouring himself another drink. Richest man in the Cloud, and before he could even bathe someone had to sweep the shower head for detonators and check the water for trace poisons.

"Come on Aldin, don't worry, be happy," Mari said, settling down by Aldin's side.

The group groaned inwardly at her inane comment.

"Well she is right in a way," the Xsarn said. "I dare say this is the finest pleasure world I've ever seen. Climate is perfect, it's isolated, and this palace has every convenience ever created."

Aldin looked around the feasting room and nodded glumly. The Xsarn was right. The palace had been created half a millennium ago by a Gaf Koh and forgotten until Aldin had picked it up and poured in several tens of millions to reactivate the servobots who maintained it and replaced the thousands of panes of glass. The main palace covered several acres, all the exterior walls made of glass that at the touch of a button could become transparent to reveal the tropical splendor outside. Every possible amusement imaginable was here, from holo theaters and floating beds to fountains of wine and giant whirlpool baths big enough to hold several hundred at a time. There were even half a hundred of the highly illegal Human and Gaf replicated bots in the gaming room in the basement to make the casino a little more lively and also to add a little sense of happy crowds enjoying themselves. They also kept several of the samurai and Gaf bodyguards happy in other ways with their remarkable talent to perform actions that were more than a bit impossible for a real female. Since one could not really call it cheating, Aldin did find a couple of the experiences to be rather interesting, though he would be far too embarrassed to let anyone know he had tried them out. One of the female bots went scampering by outside, a samurai bodyguard in happy pursuit. The bot jumped into the ocean, the samurai, peeling off his robes, jumped in after her, and they drifted away with the current.

The oceans were luxuriously warm and free of anything that might view a swimmer as dinner, but since Aldin had never learned to swim they really held no real interest for him. The mountains were covered in a lush growth of trees that had such a bizarre combination of reds and purples that they almost looked like a Gaf clothing designer had taken inspiration from them. Best of all, the planet was completely uninhabited, covered by orbital surveillance and thus about as totally secure as any place could ever be.

It was here, with his retinue of a dozen friends and samurai and Gaf bodyguards, where he was supposed to feel safe and conduct business.

Bukha rolled his eyes.

"Damn it, Aldin, unwind a bit. This is supposed to be a vacation. The hell with that latest report."

"It is only when we stop worrying that we become vulnerable," Oishi replied quietly. His tone was as always polite and courtly, but there was an insistence to it that indicated he would not be ignored.

Oishi stepped rigidly before the group. Though Aldin had argued with him for years about etiquette, Oishi still insisted upon bowing to Aldin before addressing him in public.

"An intelligence operative reported the sighting of Corbin Gablona, five former Kohs, and a hundred or more dark-robed men on the world of Parduki seven days ago. Sogio personally arrived with the report less than an hour ago."

"Which means it took that report almost as many days to reach us here, since the operative decided to hand deliver this rather than put it out on the open wave," Tia said quietly, coming up to stand by her husband's side.

"One of the dark robes purchased a derelict cargo ship on its last legs and the group left. As they pulled out, Sogio decided it was best to come straight here with the information."

"So what?" the Xsarn replied. "We know that madman Gablona is out there on the edges of the Cloud, but the bastard is powerless. Too bad the Shiga didn't get him, if that's where he really went."

"It's just that a conversation was overheard between two of the dark robes. Sogio said that one of his operatives reported that they are definitely members of the Al'Shiga cult."

That statement caused a moment of stunned silence.

"That bastard," Bukha roared, coming to his feet. "Are you telling me Corbin somehow managed to spring some of those madmen off the Hole?"

Oishi nodded.

The room was quiet.

"That's not good at all," Zergh said darkly, tearing himself away from the holo. Wiping the tears from his eyes, he switched off the opera, while Vula was shrieking out the famed, "My lover's eyes are like pools of sparkling muscatel." The contra-soprano's voice warbled in midcry and faded away, much to everyone's silent relief.

Zergh came over to settle by Aldin's side, the floating leisure chair struggling to readjust to the added weight.

"He's violating one of the major laws of the Cloud by bringing those buggers off planet. Second, he must be as insane as the psych profiles indicate. Playing with the Shiga is like lying down in a nest of snakes. They're hopping mad for revenge after the loss of their Skyhook tower."

"So he must have made some arrangement with them," Aldin said evenly. "I won't be seeing any amateurs coming after me anymore. Those people scare me to death."

Absentmindedly he rubbed the part of his body where the Shiga's impaling stick had left it's mark. That little escapade still had him waking up screaming. At least on the Hole, he knew where they were—which was all around him. Out here the Shiga could blend in, and wait. Heaven only knew how many of the crazy religious fanatics Corbin was now sprinkling around the Cloud.

"You haven't told us everything yet," Aldin said, looking up at his self-appointed protector, able to see at a glance that Oishi was more than a little worried.

"The rest is that our informant also overheard one of them joking how 'the fat one' had cooked up a surprise but he was disappointed that there wouldn't be any blood on the Shiga knives as a result."

"Is that it?" the Xsarn asked.

Oishi nodded in reply.

"So why all the fuss?" the Xsarn growled. "You had me so worried there for a moment that you almost put me off my food.

"All your samurai are here, and I dare say are rather bored and would like a little fight," the Xsarn said, as if talking about a betting game rather than his own shell being in jeopardy. "And I bet those dumb Gaf berserkers would love a little amusement time with the Shiga."

The Xsarn looked up to see that Basak, the leader of the "dumb Gaf Berserkers," was standing in the doorway, listening in on the conversation. The warrior said nothing, but a simple hand gesture that implied the cracking open of a Xsarn carapace was sufficient for the Xsarn to mumble an overhasty apology and turn his attention to his steamy dessert.

"So let him kick around out there," Bukha interjected, chuckling over the Xsarn's discomfort. "We can always arrange an accident."

"I suggest we evacuate this place at once," Oishi said coldly.

More than a few of Aldin's entourage groaned.

"What in heavens for? We just got here yesterday," the Xsarn replied defiantly.

"There is no such thing as perfect security. Security can be reasonably attained by always altering your schedule. Thousands of sources must know that our group would be away for thirty days, and from some of our purchases it wouldn't take much to figure out it's to some tropical resort, a very private resort. Conversations are overheard, schedules checked. I suspect Corbin might know where you are at this very moment. Thus we must leave within the hour. I've already alerted the ship's computer to start powering up."

Wearily, Aldin got to his feet.

"You heard him, let's get the hell out of this dump. Besides, this place was starting to get on my nerves."

He looked around the group. These were his friends, the only ones that really counted in this universe. Those he had made after his rise to Koh status didn't count. For Aldin had quickly discovered two things about wealth. The first was that anyone who put value in it was a self-deluded fool. The second was that the friendships of wealth were about as reliable as the promises of a suma drone looking for a vial.

"Well, I for one am staying," the Xsarn Prime announced. "I've heard a lot about the fine cuisine produced by the local carnivores, and I fully intend to sample it first."

"You do seem to be overreacting a bit, my courageous husband," Mari announced, coming in behind Basak, her voice edged with disdain.

"If you want to stay, that's your business," Aldin replied sharply.

"I'll run away with you," Mari snapped, "but I thought I'd married a man, not a boob afraid of his own shadow."

With a sniff of disdain, Mari stalked out of the room. Aldin's

friends looked the other way to spare their henpecked friend
further embarrassment.

"Let's get packing," Aldin said quietly. "I've got the wrong
feeling about all of this."

"Jump-point transition in ten seconds."

Chortling with delight, Corbin Gablona settled back in his
chair to ride out the turbulence. The blackness of the jump hole
snapped away, and instantly the stars of the Magellanic Cloud
formed in their myriad glory before the viewport.

"Target acquisition on line. Five degree deviation in axis rotation due to late arrival. Strike will impact 452 kilometers from
primary target."

Corbin cursed silently, punching in a command for a simulation display.

The holo field simulation showed the planet Culimir floating
in the darkness, the image magnifying down to the single continent surrounded by turquoise seas. The computer traced the
impact line in, and he watched with satisfaction as damage calculations and pressure overloads raced alongside the computer-
generated shock waves.

"Fifty p.s.i. overload still calculated for primary target," the
computer whispered. "Total destruction assured."

Corbin rubbed his fat, ring-covered hands with delight. Pushing away from the console, he floated his chair over to the forward window, joining a knot of black-robed figures who had
gathered to watch the show. The image before them was not
real—Culimir was sixty million kilometers beyond—but the
telescopic systems made it seem as if they were hovering just
several thousand kilometers away.

Jump points rarely got closer. Any attempt to travel at translight speeds so close to a planet or star was suicide with the
random bits of dust, boulders, and even the gravitational effects
attendant with all planetary systems.

"Now watch this," Corbin said, laughing. "Damn my eyes,
I wish I had thought of it sooner."

"There it goes," one of the black robes whispered.

The cargo ship, which had followed them through the jump gate, snapped past, decelerating out of translight. The ship, however, did not kick in its sublight retro thrust but continued to race straight in toward the planet at a significant portion of light-speed, a maneuver that was all but suicidal. Which was exactly the intent.

Haga, the Shiga pilot, could now be heard over the commlink, laughing out his death prayer to the Hidden Ema, calling upon him to prepare the hundred virgins for his arrival in the afterlife, an event that if all went to plan would occur in not much more than a few minutes. Forward of the ship there was a flash of light from the lone gunner, Kcuf'ha, Haga's brother, whose job was to lock onto even the tiniest particle of dust and vaporize it before the ship hit it. A thousand ton cargo vessel traveling at 0.1 light-speed would make one hell of an impact on whatever was in the way. The same could be said for a one gram cinder that happened to be sitting in the flight path.

"Just a question of mass and velocity," Corbin replied smoothly. "Take an old cargo ship of a thousand tons mass. Accelerate it up to its maximum sub–light-speed of 0.12 and aim it straight in. The result, an explosion of several million megatons on impact. Everything within a thousand kilometers totally destroyed, the atmosphere ripped away, varying levels of destruction as far as five thousand kilometers away."

Corbin signaled for a servobot to bring a drink over. He nodded to the man standing next to him, beckoning for him to help himself to a brandy. The robed figure shook his head.

"Ah, yes, of course, against the rules," Corbin said with a chuckle. "Honestly, you don't know what you're missing."

"There are other pleasures far more enjoyable," whispered Ali Hassan, once of the dreaded order of Assassins from ancient Earth and now of the Al'Shiga. "Far more enjoyable pleasures." He turned to look back at the screen, eager for the show to begin.

"It'll look like an accident," Corbin said, as if trying to re-assure his fellow conspirator. "A cargo ship, out of control, smashed into the planet. No one will ever know."

"Magnificent," the hawk-faced man said evenly. "Never in my wildest fantasy did I dream of unleashing such destruction."

"I told you to trust me, Ali," Corbin replied expansively. "Trust me, and you'll see destruction never before imagined."

"It doesn't really seem fair somehow," a quiet voice, almost at a whisper, said from the opposite end of the cabin.

Corbin looked back over his shoulder while Hassan gave a snort of disdain.

"Weak stomach, my fellow Koh," Corbin said, his voice harsh.

"Zola Faldon does have a point," Vor, one of the minor Gaf Kohs, said, coming to Zola's defense. "Aldin, I don't care about, he's vasba, lower class. But Bukha Taug's down there, and the Xsarn Prime. They're like us."

"Were like us," Corbin snapped. "After all, they did cheat all of you out of your holdings."

Several of the Kohs feebly nodded in agreement.

Trying to act expansive, Corbin guided his float chair over to where his old companions were gathered.

"The opening sneak attack in war is a time-honored tradition. Remember Yarmir at Alpha Sigma. And did Caesar send an embossed scroll to the senate telling them he was going to cross the Rubicon? Like hell, he just crossed it and marched. So my friends, let's just say that cargo ship is hitting the Rubicon."

He chuckled at his display of military historical knowledge as if it were the old days, when Kohs gamed in military simulators over brandy and cigars, as good gentlemen should, debating the finer points of history. He motioned in a jovial manner for the servobots to circulate and refill the drinks all around.

"But gentlemen don't attack gentlemen without warning," Zola said weakly, looking around the room for support and finding precious little.

"You were the one hopping for revenge," the tertiary Xsarn said quietly. "Corbin offered a solution."

"It's all my responsibility," Corbin said, not mentioning that the whole affair was being secretly recorded, and that unbeknownst to Zola the cargo ship was, through a long paper chase, ultimately registered in his name.

"All of it my responsibility." Corbin chuckled, and the others forced out a low series of laughs in reply, several of them mumbling about a need to get back to the good old days, to restore things as they were.

The group stood around self-consciously, barely paying attention to Corbin, who launched into a long monologue about the finer tactical nuances of the military reforms of the Enlightenment on Earth, which had so foolishly attached a negative value to assassination and first strike without proper warning. Several of the Kohs noticed a number of mistakes in his delivery, especially regarding Frederick the Great's lightning attack into Silesia, which he placed in 1730, but none dared to correct him; no one was in the mood for a debate, and besides, the expert in all such things, the being who could have settled the argument, was one of the targets down below.

"Impact ten seconds," the computer voice whispered. The gathering looked up from their drinks.

"Three, two, one . . . impact."

The group stood staring at the screen. There was a delay of several seconds, and Corbin silently cursed the cargo ship pilot who was supposed to drop a translight message relay to beam the image back out. The damn fool had most likely forgotten and was too busy getting worked up in anticipation of the virgins in Paradise Ali had promised him.

The image on the screen suddenly shifted. The camera zoomed in. There was a blinding flash that filled the room with a harsh white glare, dampened down a hundredfold from the reality that would have instantly blinded anyone who was looking.

Long seconds passed, the computer filtering the image down again, and then yet again. A glaring white light was rising up from the planet's surface, millions of tons of vaporized rock shooting straight up, punching out above the atmosphere, the column a hundred kilometers across.

The shock wave was already spreading out at transsonic speed, literally ripping the landscape up from the rocky surface. The widening circle hit the ocean, instantly vaporizing it into super-heated steam, pulling the water straight up from the seafloor, raising it up into a mountain a thousand meters high, the back end of the tsunami boiling away, to be replaced by the billions of tons of water further out. The landside shock wave continued outward, slamming into a high range of mountains, which in an instant became so much bare rubble.

The image of a planet dying filled the screen—soundless, ac-companied only by the gasps of the Kohs and the delighted cheers of the Shiga assassins, several of whom wept with joy for the fate of the two brothers who surely would be the envy of all in Paradise for having sacrificed their lives for such an ultimate act of destruction.

The image suddenly became distorted, the planet rushing to-ward the screen, and then went dark, as the relay drone, which had been jettisoned astern of the cargo ship with a retro system, followed its parent down into the storm and added its own mass and velocity to the Ragnarok of destruction.

"Should we go down to check for survivors?" Zola asked quietly, looking around lamely at his comrades, as if his little display of humanitarian concern would somehow exempt him from responsibility for what they had just done.

"From that?" Corbin laughed, pointing to the now darkened screen, showing only the openness of space before them. The view was ironic somehow. Culimir still glowed a tranquil green in the emptiness of space, a single world orbiting an aging red giant. It would be another couple of minutes yet before the im-age of its destruction reached them at light-speed, to suddenly flash far brighter than the sun that gave it life. The delayed view of the planet, sixty million kilometers away, still looked peace-ful.

"He's dust now!"

"What have we done?" Hultan asked, his voice breaking.

"Why, started a war of course, you damn fool," Corbin snapped. "And we've won it already. Aldin and his friends were down there—" Pausing for dramatic effect, he pointed to the steady green light of the planet. ''—and now at least part of him is coming straight up here! Let's get the hell out of here before some damn Overseer ship shows up!''

Laughing, Corbin stalked out of the room.

The assembly of fellow Kohs looked anxiously one to the other and then back to the planet. Long minutes passed, and then as bright as day there was a blinding flash of light, the light of destruction reaching out to them at last.

''We've unleashed a nightmare,'' Kulma Koh said evenly.

''And we'll spring it across the Cloud,'' Ali announced glee-fully, surveying the Kohs with disdain.

The group had been slow, far too slow for Oishi's liking. The hour deadline he had fixed had long since passed. All of his samurai and Gaf berserkers, except for Sogio, were already aboard the ship, but at the last minute Aldin's friends had started an argument outside the ship remonstrating with him to stay for just another day.

And then the alarm had been triggered, a hidden sentry bea-con parked near the jump gate showing a single vessel coming through the primary jump point and rapidly decelerating.

Back in his former life he had trained for years to master the art of protecting his daimyo. In the three years since that life ended, he had dedicated himself to mastering all the complexi-ties of this strange new reality with the sole purpose of protect-ing his new daimyo and friend.

One unannounced ship was cause enough for alarm, but then another one had appeared, coming straight in. Dropping its jump impulse, it had instantly shifted to the maximum 0.1 light-speed, which was still far too fast for anything inside a solar system. He had sent Basak to hurry the group along, watching the mon-itors as the ship just kept coming in, not slowing.

''What the hell is going on?'' Tia whispered, coming to stand by his side to watch the screen. Any traffic to this world was suspicious, that was exactly why he liked keeping Aldin here. Other worlds might have a hundred or more ships a day coming in, any one of which might be bearing an assassin. But out here, nothing could come in without drawing an awful lot of attention.

The one ship came to a complete stop, as if to try to block the jump gate back into the administrative heart of the Cloud. But evading that was simple. There were three other beacon-marked jump points from this system out to other worlds. And even if they were blocked, one could always do a blind jump from damn near anywhere and just hope for the best. Blocking one gate was useless.

Mystified, he could only shake his head.

The minutes passed, and still the second ship kept straight on, the computer softly whispering at last that if it continued there would be a rather nasty little impact on the western edge of the continent.

"Almost like the dumb-ass pilot wanted to commit suicide," Tia said nervously.

And then the terrifying reality hit him full force.

"Al'Shiga," Oishi shouted.

"Energy release at impact?" Oishi shouted to the computer.

Several long seconds passed.

"Your voice indicates stress," the computer replied laconically. "There is reason to feel that way. Energy release of one thousand plus tons instantly decelerating from 0.1 light-speed cannot be immediately calculated with software provided, but it will be rather large. Suggest that you consider moving."

Leaping from his chair, Oishi raced to the entrance ramp of the pleasure yacht.

Aldin turned away from the argumentative group at the front entrance to the pleasure dome, led of course by his wife, who was bitterly denouncing his decision to follow Oishi's request to leave, and started toward the hangar.

"Move it!" Oishi roared.

Aldin looked up at his friend, somewhat confused.

"Oh, stop the hysteria," Mari snapped peevishly. "I've still got to pack my wigs."

"Forget the damn wigs!" Oishi screamed, leaping down the ramp. Even as he raced toward Aldin he cursed inwardly. A couple of rail guns placed in orbit could have prevented this. Hit the damn thing ten thousand kilometers out and there'd be a flash, a bit of sunburn, and nothing more. Damn it!

"It's coming in now!" Tia screamed. "Cover your eyes!"

Aldin, still somewhat confused, was looking straight at Oishi, who felt as if he were running in slow motion. Looking straight at him—westward.

With a shout the samurai didn't even bother to slow and with a leap he jumped on Aldin, pushing him to the ground, groping to pull his robes up over his friend's face.

There was a flash of light across the heavens, turning the early twilight into a dazzling blur. In an instant, the world turned into the heart of a sun.

Oishi climbed on top of Aldin, shielding him with his body. Even through tightly closed eyes he felt as if the light were striking him blind.

From a great distance away he heard a thin high shriek, as if the brilliance could somehow sweep even sound away with its intensity.

There was the pungent smell of burning, and though there was no pain, Oishi realized that his hair was on fire, as well as his silken robes. He waited for the heat of this new sun to consume his body into dust, but then, ever so gradually, the radiant brilliance started to fade away.

They didn't catch us with a direct one, Oishi realized. Maybe we can still get out.

"Get in the ship!" the samurai roared, coming to his feet.

Opening his eyes, he dared a glance to the west and thought for an instant that he'd been struck blind. From horizon to horizon there was nothing but a stunning sheet of whiteness, as if he were staring into the heart of a sun gone nova.

"Move it!" Oishi screamed, reaching down to pull Aldin to his feet.

Stunned, the old gamemaster looked about.

The rest of the party stood about in silent disbelief, their clothes smoldering. Fortunately, all of them had been facing Aldin and away from the burst.

"Get in the ship!" Oishi repeated as he raced past the group.

One moment he was running; in the next instant he was down, as if his legs had been swept out from under him.

The shock wave surged through the ground beneath him with a mind-numbing roar. Behind him he could hear the ten thousand windows of the crystal palace exploding into a hurricane of flying shards. In seconds the thirty million katar building stood naked, tons of glass showering down, leaving a bare skeleton frame.

"My clothes!" Mari shouted, turning to look back at the palace, which was silhouetted by the stunning diamond-white radiance that still dominated the western sky.

"We'll buy a new wardrobe!" Zergh roared, coming out of the palace, bleeding from dozens of lacerations, his yellow and lavender pin-striped robe dangling in shreds from his massive frame. From inside the now-bare structure, dozens of servobots hooted in distress, racing about to sweep up the broken glass. Several of the illegal Humanbots staggered up from the casino below, twittering merrily, pointing at the angry sky as if it were a holo display.

"Anyone left back in there?" Oishi shouted.

"One of the Gaf berserkers," Zergh said mournfully. "Bastard was threatening to cut his own throat at the end of the opera; the shake up did it for him. I guess it's all the same. Tragic, but in a way rather artful and poetic."

Oishi ran through the group, pushing them toward the ship, the samurai within spilling out to help, and getting in the way, while Basak and his friends, hearing of their comrade's death, sent up a loud keening wail.

The ground kept tossing and bucking, and with a shuddering groan the yacht slowly settled down on its port-side landing skid, which splayed outward with a groan, the metal twisting and snapping.

The ship leaned drunkenly over to one side, its port-side landing gear collapsed beneath its massive frame. Oishi prayed silently that the ship's hull had not been breached.

Several samurai stood in the doorway and, reaching out, pulled Oishi in, while Aldin screamed for them to seal the hatch.

Oishi raced forward to the flight engineer's cockpit, and Tia looked up anxiously from the copilot's console.

"Port engine is winding down," she shouted.

Aldin gained the pilot's console and strapped himself in. Zergh, following him, was tempted to raise a protest, but Aldin's look stopped him. Aldin was finicky about anyone other than himself piloting *Gamemaster II*, and in this situation he wanted to be at the controls.

"Get us out of here now and the hell with the port engine," Oishi shouted.

The ship leaped straight up, slamming Oishi into his seat. Climbing above the palace, Aldin pivoted the ship straight west for a quick survey of the damage.

From horizon to horizon, the entire sky was a column of white-hot fire, soaring upward, obliterating the heavens.

"Too big for a pulse bomb," Aldin whispered. "What the hell did he create?"

"A cargo ship coming in at a damn high part of sub–light-speed."

"The mad bastard," Aldin whispered. "It's been joked about, but no one's ever done that, even in the ancient wars."

"Well it's happening right now," Tia gasped.

Awed, the four watched as the devastation of an entire world unfolded, while they continued straight up, going supersonic, the ship shuddering under the strain of climbing at half power inside the atmosphere.

"Here comes the blast wave," Aldin shouted.

From over the horizon it seemed as if the entire surface of the planet were being peeled away. Trees, rivers, lakes, even the very soil down to bedrock, were tearing loose, soaring outward at supersonic speed, exploding into a miles-high wall of fiery Armageddon.

"We better get the hell out of here," Aldin sighed, swinging the ship about and hitting the throttle up to full.

An instant later the first red warning light snapped on, and then an entire row started blinking wildly.

"Airtight integrity lost," the computer announced dispassionately. "Engine three shut down, number two in caution state. Repeat, airtight integrity lost in passenger section, attempt to go outside atmosphere will result in serious discomfort and/or death of all passengers. Suggest that you set down at nearest friendly authorized-dealer repair facility. Repeat, airtight—"

Aldin snapped the audio off and looked over at Oishi with stunned disbelief.

"The ground shock hit too hard, the landing skid must have punctured the hull." He sighed.

Zergh scrambled over to the emergency control station and started punching up damage control.

"Keep us ahead of the shock wave," Zergh shouted, even as Aldin swung the ship about and started to race eastward.

Groaning inwardly, Aldin surveyed the damage as it flashed across the screen.

One of the landing struts had indeed smashed clear through the hull, wiping out one engine and damaging a second, and the gear could no longer be retracted. Even the main access corridor was losing pressure; moving everyone forward was useless. He punched up the comm channel. Mari was screaming at the top of her lungs, and he pitied his friends and bodyguards who were shouting right along with her. He cut the channel off.

The caution light on the number two engine shifted to red, and Aldin immediately shut off the power feed before it went critical.

Oishi looked over at Aldin and shook his head.

"We don't have enough power in number one for escape velocity," Aldin said.

"Hell, we can't go up anyhow."

"We won't have enough to escape the shock wave either," Tia shouted, looking up from the navigation and tracking screen.

"Maybe it'll finally slow down," the samurai said grimly,

punching up a rear view. The storm was continuing behind them with an unrelenting fury, drawing closer by the second.

Aldin raged inwardly. An attempt on his life, that he could accept; ever since he got into the Alexandrian game he'd been living with that chance. But to destroy a world and all the creatures that lived on it? That was genocide. At least the poor things that lived here would never know what hit them.

He hooked into a monitor back at the shattered remains of his palace. The servobots were still racing about mindlessly, sweeping up the glass, throwing it down incinerator shoots, and going back in for more. Several of the Humanbots were now out on the lawn, the ones programmed for more provocative activities dancing shamelessly, their clothing gone, somehow keeping their footing as the ground bucked and shook, most likely thinking the roaring thunder was music. One of his favorite models was loudly declaiming poetry, an ancient Icelandic saga about the end of the world, inspired no doubt by the horrifying storm that, if one was dispassionate to the damage, held a remarkable beauty to it.

The shock wave raced in. There was a final brief image of the bay rising up, the Humanbots clapping appreciatively, and then the screen went blank. He switched back to the main screen view astern. The storm was coming up over the horizon and closing in.

"There's too much drag from the landing gear, it's going to catch us," Aldin stated. "I'd try for height and pray."

The ship surged upward, accelerating clumsily as the atmosphere thinned. Though the computer controls were rock steady, it felt as if the entire vessel were about to vibrate itself into a million pieces.

Mari appeared in the cabin doorway.

"You idiot," she growled. "You should have listened to Oishi and left immediately."

Aldin wanted to turn on the woman and scream. If it hadn't been for her damn procrastinating, they would have been long gone. But then again, it was impossible for her to ever accept any blame, no matter how wrong she might be. That was one of her more remarkable traits: to somehow, and to her most logically, figure out a way to trace the blame for everything back to someone else. Yaroslav more than once had said that if degrees were given out for transferring guilt, she should have earned a doctorate.

"It's closing in," Aldin said, ignoring his wife, his eyes glued to the aft display. "Get the hell out and strap yourself into your seat!" he shouted.

Her eyes widened as she suddenly saw the display screen, and in an instant she was gone. Aldin hit the collision alarm for the benefit of anyone astern who was not buckled in.

"There's nothing we can do," Aldin said, looking over at Oishi. "Put the ship on automatic."

Oishi hesitated for a second. Aldin reached out and patted him on the arm.

"Aldin-san," Oishi whispered, trying to keep his voice steady while he turned over controls to the computer, a system that he still viewed with the deepest of suspicions.

"Ten seconds until disruption of flight," the computer announced calmly. "According to my calculations, we crash in—" Tia slammed the computer voice off.

She looked over at Aldin and forced a sad smile.

"I always figured Corbin would think of something," she sighed. She leaned forward in her chair as far as her restraining belts would allow, pecked Aldin on the forehead, and settling back took Oishi's hand in hers.

As usual, the computer wasn't quite up to par and the storm hit at 9.91 seconds, but nobody noticed the mistake.

CHAPTER 2

"THERE IS NO CONFIRMED KILL," VUSH OF THE OVERSEERS announced solemnly.

A groan went up from the assembly of Overseers, Humans, Gafs, and Xsarns.

"So how the hell do we get our payoffs," Nugala, Xsarn Secondary of the Tala Hive, shouted dejectedly.

"I'm sorry," Vush replied sanctimoniously. "Our hidden observation drone did detect lift-off by Aldin's pleasure yacht. The vessel was then lost in the interference created by the shock wave that encircled the planet. Until we have a confirmed corpse, we have to hold on the primary bet."

"Xsarn food," Ubur Taug snapped. "Nothing could have gotten out of there. You bastard Overseers are just trying to tie up the assets on the bet so you can draw interest. Nothing could have survived that blast."

"My dear friends," Vush whispered, rising up to hover above the angry crowd. "It simply wouldn't be fair to pay off the bets when we can calculate that there was one chance in two thousand, one hundred and forty-three that the vessel reasserted hull

28

integrity and achieved space, or one chance in eighty-nine that they found safe haven on the far side of the planet.''

At least several in the crowd, those who had bet on Aldin's survival, were happy with the pronouncement. But the mood of the three dozen others was less than friendly toward Vush and the half-dozen Overseers who were running the betting pool.

"Come, come, my friends," Vush said soothingly, "we can at least pay off the side bets for Corbin successfully hitting and destroying the palace. A nice bit of astro-navigation, that. And the computers are open for a new side bet that Aldin, Bukha, the Xsarn, and/or Zergh survived. Odds on Aldin are now eighty to one, with various multiples for any combination of the others.''

"Wait a minute," Ubur growled. "You said the odds were one in eighty-nine that they found safe haven, and now suddenly its eighty to one.''

Vush looked around, a bit confused by all of this, his gaze at last fixing on Hobbs Gablona. Hobbs, who ran this gaming and pleasure planet, floated into the center of the room aboard his float chair. He looked almost like a twin of Corbin, topping out at over one hundred and eighty kilos, a characteristic that was common to most of the males of the Gablona clan, but there the comparison ended between him and his cousin. Hobbs's features were fixed in what appeared to be an almost perpetual leering grin of earthy delight. He was noted among the upper set of the Cloud for running a gaming palace second to none for exotic betting situations, luxurious treatment of guests, a tacky sense of vulgar showmanship, and a blind eye to some of the more unusual activities that his customers sometimes indulged in, especially when they were willing to pay well for his arranging of entertainment.

"House odds," Hobbs announced taking over for the thoroughly confused Overseer. "After all, there is a bit of an overhead in running these things." Laughing, he pointed to the fountain in the center of the room, filled with sparkling burgundy in which several of the Gafs were now bathing, and to the covered feeding trough in the corner around which the Xsarns were happily gathered.

"And the only damn game in town," another Koh sighed as

he bellied up to his terminal to bet on a straight ticket of all four players surviving.

There was a sullen murmur of agreements to that point at least.

"Come, come, friends, another round of bets to liven it up for a bit longer before the game finally ends. And remember, gentlemen," Vush said, "the visuals, food, and drink are free after all."

The show had indeed been spectacular. The masked remote unit placed in geosynch had relayed the most spectacular explosion to have been witnessed in the Cloud since the end of interstellar warfare nearly three thousand years before.

Connoisseurs of fine explosions who were not invited to the private gaming party had eagerly paid the Overseers' asking price of a hundred thousand credits to be hooked into the live vidlink. Some of the Kohs addicted to explosives had occasionally crashed a derelict ship into an uninhabited moon for the fun of it, but never at a speed of much more than one one-hundredth of light. No one had ever witnessed a cargo ship slamming into a life-supporting planet. The group had been awestruck by the sight, forgetting even to cheer as the explosion tore away half a continent.

Even as they grumbled at the Overseer, most of the crowd was still glued to the monitors, going over the instant replays and pointing out to each other the finer points of what was still going on. A betting pool had been quickly set up on the exact time that the shock waves would collide on the far side, and Xsarn Secondary had regurgitated excitedly when he had picked up half a million on that bet.

Several of the Kohs were already in the holo simulation rooms, where the computer could analyze the data from the blast and re-create a wide variety of vantage points from anywhere in space, or even down on the planet's surface. Wild shouts of delight could be heard from the rooms to be drowned out by the wall-shaking rumble of the shock wave blasting over the viewers.

"Gentlemen," Vush announced, looking around the room in

what he thought was a facial gesture that could be interpreted as a smile, "after all, there are still other bets to be played in this game. Do remember that though Aldin and Bukha might be dead, Aldin's estate is still the largest in the Cloud."

There was a murmur of excitement as the various Kohs and other nouveau riche beings looked expectantly at each other and started to break up and head to the wagering computers.

Though old fortunes had failed with the last game, numerous new ones had been made as well in the wild economic chaos that had followed. If Aldin was dead, and even if he was not, there was a vast economic empire waiting to fall into eager hands.

"My staff has prepared a full betting portfolio listing several hundred different options to be played against, so settle back gentlemen, all accommodations, food, and entertainment are yours here at the Overseer betting palace."

The crowd, though still angry about the delayed payoff from the attack on Aldin, could not help but give a halfhearted cheer of approval. There was no denying that the Overseer Vush had thought of everything when he had chartered Hobbs's world for the game.

"More profit for everyone," Vush said to Hobbs as he floated past, believing that this Gablona was undoubtedly delighted by the situation of additional betting.

Hobbs looked back at the screens replaying the blast, the fuzzy image of Aldin's ship staggering ahead of the shock wave and then disappearing. It gave him a slight knot in the gut. After all, in his early days he had even been a vasba for a while, and the old guild had some set rules about looking out for fellow members. A discreet tip-off was all he could offer, but it seemed as if that was now far too late. The thought of Corbin winning was disturbing enough; the thought of Aldin losing permanently was far worse.

He looked over at Vush and smiled, saying nothing.

As Vush floated from the room he gazed around benevolently at the group he had suckered into his game. However, as the door closed behind him the look of benevolence changed in an instant to horror.

"So are we enjoying our little game?"

In an instant Vush was on the floor, kneeling before the Arch Overseer, feeling like a youth who had been caught by his parents while performing some sinful and very disgusting act.

Vush looked up at the Arch, trying to read his four multifaceted eyes for some sign of what was to come.

"Oh, I knew about your little arrangement some time ago," the Arch said evenly.

"How?" Vush whispered.

"Let's just say that at the end of the last game I could see the infection of greed had been passed by the lesser barbarian races into you. I figured sooner or later you'd succumb to the sins of violence and gambling."

"I plead temporary madness," Vush said quickly. "Too much contact with their inferior breed has unsettled my mind. I'll be happy to retire to a meditation world if you will ever find a way to forgive me."

If an Overseer could have laughed, the sound coming from the Arch would have been a fairly close approximation.

"Do you really expect me to buy that rubbish?" the Arch replied, falling into the language of the humans.

Nervously Vush looked up at his master and judge.

"Tell me, what are the odds on Corbin Gablona succeeding?"

"If Aldin is dead, then I dare say there are no odds. Corbin's Al'Shiga, and his control of several dozen ships to be used as planet rams, will hold the rest of the Cloud in terror. Even if Aldin lives, which is a serious long shot, the odds are still 6.7 to 1 against him."

The Arch turned away and floated across the room.

"I tremble to think what would happen if Aldin lives. The entire Cloud might fall into civil war as the disgruntled old Kohs fight against Aldin and those still loyal to him. It would be a terrible bloodletting. It could wreck the civilization of the three outside species who now inhabit this realm of space."

The Arch turned back to look at Vush, and what passed for an Overseer's smile crossed his lips.

Vush breathed an inner sigh of relief.

"I have contended with this infection from the next galaxy for far too long," the Arch snapped out, his voice filled with loathing.

Vush floated excitedly to his feet.

"You are not forgiven," the Arch said, and Vush was immediately back on his knees.

"You've presented me with a most interesting problem, most interesting indeed."

"I was simply trying to spare you the details, and prevent the equanimity of your soul from being disturbed."

"I never knew you to be that considerate," the Arch replied sharply.

"But as I was saying. If Aldin should live, there'll be open interstellar war across the entire Cloud." The Arch looked back at his underling.

He never had agreed with the intervention to stop the last war three thousand years before. Granted he was horrified at the overt violence, but he had always felt that they should have let these noisome creatures burn themselves out completely, and then they could move in and establish order and control.

But moral arguments had won out, they had used the devices left behind by the First Travelers, and through a demonstration of sheer power, and the destruction of half a dozen planets, they had terrified the lesser species into a peace that had lasted down through the centuries.

And at what price? he thought bitterly. It was like trying to maintain order between a vast family of bickering, spoiled children. The quiet peace of the Cloud had been destroyed forever by their presence.

In the now-legendary past, beyond the memory of any living Overseer, even beyond the existing memory of the vast machines, which through the millennia had gradually lost their recall, the First Travelers had roamed the Cloud. They had created the great monuments to their power, the Rings, Skyhooks, and the vast, all-encompassing Sphere, which to them were nothing more than amusements to pass the long eternity of existence. He had often wondered who the First Travelers were. Were they simply the machines that still existed scattered throughout the Cloud, aged and worn after countless ages, or was there something even before them, endless layers of creation nestled within one another like onion skins?

The Overseers, their numbers always so small, had arrived to behold such wonders, and the machines had bowed to them and asked them to be the protectors of the monuments created. So they had settled here, curators of the entire Greater and Lesser Magellanic Cloud as the Humans called it. They were so few in number, but that had always been the way of their species, to replace one of their number only when finally, after countless time, a spirit finally slipped away to the void.

There had been two galaxies to roam in quiet contemplation, forever seeking the knowledge of the one true light. Entire worlds could be the home of a single being living in solitary meditation.

Now the Cloud was aswarm with these quarreling brawling mobs, who cluttered the space lanes, soiled the planets, and shattered the quiet of the universe.

At first the Overseers had viewed it as some great mission, to teach these creatures the ways of peace, the joy of contemplation, and the total release of nonaction. But may the Eternal damn them all, it was simply wearing too thin, he thought angrily.

And then finally they had destroyed the Tower to the world of the Al'Shiga.

The near-total destruction of the race on that planet had not bothered him in the slightest. Funny, he thought, there was a time when the Overseers had debated for centuries over the morality of eating nonsentient life-forms. Most had gone totally synthetic as a result. That, he realized, was yet another sign of their corrupting influence: now he didn't even get upset when they slaughtered each other.

But the destruction of the Tower, that was simply too much to bear. It was a sacred monument, a true artifact of the legendary First Travelers, and the Humans and Gafs had destroyed it and, in fact, had even exalted over the destruction. Holo movies showing the collapse were one of the most sought-after items now by the mob.

"Disgusting, absolutely disgusting."

"Did you say something, my Arch?" Vush whispered, looking up at his ruler.

"What? Oh, nothing, nothing at all," the Arch hissed, his voice edged with annoyance.

"Will you punish me?" Vush asked nervously.

"But of course," the Arch snapped angrily, and Vush bowed his head. Most likely he'd be sent to contemplate his sins for ten centuries on some forsaken rock. No betting for a thousand years, Vush thought dejectedly. I'll go crazy without some action.

"Oh, get up on your feet," the Arch growled. "Float with some pride, damn it."

Stunned by his leader's decadent vocabulary, Vush rose up into the air, mindful to keep himself a head lower out of respect.

"Here is your punishment," the Arch said softly, fixing Vush with his gaze. "You are to continue running this game."

Vush could not contain his exuberance, and so quickly did he rise that his head slammed into the ceiling.

"Your enlightened wish is always my desire," Vush replied ceremonially.

"There's something else," the Arch said evenly.

"Whatever it is your enlightenment wishes," Vush said, forgetting any form of decorum so that his voice was near breaking with excitement.

"We never had this conversation."

"Never had this conversation?" Vush asked quizzically. "How can that be? We are speaking this conversation at this very moment."

"A Human concept," the Arch replied sharply. "It means that in your mind you will establish a logic system that denies the reality of what we have exchanged and replace it with another reality that states you and I never discussed these things."

"Oh." Vush wrestled with the thought. His exposure to Humans had exposed him to this strange logic. But it surprised him that an Arch would be so worldly as to request such a thing.

"As you wish," Vush said quietly.

"As I order," the Arch snapped back. "Also I want you to create a situation wherein the events of the game may be altered from time to time as I see fit, especially if Aldin is still alive."

"You mean rig the results," Vush replied smartly, feeling a surge of pleasure over knowing the correct term.

"Yes, that is how they call it. This war must go on. I want these creatures to get a complete scare thrown into them in the end, if need be to push their technological prowess back to a more manageable level by the time they are done."

"You mean a real, full-blown, planet-busting war?" Vush replied.

"Yes, that," the Arch said, amazed somewhat that he had finally voiced his secret desire of centuries.

Stunned, Vush looked at his leader.

"Do the other Overseers know this?" Vush asked guardedly.

"That is none of your damn business," the Arch snapped. "We've got to weaken these creatures a bit before we can bring them back into line. Let them do their destruction on each other for a while. It's not our fault or our sin. In the end they'll come rushing to us for peace, and as the brokers of that, we'll bring better control. We thought we could rule them through the organization of Kohs, and look at what that has finally resulted in. The Koh system will be finished by this war, and then we'll simply rule directly, and those swarms of creatures out there will beg for our guidance. Maybe then we can have a little peace and quiet around here."

Vush was stunned by the extended outburst. Overseers were supposed to be reticent and above all discreet, to communicate crisply and without emotion. For an Arch, the last outburst was the closest thing to a tirade Vush had ever heard.

Even the Arch suddenly seemed embarrassed by his comments and turned away.

"I'm leaving now. I need to find a place of solitude," the

Arch said softly. "I find being anywhere near those creatures has a most disquieting effect on my soul."

Vush, bowing low, backed out toward the door.

"Keep this game going," the Arch said coldly, and then the jump-down beam encompassed him and he was gone.

"What the hell do you mean there's no confirmed kill?" Corbin yelled.

Hassan stood dispassionately by the entryway into Corbin's cabin. How he had ever found himself back in this man's employ was beyond his understanding. He had sworn to drive a dagger into Corbin's bloated belly if he ever had the pleasure of meeting him again.

But two years of struggling for survival in the wreckage of the Hole had tempered that rage. He had managed to organize a cell of new followers, and even held some sway in the power struggles that had rocked the Al'Shiga. But there was simply no way to get off that forsaken rock.

No way until a smuggler ship had alighted almost directly on top of his encampment. The offer had been straightforward and simple. Service in return for rescuing Hassan and his followers.

He had accepted; only a madman would refuse the chance to practice his craft among the unsuspecting billions who lived their fat easy lives throughout the Cloud. Yes, the fat one still had his uses, but there would be a reckoning. For the moment patience would have to do until the intricacies of travel through space had been mastered.

"That was the report issued by the Overseer. All bets are closed until it is confirmed that Aldin is either alive or dead."

"What the hell does he want," Corbin roared, "a bottle full of that bastard's dust?"

"It seems their observation remote detected a ship lifting off from the palace seconds before the shock wave hit."

With an angry snarl Corbin stalked over to the control board that dominated an entire wall of his bedroom suite. With a wave of disdain he dismissed the several girls who had been waiting for him, and as they exited the room, they eyed Hassan fearfully.

A rumor had gone through the entourage that Hassan had only once succumbed to the temptations of the flesh since he had joined Corbin. Her body had been found afterward, at least most of it: the guess was her head was floating somewhere out near the last jump portal.

The screen lit up to show the revelers on the gaming deck below. The ship was still in orbit over Aldin's pleasure world, and the passengers were continuing to observe the death throes of the planet. It had been nearly a standard day since the hit, and firestorms now engulfed nearly half a hemisphere. An entire world was dying down there, and it held a strange, perverse fascination. Even the more fastidious types who viewed real violence with disdain were engrossed by destruction on a scale so vast, it took on a certain degree of unreality.

"It is possible that they raced ahead of the shock wave, the turbulence blocking our monitors from so far out," Ali ventured. "Once on the far side they pulled straight up and away, using the planet as a shield from observation."

"Or they could have crashed on the far side," Corbin said slowly. "We've been in geosynch over the blast site watching the show."

Corbin settled back in his chair.

"Damn you, you should have thought of this possibility and suggested a sweep around the world just to make sure," Corbin snarled.

"You have lived in this universe far longer than I," Hassan said coldly, "and thus you are more familiar with such things."

Corbin was about to snap back a reply, but the look in Hassan's eyes stilled his words. He knew he needed this master of intrigue and assassination as an ally. The mere presence of the Al'Shiga on his side struck fear into all around him. But of late he was starting to wonder if he was indeed riding the tiger, and if, when the time came to eliminate the tiger, he would be able to get off his mount alive.

He forced a smile of reconciliation.

"You are correct, my friend," Corbin said warmly. "Let's

take a look at the far side. If we detect a ship down there, maybe you and your friends can have a little fun with your blades.''

Hassan smiled in reply, a smile that chilled Corbin's blood.

If there was one thing Yaroslav truly hated, it was space travel. He let out a groan of anticipation as the computer announced jump-point transition. Jump-point transitions turned his stomach inside out. He was pumped with enough motion-sickness juice to put a Gaf to sleep, but still he felt his bile rising as the forward screen suddenly washed out, went dark, and then an instant later snapped into focus.

"Merciful heavens," he whispered. Switching the forward screen to maximum magnification, he quickly surveyed the firestorm consuming the continent where Aldin's pleasure palace had been. Even from the distance of the jump-point, the monitor was able to pick up a nightmare of chaos.

"If he was down there, he's dead," the old scholar said mournfully.

The tip-off of a strike had come ten days' past. He suspected it was Jorva Taug who had passed it along, or just maybe Hobbs Gablona. The warning had ruined all of his fun.

The visit to the Ring of Alexander, and the pleasure of the conversation, had to be cut short. Ever since the Hole game, he had found it to be a rather unhealthy occupation to be one of Aldin's friends, and hanging around on remote pleasure worlds had grown a bit too boring, especially with carping from Mari about Aldin's "smelly old friends." In the end there was no place else to go but the Ring.

Alexander—now there was somebody to sit up late with and talk to. His recollections of Aristotle were revealing and most amusing. Kubar Taug's knowledge of the lost books of the philosopher Varnag were worth several articles at the very least. The only problem was that the existence of Alexander and Kubar in this time frame was something of a secret. If he published, the Ring would soon be swarming with tourists and another great spot would be ruined.

Their plans for a campaign against the Lagara over in the next continent were most justifiable, and he had been offered a staff command position, complete to the military panoply of a Macedonian general. It was most tempting. He could image a bronze statue of himself, helmeted, shield up, spear in hand. It was all going so comfortably, until the incoming message.

What had been even more disturbing was the emergency beacon flash, using Aldin's private code, that he had picked up twelve hours ago, causing him to cancel a quick side stop at Irmik for a friendly visit with an old and most interesting former student and instead push the ship to maximum speed.

He now regretted wasting the half a day on debating whether to go on what was most likely a false alarm anyhow. Now he truly regretted it.

"We've got something!" Corbin shouted. Excitement rippled through the room as the various Kohs and fellow conspirators pushed around the screen.

In an instant, odds of fifty to one against survivors were offered and millions were wagered. Side bets started to spring up as well on the possible outcome if Hassan's assassin team had to go in to finish the job.

"There's a ship down there, and it matches the profile," Corbin said, scanning the board.

"Any signs of life?" the Kohs shouted excitedly.

"Can't tell, atmospherics are going crazy down there."

Corbin spun around in his seat and looked at his companions.

"It's in the middle of a swamp, and there's no place to land this ship. Jump-down beams aren't the healthiest thing with atmospheric conditions like that—you might materialize with a bucket of hail in your chest."

He fell silent for a moment.

"I'll go down on the docking ship to check things out," Hassan said. There was a strange look in the assassin's eyes.

Though trying to act jovial, Corbin was deeply embarrassed that he had not thought to do a simple sweep of the far side, just to make sure. In the excitement of a possible ground fight the others hadn't noticed, but later there would be comments about this lack of efficiency, and there was no one he could possibly pass the blame to. He could see that Hassan was fully aware of this. He half suspected that Hassan had thought of this alternative even while the primary shock wave was encircling the planet but had kept silent to embarrass his master.

"Take him alive," Gubta Koh shouted gleefully, interrupting Corbin's thoughts. "Then we can space the bastard and place bets on how long it takes him to die in vacuum."

"Droll, but childish," Umga, Xsarn of the Polta Hive, announced. "A lot more fun it would be to shoot him into that black hole over in the fourteenth quadrant. His going over the event horizon would be worth quite a few laughs."

The group broke into a round of good-natured joking, even though with Aldin technically still alive bets worth millions were riding on this. If he got off the world, and even if they later caught and killed him, it would be ruled that Corbin had not destroyed him as a result of the first attack.

"Well, let's send Hassan down. If there's anything left, we'll take him alive," Corbin said expansively.

"And your beautiful cousin?" Hassan asked softly.

Corbin looked over at his master assassin and the room went silent.

He had written her off long ago. She was still a distant blood relative, though, and in what little corner of his heart still had feelings for her, he had simply hoped that she would be vaporized with all the others.

"Kill her," he said quietly, and the room went silent. There was something about his pronouncement that disturbed even those who had been his companions of late.

"But make it swift and painless," Corbin added, as if in an afterthought and, standing, he stalked out of the room.

With a sardonic smile Hassan surveyed the assembly, many of whom looked away as his gaze fell upon them, and turning, he followed Corbin out of the room.

"Aldin, I think I hear something."

Groaning, Aldin Larice opened his eyes and saw Oishi kneeling over him. Sitting up, he rubbed the walnut-size lump on the back of his head. For that matter nearly every square inch of his body was covered with bruises. The last hour of his once-priceless yacht's flying time had been the ride of a lifetime. All inertia dampening had been lost when the shock wave hit, so every toss and turn had thrown the occupants about the cabin and rolled them into a tangled jumble.

How the nav system had ever managed to set them down was to him a miracle. The salesman had told him that the Vax 8 autopiloting and emergency backup controls, designed to deal with one hundred and twenty-two types of emergencies, was the latest thing on the market. The manual actually did declare that it could handle surprise black holes and acts of God such as random asteroid impacts on planetary surfaces, though no legal liability was intended by such claims. His frugal nature had almost dismissed the pitch, but Oishi had agreed with the dealer, so to shut the polyester-clad Gaf salesman up he had signed for the six hundred thousand katar system, which at the time he felt was nothing more than a frill to keep Oishi happy. If he ever saw that Gaf again, he swore that for the first time in his life he would actually get on his knees and kiss the boots of a space-yacht salesman.

Aldin came to his feet and moved aft. The stench of unwashed bodies living in the emergency shelter area was near overpowering. Fear and excitement, especially for Gafs, immediately triggered an incredibly strong musky smell. It was possible to go outside, but the storms of hurricane proportion outside were simply too dangerous to venture into.

Going over to Tia, he knelt down by her side.

"How we doing this morning?" he whispered, taking her bandaged hands in his.

"Like cooked Xsarn food," she replied, forcing a smile through cracked lips. "Is it daylight out there?"

"A bit stormy, but the sun's up," Aldin said cheerfully, trying to hide his concern. She'd taken a cut in one eye, and Zergh had insisted that both of them be bandaged up.

"Sun's up?" Mari snapped peevishly. "We're stuck here for

the rest of our lives, and now the climate on this place stinks. You realize how much money you lost in this world? I figure it'd be at least a hundred and fifty million . . .''

Aldin looked up at his towering wife, and for once the anger in his eyes silenced her tirade.

Somehow he thought inwardly, if he had simply stayed poor, this woman would have been perfectly happy to buy another tavern on a safer world than the Hole. They could have settled in and undoubtedly been completely happy.

The problem was that Mari was an incredible financial manipulator, having already gained the reputation as a class-one money shark, but her taste was worse than any Gaf had ever dared to display. Within Gaf circles she had gained quite the reputation for haute couture and had even opened a fashion line that was famed for its swirling paisleys intermixed with mauve and yellow polka dots.

''There it is again,'' Oishi whispered.

Aldin came to his feet and went through the airlock to stand next to the outer door.

There was the sound of the storm outside, but there was something else as well, a high-pitched whine growing louder by the second. There was a booming throaty roar, and a vibration ran through the vessel. It was a ship going into a full reverse thrust.

In an instant his entourage of samurai guards was on its feet. Most of them now carried the modern accoutrements of a guard—Erik 15s, and the favored heavy weapon of the Gafs, the Ulman Scatter Sweeper, which put out a beehive cluster round that could knock over anything in a sixty degree spread for more than a hundred yards. The only problem with that weapon was that it couldn't differentiate between who was friendly and who was not. Oishi still held to the old form, even though there was an Erik tucked into his waist. Sweeping out his sword, he approached the door cautiously.

''If it's Corbin's people, we better go out to meet them,'' Oishi stated, as if merely discussing some minor point of strategy rather than an issue of life or death. ''In here they could simply place explosive charges on the hull and be done with us."

Aldin cursed silently. There had been a hold full of armaments on board, including a highly illegal ship-to-ship laser cannon; all that was now buried under thirty feet of muck in the collapsed stern of the ship.

Oishi grabbed hold of the door with one hand and held his blade poised with the other.

"Let's go!"

The door slammed open. A bent, shriveled form stood in the doorway. With a backhanded sweep Oishi brought his blade up for the kill.

"For heaven's sake watch that damn thing!" Yaroslav roared, tumbling over backward to avoid the blow.

The samurai behind Oishi leaped through the doorway, weapons poised to be confronted by a wiry old man who came back up to his feet and then doubled over with laughter.

"Scared the hell out of you, didn't I," Yaroslav chortled.

Aldin didn't know whether to curse him or knock him off his feet with an embrace. Finally, he chose the latter.

The now-ecstatic group piled out of the ship, and despite the near hurricane-force winds and driving rain gathered around their rescuer, barraging him with questions.

"We don't have time for it now," Yaroslav yelled, trying to be heard above the commotion, "there's another ship that'll be here in ten minutes, and the occupants are less than friendly."

"Corbin?"

"I think so, he was closing in when I shot by. He'd be blind not to pick me up and follow me in."

"That fat slob," Mari roared, standing in the doorway. "I want to stay here and give him a piece of my mind. Look what he did to our ship. He's gonna pay for this! I'll sue the bastard for damages. Our lawyers will eat his lawyers alive."

For just a brief moment Aldin was tempted to leave her. She'd most likely be more than a match for Hassan.

"Let's get moving!" Oishi shouted. He rushed back into the ruined ship and quickly reemerged, carrying Tia.

Aldin looked around the impenetrable swamp.

"Just where did you land?" he shouted.

To his amazement, Yaroslav pointed straight up. Resting directly on top of the wreck stood the old man's tiny personal transport.

There was no time to argue whether there was room for everyone or not. Scrambling up the side of the shattered yacht, the group started to pile in through the airlock.

Rushing into the control room, Aldin slipped into the copilot seat and started punching in the lift-off commands.

"Looks like company," Zergh suddenly announced with a groan, coming in alongside of Aldin and pointing forward.

Looking through the forward viewport, Aldin saw a heavy ground shuttle hover into view.

"Everyone's aboard," Yaroslav announced.

"Punch us out now!" Aldin shouted.

The ship lurched off the ground, standing nearly on its tail to avoid smashing into the landing craft. For an instant Aldin found himself staring into the control booth of the other ship, not a dozen feet away.

"Hassan!"

The hawklike eyes gazed into his, and he felt a cold shudder of fear. Oishi snapped out a curse in Japanese and brandished his sword. But Hassan did not respond, his remorseless eyes still locked on Aldin.

Zergh started to spin the ship on its axis and hit the emergency jump-out engine into life.

Unable to resist the impulse, Aldin leaned over and flashed a universal gesture of contempt at the assassin, and then the vessel disappeared from view.

Within seconds the planet was dropping away. Punching up through the atmosphere, the ship quickly gained escape velocity.

"There's Gablona's yacht," Yaroslav announced, pointing to a converging blip on the screen. "When he saw me swinging in, you should have heard him rage. This little ship always was good for getting in and out of tight corners quickly."

Aldin leaned over and hit the commlink.

"Corbin, are you picking me up?"

There was a moment of silence, and then the screen before Aldin lit up to reveal Corbin Gablona at his angriest.

"What the hell did you do it for?" Aldin asked.

"Why not?" Corbin replied, his angry features suddenly relaxing into a show of outward calm.

Aldin could only shake his head in disbelief.

"You should have left me to die back down on the Hole," Corbin said smoothly, a smile lighting his features. "But then again compassion always was one of your weak points."

"I'll see your head lying in the dust!" Oishi roared, stepping up to the screen.

Corbin recoiled in mock terror and started to laugh.

"As the old tradition must still hold," Corbin replied, "do consider my little present to your world as a formal declaration of war. All your holdings are now fair game. Since it seems I failed to eliminate you in this first strike, I'll simply have to stage a repeat on some of your major holdings as a result. I've got a dozen more ships ready to crash at selected points around the Cloud."

Aldin simply could not reply.

"It'll make a hell of a vid," Corbin continued. "I'll title it, *A Study in Destruction: Holos of Worlds Being Destroyed.*"

"You're sick," Aldin roared. "Let's just settle it here. Your people and mine back down to the planet. You're killing millions of people who have no part in this is even beneath you."

Corbin started to laugh.

"Oh, we'll get around to that eventually, but how do I know what weapons that little rescue ship's got on board? No, it's been three thousand years since this Cloud's had a good gut-busting war, now I'll give it to them and simply declare myself ruler when everyone is thoroughly intimidated."

"What about the Overseers?" Aldin cried. "They'll never allow it."

Corbin leaned back laughing, his mass shaking in great convulsive waves. Wiping the tears from his eyes, he looked back at the monitor and smiled.

"You figure that one out. You know where to reach me when you want to surrender. My terms are simple, the ceding over of all assets to my name, recognition of my rightful place as ruler, and my confederates as Kohs and cabinet members in my government. Finally you, Yaroslav, Zergh, Bukha, the Xsarn Prime, and Tia will face punishment by my hand. Think about it." The screen went dead.

Stunned, Aldin looked over his shoulder to the group that had gathered to watch the exchange.

"Do we have any ship-to-ship weapons?" Aldin asked.

He already knew the answer, but he could always hope that one had been concealed on board, despite the three thousand year injunction against such devices.

The cabin was suddenly illuminated with a blinding light.

"He sure as hell has one," Zergh roared, as the nav system automatically sent the ship into evasive maneuvers. At any distance greater than twenty thousand kilometers, ship-to-ship weapons were next to useless, since a good navigation computer could punch in a dozen lateral shifts per second. At anything more than a tenth of a second between radar pulse to lock on, firing was simply pure chance. Only the luckiest of shots would have an effect. Corbin had made the key mistake of hovering in geosynch rather than coming in low behind the landing craft for the kill—or he feared that Yaroslav might be armed after all and didn't want to take the risk.

Aldin thought about that for a moment. Both he and Corbin were masters of archaic warfare, but space combat was something they had never toyed with before. It was a lost art. An art they were all going to quickly learn.

Within seconds it was obvious that the lighter mass and maneuverability of Yaroslav's ship, even with sixty refugees crammed aboard, would quickly outrace any attempt at closing.

Aldin turned away from the conflict to look at his friends.

"I'd even suggest ramming the bastard," he said evenly, "but we'd get fried first."

Oishi nodded in agreement, even though the contemplation of it implied suicide for Aldin and everyone on board.

"Look, I didn't volunteer for another nick-of-time rescue just to get suicided for my efforts," Yaroslav replied.

The old man, however, breathed a sigh of relief at the rejection of such an idea.

"What are we going to do?" Aldin asked.

"Fight a war," Bukha said grimly. "He's taken the gloves off, so now we'll take them off as well."

Disgusted with only this alternative, Aldin settled back into his chair.

"The Overseers?"

"You heard him," Zergh interjected. "They're standing back."

"I find that hard to believe," Aldin said. "Sure, I know they're secretive, that they're most likely weaker than we ever realized, but if they don't nip this in the bud, they'll get fried in the end as well. If Corbin can destroy us, he'll turn on them next."

"Maybe they want us to fight it out," Yaroslav said, examining the quality of his manicure even while the ship continued to weave and bob, the inertial dampening all but dissipating the rapid movements. The nav system was already locked onto the nearest jump gate and was rapidly closing in, with Gablona more than fifty thousand kilometers behind and falling away.

"I think we need a drink," Aldin announced, wanting to take the time to contemplate what had just occurred. A servobot quickly appeared toting a tray of drinks, and everyone was glad for the round of brandy.

"I'm just glad someone got your emergency beacon going, otherwise I would have really been late this time," Yaroslav said, leaning back in his chair and holding his snifter up to examine its contents.

"What beacon?" Oishi asked, leaning forward. "We never set it out. If we had, Corbin would have definitely come looking for us earlier than he did."

Amazed, the group looked at each other.

"Maybe it was the Overseers, triggering one outside the

system so Corbin wouldn't detect it,'' the Xsarn announced, shaking his head. ''They wanted all of us to live.''

''So the game could continue,'' Aldin said in stunned disbelief.

CHAPTER 3

"I DON'T LIKE THIS ONE BIT," YAROSLAV WHISPERED GRIMLY.

"It's too late now," Aldin snapped in reply, and he pointed forward to where the fifty-meter-wide boulder tumbled in on its trajectory.

The battered ship they were riding in continued to shake as the reverse thrusters rapidly slowed their approach to the planet.

"Damn inertia dampening is shot to hell," Aldin mumbled to himself.

He had to confess that being the most powerful Koh in the Cloud once had its advantages. His yacht had been a finely tuned masterpiece. He had even been able to afford the standard fifty jump overhauls, and the always-outrageous costs of jump engine tune-ups. But that was gone now. In the last six months, since his escape from Corbin's first raid, nearly every ship, repair port, and terminal once under his control had been smashed to oblivion. And as for independent stations, the mere sight of him approaching set them into near convulsive fits, with much battening of hangar doors. No one was crazy enough to want to service anything belonging to Aldin the Hunted, as he was now referred to.

The Hole had been bad enough; now the gaming field was the entire Cloud. Corbin had not really needed to kill all that many, just a couple of service station managers found on Shiga impaling sticks had convinced everyone that doing business with Larice, or even allowing him landing rights, was a sure method to get a visit from the "black robes."

At least he could be thankful that after the planet-buster of the opening round, Corbin had toned things down. Some of the operations had been drop-in assaults designed to take out important personnel in Aldin's organization. Others had been surgical strikes designed to take out key locations. So far noncombatant casualties had been kept to a minimum, except for the murdered station attendants, landing-field operators, parts suppliers, and any banker willing to allow a credit transfer, but Aldin feared that most likely after today that would all change.

To be sure, he had wanted to strike back, but the problem was where to strike? Zola pleaded all innocence, as did every other Koh, and despite Oishi's demands, he could not bring himself to do a raid in those areas. Being a vasba, he found, dragged with it a certain code of honor about innocent people never being used in games. Even the supposed proof of a badly reproduced holo tape of Zola and a dozen minor Kohs being aboard Corbin's ship was not evidence enough. The damned problem of it all was that Corbin's operation was wonderfully designed to be clandestine. Having lost all his assets in the last game, the man really had nothing to lose, no place to really call home. There was occasional evidence of a temporary base in some outback region of the Cloud—he had even used the Kolbard Ring for a brief stay—but other than that, the bastard was simply a rumor, a ghost, hiding out in some unknown bolthole in the untraveled areas of the Cloud; yet always possessed it seemed with the uncanny ability to figure out where Aldin was.

At least until now.

"It's hitting the atmosphere," Oishi announced, a flicker of triumph in his voice.

A brilliant streak arched across the evening sky of Hobbs's

Pleasure and Amusement World Emporium, followed by a sharp snap-flash of light at the impact point.

"All right, let's get down there," Aldin snapped.

The forward thrusters were kicked in. Aldin felt his stomach turn over, and swore he'd get this bucket fixed at the first opportunity.

"On the mark," Oishi announced, looking up from the radar screen. "It took out the rail gun they were mounting beyond the port. There's some shock wave damage but collateral effects are nominal."

Aldin looked over at his samurai companion and smiled. Oishi on most any other occasion would still voice his opinion in the formal speech of a Japanese warrior from the late seventeenth century. But in this new form of warfare, he had quickly mastered the technical skills and jargon necessary for command.

The *Survivor* swept into the atmosphere, riding through the shock wave, and then swung out over the ocean for final approach on the base and amusement halls.

"Ground-assault team make ready," Oishi commanded. Leaving his seat, Aldin went aft to watch final preparations.

Basak and his berserkers were beside themselves with joy, now that the first offensive was about to be launched. Almost all the berserkers and samurai were armed with modern weapons and battle armor, but Basak still preferred his massive two-handed battle-ax, claiming it would create the proper mood for the occasion, while Oishi, still in the tactical battle seat, was wearing both swords. As Aldin looked the towering Gaf over, he could only agree.

The aft cabin switched to red light, and joyful shouts of anticipation emanated from the group.

Oishi came aft, and like his Gaf companion drew his blade.

"Remember," Oishi commanded, "we hit the repair sheds, and set charges to blow any ships, though if there's something in there undamaged and better than this bucket we'll swap. Remember to hit the repair equipment. If we get Corbin here, all to the better. If not, this is one of Corbin's hidden repair bases for this section of the Cloud. We destroy this and we might have a chance to get some control back in this region.''

Oishi looked over at Aldin, ready to say something, but the look in the old Koh's eyes was enough to end the argument. Oishi had gone near insane attempting to talk Aldin out of coming on this strike, but no argument would prevail. Aldin wanted to be in on the raid.

''I'll be with Aldin for the hit on the gaming center and resort facilities. Remember we have fifteen minutes to place our charges and to get out. Who's ever down here already sent out an alarm.''

A warning Klaxon sounded through the ship.

''Final approach,'' Zergh called through the intercom. ''Ten seconds.''

Aldin felt his knees going weak. Some insane pride had pushed him into doing this little adventure. Now there was no telling what would come of it.

A jarring *thud* ran through the ship, drowned out by the wild shouts of delight from the Gafs. The airlock popped open.

What Oishi had called collateral damage stunned Aldin with its magnitude.

The entire landing area was a shambles, even though the hit had slammed in nearly half a kilometer away. An old cargo ship, caught out in the open, was blazing with a hot white heat, lighting the tropical evening like a beacon. The dozen flimsy hangar sheds lining the field had caved in from the blast, the delicate ships and personal yachts within reduced to twisted piles of rubble.

The Gafs swarmed past Aldin, shouting with glee at the destruction already created. Teams swarmed out across the field, rushing toward the repair sheds.

''Let's go,'' Oishi shouted, drawing his blade and pointing toward the infamous Hobbs's Pleasure and Amusement Palace.

Within seconds Aldin was regretting his decision as he pumped his spindly legs to keep up. The glass walls of the palace were riddled with gaping holes and glass was still tinkling down, adding an almost cheery counterpoint to the explosions rocking the field. It flashed back a memory of his own palace disintegrating, the demented servo- and Humanbots wandering around before the shock wave hit. It was the same here. A distraught servo was outside, attacking a pile of glass with a near-demented fury, loading up, and then pausing to look around, wondering where it should deposit the mess.

The lead element of samurai hit the front doors, which slid open at their approach. The entire portcullis of the castlelike structure suddenly lit up in a gaudy display. Thousands of lights flashed on, forming a single word, HOBBS, though the second *B* and most of the *S* were missing. Wild calliope music filled the air, though the computer that controlled it must have had a couple of links jarred loose, for the music was pumping out at at least three times normal speed.

"Welcome to Hobbs," a booming voice echoed, so that the assault team slowed in bewilderment.

The shifting lights on a massive billboard over the entrance clicked into a wild exotic show. Couples appeared to be dancing, dice and playing cards flickered across the screen, roulette wheels spun merrily, while female Humans and Gafs appeared in a chorus line that quickly degenerated into a most unusual interspecies erotic display.

Oishi charged through the group, pushing it forward, and the team disappeared into the cavernous maw of Hobbs's shattered glass castle.

The gaming tables were empty, chips worth hundreds of thousands of katars littering the floor.

"Aldin, you son of a bitch." Oishi whirled around, blade drawn, the other samurai pointing Erik 15s at the protesting form that floated into the room, the Gafs leveling their cluster round launchers.

At the sight of an old comrade from his early days as a vasba, Aldin almost felt a touch of nostalgia. Hobbs was yet another distant cousin through his first marriage into the Gablona clan. And as was typical of the Gablona line, to call this man portly was an understatement. The owner of the amusement resort floated into the center of the room, riding a lift chair, which groaned under a mass that made Corbin look like he had been to a reduction clinic. The chair, a gaudy model with genuine gold gilding, carried Hobbs across the room.

Hobbs's piglike eyes squinted out through roll after roll of flesh, his head so massive it was impossible to discern where his jowls ended and the rest of his body began.

Several guards came out, flanking their boss, but at the sight of the heavily armed samurai and Gafs confronting them, their resolve weakened. Hobbs, with a wave of his beefy hand, dismissed them.

"I'll sue you," Hobbs shouted angrily. "I'll sue you blind."

Wearily Aldin shook his head, coming up to stand beside an old acquaintance he had not seen in years.

"Sorry you got in the way, Hobbs," Aldin said in an almost self-deprecating manner. "It had to be done."

"What in the name of the Cloud does my innocent emporium have to do with your little squabble?"

"Corbin, is he here?" Oishi barked, coming up to face the giant who floated before him.

"Check my register, you imbecile," Hobbs roared. "He left yesterday! So why did you have to smash my place up?"

Oishi went over to the desk and punched up the guest register. He scanned the list, saw Corbin's coded entry, and angrily smashed the keyboard with his fist.

"Damn, we missed him."

"I'm just a poor cousin, the same way you were when you married into the family," Hobbs shouted, his voice taking on the whine of an injured child. "I got my life savings in this joint, and now because of the two of you I'm wiped out."

"I'll make good on it once this is over," Aldin said, trying to calm the man down. "You and I both know Corbin's been using this place to refit his ships with weapons. I had to take it out even if he wasn't here."

Hobbs fell silent. He knew that protesting his innocence on

that point was useless, the shattered evidence lay everywhere out on the field. Corbin had offered him far too good a deal, to slowly cut back the entertainment business and then use the amusement center as a cover.

"And besides," Oishi interjected, "we heard how you threw a gaming party the day the war started."

Hobbs looked around guiltily.

"Family pressure," he replied lamely.

"If the Overseers ever found out about what you were covering for here, you'd be in reeducation and weight loss," Aldin said coldly.

Hobbs leaned back and started to roar with laughter.

"What's so damn funny?" Aldin inquired.

"I can't say," Hobbs said, a touch of mirth in his voice.

"All right, sweep the place," Aldin commanded, looking back at his warriors.

The samurai moved out, storming up to the second floor where the guest suites were located.

Seconds later shrill cries filled the gaming room, as dozens of entertainment girls came rushing in, circling around Hobbs as if their boss could actually offer some protection from an armed assault team. Aldin eyed the Human and Gaf females with interest. He thought back to the night he had first met Hobbs, and what they had accomplished at a little entertainment dive on Luxot, and as if the purveyor of amusement had read his mind, the two smiled.

"Bit too old now for those days," Aldin said wistfully.

"Damn me, Aldin Larice, come back when your little skirmish is over with my cousin and I'll show you you're never too old."

Aldin chuckled softly.

"I'm married, you know."

"Yeah, I heard about her. Miss Amazon. It'll never last."

Aldin nodded sadly.

His reverie was suddenly shattered by the angry bark of an Erik 15.

Screaming, the crowd of girls scattered in every direction.

Aldin ducked low, drew his weapon, and scanned the cavernous room.

"Upstairs," Oishi roared, moving up alongside of Aldin.

"I guess you found my guests," Hobbs said, trying to feign a superior boredom. "I didn't think they'd be so stupid as to start shooting."

Wild shouts echoed from the next floor, and moments later Zola Faldon appeared at the top of the stairs, flanked by several samurai.

"How dare you come barging in here like this," Zola shouted, clinging to a towel around his waist. His cry of protest was broken off as the samurai pushed him down the stairs.

Aldin looked over at Hobbs, who gave a weak smile.

"You ain't gonna like what else you'll find up there," Hobbs said quietly.

"Aldin-san." One of the samurai beckoned.

Ignoring Zola's shouted protest, Aldin raced up the stairs, Oishi by his side.

A cluster of samurai stood around a doorway out of which steam was pouring.

Entering the steam bath, Aldin gasped for breath. The far wall of glass was blown wide open; shards of glass had sickled the length of the room, all the occupants within having sustained a bloody range of injuries. Med servobots were already at work, patching up the dozen or so occupants.

A Gaf body lay spread-eagled by the door, a gaping hole in the middle of his chest. It was Kulta, a minor Koh of the Gaf-dominated Nagamak sector.

"He had a weapon under his robe," one of the samurai said. "There was nothing I could do."

Now it was really going to hit, Aldin realized. A Koh had finally been killed.

At the sight of Aldin, the half dozen other Kohs in the room broke into wild taunts and threats. Aldin looked around the room with disdain.

"So how much have you made off the gaming so far?" he snapped angrily.

"Not as much as I'm going to collect when you're dead," Zola shouted from out in the hallway. "The Overseers are going to send you up for life on this one!"

Zola barged back into the room and pointed to the now faintly visible far corner.

Aldin saw the second body and his heart froze.

The glass beneath his feet crackled loudly as Aldin nervously approached the body. He had never seen one face-to-face before, and now at last he was looking at an Overseer. A dead Overseer.

The room became as quiet as a tomb. The being had been decapitated, his multifaceted eyes looking up at him a half dozen feet away from the rest of the body. Aldin looked back at the Kohs who gazed at him accusingly.

"They won't stop till you're hunted down," Zola hissed excitedly.

Aldin looked at the group with disdain.

"You helped to let the genie out of the bottle," Aldin snapped back. "We gamed for hundreds of years as a gentlemen's sport. Then Corbin got greedy and cheated on the Alexandrian affair. So all of you in your wisdom put us into a fight. Now Corbin is triggering an interstellar war and you damn fools are gambling on it! Now we're all involved. Just what the hell was that Overseer doing here?"

The group looked back defiantly, but stayed silent.

"Gambling with you, is that it?" Aldin shouted.

Several of the Kohs looked nervously at Zola, and in that moment Aldin understood.

"Larice!"

The shout was from outside the building. Going over to the shattered wall, Aldin looked out to see Basak. On the far side of the landing field a hangar boiled up in a fireball of light, illuminating the berserker in a sharp red glare, and showing all too clearly the struggling form that he was holding up with a single hand.

"Caught him trying to sneak aboard an undamaged yacht," Basak roared. "Should I throw him back in the fire?"

Aldin stood frozen, unable to respond. The grinning berserker was holding the kicking, struggling form of an Overseer up in the air with his one hairy paw.

"Oh, gods," Aldin groaned. Now they were really in it for certain.

"Go ahead and play your damn game," Aldin snapped, looking back at the other Kohs and figuring that since he was in it so deep he might as well try to bluff them into intimidation.

"Overseers here proves one thing beyond doubt, those bastards are in it, too. That stiff in the corner won't talk, but the other one didn't get away."

The Kohs looked nervously at each other.

"Now I wouldn't go blowing this out of proportion," Zola said in his high-pitched whine, coming up to Aldin's side even as he stalked out of the room.

Aldin looked over at Zola.

"Look, Zola, the other Kohs never gave you any respect in the old days, but I never did anything wrong to you. I even arranged a couple of games for you at discount, which was strictly against my contract with Corbin."

Zola nodded, obviously torn between fear of the dead Overseer, the captured live one, and what Aldin might be getting them all into.

"I want the truth from you, just this one time, and I'll never ask again," Aldin said softly, drawing Zola down the glass-covered corridor and away from the other Kohs. "Just answer me this: are the Overseers in this game against me?"

The diminutive Koh looked nervously back at the steam room.

"You tried to rig the last game to your own advantage and I lost a good samurai and a friend as a result," Aldin whispered. "I've never told my friend Oishi that." He nodded significantly to where his bodyguard stood in the corridor.

"If I blow that to him now, that you were instrumental in killing his brother, I think he'd kill you out of hand."

"You wouldn't do that, would you?" Zola whispered.

"Watch me."

Zola licked his lips nervously, still clutching the towel around his skinny waist, and motioned for Aldin to follow him over to a corner of the hallway.

"The game was the Overseers' idea," he whispered. "We all know Corbin's nuts. All of us were just hoping he'd run into an uncharted rock during a jump outside of the lanes or something like that. Hell, Aldin, we all hated you for wiping us out, but in a good-natured way, if you get my meaning. We cheated you, you cheated us; isn't that what business is all about?"

He smiled woodenly, and Aldin forced a smile in return to hide his disgust.

"Then we heard that Corbin had sprung some Al'Shiga. Now that got us nervous."

"And you never bothered to tip me off about Corbin or the Overseers, damn you."

"Honestly, I was getting set to pass a message along. But then a small group of us was suddenly visited by an Overseer. He proposed to us a little betting venture"—Zola shrugged his shoulders—"and the offer was just too good to refuse."

"A little excitement, is that it?"

"Well, you must admit we've never seen a game anywhere other than on a planet. This had all sorts of exciting permutations. The only time we've ever bet on space combat was back in the old days when Yaroslav made up a couple of those historical computer simulators of the war of the three races. This Overseer promised us the real stuff, and at house odds with only a 2 percent commission. Hell, Aldin, that's even better than your old rates."

Zola looked up at him as if he should of course understand the logic of it all.

"I suppose a gentleman really couldn't pass up such a chance," Aldin said, his features creased by a thin smile.

"Exactly!" Zola said eagerly, clapping Aldin on the back as if he were the most understanding of fellows and that all was forgiven.

"And now it's out of control," Aldin roared.

Zola drew back fearfully.

"We figured you'd get hit in the opening round," Zola said

nervously. "Nothing personal intended, of course, or given your resourcefulness you'd knock him out inside of a couple of weeks."

"And, of course, you bet on my winning."

"Oh, but of course."

"At last count, seven worlds have been hit by asteroid shots, another twenty-five by ground landings, and one entire planet damn near wrecked," Aldin said sharply. "Things were bad enough with you and the other Kohs ruining the economy; this on top of it all is creating chaos. You make me sick to think you're betting on this."

"Don't give me your holier than thou," Zola retaliated. "We saw thousands die on primitive worlds during the arranged matches of old. Easier when it's primitives dying, is that it?"

Aldin fell silent. Suddenly he felt very, very old. Wearily he turned away.

"It's got to stop," Aldin said softly. "Try and arrange a set match with Corbin. We'll meet on a planet, his people against mine, winner take all."

"Always the romantic," Zola replied haughtily, the whine of a true upper class gentleman returning. "Corbin's insane. I half think you're nothing but an excuse for him to run rabid through the space lanes."

"So how do we stop him?" Aldin asked.

"Kill him," Zola replied sharply.

"And the Overseers?"

"That's your problem to figure out," Zola replied, a malicious grin lighting his features. "In all our recorded history, no one's ever killed an Overseer. I wonder what they plan to do about your little precedent-breaking act?"

Aldin was at a loss for words. Turning around, he started down the stairs. Hobbs waited for him at the bottom of the sweeping staircase, surrounded by his entourage of exotic performers.

"So now you know what you've done," Hobbs said, a genuine touch of pity in his voice.

Aldin looked around at the wreckage.

"Hobbs, I suggest you get out of here," Aldin said. "The Overseers might not like witnesses to this little transgression of theirs."

The man's jowls quivered nervously.

"What about my place?"

"Put it on my tab," Aldin said, a thin smile creasing his face.

"How can I get out of here?" Hobbs moaned. "You've smashed every ship."

Aldin looked around the room. If the Overseers had gone so far as to actually instigate a game, the last thing they'd want would be witnesses, now that one of them had been killed and another was in the hands of his berserkers waiting outside. His plan of action was already being formed by the turn of events, and Hobbs could be a witness that just might help.

He owed the man at least that for all the free meals the impresario had placed before him at one time or another.

"All right then, damn it, come along."

Hobbs let out an excited cry.

"Been years since I've been up," the amusement director said. "Maybe seeing space will do me some good. Come on girls, let's get moving."

"Oh, gods," Aldin groaned. If Mari ever heard about this, the screaming would go nonstop for days.

Aldin looked up the staircase to where Zola and the other Kohs stood.

"The rest of you bastards can stay here," Aldin snapped.

"You're taking the girls with you?" Zola whined.

Aldin grinned wickedly and turning, strode out of the palace.

The outside grounds were as bright as day. Dozens of ships and all the docks and repair sheds were awash with flames. The Gafs were streaming back to the ship, ecstatic with the destruction and arson that they had helped create. They were in such an exuberant mood that he suspected they would even forget their demands for pay, which had been rather in arrears since the start of the war.

Basak came around the side of the building, still holding the kicking Overseer.

"No casualties," Basak reported. "They all ran away and wouldn't fight." His voice was full of disappointment.

A flash of explosions rippled through a hangar, and the building collapsed, crushing a magnificent yacht in a tangle of broken beams.

Basak smiled approvingly and then looked ruefully at the struggling form that he was so easily holding aloft.

"Just what is this thing?" Basak asked curiously.

"Put me down, you oaf," the Overseer said evenly. "Such action is a guarantee of reeducation for all of you."

"Ah, shut up!" Aldin snapped.

The Overseer turned his attention back to Basak.

"I'm an Overseer," he said icily.

Startled, the Gaf let go, dropping his captive to the ground, where he crumpled up in a heap. Full of superstitious dread, Basak let his ax drop from his other hand, and reaching down solicitously, he helped the being back up, nervously dusting him off, all the time mumbling incantations against unseen evils.

Furious, the Overseer looked back at Aldin.

"You murdered one of the select, you'll be reeducated until you die," the Overseer hissed.

"And you, my dear Overseer, have been caught in the middle of a gambling arrangement around our little war." There was a note of disgust in Aldin's voice. "Now everything will break down because of this, the peace of three thousand years shattered by your greed, so don't even try your damned sanctimonious threats."

"What are you going to do?" the Overseer asked nervously.

Aldin was at a complete loss for words. In his hands were a responsibility and power he never imagined possible. All because of this damned raid. If he let the truth out to the entire Cloud, any hope of the Overseers intimidating everyone back to a semblance of peace would be lost. Yet if he did not reveal the truth, he'd be branded a murderer of an Overseer and hunted from one end of the Cloud to the other, not only by Corbin, but by every citizen of the Cloud eager for the reward that would be on his head.

"You're coming with me till I figure it out," Aldin whispered.

"You're a dead man for this," the Overseer hissed.

Aldin looked back at what had once been the symbol of peace and order for the three races.

"Just shut up and listen to Basak here, or I'll find a juice suit and wrap you up in it."

Horrified, Basak looked over at Aldin, and then, still mumbling his incantations, he nervously beckoned for the Overseer to follow him, so intimidated by the responsibility that he completely forgot about his precious ax and one of his warriors had to bring it along.

"Now what are you going to do?" Yaroslav asked, coming out of the ship to join his friend.

"Damned if I know," Aldin replied, shaking his head in confusion.

"I say kill him."

Stunned, the other Overseers who had gathered together for the emergency meeting of consensus looked at the Arch. Never had such words been uttered by the master of a race allegedly dedicated to contemplation and the insurance of peace.

"How have we come to this?" Yu, oldest of the ageless, whispered sadly. "We came to this magnificent Cloud to find quiet contemplation, escaping from the teeming of life in the mother galaxy. And then they followed us here, behaving as they always did, like brawling children. So we came to realize that we must teach them our ways, to control them if we were to survive. It was either that or try the impossible, an uncharted trek to a galaxy far distant, where we would, without doubt, meet the same experience yet again. We knew the task to bring peace to their hearts would take millennia, but it was the only way."

His voice trailed off, and if it were possible for an Overseer to weep, he would have done so.

"Yet, instead, it seems as if they have triumphed over us, polluting us instead of our saving them from themselves. I am saddened that our Arch would contemplate such a thought as violence.''

"It's time to be realistic,'' the Arch snapped back peevishly. "The death of Loysa was easily covered up, but the killing of Retuna, and the capture of Vush on that disgusting game world, is known by hundreds, perhaps thousands.''

"Perhaps we can still negotiate something,'' Yu replied, but his words were met by looks of disdain from the hundreds of Overseers gathered in the audience chamber.

"The myth of our infinite power and our shield of invincibility are gone,'' came a soft voice from the back of the room. The Arch looked up to see that it was Mupa, one of the younger Overseers and a meditation companion of Vush.

"We must establish our dominance again, immediately, otherwise these lower creatures will run roughshod over us,'' Mupa continued, his voice rising in a tone of self-assured insistence.

"Mupa is right, they'll hunt us out in our private meditation worlds and make sport of us,'' another replied. "We'll have no respect.''

There was a loud chorus of agreement.

The Arch nodded slowly as if weighted down with some great burden. Yet inwardly he was near to rejoicing. Throughout the millennia the numbers of the outsiders had increased at a relentless rate, while of the Overseers there were never more than five hundred in number. Only half a dozen had been born since Mupa, to replace those who, after tens of thousands of years, finally grew weary of life and either "spaced'' themselves or just simply disappeared. Control had only worked through the order of Kohs, an arrangement he had never been comfortable with. The arrangement was by accident as much as by design, both sides finding an accommodation with the other, a status quo maintained by the illusion of invincible power and underneath it all the conservative nature of the Kohs, who realized they had a good thing. Their gaming had been viewed as a safe outlet, though a certain decorum had to be maintained, and occasionally one of the Kohs was sent to a "peaceful reorientation'' center to keep the rest just a little off balance and fearful.

But it was, after all, a hoax they had been perpetrating, presenting an aura of limitless power to keep the Kohs in line, who in turn kept the peace and made sure the Overseers and their private meditation worlds were never trespassed upon.

But the Arch had become enough of a student of these distasteful species to know that the bliss of changelessness was anathema to them. Though they could be held in check temporarily, sooner or later the latent pressures of their social system were bound to trigger change. The Xsarns, as a hive species, were somewhat manageable, but as for the Gavarnians and especially the Humans, such hopes were impossible. The old monied families of the Koh class had been facing ever rising pressure from the emerging classes of the nouveau riche, who would not have the tradition of hundreds of years of social breeding to keep them in check.

Gablona had been one such case, as was Zola, never content to simply retain their vast holdings, but always grasping for yet more. Out of such individuals conflict would eventually come. Once there was conflict, sooner or later the mask of unlimited power would be pulled back to reveal just how thin was the true range of power the Overseers controlled.

He knew Vush's idea of triggering a fight was a risk of the first order. But he had hoped that such an action would generate chaos and then the Overseers could come in, offer some minor demonstration to awe the natives, and in the aftermath reestablish an order of Kohs that could again be controlled.

But then again he knew in his heart that he had harbored a darker fantasy: that the war would simply explode in an orgy of destruction that would cripple their economic system and technological base for space flight, so that once again the infinite reaches of the Cloud would be hospitable to the silence and loneliness so eagerly sought by the Select.

Now the plan had gone in a completely unforeseen direction. What little he understood of Human military theory—a subject that the mere contemplation of inevitably created an upset stomach—should have warned him that one of the fundamental principles of war is that whatever has been planned will usually be transmuted into paths unforeseen.

And, as if in some dark accordance with that fundamental principle, events had evolved into something no Overseer could ever imagine—one brother of contemplation killed by the outsiders, another prisoner. It was true that Loysa had died in the collapse of the Skyhook. But his body had never been found, and to reveal his death would have also revealed their complicity in those events.

Vush as a prisoner, he thought darkly, was far different. It was Vush who had first been seduced by the gaming of the Humans and who had found in the acquisition of money a sense of joy. Most all the others were totally mystified by that one. What good was money? No Overseer ever had a need for physical objects. What the mysterious First Travelers had left was sufficient for them, the creation of new things anathema to their beliefs.

All had been stunned when Vush had appeared at a meeting for contemplation wearing a robe of Gavarnian fabric, riding aboard a yacht of Xsarn design. So unlike the quiet simplicity of their own ships, this one was far too overpowered, and filled with the gadgets the lesser species took such perverse delight in. There was even one of their replicated machine Humans aboard, designed along the exaggerated lines of a Human female wearing a most strange costume of leather. It was not even possible to formulate the words to ask what that was for, and for his own sense of tranquility he found it simply best not to ask. And now Vush was in the outsiders' hands. What could they do to him, to corrupt him even more—and for that matter, what might he say as well?

They must reach Vush. For even though he had been seduced halfway, no one could imagine what he might finally turn into, or whom he might turn against after undue exposure to the noisome influences of the outsiders.

The room had fallen silent while the Arch floated before them, lost in his thoughts. He looked down to see that all were waiting for his pronouncements, which would guide their final consensus.

"We must create an object lesson," the Arch finally said, controlling the mounting anger he was feeling. The mere fact that he was feeling anger made him angry. As an Overseer he had spent tens of thousands of years in contemplation just to control such feelings; the outsiders were ruining all of that work.

"First a reward for the capture and presentation to us of Aldin Larice must be posted."

"There is a problem," Yu whispered in reply. "So far there has been no public announcement as to the capture of Vush."

The Arch nodded in reply. Thank the Unseen Ones that at least the Kohs and their distasteful vasbas had kept that fact secret. All were terrified at the prospect of one of their brethren being dragged before a public tribunal, thereby shattering forever the mythical aura the Overseers had granted to them in relationship to the masses. Even though Aldin was a vasba upstart, and as such of no real concern, he could still spill far too many secrets and implicate others, including one of the old school—Bukha Taug, who though an ally of Aldin's was nevertheless a Koh of the highest breeding.

"That leads me to the second consideration," the Arch replied.

"And that is?" Mupa asked, the slightest note of anticipation in his voice, as if he could already imagine what was to be said.

"We shall announce that Aldin Larice and his confederates have kidnapped one of our brothers."

"That will make us look weak," Yu said, shaking his head in disagreement.

"No it will not," the Arch replied forcefully. "For at the same time I shall announce that there will be a demonstration of our wrath for this heinous crime."

"A demonstration?" several of the Overseers asked, curious and excited, but not yet quite sure if what they heard was what he was truly suggesting.

"Exactly," the Arch said.

"What do you have in mind?" Yu interjected.

"Oh, I don't know yet. Blow up a planet, smash a star, some such thing to get our point across. That ought to get their attention."

Mupa, breaking a decorum that had not been shattered at a meeting of consensus in thousands of years, floated up and let out a whoop of delight, while Yu, shaking his head and mumbling a curse, floated out of the room.

"You mean a First Traveler device?" Tulbi, third assistant to the Arch, asked nervously, bobbing into the air excitedly as he spoke.

"We have no more of those terrible devices that can destroy planets," another voice called. "I was on the team that retrieved the device from the sacred Sphere of the First Travelers. When we destroyed the worlds three thousand years back, we used everything we had except for some small tracking missiles that can make themselves disappear. They have not the power for what you are considering. We have nothing, which has been the fortunate bluff that has maintained our position of awe over the barbarians."

"Yet there are other devices," the Arch replied, looking over to Mupa for support.

He knew that most of his brothers were now totally out of their depth with this issue. All but a handful of them eschewed the technology and miracles of the First Travelers. Very few across those thousands of years had ever had the slightest glimmer of curiosity to study the wondrous creations.

The creations of the First Travelers were, to a certain degree, held in reverent awe, even at the same time the Overseers' antitechnological minds had recoiled from the very devices that had given them intergalactic travel, an unending supply of physical comforts, and the myriad of machines to serve them in their isolated meditations. Yet they were material things, and, of course, all that was material must be illusion in the pursuit of inner knowledge and the dreamed-for mindless consciousness that all sought.

The Arch looked over to Mupa, his first assistant, and nodded.

"There is a device I have managed to decipher, and brought back with me thousands of years past," Mupa said, floating up to join the Arch upon the platform.

Mupa was viewed with some slight disdain by his brothers, for he had, like Vush, become somewhat captivated by knowledge other than the search inward. Vush and he had on several occasions even journeyed across the sacred Sphere. Their last visit of nearly four thousand years past had lasted for centuries. They had explored the vast holding bays and storage vaults of the First Travelers that stretched for hundreds upon thousands of miles. If he could have smiled he would have done so with the memory of that time.

The last visit had been slightly unsettling, something had not seemed quite right with the Sphere, as if the machines that were still building it were not working in unified efficiency. That had been a puzzlement, as had been the two small boxes they had brought back with them, along with a number of other curious artifacts. He had offered the boxes when they had smashed several planets to scare the barbarians, but then Arch Yu had deemed them to be too unreliable and had opted instead for the planet-busting devices that they better understood. Now at last he would have a chance to try out his curious toy.

"I have come across a device of the First Travelers," Mupa continued, "which has properties I do not completely understand. It appears that one can place it at a given position in space. Then one removes himself from that area, after carefully pointing it at an intended target. Upon activation, using the control box, which you keep with you, it opens a tear in what I would crudely call the dimensional fabric of time and space, sucks the chosen object through, and then instantly places it somewhere else."

The assembly looked at each other in confusion, staring at Mupa as if he were speaking an unknown language.

Not even noticing their responses, he continued, warming to his subject.

"It is really quite remarkable. I just hit these buttons, it turns on, and in that moment an entire planet disintegrates, travels, if

I wish, light-years away, and then shoots out the other side. It appears as if the First Travelers used it to transport matter to be used in the building of the Kolbard ring-world and the Sphere.

"Is the planet that is moved thus still intact?" Tulbi asked, unable to contain his curiosity.

"Oh, I don't think so," Mupa replied innocently. "I would guess that such a quick trip, for something the size of a planet, would crunch it into dust. But it sure would be something to see."

He fell silent and cleared his throat nervously, ashamed for having become excited.

"Thank you, brother, you have given us our solution," the Arch interrupted, motioning for Mupa to return to his proper position beside the platform. "So you see it really is quite simple," the Arch said. "We take this device, point it at some uninhabited world or a star, and disintegrate it.

"The barbarians will be properly impressed by our power. We can then simply position our ships near their major banking worlds and threaten to do the same. I promise you, my brothers, that within a very brief period of time they will come to us begging for forgiveness. I therefore propose for consensus that within ten standard days we pick an appropriate planet or star as a demonstration to all the inhabitants of the Cloud that we are not to be trifled with."

And this time, the Arch thought, we'll settle it right, by getting rid of any Koh that had grown too upstartish, and above all else that would mean Gablona, and the gamer Larice.

"You sure this device is easily managed?" the Arch asked, looking down at Mupa, ashamed to ask the question in public but nevertheless feeling a need for reassurance.

"Oh, my, yes indeed. Just push all the buttons in the control box for on, and push them again for off, it's as simple as that, and good-bye to a planet. Though I believe that using it on a sun would be far more dramatic and exciting."

If the Arch could smile, he would have.

"Come on," Basak said in an almost begging tone, "try some, you'll like it."

Vush turned away with revulsion at the proffered hunk of meat that the Gaf berserker offered him on the point of his knife.

"Can't you get it through your thick skull that they don't eat meat," Hobbs said wearily, even as he leaned over, scooping the nearly rare steak off the knife point and into his mouth.

"Poor things, just skin and bones," Basak said in a worried tone, looking over at Vush with open concern.

"Why, when I hoisted him into the air I thought I was picking up an empty doll, I did."

Vush, struggling to control himself, in what was an increasingly vain effort to remain aloof, turned away and started for the door.

"Now, now," Basak said, coming to his feet. "You know as well as I do that Aldin said you weren't to leave this room."

The Gaf berserker grinned good-naturedly at Vush, but it was evident from his voice that he'd enjoy hoisting the Overseer into the air again with one hand and holding him aloft for an hour or so for the fun of it.

Hobbs looked over at Vush, and with a nod of his head motioned for the Overseer to rejoin them at the table.

"This is absolutely humiliating," Vush whispered, trying to keep the growing despair out of his voice.

"Ah, so he can talk," Basak roared delightedly. "Seven days we've had you as our guest, and finally you decide to speak. And I'm the one who brought you around."

There was a look of triumph on Basak's face like that of a little boy who had finally solved a puzzle. The half-heard legends of the Overseers had caused him to build up in his Gaf-warrior mind the image of a towering foe who could smash entire planets at the snap of a finger. He had heard Aldin speak of them often enough with awe. He had to confess to himself that his warlord Aldin had been a disappointment the first time he had laid eyes upon him. But by the time Aldin had finished with those damned Al'Shiga, the old man had grown in Basak's thinking to someone at least as powerful as a good Gaf with an ax.

He was still waiting for this Overseer to demonstrate something to put him in awe, but so far he had been disappointed. The eight-foot stature of the being had some promise, but he was nothing but skin and bones, covered in a long white robe that clung to his diminutive frame. The only thing that was unsettling was the multifaceted eyes, sort of like those damned inscrutable Xsarns, Basak thought darkly.

Looking over at Vush he gave him a friendly grimace, revealing his twin rows of sharp yellow teeth, and at the sight of Basak's smile Vush backed around to stand behind Hobbs.

With a snort of disgust Basak went back to his meal. Slicing off another hunk of meat from the leg joint of some unidentifiable creature, he set into eating with the obligatory grunts and smacking noises that those of his clan felt any gentleman should use to express his appreciation for a damn fine meal.

At least the food stocks they had taken from Hobbs's kitchen before beating a hasty retreat had managed to fill all tastes, even this delicacy, whatever it was, Basak thought dryly as he set to chewing.

"I am hungry," Vush whispered.

"Ah, so you do eat!" Hobbs cried excitedly.

"I will not do so in the presence of barbarians," Vush replied indignantly. "I wish to speak to your preparer of foods in private."

Vush gave a shudder of revulsion for this admission. To the Overseers, all natural functions were viewed as being somehow unclean, and were to be practiced in the utmost of privacy. To even admit to having to eat was traumatic; how could he ever admit that for the last four days he had to fulfill another function that was driving him to absolute distraction?

Cheerfully Hobbs brought his chair around to face Vush.

"Aldin said you'd talk sooner or later. Now, let's see, would you care for some boiled lassa, a wonderful delicacy, fit for only the wealthiest Kohs?"

"What is lassa?" Vush asked, unable to contain his curiosity.

"Centipedes found on Odak. The meat comes out all fluffy pink—served with drawn butter it's a delight."

Retching, Vush turned away.

Basak roared with delight at the Overseer's discomfort, but Hobbs shouted for him to be quiet. Sulkily Basak returned to his meal. Balefully he looked over at Hobbs, still not sure if he liked this blotted hairless one; such decisions usually took time. But at least the Gaf females who traveled with this hairless one had proved to be a fitting diversion, so as such he would not insult him too much.

"All right my friend," Hobbs said, propelling his chair to the corner of the room where Vush stood. "Listen, one of my girls is a real charm with near any dish you can imagine. You just tell her what you want, and she can mix it up for you."

"But she's a female," Vush blubbered.

"So?"

"It is not proper," Vush replied. "We have no females among us."

"Damn, what a bore. I'd go mad," Basak roared. "How do you make little Overseers, then?"

Horrified, Vush could not even reply. Female Overseers had left for another galaxy eons ago, claiming a need to remove themselves from the presence of "exploitation," as they put it. He could barely even remember them. As for reproduction, far more sanitary methods of cloning were of course preferable— at least he thought so.

Vush looked over at Basak beseechingly, as if begging him not to pursue this line of the conversation.

"What the hell do you mean no females?" Basak continued. "Or do you fellas only like each other?"

"That is enough!" Vush shouted. "All of you disgust me, absolutely disgust me." And with a wild cry he fled to another corner of the room, curled up in a ball, and started to rock back and forth.

Hobbs gave Basak a sharp look of rebuke.

Basak merely shrugged his shoulders in reply.

"Well, it does seem kind of strange to me," he said defensively, and picking up the hunk of meat off his plate he walked over to the door, punched the access code, and stepped out into the ship's main corridor.

Hobbs gave a quick scan of the room to make sure there were no sharp implements left behind by the Gaf, and guiding his chair he floated to the exit.

"I'll tell you what," Hobbs said. "I'll whip up something without any meat in it, no fish, no nothing that moves. Just some nice greens, how does that sound?"

"It can only be harvested after it has died or has fallen," Vush whispered, raising his head.

"Count on it," Hobbs said soothingly, and leaving the room, he made sure to rescramble the code on the door before proceeding up to Aldin's stateroom.

"Well, did you hear that little exchange?" Hobbs announced, coming through the door without knocking.

Aldin looked up from the viewscreen and smiled.

"At least it got him talking."

Punching in for a servobot to bring a double brandy, Hobbs guided his chair into the center of the room.

"I feel somewhat sorry for him," Oishi said gently, rising from the shabby divan facing the forward viewport and coming over to stand alongside of Hobbs.

"I find that surprising," Aldin said.

"Oh, I know," Oishi replied. "If it hadn't been for their damn meddling, or perhaps lack of meddling, Corbin never would have gotten as far as he did in starting this war. In some ways he reminds me of the holy monks of my old world who removed themselves to hidden places and attempted to find release from the world. I feel more empathy for him than for some others present."

Oishi looked over at Hobbs with a jaundiced eye.

"I already told all of you, I had nothing to do with it. Corbin simply asked me to jack my rates up so the usual clientele would go someplace else, and he'd make up the difference. Hell, I was so busy running the damn place I wasn't even having any fun. Corbin's offer gave the girls and me a chance to relax for a while."

"Why, I never even saw my dear cousin until after he started the war and it was too late to get out of the deal," Hobbs said quickly. "Yaroslav flushed my systems' memory banks, they'll confirm it. It was all done through one of Corbin's old lawyers, curse the damned breed. It was only in the last couple of standard months that those ships dropped in with their damn Al'Shiga, and that gun was emplaced and the supplies started to come in. Next thing I knew I had an illegal military base in my backyard. Light transports would come in, and a couple of weeks later would leave, rearmed with laser weapons and tracking missiles.

"So what was I supposed to do, go out there and chase 'em all away? I'm not even that crazy. They stayed on the base, I just hid in my pleasure house.

"Then that damned Zola and his confederates show up, to evaluate the base, have a good time, and meet with those two Overseers. Then you people drop in and wipe me out."

Hobbs's face started to crinkle up, and there was a groan of disgust from the others in the room. The last thing they felt like listening to was another breast-beating on how his life savings had been wiped out in the hit.

"It's all the truth, Aldin. I know you uploaded my memory systems before you took off, it's all in there." He looked over at Yaroslav for support.

"Hobbs, I've known you for nearly forty years," Yaroslav sniffed, "and from the first day I was convinced you'd charge admission to your own mother's funeral if you thought you could make a katar out of it. When we were teaching together at the university, you were accepting bribes from students in your literature classes to jack up their grades."

"Well, they paid, didn't they?" Hobbs said defensively. Looking injured, he sank into his chair.

"But your records were clean," Yaroslav finally admitted, "even the coded access ones I finally managed to crack this morning."

"You cracked my private files?" Hobbs asked, looking slightly embarrassed.

"It's a good thing Bukha isn't in this room," Yaroslav said with a wicked grin. "Your little holo vid journal with that Gaf delectable, Peaches I think you call her, would definitely outrage his sense of morality."

Guiltily Hobbs looked around the room. Interspecies sex did occur—at least between Gafs and Humans; if anyone had ever tried something with a Xsarn there was no record of ever admitting to it—but to the vast majority of puritanical Gaf males, such actions were an outrage.

Basak stopped his meal in midbite.

"Peaches," he growled quietly. "You mean my Peta? Did you say something about my Peta?"

"I think it's the one and same," Yaroslav whispered, leaning over Basak's shoulder.

With a growl Basak started to come to his feet.

"Now, now," Aldin said, extending his hand. "Remember, Basak, different people, different customs, you've got to honor that when you're with me."

Basak shot Hobbs a nasty look and then sulkily settled back into his chair.

"At least your little idea worked," Yaroslav said, looking over at Aldin and shifting the topic.

"Yeah, it was a fairly good one at that," Aldin said, a grin lighting his features. "Just stick Vush in a locked room for a day with the two most disgusting beings aboard this ship and he'd be bound to crack."

Basak's mane, trapped beneath the folds of his Day-Glo yellow jumpsuit, bristled up with pride at the compliment Aldin had paid him, while Hobbs, caught now between his anxiety over Basak and a sense of being outraged, simply was too confused to respond.

"Interesting comment about no female Overseers," Yaroslav said, as if almost to himself.

"Sounds like they have a problem, if you ask me," Basak interjected as he noisily sucked on the remnants of the bone he had been chewing on.

"It is a point," Aldin replied. "Now that we at least got him talking about something, perhaps we can loosen him up further and start pumping for information about the Overseers."

"So you've decided to give him a free passage out?" Oishi asked with a note of concern.

"Call him a guest for right now, but first chance that we can get him back to his people, I'm letting him go," Aldin replied, coming to his feet and walking over to the forward viewport.

The Overseer had been a point of contention between Oishi and Aldin. The samurai felt the best possible way to handle the situation was to hang on to him and use him for a bargaining chip. At first Aldin had felt the same way, fearing a massive manhunt across the Cloud the moment he no longer had Vush as a shield. But on the other side it was the first direct exposure he had ever had to the hidden power-holders of the Cloud, and he could be a possible source of information, and at least could tell their side of the story if he felt he had been treated fairly.

Lost in thought, Aldin gazed absently at the panorama outside the forward viewport. The great Core Cluster of the Cloud filled the entire window with a swirling mass of brilliance. The jumpout had taken several long days into this almost-unknown transit point going outward toward his favorite spot, the Kolbard Ring of Alexander the Great. The next jump point could take them straight in, or by swinging over to the one other track would simply lead them out into unexplored reaches of empty space. It was, Aldin hoped, the safest place he could find for the moment. He knew that the Overseers would respond to the death of one of their comrades and the kidnapping of another. When the time came, he did not want to be anywhere in the Cloud, for though he had lost all fear and respect for them, still he was not quite sure of what technology they had up their sleeves for locating someone they really wanted to find.

He knew as well that Corbin would be scrambling after the hit, and that even though Corbin was innocent of the death of an Overseer that perhaps there would be a backlash against him as well.

"Aldin, something's coming in through the commlink," Tia said, looking up from the console set in the far corner of the room.

Aldin, his joints cracking, went over to join her.

From Aldin's expression while he looked at the screen, Oishi and the others saw that the news on a general broadcast channel was less than pleasant.

After a long moment Aldin turned to face his friends.

"Well," he whispered, "I guess we're really in the fire now."

CHAPTER 4

"OF COURSE, YOU MUST UNDERSTAND THE SHOCK, THE DIS-
gust I felt when his horrifying actions were made known to me,"
Corbin Gablona said silkily, his face a mirror of humble piety.

Tulbi, envoy of the Overseers, the voice of the Arch, struggling to control his inner feelings, said nothing. He knew this
barbarian was inwardly gleeful at the discomfort the Overseers
were now experiencing. He wished as well that somehow the
tables were back to where they should be, with this barbarian
groveling in fear before a representative of the Arch.

"Do you have any suspicions of where this Larice person and
his fellow conspirators might be hiding?"

"Upon my word as a gentleman, believe me if I even had the
slightest hint, I would most certainly have rushed to get word to
you immediately and sortie out personally in an attempt to save
your comrade from any further indignity," Corbin replied almost breathlessly, while holding up his bejeweled hand, as if
examining the thirty carat stone on his pinky for a flaw.

"You've heard the broadcast that went out to the entire
Cloud?"

Heard it? It had turned his stomach with abject terror. At first he had thought the Overseers would lump him in as an offending party as well. But when the full details came in, branding Aldin as the sole culprit, he relaxed. Though it was rather curious, Bukha was not mentioned at all. And the part about one of them being sliced up at Hobbs's in front of that squealy-voiced Zola and half a dozen other Kohs—no mention of that at all. Just the "kidnapping" of Vush, and nothing else. He half suspected they were playing a divide-and-conquer game, but if it eliminated Larice, then let them demonstrate their power; he could play along for now. And it seemed that in their stupidity they were actually offering him a pardon for the war, and would act as if everything had been Larice's fault. Their demonstration would shake everyone up to be sure. And if he played his cards right, when everything settled down they'd make sure he was back in as one of the leading Kohs.

The thought filled him with anticipation. That's how they'd have to play it out. Smash a planet, scare the Xsarn food out of everyone who would then come groveling. Then they'd point out some of the old trusted leaders and reestablish order. It'd be just like the old days again.

Of course, Larice would be gone, and he would get back all that was taken by that upstart. And then the others would go as well. Oh, I'll bide my time, Corbin thought, not allowing his expression to change into one of anticipation. Hassan and the others would have to be put on ice for a while, if need be an accident could be arranged to get rid of them and make himself look respectable. But after a time, he could let Hassan, or his replacement, take care of all the others, one by one, starting with Bukha, Zola, and the Xsarn Prime. The art of revenge had to be upheld, Corbin realized; it was, after all, a family tradition.

"A righteous response and well called for. Yet again a demonstration of your infinite wisdom," Corbin said, allowing the right tone of fawning awe to creep into his voice. "I knew that gutter-bred Larice would be the downfall of the Koh system. That is why I tried to resist him for so long.

"Oh, he is a skillful one," Corbin continued. "His people

made it appear as if this conflict were all my doing. But believe me, I have the evidence to prove that he started it all."

"Of course you do," Tulbi sniffed in reply.

"So what do you want of me?" Corbin asked, knowing they were now at the real heart of the matter.

"In three standard days we will make our demonstration of power. If you wish to be in the same system to witness it, you may be my personal guest."

"I wouldn't miss it for the universe," Corbin replied with an almost childlike joy.

It was going to be a real planet smash, and to his jaded senses such an event couldn't be missed. What they were promising was going to make his cargo ship "accident" look like a child's firecracker in comparison. Granted, the event would be broadcast live throughout the entire Cloud, but it was never as good as being there. Anyone who wished to maintain his reputation for being on the in at exotic events simply had to attend.

"In fact we command that you be there, along with all the other Kohs, so that all of you can see what can be done if our ire is provoked."

"As you command," Corbin replied, going so far as to incline his head as a token of respect.

"There shall be an investigation," Tulbi continued, "and if I do remember correctly, there is the little matter of your breaking out of a reeducation seminar just before that disgusting business on the planet of the Al'Shiga."

Even though he was in a heavily-armed ship, Corbin felt a twinge of fear. The Overseer had arrived alone, aboard a Xsarn-piloted yacht, with a guarantee of noninterference. But the thought of being back in an Overseer juice suit made his skin crawl.

"I ain't got nothing to do with that. Hell, I wanted to stay, that damned Zergh and his friends kidnapped me. I'm innocent, I tell you."

"I just want to remind you that you still owe us something like three thousand standard days of reeducation."

"Now you aren't thinking of sending me back there?" Corbin

growled, his tone suddenly belligerent. " 'Cause if you are, I ain't going."

Tulbi looked coldly at the creature seated before him, amazed at how quickly, and childishly, he could shift from simpering to threats. Typical of the species. He was inwardly disgusted with having to deal with this renegade, or for that matter any of the three species. But for now it could pass. They already had their plan within a plan to deal with him when the time came. At the present it suited their purposes to act as if they were going to overlook his multitude of transgressions. For one thing, it would completely unsettle the other Kohs to see Corbin apparently forgiven, if he performed the necessary acts of obeisance. They could use him then as the spy to keep the others in line, and, if need be, eliminate other Kohs. In the end, of course, they would have him in the juice suit for the rest of his life, if he was lucky enough to survive.

"Come, come, I was not even considering reeducation," Tulbi whispered soothingly.

"So why the threat then?" Corbin retorted.

"Just a reminder that we are willing to overlook certain little mistakes if you demonstrate a new understanding of our needs and are willing to cooperate in our new universal order."

"Who said I wasn't willing to cooperate?" Corbin snapped back.

These barbarians, Tulbi sighed inwardly. When all of this was done, he knew he'd need at least a hundred years of complete solitude and meditation to wash their filthiness from his soul.

"It's just we want to recover our brother intact," Tulbi said quickly, trying to steer the conversation back to its original point.

"So why didn't you say so in the beginning?" Corbin laughed. "That'll be easy to arrange."

"That's all we ask of you in return for certain considerations."

"Like washing my slate clean."

"Washing your slate?"

"You know, letting me off the hook."

"That sounds horrible. We would never put someone on a hook," Tulbi said in the most sanctimonious of tones.

Corbin sighed. "Forgetting about my sentence."

Tulbi nodded at last in understanding.

"Yes, the slates will be clean."

"I would be remiss if I did not offer my services in other ways as well," Corbin said, his voice silky.

"And what additional services are you referring to?"

"Larice's financial management has left the Cloud in chaos. It will take a lifetime to straighten out," Corbin said, with a heavy tone, as if the responsibility of it all were already weighing him down. "Now as for myself, I have had a lifetime of experience in such economic concerns, which, besides creating prosperity, also builds harmony and understanding.

"Since most of those corporate concerns were mine to start with, before this upstart so vilely cheated me out of them—" He paused for a moment, his features reddening, and then regaining control he continued. "—I know that it will help the cause of peace if I assume control of what I ruled before all this unpleasantness started."

Trying to keep from gagging, Tulbi continued to nod.

"That was our intention, but it is important that our brother be returned intact to us, otherwise we will be most deeply distressed, and in such a moment I cannot say what the consensus of my brothers might be.

"You do know how such things can be," Tulbi said, as if speaking now to a close friend of such superior intellect that it was almost not worth bothering to say. "Perhaps the wrong people might get blamed, perhaps even all the Kohs might be found at fault."

He smiled, if such a thing was possible for an Overseer, and Corbin felt as if the temperature in the room had suddenly dropped.

"When you said intact, I assume you mean you want Vush back alive and unharmed."

"How did you know his name?" Tulbi asked, unable to hold back his curiosity.

"Oh, word gets around," Corbin said, chuckling at the Overseer's discomfort. "Remember there were a couple of dozen witnesses to his abduction, along with the security holo cameras that Hobbs forgot to erase."

The fact that Vush had given his name to barbarians, the fact that he had even met with them in secret to gamble on the war, was shocking to Tulbi's sense of orthodoxy. Surely Vush himself might wind up in reeducation, something unheard of for an Overseer in a score of millennia. But before the barbarians it must never appear that a brother had actually strayed from the path.

"I heard he even had a couple of shots of liquor at the party just before the strike on Larice's planet, and then there was that scene with his Humanbot, but good taste prevents me from elaborating on that, the code of gentlemen you understand," Corbin interjected, guessing that little lie would surely cause a reaction.

He struggled to control a grin at the obvious shock of Tulbi, who nervously ran his hands up and down the sides of his robes, struck speechless by the thought of an Overseer behaving in such a manner.

"And this is on holo tapes?"

"I heard there's copies floating all over the place."

Tulbi actually twitched, and Corbin sat back, examining his curled fingernails for a long minute before pressing on.

"Some of the Kohs said that given a couple of more days your Vush would have been one of the boys, indulging in all sorts of delightful vices."

"Enough!" Tulbi roared.

"Now, now," Corbin cried, holding his hands up in a soothing gesture. "Just thought you should know that one of your boys was maybe out making a little hay on the side."

That phrase had Tulbi thoroughly lost, but he did not even wish to inquire, fearful of what "making hay" might really mean.

"Don't worry though," Corbin quickly continued, "his little mistakes are safe with me. My boys are tracking down the tapes and destroying all of them. Gentlemen, after all, don't keep such information on other gentlemen. It's terribly embarrassing for everyone if that type of scandalous material gets into the hands of those damn news people." He gave Tulbi a conspiratorial wink.

Completely lost at the significance of certain barbarian phrases and body gestures, he floated into the air and drifted to the door, signifying the interview was at an end.

"Just one question though, your excellency, before you leave."

"And that is?"

"What do you want me to do about Aldin Larice, Bukha Taug, and his other hangers-on? After all, if we do manage to find your brother Vush, chances are the others will be there as well."

Tulbi still could not believe the orders the Arch had directly given to him regarding this question. He had hoped it would not be asked, that the unspoken implication would be message enough, and thus he would not have to carry its burden upon his destiny.

"Whatever you wish, we will not interfere," Tulbi replied, using the Arch's exact words.

"I was hoping you would say that," Corbin said cheerfully, and Tulbi shuddered inside as he drifted from the room. Turning in his chair, Corbin looked up at the holo camera lens, no bigger than the point of a needle in the wall, and smiled.

"I can't believe this, they're mad!" Vush cried, bursting into the forward cabin, holding his head bobbing up and down in an agitated manner, with Hobbs and Basak following behind him.

"If Mupa's doing it, it's insanity."

Shocked by the sudden emotional display of an Overseer, Aldin remained quiet, glad that his guest had finally broken at last. After Hobbs had told Vush about the Arch's announcement, Vush had emitted one loud shriek and then curled up in the far corner of his room, rolled into a tight ball, and started to shake—until now.

Stunned, the group looked at the Overseer. Yaroslav, in a

most nonchalant manner, poured out a tumbler of brandy and offered it over. Somehow the Overseers could manipulate objects within very close range with a remarkable dexterity. The tumbler drifted out of Yaroslav's hand, floated up, twirled several times to coat the inside of the glass, and then tilted up to Vush's lips.

"Remind me not to play roulette with you ever again," Hobbs growled.

Still floating, Vush looked around the room, coughing slightly from the drink, which he downed in a single gulp.

"The announcement said that my brothers were going to smash a planet?" Vush asked nervously.

"Forty-eight standard hours from now."

As if disbelieving what he was hearing, Vush violently shook his head.

"They don't know what they are doing," Vush whispered nervously.

Aldin could sense that he was treading somehow into completely unknown areas of Overseer powers.

"Why do you feel they don't know what they are doing?" Oishi asked, trying to keep the nervousness out of his voice. "You chaps have done this thing before."

Vush looked down at Aldin, fixing him with his gaze. He knew that he was in deep enough trouble as it was, and upon his return to his brothers would be viewed as an outcast for millennia to come. Though in his age-long pursuit of inner knowledge and contemplation he had grown used to the self-imposed isolation of the Brotherhood of Searches, this was somehow different. Now he truly was alone, rejected most likely by the only social system he had ever known.

"You must get me in touch with my brothers," Vush said, with a decided note of pleading in his voice.

Aldin was on the edge of rejecting the request out of hand, but some inner sense stopped him. He could actually sense fear in this one.

Oishi shook his head and gave a snort of disdain.

"Oh, most certainly. There's a price on Aldin's head and all of us are in this up to our necks. The announcement claimed we kidnapped you from your ship and are holding you hostage. The moment we allow you to make a commlink transmission, every fortune hunter in the Cloud will flock to where we are.''

"If I put you in touch with them, I'd be placing myself at risk,'' Aldin said. "I'm way the hell out here to give me a little breathing room. If I drop a transmission for you, it'll be like a beacon advertising my presence.''

"You could always jump out right after you sent my signal,'' Vush said.

"Look, you might not know the translight jump-point system, but I do. There's only one line out this way, and heaven knows how far out it continues.''

Without asking permission, Vush floated over Tia's shoulder and looked down at the nav screen.

"Why did you choose out here?''

"Seemed safe,'' Tia replied, a bit testy at the Overseer's tone. "No one comes out this way, and if they did we could jump to the next gate and then turn into the Kolbard Ring.''

"The next jump gate out will take you straight to the ring-world or off into nothing.''

Aldin, though his face-to-face contact with Overseers was limited to this occasion, sensed that there was something behind Vush's curiosity. A probing as if Vush were trying to find out if Aldin knew something more than he should have.

"Oh, of course,'' Vush replied, looking straight at Aldin with his unfathomable eyes, the sight of which made Aldin feel as if he were a specimen on a dissecting table.

"I need to send a message, it's essential,'' Vush said, and again there was a pleading to his tone.

"I send the signal, everyone knows where I am. It'll take me a day and a half to jump down to a major nexus point, and what'll I see? Either your people or Gablona's waiting for the kill as I come out of null. Thanks but no thanks.''

"You'll regret this, all three of your barbarians species will regret this,'' Vush replied, without any threat in his voice.

"Why?'' Zergh sniffed. "Because you're going to bust a

planet? Hell, I know your species well enough now to realize you'd never have the moral turpitude to smash a planet with any type of life on it. So you'll blow some lifeless rock apart. All us ignorant savages will shake in our boots. The war between Gablona and us will end simply by the pressure the other fearful Kohs will finally exert. This is exactly what we want. Once things cool off, we'll let you go."

"You were going to do that?"

Aldin shook his head.

"What the hell do you think we are? Barbarians?" He looked at the Overseer, not sure if he should be angry at the insult to his own integrity.

"Finding you down there was an accident," Yaroslav interjected, "so don't go inflating your ego by thinking that we blew up Hobbs's place just to get at you. Isn't that right, Hobbs?"

Hobbs, who sat in the far corner of the room, roused himself from an alcohol-induced daze long enough to nod in agreement.

"He was after my cousin Corbin, the shipyard, and supplies. You were an accident and I got caught in the middle."

The Overseer looked back over at Aldin.

"You mean you didn't really want me?"

"It was an accident." Aldin sighed. "The death of your fellow Overseer an accident I never wanted. We dropped the rock in to destroy the automatic ground defenses. If we really wanted to kill everyone, we would have landed the rock square on the pleasure palace."

Hobbs nodded in agreement, a sentimental tear streaking his face at the memory of his home.

"You'd have never hurt your old friend, would you Larice?"

Aldin smiled and shook his head.

"Knowing my dear cousin," Hobbs said dryly, "if he had arrived after the raid and found you there, he might have killed all of us and then blamed it on Aldin, so consider my vasba friend there as having perhaps saved your life."

Vush, thoroughly confused by the logic of individuals who almost kill him and then claim to have saved him, was silent, looking back and forth around the room.

"Look," Aldin said, actually reaching up and patting the Overseer on the side, an action that caused Vush to recoil in horror. Aldin held his hand out in apology.

"Once things cool off, and I can figure out a way to get you back to your people, I will. If I just let you go, chances are Corbin might knock you off so I can be blamed for it. It's that simple, so why don't you just relax and enjoy yourself."

"Oh, the holo tape I have of him will show you just how much he can enjoy himself." Hobbs chuckled, and several of the girls with him laughed in a decidedly lewd manner.

"The only thing I'd ask of you is that when you get back to your people that you explain my side of things," Aldin continued. "None of us is going to accept reeducation, that's for sure. Just leave us alone, make sure Corbin and his murderous cutthroats are kept off our backs, and we'll just quietly disappear."

Even though the war would be over, Aldin thought, he was finished anyhow, and would be the scapegoat for everything that had gone wrong over the last several standard years. At best he might be able to sneak back to the shattered remains of his pleasure world, where he had had the foresight to stockpile a fair supply of portable assets. At least his old days as a gaming vasba had taught him to always keep a little cold cash hidden away in case he had to get out of town on very short notice.

There were enough gems, gold, and credit units there so he could at least live out his retirement in some comfort. The only question would be where to go. No space-faring world would be safe, since wanted postings and that twenty million katar reward were enough to have almost anyone turning in his own grandmother. Perhaps the Ring where even now Alexander the Great still lived would be the place to go. There at least, he and his friends could live comfortably, and the company of Alexander would be interesting to say the least. And besides, he realized somewhat sadly, he actually didn't want the old life back anymore. He had achieved everything, and found that without any interesting challenges it was far too boring. Life had simply become a process of trying to hold on to what he had already won. In a perverse sort of way the war had actually given him something back. Mari, with a couple of Gaf guards, had been disembarked, so at least there was quiet. As for the rest, he pushed the thought aside—there was no use going over his own angst of existence yet again—and looked back at Vush.

Amazed with what he had just heard, Vush nodded his head in agreement, having learned that was a signal to Humans of agreement.

"But will you send the signal now? I must talk to my Arch," Vush asked, a note of pleading creeping into his voice.

"What do you want to tell him?"

Vush struggled with the temptation to tell the full truth. If his guess was right, this little demonstration would be engineered by Mupa. As one of the youngest of the brothers, he had expressed interest in First Traveler technologies, which the others used but never really attempted to understand. If an Overseer could have a friend among his comrades, Mupa would fill such a position. There had been a time, in the very beginning when the five hundred of them had first come to the Cloud, that he and Mupa had been enthralled by the great workings of the First Travelers. They had spent several millennia together, walking about the Ring. And then it was Mupa who discovered the Great Sphere, and the Ring had then paled in comparison.

The sheer magnitude of the greatest edifice ever created by the First Travelers, or any sentient beings, had come very near to seducing him with its technical wonders. The fact of the matter was that in his heart he knew it had indeed seduced him. The Great Sphere was over two million kilometers in diameter, with literally billions of kilometers of corridors, living areas, and, curiously, abandoned cities that might have housed trillions. It had been a quest for him and Mupa. The other five hundred had wandered off to uninhabited worlds, unsettled by the sheer magnitude of something beyond their power to create. Mupa and he had been alone, claiming the entire Sphere.

It had been a most haunting, chilling reality. Two alone in a vast structure, the greatest in the entire Cloud, and not once in their millennia of exploration had they encountered another sentient living soul. They had indeed met what they believed was a First Traveler machine, but it had expressed no interest in either of them, other than a strangely feeble attempt to get them to indulge in some foolish pastime that they had of course ignored, looking instead for more insightful experiences. Other machines, vast arrays of them, quietly traversed the labyrinth world, repairing, and in many areas, still building, for nearly one-eighth of the great structure was still open to space, like a piece of fruit with a section of it peeled off. In one of their last visits something had seemed wrong with it all, here and there a machine working at cross-purposes, but that visit had been too brief to contemplate the significance of this anomaly. The devices to destroy half a dozen planets were found in a great storage building.

The unsettling question beneath it all was why? Just why had the First Travelers set about to build such things, and then disappeared? He knew that the Ring was older, perhaps a test structure before setting out to totally encase an artificially created star. They had started the Sphere, it was still not finished, but there was no one there.

When technical questions regarding a First Traveler artifact forced their way into the attention of the Overseers, Loysa, who was far more of the scholar, was usually consulted. It was he who had used the devices for the first demonstration to overawe the three barbarian species. But Loysa was now dead in the collapsed Skyhook. Only Mupa was still around. And Mupa was an immature fool who held even less knowledge than Vush did.

When confronted by First Traveler technology, Vush felt, at best, as if he were gazing at some vast and impenetrable mystery. He knew that their machines ran flawlessly, and at times he could occasionally push a button to perform some task, but as to the hows and whys, that was simply beyond him.

The Arch had finally ordered them away from the Great Sphere, claiming that it was having a detrimental effect upon their spiritual quests. Yet in the nearly three thousand years of contemplation that followed, still he found his inner curiosity harkening back to the great corridors, and the awe-inspiring sight of standing on the inner surface of the Sphere, looking up at the tiny sun that filled the vast inner room. How strange that had been to him. A sun artificially generated, contained within a vast metal ball. Ascending into the great towers that punched above the atmosphere, he could gaze in wonder at the magnificent panorama of the interior surface of the Sphere.

No wonder it had seduced him, Vush thought quietly. The three barbarian species had thought the Kolbard, or the now-destroyed tower, to be the epitome of First Traveler wonders. The Sphere was something so far kept hidden, it was a wonder beyond their imagining. If they had looked more closely, and gone several dozen more jumps down this very lane Aldin was now on, they would at last detect an infrared emission, the dissipation of heat from the outside of the jet-black surface of the Sphere. But no one had ever thought to push onward, the Kolbard Ring always diverting them. He had been tempted at times to remove the navigational buoys that marked the jump lanes, yet another accomplishment of the First Travelers, and thus hide away the Sphere forever, but he was always afraid that if he did so he himself would never find a way back.

Vush knew the place had seduced him, but he knew as well that Mupa had been completely captivated heart and soul, like a Human Soma-addicted drone, by the power it represented. When the barbarians had first gotten out of hand, it had been Mupa who had suggested the planet-smashing devices found in the Sphere, which had then been turned over to the steadier hands of Loysa. That had indeed made Vush uneasy, even though he had agreed with the others that only through such a raw display of power could they gain their ascendancy over the barbarians.

Yet there had been that other device that they had deciphered, or at least thought they had deciphered, which now had him truly frightened. Mupa had found it, a remarkable tool. Both of them had agreed to leave it where they had found it, frightened by the power it contained. And now? Mupa must have taken it back with him after all and offered it to be used. There were no more planet smashers, they had set all of them off and had been bluffing ever since. If Mupa thought he could effectively play with the machine, and had convinced the others, then they had all gone mad.

"If you tell me what it is you wish to share," Aldin said, interrupting Vush's contemplation, "I'll take it under consideration."

"They're making a mistake trying to smash a planet," Vush said cautiously.

"Well that certainly is pressing news," Aldin retorted, unable to contain the irony in his voice.

"I must try to present to them that certain—how shall I say it?—mistakes might be undertaken."

"How do you know this?" Aldin asked cautiously.

"I just know."

"You'll have to do better than that."

Vush took a deep breath and tried to center his thoughts. Among his comrades a conversation of this great an importance could take months, even years, with pauses of weeks or more as both considered the most precise way of communicating. That he felt was the greatest hindrance in dealing with these barbarians. If you stopped speaking for more than several minutes, they grew extremely agitated. A six-month conversation would drive them to the point of insanity.

The beauty of words was to find the precise one. Across the eons the Overseer vocabulary had grown to tens of millions of terms. A simple Human utterance such as, "A scarlet sunrise above an azure sea," could of course conjure up a mental picture of an event worthy of contemplation. But it was so crude, so imprecise. After all, there were a thousand worlds where such an event could happen, each one with shades of nuance, of smell, of particular wavelengths of light. To search for exactly the right description to fully convey all the essence of an event like that took time. The state of the observer was crucial as well, his health, his length of silent contemplation before observing the event, even the type of clothing he wore to reflect his mood. All of that could be formed into one word, which by its power would fully impart the entire experience, but to find that word took infinite care. It was an art, and the three species were totally artless.

"I think I know the device they plan to use; it is not stable." He felt entirely frustrated. There was so much urgency to what he felt, and yet also so much that he had to conceal, and their damned language was not up to it. If it were, a single utterance would convince them.

"I do know something of history," Aldin replied. "You fellows used some form of antimatter detonators the last time, balanced to the mass of the planets you were destroying. What could be more simple than that?"

"This one is different."

"In other words, you ran out of antimatter detonators, and now your people are using something untested," Yaroslav interjected.

Taken aback, Vush fell silent, afraid he had already given away far too much.

Aldin came to his feet.

"I'm not going to allow you to contact your people just on the basis of that little tidbit. I want the full truth."

Torn, Vush was unable to speak. He could never reveal that their power was based simply on the cannibalizing of First Traveler technologies they barely understood.

"It's just untested," he replied, trying not to reveal anything else. "I have perhaps a better grasp than my brother Mupa as to its operation. I wish to consult with him."

"Oh, now it's not just a signal, it's a consultation," Oishi replied, growing more suspicious.

"It is the only way," Vush replied, a pleading tone coming into his voice.

"I'll think about it," Aldin stated, heading for the door.

"You'll all regret this if I can't speak to my Arch," Vush replied.

"Is that a threat?" Oishi snapped.

If Vush had been capable of cursing, he would have done so at that moment. How cumbersome this language of the barbar-

ians was. The slightest mistake, or the improper mimicking of
tonal inflection, could convey an entirely wrong meaning.

"It was not intended as such," Vush replied hurriedly.

"At least head into a jump-point intersection," Vush continued. "With any good fortune there might be a delay. If you then
agree with me and allow me to contact my Arch from such a
point, you could jump in any number of directions and no one
will be the wiser as to where you have gone."

"I'll consider it," Aldin replied.

"And that's it, you'll consider it?"

"Exactly," Aldin said, as if weary of the whole conversation.

Rising back up, and setting his body at the proper angle to
display angry disdain, the Overseer floated out of the room, the
door sliding shut behind him.

"Head us back in," Yaroslav said quietly, coming up to Aldin
and offering him a drink.

"You know if that son of a bitch hadn't caused so much trouble I might actually grow to like him," Aldin said, slipping into
his chair with a sigh of exasperation.

"Why should we head back in at this time?" Oishi asked.
"Going to an intersect point we might meet someone that could
report our location."

"I never liked the idea of our skulking out here beyond reach
of any action to start with," Yaroslav stated. "Gablona could
be doing all sorts of trashing about."

"That strike of ours pretty well destroyed his facilities, and
there hasn't been any indicator of a response since," Zergh
replied.

"Go back in, pass any ship, even give the slightest whisper
of where we are, and everybody in the Cloud will be out after
us," Oishi responded.

"Just look at the holo tape of that conversation between Aldin
and Vush." And so saying Yaroslav went over to a console,
punched in a series of commands, and what appeared to be a
solid image of Vush appeared in the middle of the room.

"It's hard to read a voice-stress analysis on these creatures, but even a cursory examination will show Vush is half out of his mind with anxiety.''

"He's a prisoner of us so-called barbarians," Hobbs replied, drifting over in his chair to hover alongside the image of the Overseer. "Of course he'd be nervous. Good heavens, you should have seen him and his companion when they first showed up at my pleasure world. A couple of the girls came bounding over to them, wearing not much more than their birthing suits, and I thought the poor creatures were gonna die." Hobbs chuckled at the memory.

"But the stress indicators shoot out the roof once he starts talking about this planet smashing," Yaroslav said, pointing to the image in the holo and then to a computer screen that was punching out an analysis even while the tape played.

"Something big's going down here," Yaroslav continued.

"More than he's willing to discuss," Aldin said softly, watching the holo image. "All right, we go back in."

"It's about time for a little action," Basak growled from the back of the room. "My boys have been getting a bit bored drifting around out here."

"How long to get down to the first jump point with at least three alternate lines running out?" Aldin asked, looking back at Yaroslav.

"We'll get there approximately six standard hours before this little demonstration."

"If nothing really serious has happened as a result, we'll simply come back out here and settle back in. If not, we'll at least have some options to work with."

"What options?" Tia asked quietly.

Aldin could only smile and shrug his shoulders.

Oishi came up to the holo image and studied it carefully.

"I think we are all going to get a lot more than we bargained for out of this."

CHAPTER 5

Mupa could not help but feel amazement at these barbarians. Hundreds of ships, ranging from vast cruise liners
packed with tourists, to the elaborate pleasure barges of the
Kohs, had come from every direction of the Cloud, like flies to
honey in order to watch the show.

He could easily remember the last time they had blown a
planet. Then the action had created abject terror throughout the
Cloud, causing a near-instantaneous cessation of hostilities.
Either these barbarians had became jaded, Mupa thought, or
they were insane. At least all the Overseers who had shown up
were showing some modicum of decorum, just as he was.

The object of this exercise, a cold gas giant, hovered before
him, several million kilometers away. Beyond it Beta Zul, a vast
and highly unstable red giant star, filled the darkness of space
with its red orb.

The giant had been a cause of some concern when the Arch
had first selected the location, but Mupa had felt it best not to
raise any real objections. The proximity of Beta Zul to the Core
Cluster, which was the inhabited heart of the Cloud, made the
demonstration, if anything, a little more immediate rather than

out at the fringe of the Cloud. Somehow it implied that with the mere flick of a finger such destruction could be visited on any of the space-faring worlds filled with the three barbarian species.

Even as he did a final run-through on what he hoped was an accurate checklist, Mupa could hear his brothers exclaiming about the hundreds of ships that were still pouring in through the dozen jump points that converged in this particular system. An hour before there had been a most unfortunate accident when two ships had consummated certain statistical probabilities by jumping down in the same spot at exactly the same instant.

The flash of instantaneous destruction had been most impressive as five hundred Gaf tourists, who had won their privileged seats in a hastily conducted lottery, and a hive ship of Xsarns suddenly got far more than they had bargained for.

*Ooh*s and *ah*s had echoed across the commlinks, as some of the witnesses assumed that the brilliant flash had been an opening warm-up for the show. Tourist ships were already scrambling over the area, picking up tiny bits of wreckage as souvenirs of the big event.

"I do hope that everything is in order?" Mupa looked up to see the Arch hovering over him.

Mupa swallowed hard and nodded.

"The triggering device that will activate the opening of the transfer gate can be launched whenever you desire," Mupa replied nervously. "Once it is dropped into the planet's atmosphere, all I need do is flick these buttons." He let his hand touch the small protrusions coming out of a golden box that rested in his lap. "That will open the gate. As I understand this system, the gate will instantly attach itself to the primary gravitational body within its region and quite simply devour it."

Mupa paused. What a wormhole or transfer gate was remained a mystery to him. Even the term was beyond his understanding, picked up back when Humans had first come to this region of the Cloud. One of their great scientists from their ancient world had somehow managed to replicate the process, but he was now, of course, long dead. The name they had for it conjured in his mind the image of an actual worm reaching out to devour the great yellow-green planet before him. He knew the Human term was not quite accurate, but the effect seemed the same and it had somehow stuck in the public's mind as well to describe what was going to happen.

"And where does it go?" the Arch asked, as if seeking reassurance.

"Into another dimension. If the wormhole is rotating at a significant portion of the speed of light it will even go into another time."

"But where?"

"Oh, somewhere out beyond the Cloud," Mupa said vaguely, and he fingered the golden box nervously.

The Overseer looked at how casually Mupa's hand danced across the device.

"I'd rather if you didn't touch it until we were ready," the Overseer said, trying to keep his voice even.

"Oh, nothing to worry about," Mupa replied, and with an audible click he threw the trigger over.

In spite of himself, the Overseer backed up.

"I've got to push these keys on the side first," Mupa said, holding the box up.

"How do you know that?" the Arch snapped testily.

"Just figured it out, that's all." If a lie was possible for an Overseer, Mupa had just committed that heinous sin. By "figuring out" he simply meant that he and Vush had discovered the box and the small instrument pack that actually activated the wormhole. A First Traveler machine, a most annoying thing actually, had been nearby when they had found it. It didn't seem to be working quite right, had pestered them a bit at first, and then left them alone. The machine kept replaying a holo projection of the operation of the device. However, it insisted upon shocking them whenever they attempted to pick it up, until he had, in a rare display of Overseer impatience, screamed at it to leave them alone, and it had drifted away.

"Don't worry about it, everything is under control," Mupa said, trying to sound as self-assured as possible.

"Well get the thing launched," the Arch retorted, trying to

decide whether he was furious or frightened. The mere thought of either emotion made him ever angrier.

"Damn these barbarians," he cursed under his breath as he stormed from the room.

"We're not going to make it," Yaroslav said, coming up to stand beside Aldin as they pulled through their fifth jump-through in as many hours.

"Well, I never expected us to," Aldin replied, swinging his chair around to look at his old companion. "Don't tell me that Vush has made you nervous as well with his dire predictions."

"Absolutely yes," Yaroslav retorted.

"Even if we did get into a safe place to transmit, and even if I were then willing to break commlink silence, do you actually expect that anything Vush said would change what they plan to do?"

"The display of our intention might make a difference later on," Zergh said.

Oishi swung his chair about to look back at Vush.

"You will tell them of our effort, won't you?"

Vush, who had remained silent since his outburst of two days past, did not reply.

Zola and most of the other Kohs, who were aboard a yacht escorted by several of the small Overseer vessels, could not help but look nervously at a distant ship hovering on the far side of the gas giant, parked in among several hundred sight-seeing cruisers. It was Corbin Gablona's battered yacht, escorted as well by half a dozen Overseer craft. Both his own vessel and Gablona's had been inspected by Overseers before departure to insure that no contraband weapons were on board. The fact that he was defenseless made him decidedly uncomfortable, especially with Corbin less than half a light-minute away. If anything, it showed him how much Corbin had changed everything, thus necessitating this demonstration.

A heavy Xsarn cruise ship drifted by in front of his vessel and came to a stop.

"Damn Xsarns, always pushing ahead of others," Zola growled, and punching up a commlink, he soundly cursed at the pilot of the bulky vessel. Seconds later it moved on, parking a kilometer to his port side. With all of space to choose from, it was getting rather crowded in the area as everyone hugged up close to the safety line set by the Overseers. Thousands of ships were jockeying for position on the equatorial line so that both hemispheres would be clearly visible.

There was a brilliant flash several hundred thousand kilometers above the northern pole of the gas giant, and everyone let out an excited shout, expecting that the show had begun. Tracking cameras swung onto the point and quickly jacked up the scale, projecting it onto forward viewscreens. The room filled with groans, and then with several appreciative chuckles when the image resolved into a glowing sign, an advertisement for a chain of space yachts manufactured by one of the usual characters who took delight in portraying himself as a madman who would give away his ships at below cost. The commlinks chattered with inquiries from angry Overseers attempting to ascertain who set off the display, an action that only caused additional hilarity and ribald responses, as if the pilots of the hundreds of ships that had gathered were covering for a schoolboy who had pulled off an entertaining prank.

Zola made a mental note to buy stock in the man's company; sales were certain to go up since what was going to happen here would certainly prove to be one of the most-watched broadcasts in all the history of the Cloud. Tens of millions of katars had already been made on commemorative drinking mugs, souvenir shirts with an imbedded holo of the gas giant imploding into a shocking chartreuse that the Gafs were going crazy over, and even Xsarn food trays were being decorated with stenciled images of the planet that shrank and disappeared when the owner sucked on the feeding tube.

It certainly was helping to maintain the decorum of the situation, a fact that, if it were possible, annoyed the Overseers to no end, and Zola could not help but find the whole thing vastly amusing.

"This is not supposed to be funny."

Zola looked over his shoulder and saw the Overseer floating in the middle of the room, and he immediately wiped the smile from his face and nodded in serious agreement.

"Shockingly childish," Zola said, and, of course, all the others agreed.

Feeling a flutter in his stomach, Mupa watched the monitor as the instrument pack that would open the transfer gate moved down toward the gas giant in a long tightening spiral. He wasn't sure if the flutter was from fear, excitement, or just simple hunger, for, after all, a proper Overseer spent thousands of years learning to suppress any and all emotions and direct contact between one's bodily reaction and the higher planes of intellectual contemplation.

The monitor flashed green, and on another linked display a tracking camera showed the instrument pack's retro system firing, stabilizing the machine in orbit around the giant, barely skimming above the swirling atmosphere of poisonous chlorine and ammonia. There was a ripple of excitement as dozens of his brothers all tried to float ever so much closer to the forward viewport, feigning disinterest and yet unwilling to move aside as more Overseers came into the room to watch. Even old Yu, who had stayed in the far corner of the chamber, rose up ever so slowly, his body turned as if looking in the other direction, yet tilting his head just enough to be able to watch out of the corners of his eyes.

Mupa looked over at the Arch and nodded. A holo camera, controlled by a Xsarn crew member, was flicked on, and the Arch started into a brief sermon that was going out across the entire Cloud, explaining the sinful ways of the three species, the heinous crimes of Aldin Larice and his compatriots, and the sad necessity of having to destroy a planet as a demonstration of their ire, closing with the promise that if order was not reestablished, the instrument of destruction would next be turned on some of the banking planets.

All the time the Arch was speaking, Mupa nervously held the

box of control switches. He was barely aware of it when the Arch finished his hour-long preaching and the light of the camera swung onto him.

With a start he looked up, almost letting the focus of his thoughts on the firing box drift away. Behind the camera, the Arch was bobbing up and down as if motioning for him to get started. There was an expectant hush.

Mupa floated up, the box floating with him. He looked straight at the camera.

"Behold the power of the Overseers," he announced in the deepest voice he could muster.

He reached out to the box, and with grave deliberation pressed down on the first golden button as he had seen it done on the ancient First Traveler holo record. There was a barely audible click and the button popped back up, a small light alongside of it flashing white. He pushed the second and the third, the lights flashing beside each. And then with a melodramatic flourish, he poised his finger—or what passed for an Overseer finger—over the fourth button on the side of the box. He pushed down. It didn't move. He tried again, and still it refused to budge. Nervous, he looked up at the Arch, who started to bob up and down in a most agitated manner. Feeling totally ridiculous, he slammed down hard on the button, muffling a yelp of pain. He suddenly had the strongest of feelings that all the members of the lesser species were howling with delight, and he wasn't far wrong.

Floating back down to the ground, he placed the box on the floor, and then kneeling over it he rose back up into the air and willed himself to drop. Coming down full force, he slammed the button with extended arm. There was an audible *snick* as the button slammed down, the sound of which was hidden by the louder crack of his finger breaking and a most Human curse of pain escaping his lips.

All four lights on the box started to blink in unison, shifting through a broad spectrum of colors. Nursing his broken member, Mupa sat on the floor staring at the box and then at the holo screen.

"Nothing," one of his brothers whispered. "Absolutely nothing."

Wiping the tears from his eyes, Zola rocked back and forth in his chair while the other Kohs raised mock toasts to the gallant Mupa. The lone Overseer aboard the ship shouted in a shrill voice for respectful silence and was greeted with hoots of derision. Yet even in his mirth, Zola felt worried. If this was a show of Overseer power, then the mysterious power they claimed to hold was a sham. And if that was the case, then the last three thousand years of peace that they had been able to enforce was a sham as well, a paper cutout without substance. He didn't know whether to be furious or frightened by all that this implied.

And then suddenly all of it was driven from his mind.

Above the surface of the gas giant, there was a flicker of light—nowhere near as impressive as that of the yacht salesman's sign—just a tiny flash. Completely unnoticed at first, since the field of the effect was barely a meter across, the wormhole transfer gate opened, and the photons of starlight streaming past the field were twisted into a spiraling loop. It was a remarkable event, since the instrument pack that should have been crushed within a millionth of a second into the size of a single hydrogen atom nevertheless maintained its structural integrity. It fell. After all, that is what it was designed to do, to plummet into the heart of whatever it was expected to alter, burying itself into the very core of its gravitational field.

The chlorine and ammonia atmosphere of the gas giant offered not the slightest resistance. The hard molten surface of liquid chlorine and the compressed solid chlorine beneath it posed not the slightest problem for the field as it punched straight into the core and pulled along with it anything that was encompassed within the meter-wide band of the wormhole effect.

Yet there was something missing; within its own system of memory and logic the First Traveler package could not sense the proper connections. A signal of inquiry raced outward, back to its control station. A microscopic servo and computation unit acknowledged the inquiry, calculated that there was a mistake in the entire operation, and rolled a switch. And that micro-size switch broke, coming up against the unyielding bottom side of the fourth button.

Its creators had made things to last for eternity, but even the most simple device, such as a simple button, can corrode ever so slightly after millions of years of waiting to be pushed, or worse yet, hammered down. It was now firmly locked in place, which to the logic system of the controlling unit meant that the creator of this miraculous device was simply overriding the command to disengage. It took but thousandths of a second for the system to call up the alternate program for such a contingency. And yet the program was not quite as it should be. Several million years of waiting while random X rays bounce through space might nick and damage a dense-packed system that moves its commands on through circuits built around systems the size of single molecules.

Or in simpler terms, the machine hiccuped and then sent a rather unusual signal back: to run full bore until there was no more material left to take. The problem was that there was no command to send that material anywhere, the necessary part of the unit was missing, therefore it would have to just feed on whatever was available and pack it in around itself.

The instrument pack now received its command, a most unusual command. It had found a place to nest, now it had to find something to feed upon. A tentaclelike finger of spacial distortion, a wormhole in search of another end to anchor upon. Not even a millimeter in diameter, it snaked out and away in the opposite direction from the gas giant, and as if it were a living creature tracking down a scent, the tentacle of distortion raced toward the gravitational center of the great red giant star. In its outward track it deviated ever so slightly, like a wave running down a tautly drawn string, dawn to the mass of a Xsarn cruise ship of ten thousand tons, drilling a hole through it not much wider than a pinhead. If it had had time to even observe what was occurring, a Xsarn tourist, who was busy slurping on a feeding tube of a souvenir tray, would have seen the wormhole distortion pop through the hull of the ship, straight through his tray and the contents within, then through itself and out the other side of the vessel. Within one ten thousandth of a second two thousand Xsarns, tons of Xsarn haute cuisine, two thousand souvenir trays, and ten thousand tons of ship were sucked into the wormhole and flashed out of existence.

The tentacle of distortion snaked onward, almost drawn in by another ship, but overridden by the stronger gravitation anchor of the sun. Straight as a laser beam it dove across space, its event horizon bulged now by the churning hyper-compressed atoms of Xsarns and their ship. Already functioning in the other dimensional reality that was the same used for jump transition, an instant later the probing end of the wormhole punched through the chromosphere of the sun and leaped straight into the core of the helium-fired inferno.

It had all taken less than the time of half a dozen heartbeats.

"What the shit was that?" Zola gasped, coming to his feet. The other Kohs, who but several seconds before were laughing hysterically, had stopped; the sound of drinking glasses shattering on the floor echoed in the room, counterpointed by the angry hoot of a servobot, which was instantly responding to the mess.

The Xsarn cruise ship, whose pilot he had soundly cursed not an hour before for parking too close, was gone. It just disappeared. The effect had been startling, disorienting, reminding him of a picture on a flat commlink screen at the instant it was turned off; the picture would drop in upon itself to form a tiny point of light before disappearing. It was as if the Xsarn ship had suddenly compressed in upon itself and then winked out of existence. There had been a momentary streak of light that he thought had curved toward him before going over the port side of the ship.

"Look at that!"

One of the Gaf Kohs was pointing to a monitor to one side of the main screen. In the center of the monitor was the red giant, and what appeared to be a string going straight into it. It was not a string of light, it was not even really visible, rather it was a distortion, almost a sensing that something was wrong with the fabric of space.

"Get us the fuck out of here!" the Overseer cried.

It was, after all, nothing more than a moving machine, a play toy of its creators, designed to take entire stars and move them in a godlike manner. It was how they had transported the tremendous mass necessary to build the Kolbard Ring and later the Sphere. It was also a play toy used to combine one star with another for the mere entertainment such an act might provide. When the jump lanes were first being cleared, it was a simple means of moving out unwanted and dangerous material, consigning it to a cosmic dump yard where it could do no harm. Or, when more godlike activities were desired, it could heal an aging star with an infusion of new matter, simply to save an orbiting planet that they found appealing, or for the act of saving a star for no other reason than to save it.

It could be a work of art, the altering of suns for no other reason than to do it. Or, if in a mischievous mood, to pump a star so full of mass as to cause it to collapse upon itself and then detonate it into a supernova, to set off the biggest firecracker in the universe for the sheer spectacle it might provide. Such an event had been one of the First Travelers' last playful acts more than a hundred thousand years ago.

When one could engineer the design of an entire galaxy, such things were necessary to relieve the tedium. All one needed to do was place the proper instrument pack at the destination point and place a companion piece at the star to be moved and stand back and throw the switch on the control unit. But no one had ever been foolish enough to use the one instrument pack without the other, compounded by a little overenthusiastic hammering upon a sticky switch.

The link was not complete, and like a cosmic garden hose transporting the raw matter of stars, the pump was activated down the wormhole line. Matter that was compressed into thousands of tons per cubic centimeter was compressed yet further as it fell into the event horizon of the suction end of the wormhole. In an instant it snaked up the line, traveling far faster than light-speed, bulging the wormhole line out, the mass expanding the diameter of the event horizon and in turn generating an ever-increasing range of distortion, pulling in yet more matter from its surroundings. Racing up through the surface of the star, it flashed on up the line, snapping across space and then plummeting down into the very heart of what had been a cold gas giant. Within the first second, a million tons of active thermonuclear matter was deposited into the gravitational core of the planet. Though the gas giant was indeed cold, its center, under tremendous gravitational pressure from its own weight, was a chain reaction waiting to happen. Like superheated steam shot into a block of ice, the emerging mass of the sun, compressed to millions of tons per cubic centimeter, underwent two simultaneous experiences, rapid expansion when the gravitational pressures of the wormhole were behind it, and a rather interesting experience created by a thermonuclear reaction suddenly inserted into the heart of a planet.

Barely a dozen seconds had passed since Mupa had finally managed to push the button down. For long seconds he looked up at his Arch, expecting a berating unlike any experienced by an Overseer in ten thousand years. After all, he had managed to make all of them look like fools in front of all the barbarians. How could he ever explain that testing these types of devices was rather impossible, since testing them meant actually using them.

Suddenly he heard a squawking voice on the commlink, and then a rippled gasp go through his brothers. Floating back up, still nursing his injured limb, he looked at the main viewscreen. The instrument pack should have been above the planet. It was gone. Another screen showed an empty stretch of space, an ever so thin streak of light cutting straight across it.

"What is going on?" Mupa whispered.

The Arch looked back at him, his eyes showing confusion.

"I thought you were supposed to know."

How could he ever admit that he wasn't really sure?

"Replay that one!" somebody shouted, pointing to the screen with the line going through it.

The image went into reverse.

"Hold it!" several cried.

The image snapped through several enlargements. A ship was there, it looked like a Xsarn design.

The image started forward again, this time slowly. In the span of less than a single frame the ship disappeared, replaced by the line.

The Overseers all started to look back at Mupa for an explanation.

Other commlink screens were showing where the instrument pack was supposed to be—emptiness. Several showed a straight line emerging out of the planet, one of the cameras tracing it all the way across hundreds of millions of miles toward the red giant. Another link, the one hooked into Zola's ship, was showing complete pandemonium, panicked screams, and Zola hysterically calling for the pilot to jump them out, the hell with collisions and gravitational distortions.

Something was unraveling here—but what?

"Put the forward screen on real time!" Mupa shouted.

An instant later the vast forward viewscreen dropped all the other images to show what was actually in front of them, rather than signals that were jumped at translight speed. With the planet nine million kilometers away, it was thirty seconds until a real time view of the planet would arrive. Just about now, he realized.

The high-gain cameras mounted aboard the ship were superb Xsarn workmanship and could pick up every detail.

There was the flash where the instrument pack was supposed to be, and then nothing. Long seconds passed, while from the jump commlink images everything seemed to be going into chaos. He could sense the panic building.

There was a flash to forward, a ship accelerating up to jump velocity passing a dozen kilometers in front of their own vessel, a streaked blur of light, and a crackling voice screaming obscenities.

In real time the image of the planet filled the entire forward screen.

"What is that?" somebody whispered.

It appeared as if an arrow of distorted light were cutting straight from the surface of the world, driving across space to the sun behind them.

The flow through the wormhole was increasing at a near exponential rate, driving up to its peak load, for that given transfer distance, of trillions of tons of mass a second. What pulsed through its narrow corridor was in a highly compressed state not much more in volume than that of a Gaf's body, though a Gaf's body that would be very heavy indeed. In its own environment, inside the heart of a red giant star, this mass would be reasonably stable, but in the far less dense heart of the gas planet, when released, it would not only create tremendous gravitational distortions but would also explode outward, like superheated steam uncorked from a jar, while at the same time releasing a stunningly large nuclear pulse of heat and light. It was enough to give any planet a serious case of indigestion. Sooner or later it was bound to get sick.

One moment the surface of the planet looked just about like any other gas giant with its swirling poisonous clouds. The surface of the planet seemed to bulge outward with a certain slow-motion majesty at its poles, the energy of internal events first racing up the magnetic lines. The top and bottom of the planet peeled back, exploding into light.

Mupa, far more excited than he could ever remember, started to bob up and down.

"It's working, it's working!" he shouted triumphantly.

As if his words were a cue, the other Overseers let out a cheer, forgetting all sense of comportment and dignity, an event that made the Arch glad that he had, at least for the moment, shut down the link.

"Dignity my brothers, dignity!"

The room fell silent.

The Arch nodded to the Xsarn operating the camera, and it was flicked back on and turned toward the Arch, who floated before the forward viewscreen, the image of the erupting planet behind him.

"What you are witnessing is the destruction of an inhospitable planet," the Arch said solemnly.

He paused for a brief instant.

"By the mere flick of a finger this is what we can accomplish. If certain terms are not agreed to, we can arrange the same thing to happen to any of the worlds you now inhabit, or for that matter, all of them."

He floated in silence, letting his words sink in as they instantly flashed across the Cloud. Yet in the background, other commlinks were conveying a rising sense of panic from the hundreds of ships, news stations, and yachts that had gathered to watch the event. Good, it was having the proper effect, the party atmosphere of moments before now dispelled.

A shudder raced through the ship, the gravitational pulse arriving without warning, giving no time to the inertial dampening systems to compensate. A number of Overseers were knocked head over heels. The Arch, though floating, was slammed against the forward viewscreen and slumped down, the wind knocked out of him.

The explosions were rippling out across the entire planet's surface, vast plumes of star fire racing straight upward, the total mass of the gas giant not yet sufficient to turn the plumes back in upon themselves. Within the heart of the dying world position was everything. The instrument pack, contained within its field, was still very much intact. Around it, density was so intense that even light itself was near to coiling and looping back upon itself. But meters away the outward explosion of energy was pushing matter straight up at the speed of light, while up upon the surface vast eddies of chlorine and ammonia were plummeting straight back into the core, drawn downward by the vast gravitational forces now being generated. Long streams of icy gas would strike the upward currents, flash into nuclear incandescents, and be flung straight back up again.

The planet was a star forming, but unlike anything that normally occurs, this was the birthing of a billion years compressed into seconds. A balance had yet to be reached between the outward thrust of the thermonuclear furnace within and the gravitational forces that held the star stable and together. It was simply a writhing mess that was not quite sure what it wanted to become.

But for the moment, at least, exploding seemed like a good idea.

The gravitational distortions were continuous, the dampening systems of the lurching ship unable to compensate. Mupa looked about, reminded of bad holo films made by the Gafs that showed crew members of crashing ships flinging themselves back and forth across a set, while the recording camera gyrated to simulate a ship out of control. It was decidedly unpleasant, though.

He looked back at the planet. Streams of material were ejecting straight outward, the clouds on the planet's surface churning, some of them looking as if they were turning into whirlpools sucking straight down into the planet's core.

Of course the device had to be responsible, but since he had never actually seen a planet swallowed by a wormhole transfer gate he wasn't quite sure if what he was seeing was what he was supposed to see.

The dampening system ejected a sensor to be positioned ahead of the ship and thus relay warning of the approaching distortions. The lurching of the ship gradually steadied, though there were still occasional rumbles, the ship echoing to the creaks and groans of stressed metal.

"What is that line?" someone finally asked, disturbing Mupa's rapt attention upon the phenomenon on the planet surface.

"The wormhole, of course," Mupa said with a superior air.

"Oh." There was a pause. "Why is it going to the sun? I thought this was supposed to dump things into another dimension."

"I don't—" he stopped himself. "I don't believe that it is necessarily going through the sun,'' he replied, realizing that his words were being broadcast across the Cloud, and that the response didn't quite have the authoritative tone of an expert.

There was another pause.

He started to worry. Just what was actually going on here?

Another commlink line flashed into life, a distant voice talking. It took several seconds to register.

It was Vush!

Startled, Mupa turned to look at the screen, the sight of the kidnapped Overseer turning the attention of nearly everyone from the spectacular display of the planet.

He could barely hear his friend's voice above the insane chatter of the dozens of other monitor lines.

''You damned idiot, it's only half the machine . . .'' was all they heard before another gravitational pulse rocked the ship and distorted transmissions, drowning out Vush's words.

Mupa looked forward. The entire surface of the planet was glowing, churning, and then started to lift outward.

Outward?

The wormhole was supposed to be eating the planet, collapsing it inward, not outward.

The rather unique sensation of queasiness coursed through Mupa. Too much was happening, and he was starting to feel overloaded. Voices on the commlink shouting, Vush yelling, the Arch turning toward him trying to say something, and a Xsarn crew member pointing at a monitor that showed that the gravitational pull of the planet was in fact increasing at a rather alarming rate.

A steady pump was now operating, running at maximum design load. Already a minute but discernable fraction of the red giant had coursed through the line, and the star's core was beginning to collapse in upon itself. It would take long minutes for the gravitational variation to take effect out at the outer edge of the chromosphere, a hundred million miles away, but red giants were balancing acts: the outward pressure of their internal reaction balanced with the gravitational effect. If enough reaction mass is lost at the core, outward pressure decreases and gravity takes over—the star collapses.

As for the wormhole, a tremendous amount of mass was now pumping down the line, enough to set up its own gravitational field. The Xsarn ship had been unfortunately in the line of its creation, and trace elements and all the component atoms of two thousand Xsarns were now blowing up through towering columns of radioactive bursts, leaping far above the planet's surface. The wormhole was spinning upon its long axis, bulging and twisting in a sinuous motion like a tornado weaving across an open prairie. Within the effect of its field even smaller wormholes would occasionally twist out from the main trunk, lasting perhaps for a millionth of a second, in a highly unstable state, and fall back in or disconnect. Some might run rampant for as long as a second or two, either bouncing across a hundred thousand kilometers of space and shooting matter back into the mother of all wormholes or existing a brief moment in total freedom. Of course, whatever these free-agent wormholes caught, even if disconnected from the main line, would fall in one end, and emerge out the other in a rather disorganized and thoroughly pulped state.

A pleasure yacht of half a dozen Gafs, who had told their wives they were at a business meeting, making no mention of their female companions for this trip, were more than a thousand kilometers from the main wormhole when they received a short visit from a disconnected line, which in its brief tenth of a second of existence never measured more than ten centimeters in length and barely a millimeter in diameter. The entire Gaf yacht fell in one end, and popped out the other, the ship turned inside out and backward, with Gafs, their ship, polyester clothing, and muscatel all churned into an unpleasant soup and sprayed with such velocity that another Gaf ship, fifty kilometers away, was hulled by the puree, resulting in a disconcerting decompression experience for all aboard.

For a brief instant it appeared as if the planet was racing in upon itself.

Mupa felt a momentary surge of reassurance at the sight. Of course that's what would happen. And then there was the snap of light, the blinding sight of a star being born. And in that instant he knew.

The Xsarn crew members were already reacting, screaming in panic, spraying the ingredients of their last meal upon anyone within range. One of them was pointing at the monitor, shouting that the wormhole was out of control and rather than sucking the planet up it was, instead, sucking the heart of the red giant straight into the planet.

Mupa barely heard shouted comments about novas, supernovas, black holes, and radiation.

The Arch was before him, holding the control box, shouting at Mupa to do something.

Numbly he took the box. The lights were flashing wildly, the fourth button still jammed down. And it was absolutely flush with the surface of the box. Typical First Traveler engineering, so finely crafted that unless someone knew the button was even there, it would be invisible. It was jammed and there was no way to get it back up.

Mupa looked up at the Arch.

"It's broke," he said weakly.

"What do you mean 'it's broke'?" the Arch roared, no longer even aware that the commlink camera was still running, broadcasting the entire event live across the Cloud.

"It's broke," Mupa whispered, unable to say anything else.

"Then fix it!"

Mupa studied the box intently, barely aware that the light in the room was shifting, growing brighter.

Rather clumsily he tried to pry the button back up, going so far as to bring the box up to his mouth and then try to suck it back up.

It was thoroughly and completely jammed.

"I can't."

He looked back up, and at that instant the planet made its transition into a star, flaring into a brilliant and, from a purely objective viewpoint, beautiful flood of light.

"I suggest we leave," Mupa said. "I think something very bad is going to happen."

He handed the box back to the Arch, as if somehow showing that he was washing his hands of the entire affair.

The Arch let the box drop.

"Oh, shit," he whispered, and then floated out of the room.

Zola, still sweating with fear, poured another drink to steady his nerves. He was out of danger, at least that's what the ship's navigator claimed. It was the first time in his life he had ever experienced a full transition jump from within the close gravitational field of a planet, and worse yet, a blind jump through totally unmarked space. He had always been told that such an experiment would always produce one of two events: either you came out the other side, or before your nerves could even register the moment, you were vaporized. He was still alive and able to pour the drink, even though his hands were shaking violently. Most of the drink was spilling onto the carpet, to the dismay of a servobot that was holding a tray with one tentacle while trying to mop up the spill with another.

That was half of his fear. The other half was the thought of how the Xsarn ship had simply winked out of existence, not much more than a kilometer away, and the impression that whatever had hit it had almost hit him as well.

The jump had taken them a tenth of a light year out, dropping them back into a main jump line back toward the Core Cluster. The commlinks, with their near-instantaneous transmissions, were jammed. A "We Are There for You" news crew was running several images on the same screen. The gorgeously coiffured main reporter—who allegedly could not even read a cue note but nevertheless managed to somehow project an image of infinite wisdom—was openly weeping while describing the destruction of the Xsarn ship, which their cameras had recorded. The reporter looked absolutely sincere and was obviously angling for a major award. The tears streamed down his angular and well-tanned face to dangle on the edge of his mustache. An instant later the signal died and was replaced by a rival news system, with another emoting reporter showing footage of the "We Are There For You" ship being pierced by an errant wormhole. An ultra-high-speed camera replayed the footage in fascinating detail: the ship looked like a balloon that was slowly being sucked into a straw.

"Anyone wanna place a bet on what's going to happen next?"

Zola looked up to see that his fellow Kohs were recovering from the shock of their narrow escape.

"Ten thousand katars that ten to thirty ships are destroyed," someone shouted, and his bet was quickly covered at four-to-one odds.

Though the Overseer on board shouted his protests at the impropriety of gambling on such a tragedy, he soon fell silent with the realization that he was now being totally ignored.

Hassan smiled. He looked into Corbin Gablona's face and saw that the fat man was smiling as well, but underneath it all he could also see the fear.

"Why did you do that?" Corbin whispered.

"I wanted to see what it was like," Hassan replied, wiping the blade on his sleeve before sheathing it.

"You know what you've done?"

"They're powerless now. All of you people have been shaking in your boots for three thousand years."

He pointed to the monitors, which showed the planet exploding into a sun, the destruction of several dozen ships, the cries of panic, and most important of all the mad pandemonium aboard the Overseer ship, which had already turned about and was racing toward the nearest jump gate in order to escape, even as the Arch's last words reverberated across the Cloud.

"If we were close enough, I'd say destroy them in that ship and be rid of them forever."

Corbin Gablona felt an inner quaking of fear. Far worse than all that had happened outside the ship, it was what was happening inside it, and all that it implied, that terrified him far more. The Overseers were powerless, they had no understanding of what they had done, they could not control it, and, from what little he understood, there appeared to be a disaster of monumental proportions in the making.

It also meant that the entire structure of power as he knew it was forever altered. Though he had broken the bounds, there was still the question of dealing with the Overseers, even if some of them had been corrupted into the playing of the games. But this was different.

The Overseer Tulbi lay at Hassan's feet, the body still twitching spasmodically from the knife blow to the base of the skull. It finally grew still.

"You've killed him," Gablona whispered. "You've killed an Overseer."

"An Overseer?" Hassan laughed, his voice harsh. "I killed nothing, absolutely nothing, as I would kill any insect that boasted that it had power and yet could be crushed by the back of my hand. The old order is dead."

He paused for a moment.

"And I am the new order."

He looked at Gablona and smiled.

"In service to you, of course. Do you have any problems with that?"

Gablona looked around the room. All his guards were Al'Shiga, led by Hassan of the ancient order of Assassins of Earth.

He looked back into the man's hawklike eyes.

"You still need me if you want to survive," Corbin said, trying to hide the fear in his voice.

Hassan smiled.

"Of course I do, my lord Gablona, of course I do."

Hassan started to turn away.

"You saw that commlink message of the Overseer Vush. He is obviously still with your old friend Larice. You have the means to trace that signal; I suggest we do it now, and perhaps we can run him down."

Corbin could tell instantly from the tone of voice that it was not a suggestion—it was an order. And he did not hesitate to comply.

CHAPTER 6

THE COMMLINKS HAD BEEN JAMMED WITH THE NEWS FOR THREE standard days. The plan had been forming, but the thought of it gave him a cold gnawing in his stomach. A strange sensation, that—to be cognizant of one's stomach, such an unpleasant sensation for an Overseer, and he found it deeply disturbing. The door to his room slid open, and Vush looked up expectantly as Hobbs came into the chamber, a servobot behind him toting a tray of wilted salad.

"Dead before it was plucked," Hobbs said.

"Thank you."

Vush swung around from his sleeping pallet and, taking up one of the Human eating instruments, forked a piece of dried fruit and chewed on it meditatively, a bit shocked that he was actually enjoying the taste of food.

"Been watching the news?" Hobbs asked.

Vush nodded.

"What does it all mean?"

"Something's broke and Mupa doesn't know how to turn it off."

"Well I think that's kind of obvious," Hobbs sniffed.

It was more than obvious. No one was quite sure yet, but somewhere around twenty to twenty-five ships had disappeared, not counting several that collided in the mad panic to get away.

The former planet was now a highly unstable yellow star, which was continuing to grow; its companion red giant, linked by the wormhole line, was collapsing in upon itself. The more disturbing question was, what would happen when there was no more mass from the draining red giant? Would the wormhole shut off, or would it snake out to look for yet more items to devour?

Vush finally worked up his nerve.

"I'd like to talk with Aldin again."

"Well, it's about time," Hobbs said cheerily. "And then afterward how about a good stiff toddy to take the edge off things?"

"How about one before?" Vush said nervously.

"So what are we going to do?" the Arch asked, for what he knew was at least the hundredth time.

Mupa, if he had shoulders, would have shrugged them.

"Nothing we can do," he finally admitted.

"What's going to happen?"

"The barbarians' news reports are most likely right. First the star will disintegrate when its gravity can no longer hold the chromosphere. Anything within a quarter of a light-year would be in trouble when that happens. Fortunately there are no worlds that close by."

"Oh, yes, most fortunate."

The Arch looked away for a moment.

"When will it happen?" the Arch asked.

"Days, maybe ten or fifteen at most. It might even get to the point that the gravitational force of the new star will even start to pull the side of the red star closest to it in on itself. It should be a beautiful sight," Mupa said with a sigh.

"And then?"

"Once the red star dies, one of two things. The wormhole will lose its anchor and collapse back in on itself and that is it."

"Or," the Arch prompted him.

"It will just snake outward. There are half a dozen stars within half a light-year or less, several of them have mining outposts. There are no major barbarian centers, but you know how it is, if there's something to be mined on a world, they'll be there."

Damn Humans and Gafs were everywhere, the Arch thought dryly. The First Travelers had accomplished so much, but they had committed one terrible sin: their demand for various metals, the exotic ones beyond the ever-plentiful iron and nickel, had led them to harvest nearly every vein of metal on all the planets of the Cloud. Perhaps, he mused, that is why they eventually moved on, they had simply run out of certain key components for building, for though they could make nearly anything, the creation of raw elements was a rather laborious process. As a result, there wasn't a world that didn't have some prospectors on it, looking for a precious vein of gold or lead or copper. It was impossible to ever feel any real sense of privacy. You could go to a world, think you had solitude, and then some Xsarn prospectors would wander into your encampment.

He looked back at Mupa.

"So it will attack another sun?"

"It'll lock onto one of those suns and suck it dry, and then on and on. Beyond those six suns we go straight into the Core Cluster, the red giant is right on the edge of it and could be called part of it as is. Hundreds of worlds there, including the banking centers of the barbarians' civilization. But chances are it wouldn't go that far."

"And why not?" the Arch asked, as if almost hopeful.

"There are two black dwarfs nearby."

"And pray what are those?"

"Suns that have burned themselves out. Their rather large mass is condensed into an incredibly small area. We've always avoided them since their gravity is thousands of times standard. Anyhow, they're almost solid compressed iron. Once the wormhole hits one of those, it's all over."

Mupa fell silent and the Arch looked over at him in an agitated manner, waiting for the rest of the information, not willing to admit to his own ignorance of such things.

"The core of a sun can burn every element up to iron. Start pumping in trillions of tons of iron and it shuts the nuclear furnace down. This dampens the outward pressure that holds a star up. Everything rushes into the center, pressure builds to an unbelievable rate, and then we have an exciting explosion."

"Supernova?"

Mupa nodded. "Poof. A supernova. The last one in these parts was well over a hundred thousand standard years back."

The Arch nodded—the one that many suspected the First Travelers had triggered.

"I can't make an accurate projection," he admitted, "but the lesser species' news reports are full of it. The shock wave from the supernova will slam into the galactic core, it might even tear some stars apart. It'll definitely douse everything within fifteen odd light-years with a lethal dose of radiation. It will shatter their civilization. Their key worlds of finance and the intersection for hundreds of jump points converge there. They'll never recover and billions will die."

"What I thought I'd hear," the Arch replied.

Mupa looked up at him fearfully, fully expecting that after this particular confession of just how far he had truly managed to bungle things, that he would be banished for the full extent of his natural life to some barren rock.

The Arch looked at him and then drifted out of the room without a word.

Mupa sat in stunned silence. He was positive that for the briefest instant the Arch had actually smiled.

"So you're telling us that it'll just keep going on until the damn thing blows and then the Core Cluster gets the blast?"

Aldin sat back in his chair and exhaled, his cheeks puffing out. Every one of his group was present, filling the small room: the surviving samurai and Gaf warriors, Oishi, Zergh, Tia, Hobbs and his companions, Yaroslav, and even Mari, Bukha, and the Xsarn Prime, whom they had picked up when the Xsarn's private yacht had managed to rendezvous and drop them off.

Vush nodded his head, already learning to fit in somewhat

better with these creatures. He took another sip of the steaming toddy that Hobbs had cooked up for him, and he actually found that he enjoyed the sensation of it going down his throat, warming his stomach, relaxing his mind.

Vush bobbed his head in reply to Aldin's question.

"As we surmised," Yaroslav said. He looked over at Aldin. "How do you think everyone will jump?"

"Gablona will have the time of his life," Hobbs interjected. "If it all goes to chaos, he'll tear out whatever pieces he can from the dying beast. He went outcast when he started this war. He'd be a fool not to know that even if he won, and everyone put up the front that he was one of the boys again, it'd never be the same. Now he has the breakdown that he wanted."

"And the other Kohs?" Aldin asked, as if looking for a reassurance of his own dark beliefs.

"They'll grovel to whomever is the strongest," the Xsarn said, his mandibles clicking in a display of extreme anger. "The Overseers have shown themselves to be fools, and beyond that, the truth of how they've controlled events is finally sinking in with my brother Kohs. We've been trembling in front of a hoax ever since we arrived in the Cloud. Gablona and his like will never allow them to run things again."

"Simply put," Oishi said, his voice cold, "it means war."

"The Overseers, what are they really doing?" Aldin asked, putting his hands together, fingertips touching, almost as if he were praying.

He looked over at Vush.

"Do you really believe it was an accident?"

It was, of course, impossible to read this one the way he could so easily read another Human, a Gaf, or even a Xsarn. He had no experience in this, to be able to pick up the slightest nuance or gesture that could reveal far more at times than words.

"If they listened to Mupa, it was certainly an accident."

"How is that?" Hobbs asked, smiling and prompting Vush along.

"Because he is immature, foolish, everyone knew that, especially our Arch."

"Yet you claim that this Mupa was your closest friend, if such a thing is possible among the Overseers."

"That is why I can say what I said." He paused for a moment.

"Go on," Hobbs said quietly.

"I was with Mupa when he found the wormhole device."

A bit surprised, everyone in the room stirred.

He then went on to spill it all, the hidden Sphere, the decrepit First Traveler machine guarding the device, and his own suspicions of its faultiness.

The room was silent as he finished, and Vush looked around nervously, suspecting he had told far too much, but no longer really caring. Upward of ten thousand beings might have died when the machine was set off and the various ships were swallowed. Billions more might get it in the not too distant future. He was fed up with all of it.

His back started to convulse and he lowered his head. Crying was impossible for an Overseer, but he was doing as close an imitation of it as was possible for his race.

"The Sphere?" Yaroslav asked, his eyes shining with excitement. "I've heard legends of it, fragments. An artificially created star completely encased inside a hollow ball millions of kilometers across."

"It dwarfs the Ring of Kolbard," Vush whispered. "The most magnificent creation ever rendered by the First Travelers, only the Prime Mover could have done more."

"Where is it?" Yaroslav asked, fidgeting in his chair like an excited child who had just been told that a long-dreamed-for gift was waiting on the doorstep.

A bit startled, Vush looked at Yaroslav and then around to the others in the room, all of them leaning forward.

"I can't," he whispered, half curling up into a ball. Hobbs motioned for the servobot to bring another toddy. The machine glided over to Vush and held the drink up. The Overseer ignored it, and the bot, not sure of itself, just waited patiently.

"I could make you talk easily enough," Basak growled, and as he spoke he stood up, stretching out his arms, the muscles rippling under his shaggy, matted hair.

Vush looked at him wide-eyed, while Oishi cut across the room and quickly shoved the Gaf berserker and his comrades out of the room.

Vush again curled up into a tight ball.

"Perhaps we can find an answer there," Aldin said, in the most soothing voice that he could muster. He knew that just a little part of him was lying. The Ring had held him in awe. There had been rumors of the Sphere, but he believed them to be nothing but rumors. Such a thing was impossible, requiring thousands of times the mass of the Ring. Gods, to be able to see it!

He suspected that Vush could see the avarice in his eyes and he looked away.

"You are pledged to nonviolence?" Oishi asked, coming back into the room, breathing a bit hard and stepping around in front of Aldin.

Vush looked up at the samurai. He had seen him before wearing his swords, but this time the man had no weapons. He found him somehow pleasing. There was a masterful bearing and grace to him. For this occasion he was dressed in the ceremonial garments of his old world, a simple robe of white silk decorated with a stylized blue flower. It was vaguely reminiscent of the flowing robes of the Overseers. He suspected that the man was wearing it because it might be familiar, but it disarmed him nevertheless.

"It was obvious that not one of your people understood how to operate the machine," Oishi said, just the slightest tone of accusation in his voice. He had mastered the common language of the Cloud in a remarkably short time, no longer needing the translation implant, but the hint of Japanese was still there.

"Do you honestly believe that Mupa could go back to this Sphere, discover his mistake, and thus prevent a catastrophe?"

Vush hesitated, and taking up the toddy that was still waiting, he downed a long drink.

"No," he whispered sadly.

"One of us can."

Vush looked back up, staring straight into Oishi's eyes. It

would not have been all so long ago when such a gaze from an Overseer would have had one of the three lesser species blubbering in fear, ready to confess to whatever sin he had committed. He sighed inwardly. Those days were obviously over with.

"I could take you to the Arch; it should be he who decides this," Vush replied, trying to find some sort of fallback position.

"Do you honestly think he would agree to that?" Yaroslav interjected, trying to force down his excitement about the Sphere.

Vush hesitated. He did not want to truly confess his darker fear, and he buried it.

"I don't think so," he finally whispered.

"Will you show us then?" Yaroslav asked, his voice becoming insistent. Oishi looked over his shoulder as if to silence him.

"Remember, a nonaction that creates evil and violence is as reprehensible as an action that creates the same. If you stand by and do nothing, the tens of thousands of years of cleansing your soul will be for naught. You might as well start all over again and take a million years while you're at it. A billion deaths on your soul, and you who worry if the salad you eat is dead before plucking."

"A million years trapped in the Hole of the Shiga would not be enough to atone for all the deaths," Hobbs whispered, even as he smiled and leaned back in his floating lounge chair, motioning for one of his young ladies to rub the rolls of fat around his neck.

Vush started to shake again, and if he could have curled into an even tighter ball and simply disappeared from existence, he would have willed it so. He did in fact try to will it, but nothing came of the effort other than a pulled muscle in his back.

He finally looked back up at the silent gathering.

"I'll do it," he sighed.

Yaroslav grinned, slapping his knee with delight. There was an audible exhaling of a collectively held breath.

"But . . ." Vush whispered.

They all stopped and looked at him.

"I will tell only one person," Vush said, looking over at

Hobbs. "He will navigate the ship. He must swear a solemn oath never to reveal his knowledge, and all ship memories are to be purged."

"I'm honored by your friendship," Hobbs replied with a good-natured grin.

"But of course," Yaroslav said.

"Not him," Vush said. "Oishi."

"Damn it all," Yaroslav groaned. "He'll keep his word, too."

"Precisely," Vush replied, feeling relieved. He looked up at Oishi.

"Swear on what you honor most that you'll agree to these terms."

Oishi, his eyes shining with pride, bowed low, and then hesitating, he looked over at Aldin and bowed again.

"Am I released to make a pledge that I cannot reveal, even to my daimyo?"

"Of course," Aldin said, feeling a wave of relief.

"Then excuse me for a moment."

He left the room and returned a minute later, reverently carrying his swords, the Gaf berserkers crowding in behind him, hoping that there was going to be a fight of some sort or, better yet, a beheading.

Oishi unsheathed the two swords and placed them on the floor in front of the Overseer and then knelt down before him. Reverently he bowed to the blades.

"These were fashioned by Marimosoto, master of blades; his spirit, the spirits of my fathers, reside in them. In front of them I now pledge my word to keep secret whatever you reveal to me."

Without hesitation he took the short blade and cut open his arm, letting the blood drip on the long sword resting before him. A servobot, disturbed by the scent of the blood, turned to look and started to move over to wipe the mess up. Sogio reached out and grabbed the machine, which struggled and hooted weakly.

"I swear by my blood, the blood of my sires, the spirit of my blades to honor my word to you, and if I fail, to die by my own hand."

Vush was impressed and appalled by the ceremony. Still barbarians, drawing blood, swearing oaths. Yet there was a dignity and power to it that convinced him. He looked about the room and saw the respect that the others held for this Human.

"I will tell you as soon as you wish to speak with me," he said, and rising up unsteadily, not sure if it was from the heavily spiked toddies or from a more disturbing phenomenon of emotion, he floated out of the room.

He paused at the door and looked back nervously.

"By the way," he said sheepishly, "there is one other condition."

"What is it?" Yaroslav groaned.

"I have exclusive right to arrange any gaming possibilities that come out of your little expedition."

"Well I'll be damned." Hobbs laughed, slapping the side of his chair. "An Overseer vasba."

Aldin, taken aback, could only grin and nod his head in agreement.

Vush tried to manage a graceful turn, bounced against the door frame, and drifted out of the room.

"Damn it, Oishi, you would have to go and promise like that," Yaroslav snapped peevishly.

"Well at least you'll get to see it," Oishi replied good-naturedly, coming to his feet.

Approaching respectfully, Sogio picked up Oishi's swords and with head lowered held them out to Oishi, who took a silk cloth from his robe and wiped them down before resheathing them. Tia, coming to his side, started to fuss over the cut, but a look from him was sufficient to tell her that she was to stop.

The Gaf berserkers, their respect for Oishi going up yet higher, gathered around him, several of them furtively touching his wound or bloodstained robe and then withdrawing hurriedly to their private chambers to touch the blood to their weapons and thus give them more power.

"It'll be tough getting there," Bukha said, his voice cold.

Oishi looked over at him.

"The Arch."

"They don't have any weapons, other than some disabling equipment on some of their ships," the Xsarn replied.

"But Corbin does," Aldin said.

"Why, Corbin, he'd never figure out how to get there. Hell, we've lived in the Cloud for three thousand years and no one has ever stumbled across it."

"The Arch will tell him," Yaroslav replied.

Aldin looked over at his old friend, a bit sad to realize that both had come to the same dark conclusion.

"And when we do get there, just how the hell are we to figure this thing out?" Tia asked. "I mean, if Vush spent thousands of years prowling around the place and couldn't figure out this wormhole machine, or any of the other things of the First Travelers, how are we suppose to?"

"It's simple," Aldin replied. "We can't, but someone else can."

"Who?" Yaroslav asked, caught off guard, not willing to admit that when it came to trying to master how to shut down the wormhole, that he was as totally confused as everyone else.

"Yashima Korobachi," Aldin said quietly.

"But of course," Yaroslav said, ashamed to admit that there was someone better than him at unraveling mysteries, but thrilled at the prospect of what this implied.

Oishi looked over at Aldin, not sure why Zergh, Yaroslav, and his daimyo were excited.

"The name, I do not know it," Oishi said.

"Oishi, we're going back to Earth. We're going to jump down to the twenty-third century, using the same machine that Zergh flew to bring you through time."

"Earth? You mean back home again?"

"Japan, A.D. 2220," Yaroslav interjected. "Just before the beginning of the great wars. Korobachi cracked the secret of control of the event horizons of black holes and wormholes. He supposedly even generated a wormhole and successfully navigated through one. No one knows how he did it; the information was lost in the wars when the Gafs bombarded Earth.''

He paused for a moment, looking over at Bukha.

"Don't blame me," Bukha said wearily. "I wasn't even there, and remember, you did it to us first.''

Aldin could sense an argument coming and held up his hand for the two to stop. After three thousand years, whenever the topic came up, tempers usually started to flare. Ancient history could still rub a sore spot, even now.

"Yeah, but your grandfathers were," Yaroslav mumbled.

"And so were yours," one of the berserkers growled.

"Enough, damn it. After all, we are civilized gentlemen," the Xsarn interjected hotly, and everyone backed down, not willing to be subjected to the spray from a Xsarn made angry.

"Even though both your ancestors did the same to mine," the Xsarn whispered underneath his fetid breath.

"We go back, snatch the guy, bring him with us to the Sphere, and let him figure it out," Yaroslav said excitedly. "Damn, I'd love to see him at work. Heaven knows what he might be able to figure out inside that thing. He'll shut down the wormhole in no time, and then we can take over the First Traveler stuff for ourselves.''

"There's just one problem," the Xsarn said.

"What's that?" Yaroslav asked.

"There're only two ships to go back in time, one of them parked on my home world.''

"Well, we'll just have to sneak down there and get it," Zergh said. "I've flown it before.''

"You forget you're outlaws and Alpha Xsarn is in the center of the Core Cluster.''

"I guess sneaking us in is up to you," Aldin said. "There's no other way around it.''

"We'll have to abandon this ship and pile everyone aboard mine," the Xsarn said.

"Gods, a Xsarn hive ship," Hobbs groaned. "The stink will kill us!''

Aldin found himself hesitating. It was going to be hell.

"There's no other alternative," the Xsarn said. "We blow this ship up to cover your traces; it should throw the pursuit off for a while."

Several of the Gaf berserkers fell into making retching noises, but an angry look from Oishi silenced them.

"It will have to be that way," Oishi announced as if the argument were closed.

"Let's get started moving our gear," Aldin finally said, his mouth going dry at the thought of being aboard a Xsarn ship.

With a clattering shrug of his six arms, the Xsarn nodded and walked out of the room.

"So who has the other time-jump ship? We can always get that if going to Xsarn prime is too dangerous," Hobbs said as if offering out a hopeful alternative.

Aldin chuckled sadly and shook his head.

"The other one is most likely in the possession of Corbin Gablona."

It had been twenty years or more since he had been to the Prime Hive World of the Xsarns. He was not looking forward to it.

The traffic patterns through the jump points in were not at all what he expected. Interstellar fares had quadrupled for any passage originating from those planets closest to the runaway wormhole to any that were further out. There wasn't a yacht, freighter, cruise ship, or junk scow that wasn't converging in to pick up passengers who would pay damn near anything to get out. Most of the old corporation ships were busy pulling out their upper-level management people and giving a high priority to valuable office equipment. Traffic control had broken down, with ships leaping through holding patterns and the automated sentinels handing out tickets at a record rate.

One Xsarn yacht, heading in the opposite direction, needed only to worry about the congestion and the possibility of somebody running on the wrong side of the lanes, thus creating a head-on collision, an event that would for a brief instant glow as bright as the convulsing new star.

The Prime Hive of the Xsarns would, at least for the moment, be a fairly safe place, at least as long as the Xsarn Prime was Xsarn Prime. Aldin had never been able to quite figure out all the nuances of Xsarn rule and society. There were times when they appeared to experience a collective mentality, something he was almost sure happened when they gathered into one of their mating balls and for their various religious ceremonies that took up a good part of their yearly cycle. There were other times when their behavior seemed erratic in the extreme. There was a very strange phenomenon that would occur at times when one of them would form a large ball of mud and Xsarn food and roll it along whatever magnetic north line was handy until it dropped from exhaustion. Then another would roll it back to the original spot. The first would revive, go back, and push the ball north again, endlessly repeating the cycle until one or the other died of exhaustion. The Xsarn Prime, when asked about this, would only repeat one of their favorite lines, which appeared to be universal to all three species but had a special appeal to Xsarn humor: "Shit happens."

Lining up for final approach behind several food import ships, which he half believed he could smell even through the vacuum of space, Aldin finally turned the con over to the Xsarn Prime. His mandibles clicking excitedly, the Xsarn guided the ship in, swooping down through the atmosphere, breaking the final approach line to dock directly at the main terminus of his own private hive.

As the hatch was released the Xsarn strode out, waving his antennae high, thousands of identical-looking Xsarns swarming about the ship. Following behind him, Aldin took one deep breath and gagged at the overpowering stench that he suddenly believed was a full magnitude worse than the stench within the ship.

"Ah, home," the Xsarn sighed.

"Not exactly what I'd call it," Yaroslav growled, putting a scented handkerchief to his face, while most of the others donned gas filter masks that were filled with various scents to block out the smell, a convenience Aldin and Bukha had to do without due do diplomatic niceties.

Stepping off the ramp, Aldin followed the Xsarn, nearly deafened by the rhythmic banging as the members of the reception committee started to beat on their carapaces with all six arms, a drumming that thundered and rolled over them like a storm. Then came the part that he was dreading—the ritual of the communal sharing of food. Five thousand Xsarns, acting as if one, sprayed up the contents of their last half-dozen meals, the air turning instantly into a dark shadow of foaming mist. The Xsarns now started to roar with delight, dancing under the rain of food, turning their faces up to catch the shower, rubbing it over themselves, the Xsarn Prime being covered from the top of his antennae to his clawed feet in a single instant.

Exuberant Xsarns ran up to the Xsarn Prime's companions and treated them to the same friendly greeting. For a brief instant Aldin could hear Mari's high shrill laugh coming from the ship as she hid within, witnessing her husband's greeting. The laugh was cut short by a wailing shriek as a Xsarn clambered aboard and gave her a similar treatment. The servobots aboard the ship hooted in high-pitched distress as the gallons of regurgitated Xsarn food sprayed across shag carpets.

Unable to contain himself, Aldin leaned over, adding his meal to the ritual, his companions whipping off their gas masks to join in. The Xsarns, delighted at such a gesture of friendliness, redoubled their efforts to make these rare guests feel right at home. Several of the Gaf berserkers, however, delighted with the absolutely overwhelming display and laughing at the spectacle, set into dancing and waving their weapons. The Xsarns, deeply moved by the good manners and enthusiasm, surrounded the Gafs, lifting them up in the air so that those pressing in from the back could project their meals onto these remarkable friends.

"Your guards are making an excellent impression," the Xsarn Prime shouted, trying to be heard above the clattering, roaring, and retching.

Aldin, almost down on his knees from the convulsions, could not even respond as he was pushed through the crowd.

"No wonder this place is so low on the tourist circuit," Yaroslav groaned.

Aldin sniffed at his clothes. He knew that they had been stored aboard the ship, and as such had not received the Xsarn greeting treatment. Though highly insulted, the Xsarn Prime had at last relented and allowed him, along with Zergh, Tia, Basak, Yaroslav, Vush, and Oishi, to depart in secret and thus avoid the even more disturbing farewell ceremony, which, if it were possible, was even more disgusting. Hobbs finally managed to get aboard ship as well with an emotional and most likely correct argument that Corbin and the Overseers would kill him on sight and that there was no place to hide until this war was over.

"In close fighting, they'd always win," Oishi said, sitting pale beside Aldin. They've got natural armor against arrows, and when it came to sword fighting range, they'd only have to greet you." He shuddered slightly, an exhausted servobot looking over at him anxiously.

"I hope you enjoyed your stay," the Xsarn Prime said, a light tone of amusement in his voice, his face filling the commlink screen.

In the background Aldin could hear Mari cursing wildly.

"Take good care of the guests," Aldin said, not able to hide a slight chuckle.

"Larice, this is it!" Mari shouted across the link. "I'll divorce you for this, clean you out for everything you've got, dumping me in this damn shit hole planet."

Though it was impossible to read emotion in a Xsarn's eyes, his drooping antennae were signal enough that he was not amused with Aldin's decision to leave Mari behind. There was simply not enough room in the ship, Aldin had argued, truthfully enough. Except for his chosen companions, Vush who was hiding in his room, and the replacement Humanbot stored below deck, everyone else was being left behind. Bukha would depart later, along with the Xsarn to try to link back up with some of the other Kohs. The samurai guards were none too happy, but the Gaf berserkers were delighted. He suspected that down deep they were most likely struggling for control, but after the riotous reception given to those who had thrown themselves into the ceremony, the others, no matter how their stomachs might feel, had to best their companions or suffer the shame of it. They were already boasting to each other how they would outdo each other in the departure ceremony, and several, to the shock of the Xsarn, had requested the honor of joining in a mating ball. Disgusting crudity was a badge of honor to a Gaf berserker.

"We'll be back in twenty days," Aldin said, nodding a farewell to the commlink screen.

"If there's anything to come back to," Yaroslav quipped.

As they gained escape velocity and turned toward the first jump gate that would start them on their long journey back into the old galaxy, Mari's cursing could be heard in the background. With a smile Aldin turned the switch off and settled back for the long journey back to the Milky Way, which shone brightly off the starboard side.

At jump-point terminus MW1, the only jump transit back to the Milky Way, a lone ship poised for acceleration. There was no need to bring others in to try to block anyone who followed. For that matter he was hoping he'd be followed, for there would certainly be a surprise at the other end.

With a nod of command, Corbin Gablona signaled the ship to accelerate up and head into the jump point. He looked over cautiously at Hassan. At least in this type of situation Hassan still needed him, could not survive without him. For the moment, at least, he was back in control.

Hitting the jump point, the vessel leaped through the translight line and disappeared, heading straight down toward the Milky Way, a hundred and fifty thousand light-years away. This single jump line back to the old system was also the only door into the past.

CHAPTER 7

Bracing for the gut-wrenching jump-down transition, Aldin Larice checked the calibration for what he knew must be the hundredth time.

It had been a laborious run down the jump line back to the Milky Way. Most other leaps were near instantaneous, but those were rarely for more than several hundred light-years, the longest within the entire cloud being out to the Kolbard Ring, a twelve thousand light-year leap. For some as yet unexplainable reason, part of the mystery of just how or why jump transition worked, duration of flight grew at an exponential rate. Given the incredible amount of energy required to maintain jump, any run much beyond that distance was totally out of the question.

How the First Travelers had ever managed to chart out the lines, discover the null points, lay out the markers and danger buoys, was beyond him. The discovery of jump was, in itself, shrouded in mystery for all three species, who appeared to have discovered it nearly simultaneously, thus triggering the outward leap from their respective solar systems, and the Great Wars for control of interstellar space, which eventually devastated most of the inhabitable planets of the old galaxy.

137

He had to give the damn Overseers their due. If they had not broken the cycle of violence in the Magellanic Cloud, the wars would most likely have resulted in the annihilation of all three species, the few survivors stranded on remote planets, reverting to prespace civilizations.

Granted, the Overseers were overbearing in the extreme with their holier-than-thou preaching, their constant seizure of the moral high ground from which to moralize. They reminded him far too much of the damned professional cause-seekers, who raced from moral issue to moral issue, weeping one month over the rights of criminal psychopaths being so cruelly mistreated by exile with their own kind to orbital prisons, the next month lamenting the insensitivity of someone laughing about Gaf trisexual cross-dressers. Anyone who disagreed with such individuals was branded insensitive, barbaric, incorrect, and Neanderthalishly phobic. He didn't mind someone telling him he might be wrong, but when someone told him he was definitely wrong, especially for daring to disagree with an accuser who knew he was morally superior, it simply grated his nerves. The Overseers had been doing that for thousands of years. He knew he'd miss the order they provided, he'd do anything to bring it back, but he could only hope that at least in the future they'd shut the hell up.

He was surprised that there hadn't been an Overseer ship blocking the jump point back to the Milky Way. There must have been some sort of security system to reveal that he had hopped right into the Core Cluster and then back out again.

It was all going a little too easily.

He looked over at Zergh and Yaroslav, who were checking the calibration of the time-transit system. This was going to be the hard part.

"Not to worry," Yaroslav said, though it sounded as if he were reassuring himself as much as he was trying to put Aldin at ease.

A shudder ran through the ship and, with a spectacular Doppler shift, it went through jump transition. They were back in the Milky Way.

He had only been here once before, and he looked over his shoulder as Tia came into the forward room, Oishi by her side.

"Last time was when we came for Alexander the Great," she said with a grin.

"And you were one royal pain in the ass," he replied with a smile.

She laughed playfully and kissed him on his balding crown.

"Where is home?" Oishi asked, his voice betraying his eagerness to see Earth once again. Cherry blossoms, unfortunately, were something unknown in the Cloud, and he had finally convinced Aldin that if there was time he could go down and try to get a couple of shoots.

"Somewhere right over there," Yaroslav said, pointing out the window. Oishi pressed himself against the forward viewport.

"So far from the center," he said, as if almost disappointed.

"The Gavarnian homeworld is closer in," Zergh interjected with a faint touch of superiority. It was a point of Gaf pride that Humans were definitely from the outback and thus of lower breeding.

"At least we don't have the Xsarn along," Yaroslav said. "They get so damn touchy about the war and what it did to their home planet, he'd most likely puke on all of us before he was done."

"Well, they did start it," Zergh said.

"Like hell, it was you Gafs," Aldin replied, sounding professorial when the topic came to military history.

"From the viewpoint of a neutral observer, you're all to blame," Vush said, floating in to join them. "After the incident at Vak, all three of you started shooting within microseconds of each other, the rest is history until we so foolishly stopped you."

It was the first time he had come out of his cabin since they had left Alpha Xsarn, and Aldin found he was almost glad to see him. The secret location of the Sphere was locked up with this one individual, and his health had suddenly become a very important issue.

"Ever been here before?" Oishi asked.

Vush tried to shake his head, but since Overseer necks did not articulate well, his entire body turned back and forth.

"If you mean to this particular vantage point, I have not. Though I did come—"

He stopped himself.

"So there is another jump point!" Yaroslav said triumphantly. "Come on, if you weren't here, there's got to be another jump point."

"I've said too much already," Vush said sulkily.

"It's all right. Now don't say another word," Oishi interjected, feeling a sort of friendship toward Vush ever since making his pledge of secrecy to him.

Vush nodded and floated over to the window. Yaroslav was tempted to ask him some more questions, but a look from Oishi stopped him.

"I'd almost forgotten how vast it all is," Vush whispered, as if speaking to himself. "So limitless, all of space. So quiet, just the four of us, the three of you and us, all that is self-aware, except for the First Travelers, wherever it is they now hide."

He looked back at the group.

"Your language is so limited, so pale to all of this," Vush said softly. "Even the ten million words that shape my thoughts cannot give justice to the grandeur of eternity."

He silently floated out of the room, the door sliding shut behind him.

"A damn philosopher no less," Yaroslav growled, though obviously moved by the poignancy in Vush's voice.

"Actually, I kind of like him," Oishi replied.

Ten days after the wormhole was activated, the inner layers of carbon-oxygen of the red giant were long gone, exploding out of the new star at the other end of the link. The next layer up of helium burning at well over one hundred million degrees K now funneled into the wormhole, coursing in an instant into the heart of the new star, boiling up through the material already there, the star shifting in an instant into the beginnings of a red giant that was already nearly two times the mass of a standard yellow sun. A flat spiral of glowing hydrogen was, at the same time, spinning down the outside length of the wormhole, pulled along by the intense gravitational field induced by the tremendous amount of mass moving at translight speed through the dimensional pipeline. Occasional flickers were still giving birth to independent wormholes, some of which ejected matter into other dimensions and even other times.

A minor footnote of Gaf history could thus be explained, when three thousand years before a yacht, carrying the lover of a Gaf princess, disappeared in the region, the incident being blamed on a Xsarn exploration ship, thus triggering the seventh Gaf-Xsarn war. The mourned lover was, in fact, now percolating inside the new star, pulled through by an errant wormhole that had jumped time. Another wormhole, flung completely out of the system, popped through a jump-transit line, crossed time, and by sheer chance drilled through a distant Earth, causing the mysterious disappearance of an ancient union leader, of dubious moral character, involved in the business of moving goods on land with internal combustion machines; it popped him, complete with smoking cigar and Cadillac, back into the boiling sun.

Inside of it all, at the very core of the event, the well-crafted First Traveler wormhole-maker chugged along.

"Time-transition jump." Aldin and Zergh gazed intently at the instrument panel, both of them holding their breath.

"Now!"

For a fraction of a second Aldin thought the machine had malfunctioned. An instant later there was a rapid Doppler shift. Unlike jump-point transitions where there was a tiny cone of visible star patterns straight ahead, everything went totally blank.

"June 18, 2220," Aldin called, double-checking the panel, "the day before the Great Wars start."

A curious vibration ran through the vessel, one that set his teeth to chattering. If jump transitions were tough on the constitution, this was far worse, and he inwardly cursed the day, so long ago, when he and Zergh playfully suggested the possibilities of time travel to their old employer—Corbin Gablona. Several billion katars later he had actually pulled it off, one of the most expensive construction and research projects in history, all to be able to bring back various generals and warriors to support the games. The theory of exactly why it all worked was still a complete mystery, even to those who had made the system.

He had chosen the date with care. Less than a day later the Vak incident would occur, and with it the conflagration that would sweep across the entire galaxy. Yashima's work had been completed, and he was living in retirement at a remote villa on the northern island of Hokkaido. The timing was such that there was no chance of disturbing history. The Humanbot could be altered to replace him and away they would go, a full day before a crazed assassin would burst into his villa and gun him down.

They soared inward, hitting the time-jump line, and with a sickening lurch the backward count of the system started to click through with blinding speed.

"Just a couple of more seconds," Yaroslav said, and Oishi stood up excitedly, moving toward the forward viewscreen, which would suddenly fill with Earth.

Before he was even fully aware of it, everything seemed to go wrong at once. The ship somehow managed to pull a full inverted roll, the inertial dampening system a full second behind, thus spilling everybody to the ceiling before sucking them back up again into their old positions. Zergh, tumbling through the air, roared a quick string of Gaf imprecations before slamming into the control panel. Like a chip of wood on a storm-tossed sea, the craft bobbed and weaved and then finally settled down.

"What the shit?" Aldin shouted, looking over at Zergh, who was slowly sliding down the side of the control panel and dropping back into his chair.

The door flung open behind them, and Vush floated in, moving horizontally rather than vertically, a trace of yellow-green blood pouring down from a cut head.

"Something's jumbled the field," Zergh shouted, cursing as

he tried to mop a spilled cup of coffee off a set of monitors, a servobot shouldering him aside to do the job.

"What?"

"I said something jumbled the field ahead of us."

Aldin groaned and sat back, nursing a bump on his head.

"I think we've got a problem," Zergh whispered, pointing to one of the monitors.

Aldin looked over at it.

"How, damn it?" he roared.

"I guess I bumped into one of the dials," Zergh said weakly, trying to force a smile.

Yashima Korobachi, overwhelmed with sadness, stepped out onto the porch of his villa. A weak sun was breaking through the morning clouds, glinting off the high-cresting waves of the cold Pacific. Angry gulls circled overhead, distraught that he who was always so free with gifts was this morning ignoring them.

Waves. He could remember as a small boy when his grandfather would bring him to this place. When the tide was rushing out, there was a small pool down in the rocks where a whirlpool would on occasion form. Perhaps that is where it all started, the fascination of a small boy squatting on a rock, throwing chips of wood in, watching them swirl around and disappear.

He smiled.

The news, damn them. Couldn't they see where his thoughts could now lead them? Infinity, the limitless universe, all dreamed of in his mind and now made within reach. And they were going to end it all.

He reached into his pocket and pulled out a crust of bread, and breaking it into pieces, he fed his friends who wheeled overhead.

He did not even hear the crackling of the beam, nor see the coalescence of the hooded man who appeared behind him, nor hear the crack of the Erik 10 that sent him into the long sleep.

* * *

"Someone jumped through ahead of us," Aldin said, cursing and slamming his fist on the console. "Once someone does a jump into a particular time, it's impossible to do it ever again through that entry point. The disturbance wake almost killed us."

"So find another time-transition point," Vush said hopefully.

"We don't know of any," Yaroslav said coldly. "Gablona got to him ahead of us. We've only got enough energy for this one jump and we just did it."

"Whatever for? Why would Gablona come here?" Vush asked, still not understanding the confusion around him.

"To keep us from getting him, stupid," Yaroslav snapped.

Oishi, straightening out his clothes, struggled back to his feet and looked out the forward window. Earth hovered before him, and he felt his eyes cloud with tears; it was far more beautiful than he ever imagined possible. He looked back expectantly at Aldin, the needs of their mission, at least for this brief moment, forgotten.

"It's home, Oishi," Aldin said, forcing a smile. Then he looked over at Zergh.

"Just when the hell are we?" Aldin asked.

"Well the date is right at least," Zergh said quietly, "It's still June eighteenth."

"But what year?"

Zergh chuckled and scratched his head.

"Either the wave disturbance did it, or . . ." His voice trailed off. "When I fell back on the panel I spun the entry date a little bit."

"To?" Aldin asked peevishly.

"A nice round change it was, we're only off by exactly four hundred years."

Yaroslav looked over his shoulder and sighed.

"June 18, 1820. Just what the hell good is that when we're looking for a wormhole physicist?"

"Well it's better than nothing," Zergh said lamely. "At least I got us here."

"This is a fine mess we've gotten into," Yaroslav said, disgusted.

"Anyhow, now that we're here," Zergh said, a sudden smile lighting his features, "there's no sense in going home empty-handed."

The sounds in the garden had finally died away. The sentry had managed his rendezvous with the serving girl, and together they had their brief moment. He was tempted to stir from bed, to pull back the shutter, lean out, and tell them to be quiet. Soldiers could be like children. He remembered when they were his children, the finest soldiers ever to march across Europe, who would look at him with adulation, their eyes damp, joyfully offering their deaths for his glory.

He could not begrudge a soldier, even an English soldier, his brief moment of living.

Living.

He sighed and swung his legs off the bed, letting them rest on the cold wooden floor. The room was dank, a slight scent of damp mold in the air. In the dark, at least, he could forget the shabbiness. How many palaces had he slept in, the poor son of alleged Corsican nobility. Paris, Madrid, Cairo, Vienna, Berlin, and the cold rooms of the Kremlin. Even his campaign tent was better—the whispers outside of it that of his old grumblers, Imperial Guard of a dozen campaigns, silencing the camp when they thought him asleep, his children watching over him like hovering parents. The night before battle he would come out of the tent, showing the outward calm, the quiet self-assurance that would then flood through his army, convincing them that live or dié, in the morn victory for France was assured.

Sleep would not come. Funny, he thought, I never really needed it before, it was the robber, sent to steal the precious hours when so much needed to be done. Now he longed for it, when the stillness of the last watch of night was at its deepest. Now it would not steal upon him and drown the pain, the memories.

Napoleon Bonaparte sighed heavily, leaning forward slightly, tucking his hands over his bloated stomach to try to hold in the pain, to prevent it from sweeping outward. Should he call his servant?

No. Let him sleep awhile longer. How many countless times had he seen men sitting like he now did, clutching their stomachs, looking up at him with watery eyes, trying to hold their lives in, knowing that the darkness was coming. Some would force a smile—"just a scratch my Emperor," "long live France," "did we win?"

He had lost all sense of pity long ago and could look upon the thousands dead and dying and not feel a stirring. If a general ever did, he could no longer be a general. Now he knew what it must feel like, the pain, and he pitied them all, and himself.

I'm dying. He wanted it to come, the pain gnawing up inside him. I've been dead for five years already. They should not have stopped me. I should have gone back up to the guard as they covered my retreat, I should have picked up the flag, as I once did at Arcola. He smiled for a brief instant with that memory. How legends had been built around that, the wonderful painting by David—his picking up the fallen flag, leading the charge across the bridge. It was hard now even in memory to separate the truth from the legend . . . the legend was better, of course.

I should have died within my legend, not lingering here. There would be no more paintings by David, no *Victory at Marengo* marches, no return to the palace, Josephine, damn her, waiting, unwashed as ordered, or so many of the others who joyfully slipped into his room. He thought for a moment of the maid out in the garden with the soldier. He had flirted with her and she had smiled at him only the day before, and he heard her whisper later how he was a charming old man. Just an old man now, he thought with a sigh. Dying from a fire within, dying chained to this damnable rock.

Five years ago today . . . Waterloo, and now this.

He tried to stand up, his spindly legs trembling, his stomach, bloated, burning, the pain cutting through. Never again would there be what was. If only there could be the release, to dream, to once again be as it was.

"To die." The words were a sigh.

"France," he whispered, "France . . . *armée* . . . *Tête d'armée* . . . Josephine."

A shimmer of light began to form in the center of the room, which until the coming of the exile had been a pigsty. For a brief second he was not even sure if it was real, an illusion, or the summoning of the angel of death.

The light took shape, a human shape, growing brighter. The air that was within the cylinder of light rushed out with a gust, fluttering the worn curtains. Napoleon tried to straighten up, to face the end standing. He smiled; there was no fear, never such a low thing as fear, though for the first time in years, and not even aware of it, he made the sign of the cross.

The light shifted through a dazzling display of colors, and then with an audible pop the shape became real.

"Are you an angel?"

"Hardly, my emperor."

The accent was atrocious. But it had called him emperor! He was willing to forgive just to again hear the sound of the words.

Aldin Larice felt a surge of joy and yet also one of painful disappointment. He was standing in the presence of the emperor, Napoleon Bonaparte. Yet such a difference from the first time he had seen Alexander. Though dying, Alexander had still retained an almost godlike beauty, a power even at the edge of death. Napoleon looked like a man defeated, an old man who was waiting for but one final appointment. And he felt a surge of pity. In this musty room languished the greatest mind of the revolutionary age, the dreamer of empires, trapped by his own ambitions and defeat.

In a perverse way this was nothing but a tourist stop. There was no use for Napoleon in the crisis of his time. What use was this dying man, when it was a wormhole physicist that he had sought? Accident alone had brought him here. But as a vasba he could not be in this time without meeting him. Before all the madness of the games had started, bringing Napoleon into the future would have been viewed as a coup, as spectacular as fetching Alexander had been. And yet Zergh, who had a fascination with Napoleon, had said it all—that while they were in the neighborhood it would be impolite not to drop in, and perhaps offer a hand. Yaroslav, however, had come close to throwing a tantrum, denouncing Napoleon as a brutal murderer, and when outvoted by the group, he threatened to stay on Earth rather than ride in the same ship with the emperor.

"If you are not an angel," Napoleon asked, "then tell me, who and what you are?"

There was a wonderful command to his voice, instantly relayed and translated through Aldin's voice implant.

"Well," Aldin said, not quite sure where to start, "we were passing through the area, and thought you might like to come along for the ride."

"A ride?"

"Call it a little trip, Excellency. A chance to get off this godforsaken rock and live again."

The last thing Aldin Larice ever expected to see was Napoleon Bonaparte cry.

"He's a hell of a mess," Tia said, coming back into the room. Though everyone else except Yaroslav was awed by the fact that the emperor was in the next room, Oishi could barely contain himself from taking Tia over to the far corner of the forward cabin where he proudly pointed out a dozen tiny saplings. Napoleon, a hundred years in Oishi's future, meant nothing. The cherry trees were far more important.

"It was still the same," Oishi said, his voice choked with emotion. "The grave of my first lord Asano still honored. A temple is nearby and monks pray near his remains. There were even fresh flowers upon it."

His eyes filled with tears and he shyly brushed them away.

"Then I walked through the town, and would you believe it, I saw a Kabuki play, a play about us, me, *The Forty-Seven Ronin.* He chuckled. "I brought the cherry saplings. Little did that woman know how precious they truly were, to a time when no such things exist.

"And then I could not help it, I had to see. If only they knew the real truth of what happened to us. I asked a man to show me the grave of the Forty-Seven Ronin, and he took me to it. There was my name." He paused. "And yet so many of us are gone," he continued, his voice quiet. "Takashi. Only thirty of us left."

"Thirty who would be dead otherwise," Aldin said, looking over at one of his closest friends with deep-felt emotion. There were times when he wondered about the morality of all that he had done. But if he had not, Oishi and the other samurai would be dead. Alexander would be dust. And the man in the next room?

"How bad off is he?" Aldin asked.

"The medbots are finishing up the examination right now."

"Those damned things," Yaroslav sniffed. "I'd be damned if I let myself get treated by one of them."

"Corbin spent a bundle on them," Zergh replied. "When we planned to bring Alexander back we figured he'd be in bad shape. There was no sense spending billions on this and then scrimp a million or two more only to let him die."

"Well, they better be good," Tia said. "He's got arteriosclerosis, some minor neural deterioration that must have been affecting his thought process, a hell of a nasty dose of tapeworms, advancing rheumatism, astigmatism, and damned if he isn't suffering from arsenic poisoning."

"Ah, yes, your typical ancient Human," Zergh said, with an air of superiority.

"Poisoning?" Aldin asked, looking up with professional curiosity.

"Damn stuff was eating right through him. His stomach was chewed to hell. The medbots will be working flat-out for a couple of days to bring him back on line. I figured we should let him rest up a little bit, tell him what's going on, before going to work on him. The guy was just going crazy with questions, especially when it finally started to sink in that we're from his future."

"The replacement unit integrated in all right?"

"He was dropped in a couple of minutes ago," Tia said. "It was a quick programming and change job, remember we thought we could just drop him off for our physicist friend who was going to get killed when the war started. This one had to be perfect, able to withstand an autopsy. It was a near thing. A guard peeked in the window just when we finished the transfer and ran off. Fortunately he'd had a couple of drinks, and his sergeant cuffed him around and then led him away."

"I heard a story about what they did to him at the autopsy. How a little something, a very little something was taken by one of the doctors as a souvenir. So thanks for letting me do that final check-over of his body before it got taken out of the mold," Yaroslav said with a smile.

"So that's why you wanted to make that change," Aldin said.

"I think it's disgusting," Tia interjected.

"He's got enough of an inflated ego as is," Yaroslav replied. "I'm glad history will think he was indeed small, indeed microscopic in at least one aspect of his life."

Zergh, at last catching on as to what Yaroslav had done to Napoleon's replacement unit, growled angrily.

"Well, now that we've got him, what the hell are we going to do with him?" Hobbs asked, his voice flat with dejection.

"Why, send him to the wormhole and let him figure it out," Yaroslav replied.

Zergh sniffed disdainfully and looked away.

"Look, as Zergh said earlier," Aldin interjected, "while we were in the area it wouldn't hurt to pick him up. You know, if ever there's a future game, it'd be great to have him around."

"It's still not going to help us any," Yaroslav said.

"You talk like he's a toy or something," Aldin replied sharply. "He's the Emperor Napoleon."

"All right. So now we have the Emperor Napoleon. We've failed to get the help we needed. We've got to go back home. It'll take months to get this bucket ready for another jump to look for someone else, say Einstein or Pradap Singh, for instance."

"Einstein," Aldin corrected him.

"As I said. By that time heaven alone knows what the wormhole will have eaten. Gablona obviously has the man we wanted, and the Overseers still have a price on our head. Civilization is about to collapse. What the hell are we going to do?''

"It sounds like you have a problem."

Startled, Aldin turned to the door. Napoleon, wearing a baggy hospital robe, stood before him. It was obvious that the man was badly shaken, and somewhat frightened by the disk of the Earth floating in the forward window. Yet, in a masterful display, he came into the room, hands behind his back, the only signal of his nervousness the twitching of his tightly interlaced fingers.

"Aldin Larice?"

His voice was slightly raspy, not quite catching the uplift of the final syllable to signify a question. He had already received the microscopic neural translating unit and had been instructed in its use, but the unit was still adjusting to the idiosyncracies of early nineteenth-century French, laced with a Corsican accent.

Aldin stood up, feeling a bit satisfied that here was someone to whom he could speak eye to eye.

Napoleon came forward and in a gracious gesture extended his hand, which Aldin took.

"I do not understand the hows of all of this." He looked around the room, giving a bit of a start at the sight of Zergh, who stood up to his full seven-foot height.

"An intelligent being from another world, sir," Tia said, poking Zergh in the ribs.

"Looks almost like an overgrown dog," Napoleon said.

Zergh growled softly.

"No insult intended, of course."

"That's quite all right, Humans are noted for such mistakes," Zergh replied, grinning with a full display of sharpened canines.

Napoleon, not missing a beat, chuckled, and releasing Aldin's hand he went over and offered it to Zergh.

The Gaf vasba smiled genuinely this time and shook it warmly.

"Would you care for some muscatel?" Zergh asked.

Oishi, clearing his throat, stepped past Zergh and snapped his fingers to a servobot.

"Napoleon brandy," Oishi ordered.

The bot put a snifter beneath the universal dispenser and rolled forward, offering the drink up.

"Napoleon brandy," the emperor said, smiling with delight, looking closely at the bot.

"Why don't we offer him some beef Wellington," Yaroslav whispered, a comment that Aldin was glad their guest did not hear.

"What is this?" Napoleon asked looking down at the bot.

"An automatona" Aldin said. "A machine to serve us and to clean up the place."

"Ingenious."

He looked back at Oishi.

"Japan?"

Oishi smiled and nodded.

"Good warriors, I heard; the best swordsmen in the world. Samurai I believe you are called?"

Oishi grunted with approval and bowed low at the compliment.

Next he turned to Tia, and smiling, he approached her; with a slight incline of his head he took her hand and kissed it lightly.

"Mademoiselle, I am honored to be in your company."

Tia, a bit flustered, looked over at Aldin, who smiled warmly, and at Oishi, who remained silent.

Napoleon, catching her eye movement, looked over at Oishi and nodded his head again.

"You are fortunate to be married to one of such beauty, and she to be married to one of such bravery."

"And you are the philosopher Yaroslav," Napoleon said, graciously dropping Tia's hand and looking over at the old man sitting in the corner.

"Philosopher?" Yaroslav sniffed. "Did Tia tell you that?"

"A compliment to disarm you," Napoleon replied, still smiling and coming over to offer his hand.

"Such familiarity from an emperor," Yaroslav said, his tone ever so slightly ironic.

"To command in this situation?" Napoleon said, looking

around, letting his confusion show for the briefest of moments. "Would it do me much good?"

"I doubt it," Yaroslav replied.

"There you have it then. You see that I have made a tactical withdraw in order to be able to gain a strategic advantage."

"Like you did in Russia?"

Aldin could sense the bristling between the two. There was the slightest of flickers, and then ever so gradually a smile crossed Napoleon's features.

"I am told that this is the future, at least for me," he said, looking back over at Aldin.

"By several thousand years, once we return."

Napoleon nodded.

"And yet still I am remembered."

"Next to Alexander, as one of the greatest generals of history."

"Ah, yes, Alexander, a worthy rival for glory and fame."

"And better looking than you, too," Yaroslav replied.

Napoleon looked back at the old man.

"You are picking a quarrel with me, sir," he said slowly.

Yaroslav smiled. "But of course."

"Someday, maybe later," he said softly. "But not now. I will confess to be in your debt. I sense there is a crisis. Such things I have faced before. I am eager to face them again."

Yaroslav was silent, Aldin looking over at him with barely suppressed rage.

The door slid open again, and Vush entered the room. Napoleon could not help but step backward in shock at the sight of an Overseer.

"They are a bit unsettling at first sight," Yaroslav said, loud enough for Vush to hear.

"Is this the Human scientist of wormholes?" Vush asked.

"Not exactly," Yaroslav replied, a trace of a grin crossing his face.

"Then what is it?"

"Oh, only a damn good killer, one of our best."

Vush looked at Napoleon, and with a groan turned and floated back out of the room, the single word "damn" floating on the air.

"You delight in annoying everyone, don't you," Napoleon said, looking back and smiling.

"It can be one of the best things in life. The more self-important they are, the bigger the bubble to burst."

"You do it well," Napoleon replied. With a flourish he downed the rest of his brandy.

"An excellent drink," he said with a smile. "And now if mademoiselle will be so kind as to show me back to the hospital, I will confess that the pain is starting to master my composure."

Nodding to each in turn, he started for the door, Tia coming up to him solicitously to take his arm, surprised by how much he suddenly needed to lean upon her for support. Yet he stopped for a moment and looked back.

"I suspect that you are indeed in serious trouble. It is easy to surmise by your need to travel into the past to find help and by the behavior of that being who came in here. You came to find someone else you needed more, and I am just a substitute that was not intended, nor I suspect viewed as any use other than a nostalgia. Fate has her reasons for casting me here. My star is not yet ready to set, and I will be of service as you need it." He nodded again and slowly, struggling for a graceful exit, left the room.

"Well, I'll be damned," Yaroslav said, smiling and shaking his head. "Before it's done, I bet that son of a bitch will get the better of all of us."

"Why don't you like him?"

"Oh, of course, I just love him," Yaroslav said. "Who couldn't, once you get past the fact that the bastard killed somewhere around a million men by the time his wars were done."

"Alexander did the same," Zergh said.

"Maybe the further back in history, the less the pain comes through. It's just I always thought Alexander was driven by a desire to unite our entire world, much as Kubar Taug did yours. To bring about a universal peace under Hellenic enlightenment."

"Napoleon started out believing the revolutionary ideals of the Enlightenment," Aldin said. "It was a dream of uniting the western world two hundred years ahead of its time and ending the reign of nobility over that of ability."

"I never quite saw him that way," Yaroslav replied sharply. "Did you see how he worked each of us in turn? He's masterful."

"And you can't quite tolerate two such individuals in the same room," Zergh replied, "especially when one of them isn't you."

Yaroslav looked over at Zergh and replied with an obscure Gaf hand gesture that was nearly impossible for Humans to make and thus elicited a roar of delight at the absurdity of it.

Tia came back into the room, a worried look in her eyes.

"That little show of his was incredible, considering the pain he must be in."

"A showman of the first degree," Yaroslav replied.

"Well, he's out of action for the next couple of days. The medbots have their work cut out for them; purging out heavy-metal poisoning is a bitch."

"And just wait for the tapeworms. Too bad we don't have a Xsarn along, they'd love it, might even see them as a distant cousin," Yaroslav interjected.

"You're disgusting," Tia snapped.

"Always a pleasure."

"Well, let's head for home," Aldin said. "We'll try and figure out what to do on the way back in.

Punching the ship around, he quickly lined up on the time-jump line, and with a forward surge, the ship accelerated, hitting its maximum speed within minutes. Three thousand years were leaped in a matter of seconds.

Pushing through the next two transition points, Aldin spared a quick break from the controls to sneak back into the med room. The medbots hovered over their charge, half a dozen working at once, the body of Napoleon covered in a maze of monitors, wires, and control units. Though it played with his all-too-weak stomach, he could not help but watch, fascinated. It was almost as if they were taking him apart from top to bottom, cleaning, repairing, draining, patching. A kidney too thoroughly impregnated with the arsenic was pulled out and replaced with a synthetic substitute, grown in the same manner as a Humanbot's organs. It was a treatment that, so unfairly he thought, only the richest of Kohs could afford, thus far extending their lives by repairing the ravages of their dissipation. He had snatched Napoleon only months from his demise; when the man again awoke his body would be as fit as it was at the height of his glory, in the heady days as first consul. Even the neural system would be revitalized, agility of thought returning from the cloudiness. Yet what will we do with him? Aldin wondered. Yaroslav, hiding his admiration in cynicism, was all too right. This was not another Alexandrian game. Civilization was on the point of a catastrophe. He had set out to find the cure and was returning with an anachronism.

"Aldin?"

He looked back at Oishi, who had silently entered the room.

"A problem."

"What?"

"Company's coming."

Stirred from his contemplation of Napoleon's fate, he returned to the forward control room and looked over Zergh's shoulder at the main nav screen.

"Someone's pushed through here; there're traces of unburned antimatter still kicking about, an engine slightly out of tune. The long jump point back to the Cloud is ten minutes ahead."

"Corbin?"

"I think so," Zergh replied.

"Damn it."

"Do you think he's armed?" Aldin asked, looking over at Oishi.

"We're not, and in such a case, I'd suggest that we assume that he is."

"Get Vush in here," Aldin said quietly.

If he's blocking the path back home, Aldin thought coldly, we can either try to run past him or wait it out.

"I'm picking up something," Zergh said quietly.

Aldin looked back at the screen. Six dots appeared, spreading out from the demarcation line of the jump point.

"Whatever it is, it doesn't look good," Yaroslav said, motioning for a drink from one of the bots.

Aldin heard the door open behind him, and there was the faint rustling of Vush's robes as the Overseer came into the room.

The six dots started to accelerate, and several more appeared behind them.

Vush looked down at the screen and then over at Aldin.

"Your brothers?" Aldin asked.

Vush hesitated.

"If Gablona came here, I think it fair to assume that they would be here as well, believing that you would come on the same errand."

"Well, that bastard Gablona got to him first," Oishi said coldly.

"That does not matter. The issue is you and the wish to rescue me."

Aldin looked up at Vush.

"Do you want to be rescued?"

Vush hesitated, looking back at the screen, and said nothing.

"Your Arch will certainly love to have you back," Yaroslav said with a light chuckle. "He can throw you in with your friend Mupa, and together you can watch everything go to hell. A million years on some forsaken rock at least. He's got to blame someone for all of this, and as they used to say, 'you're taking the fall.' "

"Turn left," Vush said quietly.

"What?" Aldin asked, looking up at Vush in confusion.

"Left, port, whatever—just aim at that star over there, the second one to the right." He pointed to the side of the forward viewport.

Aldin punched the ship around, not even bothering to ask why. According to the charts, there wasn't anything in that direction but empty space for nearly three light-years, and at the present speed they just might escape in roughly thirty years of running.

"Everyone out of this room," Vush said, looking nervously at the nav screen, which showed the unidentified ships still closing in.

Everyone looked at him in confusion.

"Oishi stays; he promised. The rest of you get out. I know another way."

"Well, I'll be damned," Zergh said. "It takes us hundreds of years to find this one jump point, we lose it for nearly three thousand years before we find it again, and then this one looks around and says there's another way out."

"Get out of here now!" Oishi shouted, and Vush looked over at him with relief.

"Well, you heard the boss," Yaroslav snapped. "An emperor in one room and a dictator in another."

Aldin and the others filed out, Yaroslav motioning for the servobot to follow.

Oishi swung into the command seat and looked over at Vush.

"I'm not sure, it's been so long, but I think we head a bit more to the right," he said, and with a sigh Oishi punched in the commands. Long minutes later he was suddenly startled when without warning the ship hit an unmarked jump point and accelerated into translight.

"Just where the hell are we heading?" Oishi shouted.

"If I'm not mistaken, I think it takes us straight to the Sphere," Vush replied with a self-satisfied tone. "A little secret Mupa and I stumbled on about ten thousand years back.

"Either there, or to the other side of this galaxy, I'm really not quite sure which."

"Just where did he go?" the Arch asked, barely able to contain himself as the first ship reemerged through the jump point back from the Milky Way.

"They turned about and then just disappeared," the pilot of the Overseer ship replied.

The Arch looked over at Mupa, who sat curled up in the corner.

"Well?"

"Vush must have been on board."

"Did you follow them?" the Arch asked, looking back at the screen.

"Where? It was an unmarked jump gate, we could have blundered around for years before hitting it."

The Arch looked back again at Mupa.

"Can you explain this?"

"Like I told you before," Mupa replied, his voice nearly whining, "the two of us wandered through there once."

"Without my knowledge or permission."

Mupa lowered his head even further.

"It's a confusing path. The wrong turn could take you all the way over to the far end of the galaxy."

"Or?"

"Straight to the far side of this Cloud and to the Sphere."

Repeating a habit he found all too distasteful, the Arch cursed to himself once again.

"And what about Gablona?"

"He claims they killed this Human who understands wormholes, took the new weapons we offered to him, and then disappeared," the pilot replied.

The Arch shut the screen off and drifted out of the room.

Too much was happening at once. Events were spinning out of control, and he had to find some means to reestablish it. They'd have to go to the Sphere, that was obvious. He'd point Gablona in that direction as well. By the simple fact of Aldin's escape it was obvious that Vush was now helping him. A brother Overseer was now in league with the barbarians. It was disgusting. He would have to be punished, as all of them would have to be punished.

At the end, there was no final bang; more like a sigh. The outer shell of the red giant, no longer held together by the gravitational mass from within, simply started to race outward, driven by the dying nuclear furnace. It was a most unusual phenomenon, a star sucked dry from within, the outer shell simply rupturing in a small novalike explosion. And then darkness.

Yet there was already another light beside it, now burning fiercely, vast explosions roaring up from below.

The vast wormhole pipeline for the briefest instant went dry. An inquiry raced out from the instrument pack buried deep within its heart. Was the job done? Should it continue? But the control system was now thousands of light-years away, and besides, the button was still jammed down, even if the message could reach it.

If an overworked machine could shrug its shoulders and with a philosophical sigh get back to work, this would have definitely done so. A quick scan probed surrounding space. There was the brief flicker of a gravitational center, and the wormhole snaked over to it. In a thousandth of a second, a shipload of Humans, who on a bet had come out to watch the show, were swallowed up. The tidbit could not possibly satisfy the need for more matter. The wormhole leaped across a quarter light-year and latched itself to a white dwarf star. At least that would satisfy the machine's requirements for a while, and then there were others beyond that. The line was now pointing straight into the Core Cluster, where hundreds of worlds and stars would serve as meals yet to come, one of them a vast ball of condensed iron, hundreds of trillions of tons worth, the burned out hulk of a dying star that had not gone supernova or collapsed into singularity. Fed into the heart of a star in convulsion, it would most certainly shut down a nuclear burn in short order, with the most interesting of results.

CHAPTER 8

IT WAS ALL RATHER DISCONCERTING AND YET SO MIRACULOUS. He felt as if he had awakened from a cold, distant dream filled with phantoms of memories. How could he even begin to explain it all, as if fifteen years of living had been peeled away from his body, and his soul. The memories, were they even real? The biting cold of the retreat that he felt he would never get out of his soul. The numbed realization of the last defeat, the musty dankness of that damned island. Was it even real? The pain?

The pain, where was it? There was none! He felt his stomach. Strange, it felt flatter than he remembered. So strange. What was the dream and what was real?

He sat up. As he did so the room was illuminated by a soft diffused light and he looked around. This is real then, and not the fevered dreams of approaching death. The room was small, neatly arranged. Some drawers set into a wall, a door without handles. And the light? He looked around; there was no candle, no lamp, yet still there was the light. He felt a shudder, and he almost slid off the bed. That's what awoke me, like a carriage lurching to a stop. The ship—that's what they called it—a ship flying through the ether of space was moving beneath him.

161

He stood up. He felt light, a coiled vibrancy, just the way it used to be—out of bed after four hours and ready to work twenty more. And his eyes. Everything was so sharp, so clear. And hunger! My God, real hunger, not the dull ache, the dread of eating, knowing the agony it would create.

In the soft light he looked down at himself. He was naked, and yet it was real, his body had changed; it looked, and felt younger. He chuckled to himself, looking about the room, stretching. Clothes?

A faint clicking disturbed his thoughts. In the corner of the room a servobot waited patiently, its electronic eyes and sensors aimed at him.

"You are an ugly thing," Napoleon said.

The machine remained silent.

"So, my iron friend, shall I walk about naked?"

The bot moved to a side wall, pushed a button, and a closet slid open.

"Delightful!" Napoleon exclaimed. Hanging in the closet was a blue military jacket faced with white, epaulets of gold, sleeves and collar trimmed with red. The trousers were buff, the calf-high boots freshly polished till they seemed to glow.

Admiring himself in the mirror, the uniform on, he felt as if the years truly had slipped away. The uniform was tailored to perfection, though the material felt strange, almost silky.

It is something Aldin would have thought of, a friendly gesture.

And why the friendly gesture? he wondered. Admiration for his skills? Of course. But what was to be his part in this strangeness of ships that passed through the ether between stars, the hint of political strife and strange beings? Everything he knew was gone, if what they said was true. The English, the Bourbons, St. Helena, even France, as distant now as Babylon and Sargon.

"Soldiers of France, remember forty centuries of history look down upon you today." That was a moment, arrayed before the pyramids, waiting for the Mamluks to charge. My world, my time, as distant to me now as the pyramids were to their builders.

Who was that damned English poet, Shelley or Byron? "Ozymandias." He half suspected it was a barb directed at him. So now I am ancient history for an Earth that does not even exist. And yet they mentioned Alexander. How did they meet him? he wondered. Did they collect the greatness of history? But for what purpose? To help them, to use us, or simply to collect us like a bored noble collecting antiquities?

The ship lurched again beneath his feet, causing him to nearly lose his balance. For a brief second he felt as if everything around him had gone into a blurred distortion, and a mild nausea enveloped him. He felt a brief shudder of fear. It was like the old symptoms, the dizziness, the nausea. Was it all an illusion, was he about to wake up and again be fat, dying, and vomiting in his own bed? He heard a distant cursing, and then shouts of excitement. No, this was real, very real indeed.

He looked toward the door. There was no sense hiding in here. A chance had been offered; the dream of old men, to suddenly have strength and youth returned to them. To be given the chance to do it all over again. Yet for all that he had built, there was no security now, the playing field was leveled again, and fresh. He could fall, not living up to the legend of what was expected of him.

It would be like beginning again as a young major of artillery, angling so sharply for the first command, the chance for glory and for power. Offensive, always the offensive, that was the path to victory. Fixing his features with a confident smile, he looked down at the bot, which sat quiet, impassively waiting for him to clear the room so it could make the bed. He patted it lightly on the side and, turning, strode out of the room, the door opening silently for the emperor.

Aldin burst into the forward cabin, Tia behind him.

"Just what the hell was that?" he shouted.

"It seems we've finished our jump," Yaroslav announced, as if it were he who had been piloting the ship. The old man, however, barely noticed Aldin. Eyes gleaming with delight, Yaroslav looked back to the forward screen, which was showing the real-time view in front of the ship.

Aldin stared at it intently for a moment, not quite sure of what he was seeing. Then he realized that the fact he was seeing nothing at all was actually quite significant. The scattering of stars and far-distant galaxies had a hole in the middle of it, a black circle of what appeared to be emptiness.

He looked over at Oishi and Vush sitting at the control consoles.

"The Sphere of the First Travelers," Oishi said quietly, as if standing in the foyer of a temple.

Vush looked at the forward viewscreen, his head bobbing nervously.

Aldin came up to Oishi's side and looked down at the nav screen. A close study of the system would help him to figure out where they were, but a look from his friend convinced him to honor their pledge, and instead he studied the dark circle in the middle. There was mass there, an infrared signature, most likely heat exhaust, similar to the backside of the Ring. It had a very slow rotation, barely noticeable, enough to create an artificial gravity on the inside. They were still twenty million kilometers out, but closing in at 0.1 of light.

Zergh came into the room and, immediately realizing where they were, let out a triumphant whoop. Within seconds the servobots were busy filling glasses for a toast. Oishi, with Vush's vague directions, initiated a shallow curving approach in toward the Sphere, and seconds later a gasp of astonishment swept through the room.

A pie-shaped section of the northern hemisphere was incomplete and open to space. As they dove in toward the gap, the interior of the Sphere came into view. From the distance of ten million kilometers it reminded Aldin of a crystal ball, veiled in black except for one small section, which revealed the mystery and brilliance within. The small artificially created sun hovered in the middle, as if dangling from a thread, its light illuminating the interior of the hollow ball.

The doorway of the control room slid open again, and Napoleon entered. He stood still for a moment, as if expecting a fanfare of greeting, and then seeing how his companions' attention was fixed to the forward screen, he quietly entered. To his untutored eyes the object before them held no real meaning for a moment; it looked like nothing more than a pie-shaped sliver of light with a glowing ball within. Yet it must be a great wonder, he realized, to hold their attention such.

He approached the screen, gazing intently at it.

"It is a sun, contained within an artificially made hollow ball, several million kilometers across," Oishi said, looking over at the emperor and attempting to interpret what they were seeing. Oishi could well understand the confusion, the awe over things trivial and the incomprehension of things magnificent. He had stood dumbstruck as well, when the reality of what the future was had finally started to settle into his heart and mind. It was a ripping away of the old world and replacing it with a new. It created heartsickness, almost a madness at times, and yet it was a constant wonder. He could only hope that this man would learn to live in a new reality not of his own creation.

"Then it is hundreds of times bigger than our Earth," Napoleon whispered, looking over at Oishi in confusion.

"Billions of times," Yaroslav said.

"The works of man pale to insignificance," Napoleon said with a sigh.

Aldin looked over at him and smiled.

"Made long before us by an unknown race we call the First Travelers. Everything of Human hand is insignificant to what they created."

"Go straight into it," Vush said, pointing toward the open section.

Zergh looked over at Vush for a second and then moved to occupy the copilot chair. Oishi might be good at his work, but everyone knew that few could outmaster the Gaf vasba when it came to piloting in what might be a difficult situation.

The dark Sphere now filled the entire heavens before them, the blackness of its exterior revealing no sense of depth, so that it felt as if they were coming up on a flat circle with a slice of light on the upper side.

"The opening is nearly a million kilimoters across," Oishi said, "but it's latticed with beams." As they closed to within a hundred thousand kilometers, the sense of the depth of the Sphere started to be apparent, the blackness of the outer shell curving away.

Inside the Sphere, the far side was three million kilometers away, glowing with a reflected yellow light, silhouetting the small star in the middle. The vast open space started to resolve itself into a latticework of support beams that interlaced and cut across hundreds of thousands of kilometers. The opening was not truly open at all; there were tiny spots of darkness, which were in fact partially completed sections, some of them tens of thousands of kilometers across. Support structures a hundred kilometers wide cut a crisscross pattern that in places was partially filled in by a filigree of smaller lines and yet smaller between them, as if a spider were gradually weaving its tenuous web into a solid mass.

The distance shrank to ten thousand kilometers and then five, as Zergh bled off speed, adjusting for the unusual gravitational effects created by the massive structure.

Napoleon went over to one of the servobots and returned to the screen with a brandy to stand meditatively watching the show.

"You look good in uniform," Aldin said.

"My thanks."

"Tia's the one who thought of it," Yaroslav said, not bothering to look back, "though I threw in the historical details, and it was the bots that actually made it."

Napoleon smiled and decided to say nothing.

Any sense that they were approaching a sphere was gone, the vast open area filling all of space in front of them. Pulling the ship up slightly, Zergh maneuvered to avoid a hundred-kilometer-wide beam. The forward nav screen revealed a jumble of debris, interlocking structures, and cables. There was movement as well, something Aldin had not expected, and he looked over inquisitively at Vush.

"Could someone be there waiting for us?"

"They're still building it," Vush replied.

"Who?" Yaroslav asked excitedly. "The First Travelers?"

"Their machines. They've been building it for millions of years. It'll be hundreds of thousands more before they are done."

Zergh slowed to a near stop a dozen kilometers out and looked closely at the nav screen before slowly picking up speed again.

From behind one of the beams a massive shiplike vehicle appeared, several kilometers in length, trailing a long filament strand behind it.

Vush rose up, unable to contain his excitement.

"I haven't been here in thousands of years. Yet you can barely see the progress, so vast it is."

The ship laying out the long filament of a support beam moved directly in front of their ship, not a kilometer away. Zergh suddenly punched in reverse thrusters.

"The damn thing's got its own gravitational field," the Gaf cried in amazement. "It's got the mass of a small planet. It's laying out the same material that they built the Ring out of." He looked over darkly at Yaroslav. "And the Skyhook as well."

Yaroslav shifted uncomfortably.

"I think that inside that ship, the building material is compressed at an atomic level," Yaroslav speculated in a professorial voice. "The matter is contained in a field to keep a nuclear reaction from igniting, and then it's trailed out behind the ship, like a spider dumping silk to form the ribs of the sphere."

The ship moved majestically on, the newly laid beam glowing briefly before cooling in the vacuum of space. Smaller objects, that looked like crosses between space vessels and pieces of multiarmed construction equipment, darted back and forth. Space suddenly seemed alive with movement.

Zergh nudged them in past the outer shell.

Awed, he brought the vessel to a stop. The entire inner Sphere was now almost completely visible.

"It is like gazing at heaven," Napoleon whispered.

The darkness of space was banished. The vast interior glowed with a golden light, the blackness of the outside replaced with a blue-green softness. All sense of scale was lost; it was simply too vast for the human mind to comprehend that what they were looking at covered an area of billions of square kilometers, all of it shaped and crafted to perfection. When he had heard of rumors of the Sphere, Aldin somehow imagined it cold, lifeless, an interior of gleaming icy metal. Foolishness. The Ring was beyond description in its magnificence. This made the Ring pale into nothingness by comparison.

He looked over at Vush.

"It is good that you kept this secret from us," he whispered. "At least let one small part of heaven remain beyond our grasp."

"Why didn't all your kind choose here to live?" Yaroslav asked, wiping the tears from his eyes.

"We believed it wrong to make our place of contemplation something made by others," Vush replied softly. "I think though it showed us our true insignificance and made us feel too humble to know that others had created perfection and we could never obtain it, either through the strength of our hands or the power of our minds."

To either side of the open section, walls hundreds of kilometers high had been constructed as barriers to keep the atmosphere in, and as the ship slowly drifted in, the view to the starboard side started to expand, the vast, limitless view gradually taking on detailed form. Mountain ranges, some punching clean through the atmosphere and soaring hundreds of kilometers high, dotted the landscape, their green slopes giving way to snow, and then finally to bare black crystalline rock. Several of the mountains had necklaces of bridges that soared across vast reaches of empty space, to anchor like a descending halo to a range on the far side of a sparkling turquoise ocean.

Spindly towers, a dozen times the height of the Shiga Skyhook, soared up from the surface, apparently constructed for no purpose other than the joy of creating them.

"One expects to hear angels," Napoleon said quietly, sipping at his drink, feet braced far apart, unable to contain the emotion of wonder from dancing across his features. A vast hexagonal-shaped section of framework a hundred kilometers across hovered to one side, a variety of multiarmed machines and what appeared to be tugs slowly moving it down, as if to lock it onto a bed of support beams.

Aldin watched it intently, awed by the manipulation of what must have been hundreds of millions of tons of mass with seemingly effortless ease.

What appeared to be a small beam layer, coming straight in from the sun, approached the hexagon. Zergh barely had time to call out a warning, when in the lonely silence of space there was a flash of light. A massive chunk of metal blew through the side of the hexagon, the beam layer continuing straight on, its side torn open, the contents from within spilling out, exploding into a flash of blinding light.

Zergh spun their ship over and accelerated, dashing in the opposite direction as the shock wave of the explosion leaped out.

"What the hell was that all about?" Yaroslav asked, gazing intently at the aft viewscreen, as the hexagon slowly started to tumble out of control. A number of ships streaked past, heading in toward the explosion, and to Aldin's disbelief, one came straight at them, causing Zergh to maneuver violently as the vessel shot past, tentacles and tool arms flailing. Two of the machines a kilometer to port smashed into each other, one of them vaporizing, the other continuing on. Yet smaller machines scurried out, apparently bent on retrieving the damaged equipment and fragments that were careening off in every direction.

The situation seemed to be compounding by the second; several of the smaller machines started to circle in on each other, as if they were dogs chasing each other's tails. They spiraled in faster and faster until finally three met, one of them bouncing out of the spiral, the other two then taking off in pursuit.

"I think there's trouble in paradise," Yaroslav sniffed.

Oishi looked over at Vush, who was obviously deeply troubled by what they were witnessing.

"They're working at cross-purposes," Aldin interjected. "It looked like some of the machines can't even sense the presence of others."

Zergh continued to pilot the ship out of the confusion, dodging through a forest of towers and converging machines.

Approaching the starboard barrier wall, Zergh spun straight up toward the sun, accelerated, and a minute later cleared the top. The confusion, at least for the moment, appeared to be left behind.

"Let's pull over here and take a break," Aldin announced.

Zergh nudged the vessel forward and finally settled it down on the lip of the barrier, thus granting them a view straight down to the Sphere's inner surface five hundred kilometers below. So smooth was the wall's surface that rotational movement of the Sphere caused the ship to slowly start to slide across the top until a final nudge of a docking thruster put them into synch with their surroundings.

It was as if they were now looking down on a planet's surface, however this surface just continued on forever, sweeping out, up, and away in all directions, until all details were lost in the vast eternal distance. Directly below, an ocean of bright blue-green glinted with reflected sunlight, a tower on a small continent in the middle of an ocean rising up clear through the atmosphere to top out at nearly the same height as the great barrier wall. A mountain range, which Aldin guessed must be at least ten thousand kilometers away, marched in a straight serrate line of snow-blanketed ridges, disappearing in the direction of the equator.

"Still going crazy back there," Tia said, breaking the awestruck silence, and pointed to a monitor that was tracking the hexagon that was starting to break into two halves, while hundreds of tiny dots appeared to be converging in upon the disaster.

"That," Vush interjected, his voice weak, "is not supposed to happen."

"Kind of what I thought," Aldin replied. "I mean, after all, this is First Traveler stuff. Nothing is ever supposed to go wrong."

"Well, that sure didn't look like a planned festivity to me," Yaroslav stated. "What's going on, Vush?"

"Something is not right, to be certain."

"If the pilot leaves the wheel," Napoleon ventured, "a ship might sail for days, but in the end it is bound to strike disaster."

"Not a bad metaphor," Zergh said.

"But that's impossible," Vush interjected. "You are talking about the First Travelers."

"Hey, you yourself said that when you and this Mupa fellow found the wormhole device, the machine that was supposed to run it appeared to be out of order," Yaroslav countered. "Well, what we're looking at here might be the First Traveler machines screwing up in a major way."

"Everything else looks so perfect, though," Tia whispered.

"It's a big place," Aldin said. "It's taken them millions of years to build it. It might take even longer for it to run completely amok."

"That should be the least of our concerns at the moment," Oishi said, looking over at Vush. "Right now we need to find the place where you found the wormhole device. So where is it?"

Vush hesitated and looked around the group. With a deliberate slowness he floated up and went over to the forward viewscreen and looked at the vista for several long minutes in total silence.

Napoleon could already see what was coming. Going to the bot, he got another brandy and took it over to Aldin.

"You're going to need this," Napoleon said with a knowing smile.

Vush turned to look back at the group.

"It's been so long . . ." His voice trailed off.

"Don't tell me you've forgotten," Zergh growled.

"It will come back to me. It's just the place is so big."

"So now what the hell are we going to do?" Yaroslav asked.

"I don't know," Vush replied, as if offended. "How about if we just drive around for a while? Sooner or later I'll get my bearings."

"So where do we start?" Oishi snapped, barely able to control the rising temper that was about to explode.

"Oh, I don't know. That way," Vush replied, waving vaguely toward the equatorial region.

With a muffled curse, Zergh shot the vessel off the wall in a shower of burned skids and smoking wall, nearly knocking everyone over with the suddenness of the maneuver. With head bowed, Vush stayed by the screen and didn't look back.

"Rather an interesting situation," Zola said, smiling for the first time in days.

He gazed intently at the screen, which displayed a complex jump-route schematic.

"Where did you get this?" Zola asked.

Xsarn Tertiary clattered its mandibles in an agitated manner.

"It took a little digging. We knew from Xsarn Secondary that Larice dropped off most of his people, picked up the time ship, and went back to the home galaxy."

"Go on."

"Some of our old gaming-net people started, shall we say, a speculation as to where Aldin was going and why."

"And?"

"The betting was eight-to-five that he was going back to old Earth to get that Japanese physicist."

"Yashima Korobachi," Zola said.

"Ah, so you do know of him?" the Xsarn asked.

"Who doesn't?" Zola replied absently, examining the crease on his purple and green striped trousers.

"He went in and he hasn't come back out," the Xsarn continued.

"Ah, well, the vicissitudes of time travel," Zola said.

The Xsarn hesitated, but Zola nodded for it to continue.

"If he was after Korobachi, then he was looking for a way to defuse the wormhole. Overseer security has been lax, they've been running like scared children. Several of them were actually killed when one of their ships touched down on a pleasure world and a mob tore them apart."

"Delightful," Zola chuckled.

"One of our people gained access to the ship's computer, and this chart to a place called the Sphere was stored in it along with some notations concerning an Overseer called Mupa and the wormhole. It wasn't too hard to put two and two together."

"Excellent work," Zola said. "I think we can safely surmise that Aldin has fantasies of saving everybody by getting this scientist chap and then going to the Sphere and trying to get an answer on the wormhole and how to stop it."

Zola looked over the Xsarn and smiled craftily.

"You didn't just drop in for a friendly visit," Zola said. "Everything's going to hell. The entire western side of the core cluster is in chaos."

"And?"

"There are significant marketing potentials in all of this," Zola replied coldly.

"Such as?"

"Come, come, my old friend, you know as well as I." Zola Faldon laughed, his voice high and whiny.

Shipping rates out of the side of the cluster closest to the wormhole were up over 400 percent. That was short-term and most lucrative. However, there was an even grander consideration. If this new star should eventually explode, some computer models were speculating that nearly a hundred heavily settled worlds in the outer edge of the cluster closest to the explosion would be in danger. Those that were closest would most likely be rendered totally uninhabitable. Projections were running that over one hundred and sixty worlds would be in this band of destruction, a further three hundred requiring at least temporary sheltering for all inhabitants. Even if the star went supernova immediately, it would still take a couple of years before the blast of radiation and debris hit the nearest prime-level world, but panic was already spreading.

Of course, the chance was always there as well that the runaway wormhole might very well sweep all the way into the cluster and start devouring planets, a speculation that had already triggered the filming of several Gaf disaster films, thereby helping to fuel the panic.

Billions of beings would have to be resettled, hundreds of

corporate headquarters and their staffs moved. One of the worlds run by the lawyers' guild was in the path of destruction, and some had suggested a boycott of ships to that world, thus leaving them to their proper fate—a concept that Zola found himself in complete agreement with.

There was barely a prime planet left in the Cloud that was not fully controlled by some corporation or guild, but as for second- and third-rate worlds, there were hundreds on the marketplace for next to nothing.

Zola smiled even as he thought of the possibilities: billions needing to move; desert, swamp, and ice planets to be bought for a song; and, with proper advertising, katars uncounted to be made providing new homeworlds for the refugees. What a chance for a killing.

"A consortium of investors, a very limited number of investors, could certainly come out well because of this," Zola said, looking up at the Xsarn.

"Precisely. Of course, it would all go awry if a certain vasba managed to shut the wormhole down."

Zola nodded in agreement.

He knew that Corbin Gablona and the Overseers were both after Aldin, along with a swarm of bounty hunters still after the Overseer reward. But Aldin had a propensity for survival against difficult odds. Odds. The mere thought of how much Aldin and Bukha had taken from him in the last game was reason enough to want Aldin taken care of.

"Don't worry, he won't get back," Zola replied.

The Xsarn Tertiary nodded, arms clicking, and he stood up to leave.

"Our assistants shall meet and draw up an investment plan. We can start purchasing planets almost immediately then; some of my field people have already scouted out a number of prospects."

"I'll get my media team to make them look like paradises," Zola replied. Gods, how he loved scams like this. It brightened his whole day.

The Xsarn left the room, knowing that the game within the

game was working as planned. Zola, watching him leave, felt exactly the same way.

"You know that the Overseers will be behind us," Corbin said, looking over at Hassan, who sat in the darkened corner of the room.

"But of course they'll follow. This Sphere is after all their precious little secret."

Corbin sat in silence. He felt like he was trapped in a pit with a snake. As long as he could convince the snake that he served a purpose, he would continue to live. But already Hassan was learning to master ship's navigation and piloting. The nuances of the political and economic webs that governed the rather haphazard management of life in the Cloud he viewed as a joke, openly wondering how for three thousand years no single agent had not simply taken control with an iron fist. As for the Overseers, he had expressed contempt from the beginning, seeing before all others that their threats and their power were a charade. Corbin felt as if he were gazing into the pitiless stare once again, an unblinking gaze that from moment to moment toyed with the idea of granting continued life or death in an infinite variety of disturbing manners.

The fat man could be jovial, even charming in a disgustingly effete sort of way, Hassan thought, looking over at Corbin, who gazed at him warily. He could always have his uses as a front—at least until something better came along.

Something better. He hoped it was soon. He had once been a servant of Corbin's, had even been in awe of him in the early days, when this universe was still all too new and disturbingly frightful. The memory of that subservience did not sit well. And the whole time that he contemplated this thought, his features did not change in the slightest.

"We can expect Zola, maybe the others to follow as well," Corbin said. "After all, the person who sold us the navigation charts most likely did the same thing for anyone else who might be interested."

Hassan nodded as if he had ascertained such a fact long before Corbin had even begun to contemplate it.

Hassan let his gaze turn back to the forward viewscreen. A thin, pin-shaped sliver of light floated before them. It was hard to grasp the size of what he was looking at; his experiences had never prepared him to even contemplate such scale. Surely, if Allah even existed, this would have been a creation that would challenge even His skill. It would be a worthy place to rule from as the Hidden Ema—remote, distant. A place to return to when he had not only stopped the Overseer device, but learned how to use it for his own ends.

Hassan smiled as the ship started its curving descent in toward the Sphere.

CHAPTER 9

"I THINK THAT'S IT."

Everyone stirred. Aldin, asleep on the floor, sat up with a groan. Oishi, who was stretched out between two chairs, sat up, his joints creaking.

The only one who had been awake throughout it all was Napoleon, sitting by Vush's side, nursing a brandy that he had poured for himself a dozen hours ago, while refilling Vush's drink at regular intervals.

It had been an illuminating twenty hours; he barely felt tired, and hunger was hardly noticed. The Overseer, who hovered beside him, intent upon watching the viewscreen, occasionally floating over to a control panel to alter course and then back again, had been reticent at first.

There had been several inquires about his role as emperor, and his frank answers, especially regarding the executions he had ordered, had obviously upset Vush, who for several hours had launched into a nonstop sermon on the sanctity of life. Napoleon had sat patiently, barely disputing the Overseer, but in the end he terminated the line of thought with an offhand reference to the billions who would die due to the wormhole unleashed in part by Vush's own actions. It was a statement followed by a long and well-crafted reassurance of how fate can sometimes cast one into roles not anticipated, and thus, by extension, remove the onus of later tragedies created by what were initially good intentions.

Much had been learned. He felt at times as if he were hearing the fantastic tales of Baron Munchausen or Cyrano. Yet it was real. The fantastic being beside him would have been greeted either as an angel or a devil if it had appeared suddenly in the aisle of Notre Dame. Here it was just a lonely creature trying to hide its fear, its pitiful weakness, behind a mask of well-cultivated superiority. It was difficult to sit and listen, an art he had known in his youth when first introduced to those who thought themselves his betters. The early days in Paris, during the Revolution, when Robespierre held the reins, that had been a time to listen, to form plans alone, to wear the masks one needed if one's head was to stay attached. It was an art he had almost forgotten.

St. Helena had never forced him to this level of self-contemplation; it was as if he were almost removed from himself, detached to gaze at his strengths and his faults. Defeat had burned too deeply to admit all the mistakes. Too much had to be defended when in front of the mocking gaze of those perfidious English. Here, here it was different. He had to know what he was, what he had done, what he now could be in order to understand. Or was it the change in myself? he wondered, unable not to sneak a sidelong glance at the reflective surface of a viewscreen in order to reaffirm the changes Aldin had brought about to his body.

Thinking was so clear again, the body tireless. I have an opportunity here, he realized, even while still listening intently to Vush. I am almost youthful again, and so painfully aware of all that has been lost, and all that might be gained. He remembered the nights alone, fully realizing that there would never be a rescue, that no French frigate would arrive offshore to whisk him back to France and to glory. At those moments, when the true realization had settled in that it was over, there had been one last dream of consolation, that in the next world it would be like the warrior legends of old. Valhalla, a gathering together of his old comrades, the grumblers, all those lost in Spain, Russia, Leipzig, Eylau, coming to his banner, and again the old battles would be fought.

And now this instead, another chance after all, a chance unlike anything even a madman could have dreamed.

Vush paused for a moment to look over at the Human who seemed lost in thought and then back at the screen. He quietly continued on, almost absently, with his lecture regarding the barbarity of Humans, Gavarnians, and Xsarns, when suddenly he stirred, bobbing up and down and shouting.

Aldin, wiping the sleep from his eyes, came up to the forward viewscreen.

"Down there," Vush announced, the conversation with Napoleon forgotten.

Napoleon, who had ignored the remarkable scenery below to concentrate instead upon Vush, looked out to where the Overseer was pointing.

The landscape below was rather remarkable, even for such a remarkable world. A vast series of concentric rings seemed to be carved into the landscape. It took him several seconds to remember the perspective from which he was looking down at this strange world, to realize that they were, in fact, a ringlike series of towering mountains, as if planted as a painted target.

"Five thousand kilometers across," Tia announced, settling into the nav chair. "The formation is perfectly circular, the mountain ranges nearly three hundred kilometers high."

Aldin noticed that there were smaller rings set further out, the landscape between each of the rings a barren, black surface, each ring a circle of light in a region that must have measured several hundred thousand kilometers across.

"It almost looks like a symbolic representation of a solar system," Yaroslav said, looking over at Vush intently.

"I should have remembered this," Vush replied. "Mupa said the same thing. In fact we spent several days running comparisons to systems in the galaxy, hoping maybe to find the home-world of the First Travelers, but it never came to anything."

"So where is it?" Zergh asked.

"The central one. The central mesa, the eye of the circle, is one vast control complex. It was there that we found it."

"Well let's go in then," Yaroslav announced, barely able to suppress his excitement.

Napoleon, like the others, found himself pressed up against the forward viewscreen. They had been weaving back and forth above the surface of the Sphere at over twenty thousand kilometers while Vush tried to figure out where to go. The land below had been a curious pattern of what he thought must be green fields or forests, oceans, mountains, and then tremendous open spaces of blackness or polished silver, regions that Vush announced were yet to be completely formed.

The ship went into a steep dive, pointing straight down at the surface, Aldin taking the controls alongside Zergh. The exuberance of the moment showed in them as well, as they threw caution aside and let the speed build. The mountains, which punched up through the atmosphere, glinted in the perpetual noonday sun, and as they dove past the top peaks the retro system fired and sent a shudder running through the ship as it started to plunge into the atmosphere.

Napoleon felt like an eagle spiraling down from a mountain aerie and laughed aloud with the pleasure of it, as the ship started to flatten out its dive, swinging in between two razor-sharp peaks and passing above high alpine meadows. A light covering of clouds whisked by, their undersides dark with showering snow that flashed into steam with the heat of their passage. Through holes in the clouds the sun shone, the world a glaring crystalline white, as Aldin guided them into a pass and weaved down it, dodging and turning, while Tia clung to her chair, cursing the pilots. Oishi laughed aloud, his teeth glinting like the snow, a faint tear barely discernible in his eyes, for it had been long years since he had seen snow and it conjured a memory of home.

The pass opened out into flower-strewn meadows so that they

appeared to rush above a carpet of burgundy and violet that swayed in the cold breeze coming down out of the high hills. The meadows in turn gave way to stands of high trees, unlike any they had ever seen, the trunks soaring upward hundreds of feet before the first limbs branched out, the leaves bright green and lavender. A cliff shot by beneath them, a cascade of water tumbling over it, plummeting in an angel-haired plume. The falls plunged a thousand meters into a circular pool that was of the deepest blue, the white foam dancing down upon it like a shower of diamonds, surrounded on the shore by a cathedral grove of elmlike trees.

The beginning of a river coursed down out of the hills, tumbling over falls, other streams coming down to join it from now-distant peaks. Though there were other things far more pressing, Aldin swung the ship about and brought it to a hover above the falls, pools, and tumbling river. Punching a button, he opened the outside hatches and let the air circulate in.

The room was suddenly awash with a fresh pinelike scent, mingled with a sharp vibrant chill of cool damp mountain air.

"Eden," Napoleon whispered, finding that for the first time in years he was moved by a sight not of his own creating.

After a few moments, Aldin reluctantly shut the hatches, turned the ship about, and raced on. The forest rolled down before them, the sharp mountain ridges and slopes giving way to a succession of gentle hills that seemed to go on forever. The ship picked up speed, racing across the open landscape, a sinewy river weaving back and forth beneath them, growing broader, turning at last toward an ocean, which was its final destiny, shining in the distance.

Aldin found it remarkable just how far they could see. It was like the Ring, of course. The horizon did not curve downward, rather it slowly curved up, so that sights thousands of kilometers away could be seen. In some ways, the Ring was more dramatic, for it curved up and away, rising straight into the heavens, with darkness to either side. But here the true scale of the First Traveler creation was far more overwhelming. As they moved across the landscape, the distant ring of mountains, five thousand kilometers across, were clearly visible, and beyond, the bowl of the world curved outward in every direction. Low to the horizon it was somewhat hazy, looking as he was through thousands of kilometers of atmosphere. But if he raised his gaze higher, the vastness of the Sphere was more clearly in view, stretching on forever it seemed. Dark places of bareness alternated with the patches of green and blue where the First Travelers had planted life, while directly overhead the sun shone, now somewhat more dimly inside the atmosphere. Its construction was the same as the sun of the Kolbard Ring, a variable artificial star with a high rate of shift, thus dimming down to a dull glimmer and ten hours later shifting back up to a pleasant warmth.

Aldin looked over at Napoleon and smiled, and neither one felt the need to speak, to disturb the thoughts of the other.

Zergh pulled the ship up slightly, gaining enough altitude to cut down on atmospheric drag. The woods had given way to a pleasant patchwork quilt of forested glens, meandering streams, and then vast open stretches of high prairie. Occasional areas of darkness seemed to move on the land, which were numberless herds of a bisonlike creature.

The sight of them startled Napoleon. He had come to think that this place was not inhabited at all, but then again he realized it already was, planted with trees and grasses, and why shouldn't there be other things here as well? As they passed over a vast open canyon, the air below was black with millions of winged creatures, some with black bodies and wings, others multihued, who seemed to be engaged in a war, towering formations of them spiraling up on rising columns of air to then swing out and pounce upon those below.

The canyon disappeared astern, the war, if it was that, gone from view.

What first appeared to be a central bluff started at last to resolve into a gentle upslope that as it climbed in a series of undulating hills, each slightly higher than the one before, some tree-clad, others covered in grass, and yet others strangely bare, revealed the black rocklike subsurface of the Sphere. The ship dove back down, the end of the journey near, all desiring to get a closer look. The upward slope suddenly flattened out, and they closed in upon it. And all stood in silent awe.

For the first time since they had entered the atmosphere, it was again impressed upon them that this was an artificial creation. The plain in the center of the five-thousand-kilometer circle was nearly a hundred kilometers across. The central cone at the center at last resolved into a black volcanolike mountain that rose up for nearly a dozen kilometers, its peak torn and jagged.

Clouds swirled around the summit, the tops spiraling up to the top and then disappearing.

"A puncture hole," Zergh said quietly. "Asteroid impact from outside."

"The damn thing must be sucking air like mad," Tia said.

"It'd still take thousands of years to have much of an effect in this region," Aldin replied, "but curious that they haven't fixed it somehow."

Aldin looked over at Vush, who said nothing, as if he had never considered the implication of this scar.

Across the vast circle on the near side of the mountain was an unending array of buildings. Some were simple upright slabs, others cylindrical, others hexagonal, pentagonal, and yet others a bizarre free-form of sharp lines and then sweeping curves. The randomness of their design when viewed as an entire system, or city, however, was strangely pleasing to the eye, almost childlike in its whimsy, as if every possible design were to be tried and then in the end fitted together into a whole. Thus no one place looked quite like any other, each vista different, and yet all seemed to fit together. The wreckage of a number of buildings was strewn up the sides of the mountain created by the impact.

"Was it like this when you were here last?" Oishi asked.

Vush nodded, still silent.

Slowing the vessel, Aldin looked back over at Vush.

"Well, I guess we're here," he said expectantly.

Vush looked around nervously.

"I'm not quite sure," he whispered.

There was a universal groan.

"It was fairly near the center, but off to one side."

"Well, that gives us a hell of a lot to go on," Yaroslav sighed.

"How about over there? It looks rather familiar," Vush announced, pointing to what looked like a small overgrown park.

"As good as any place," Aldin grumbled, and guided the ship to a soft touchdown, dust swirling up underneath the vessel.

"Comfortable temperature and air's good, a little high on oxygen content," Tia announced. "Gravity is 0.8 standard."

"Same as the Ring," Aldin announced as he swung his chair around and headed for the airlock, the rest of the group eagerly following, anxious to get outside and stretch their legs after ten days of being cooped up inside the ship.

Napoleon fell in behind them, ever so slightly miffed that they had not waited for him to go out first. Then he smiled philosophically. After all, he was not an emperor any longer, and hard as it was to bear, his participation in this little adventure was quite simply an accident.

It was like a comfortable spring day in Paris. The air was just the right temperature, a gentle breeze wafting past the hatchway. Following the others, he stepped out into the parklike setting. It had the appearance of a city to be sure, but unlike anything he had ever imagined. The buildings were vast, blocklike affairs soaring hundreds of feet into the air, where several spires broke the monotony. A number of the structures seemed worn, fissured with great cracks, and one of the spires was shattered, its rubble lying around the base of the building. In the distance, the great black mountain punched straight up into the heavens, the clouds that masked its summit roiling and twisting into streaming plumes.

Vush looked around, hesitating, Aldin and the others looking at the Overseer with barely concealed exasperation.

"Well?" Oishi asked, his voice set as if coaxing a confused child.

The Overseer floated up and turned slowly, his gown rustling and swirling out around him. Napoleon wandered off while the group waited.

"Ghostly, isn't it?"

Tia came up beside him, smiling.

"I was just thinking that," Napoleon replied. He found a memory of Moscow filling him. Marching into the city, the dream of youth reached at last, the gateway to the Orient, an empire to reach across the world—and it was empty.

The same here: empty, dead, and a vague sense that something was all wrong.

"These First Travelers," Napoleon said, "they sound to be like gods. Perfection, masters of all the universe. A mystery beyond our understanding."

"I guess you could say that. We certainly couldn't have created all of this," Tia replied, and gestured toward the incredible scale of the Sphere, which swept upward in every direction. He looked up.

A world without night, a vast room floating in space. That was how the ancient Egyptians saw the universe, the Earth inside the bottom of a bowl, the heavens the top overhead. The gods created that, and yet here, he looked around critically.

In the distance there was a glint of light and a machine floated by; looking almost like one of the servobots, it moved in an erratic pattern as if searching for something. It continued across the plaza and disappeared into a pyramid structure. Tia followed it with her gaze.

"A First Traveler machine. We found them on the Ring of Kolbard and in the Skyhook tower. They're a mystery, as is everything else about their creators."

"If they could build this, why would they allow a hole to be in it?" Napoleon asked, gesturing back toward the mountain.

"Your guess is as good as mine."

"I think of a finely crafted clock. Shooting a musket ball into it is bound to damage the inner workings."

"What I've been thinking, too," Tia replied quietly. She looked back toward Vush.

"I think the damn fool's decided," she said, and the two fell in behind the group as it started across the plaza, moving toward the pyramid that the machine had disappeared into. The pavement underfoot changed dramatically, from the seamless black stone upon which the ship had landed to a checkerboard pattern of alternating blue and white squares. The far side of the plaza was dominated by the pyramid, which soared upward for nearly half a thousand meters and was sheathed from base to top in what appeared to be gold.

"Bring back old memories?" Aldin asked, looking back at Napoleon.

"The mamluks had already stripped the polished limestone surface off by the time I got there," he replied. "If I had held on to the place, I was tempted to restore them back to their original glory. But this . . ." his voice trailed off as he looked up at the building.

"So is this it?" Zergh asked, looking over at Vush.

"You've got to remember," the Overseer said, his voice a near whine, "I've been to hundreds of worlds and all over this Sphere. It's been thousands of your years since I was last here. These things tend to blur a bit in memory. But these blue and white squares, facing the golden pyramid . . . I do remember searching a pyramid, and we saw the machine outside of it. It might be this one."

"Just how the hell could you forget something as awesome as this?" Tia interjected angrily. "This is incredible."

Vush's voice almost sounded like it was chuckling.

"There're billions of square kilometers to this Sphere, and several hundred levels beneath it. So just shut up and let me think."

Aldin roared with delight over the Overseer's display of temper.

"Keep it up and we'll make you Human yet," the vasba said. Vush gave a shudder of disgust.

Vush paused for a moment, looking intently at the pyramid and then at the surrounding city, which was silent except for the everpresent whisper of the wind as it swept toward the mountain.

"This is it," Vush finally said with a self-satisfied air.

"Well, let's get inside, find the other half of the machine, and go out and save the Cloud," Zergh said.

* * *

Four more suns had disappeared up the wormhole, along with the seven worlds that had orbited them. The last one had been inhabited, the Xsarn mining population moving out aboard a fleet of Zola's ore carriers, hired, of course, at 1,100 percent the prewormhole rate. A small fortune was lost by a Gaf consortium that had gambled at most favorable odds that the second rather than the third planet in the now-destroyed system would be swallowed first. It seemed like a sure bet, except for the simple fact that the wormhole curved slightly as it bored in on the system and simply knocked off the third planet first before going on into the sun. The mass of the new star was nearly half that of Beta Zul, and it continued to grow, relentless in its appetite, the intake end of the wormhole cutting in closer and yet closer to the Core Cluster.

"It appears as if all of this is ruled by chaos."

Corbin Gablona turned his float chair to look back at Hassan standing behind him.

The presence of the assassin in such a position had always given him a chill feeling in the back of his neck. There was a time when he would have told him so.

He looked up at Hassan and knew that the assassin sensed his discomfort. The thin lips were curled in a disdainful smile.

"The machines, they work against each other," Hassan continued, the slightest note of surprise in his voice. "Those who made the Sida, the great tower of the Hole, they made this thing as well?"

Corbin nodded, as surprised as the assassin.

"All things descend to chaos," Hassan said, "even the creations of Allah, if ever there was such a being."

Slightly surprised, Corbin looked over at the assassin.

Hassan, seeing the surprise, smiled.

"Allah, God, the First Travelers—all children's legends to be used to instill fear, to manipulate those too afraid of the darkness."

Hassan chuckled softly. That had been the ultimate secret of his order, to promise a nonexistent paradise to the fools of the lower ranks who would thus gladly throw themselves to their deaths to fulfill the wishes, the dreams of their masters.

"You've made gods of these First Travelers, and now you tremble when what they created appears to be ruled by madness."

"It has never happened before. The Overseers used the First Traveler weapons to rule us. Therefore by implication the First Travelers were almost beyond perfection."

"The Overseers." Hassan sniffed. "Frightened children like all the other beings of the Cloud, of all the universe. You saw how easy it was to kill the one named Tulbi, and then to cover up its death by what you called a jump-beam accident. They are weaklings."

"And you alone are without fear," Corbin said, frightened to challenge with such a statement, but unable to contain his curiosity.

Hassan smiled.

"Where do we go now?" Hassan asked.

"The directions said that there is only one place in this entire Sphere where there are buildings, all the rest is wilderness. We scan till we find it."

"Scan quickly," Hassan said, the command in his voice cold and imperative. "I look forward to trying out those new tracking missiles. It should prove to be amusing."

Annoyed with the squabbling of the group, Napoleon Bonaparte stood by in silent exasperation.

The entry into the great pyramid had been easy enough; the doors had slid silently open at their approach. The interior appeared to be nothing more than a vast foyer, the floor a highly polished silver surface, the room springing into light the moment they entered. A maze of corridors went off in every direction, some up and others down to subterranean levels. Vush had stopped, looked around for several long minutes, and then quietly announced that this indeed was the building. A sigh of relief had gone through the group, until he softly admitted that though this was the building where he had discovered the wormhole machine, he wasn't quite sure where inside the cavernous structure he and Mupa had finally managed to come across it.

Napoleon found himself tempted to exert command—to give an order for the group to divide up responsibility, to start a systematic search for whatever useful military stores could be found, to bring the ship inside the building for safety and to set up a patrol. He watched them shouting and arguing and, with a philosophical shrug of his shoulders, he turned and strode away.

The room was so big that it took him several minutes to return almost to the doorway through which they had entered. He paused for a moment and looked up. The ceiling vaulted upward more than a hundred feet into the air. A dozen Notre Dames could easily be deposited in this one room. What did they use it for? An audience chamber? A place for pageants? It all looked too cold, dead. A single room, silvered floors and walls, ramps leading off. No ornamentation, no stained glass, not a single painting to relieve the daunting space, to make it somehow Human. Grandness had always appealed to him, but this was a grandeur without life.

A stairless causeway led up the side of one wall, and he ventured upward. If the ground floor was a gathering place, then the upper rooms must contain the stored secrets of these First Travelers the others spoke about with such awe. The ground floor dropped away, the thin voices of argument echoing in the chamber. He laughed softly, amused that they had not even noticed his wandering off. The causeway turned and plunged into the heart of the building.

He stopped, a thrill of fear coursing through him. A machine floated before him, tentacled arms hanging limp, an array of blinking lights apparently looking at him with soulless intent.

He took a deep breath.

"So, are you the master of this palace?"

Nothing.

"What are you?"

The machine remained motionless, silent.

"As inscrutable as a Russian."

A faint breeze stirred from a side corridor, carrying with it a pleasant scent of flowers and fresh air. With a curious gesture the machine turned and waved one of its arms, as if pointing down the corridor.

"So do you want me to go that way?"

The machine's arm was rigid, pointing, and it started down the corridor.

He turned to follow it and entered into a broad passage suffused with the reflected light. He had a sudden flash of memory—it was of Brienne, school, sitting in the shade of an arcade facing the square and playing chess with Brother Louis, who taught there. It was one of the few happy memories of that place. What triggered the memory? he wondered.

The side corridor widened out, and he suddenly found himself back outside, standing on a balcony that looked out over the open square. It had a good feel to it, twenty meters up from the ground, the perfect place to stage a grand review. The machine followed him, floating to come up by his side.

The view was magnificent, the sun straight overhead, the inside of the Sphere glowing with yellow light, the buildings in the vast plaza reflecting it like burnished mirrors, the strange black mountain dominating the sky, the clouds about its summit coiling and spiraling upward.

Below, the blue and white polished squares stood out like a chessboard, twenty across and twenty deep. Chess: the memory in the corridor and now this. He looked over at the machine, wondering and then dismissing the speculation.

Napoleon leaned against the chest-high railing, his arms draped over the side.

He looked back at the machine that floated beside him, as if waiting.

"So, my mechanical citizen, you appear to rule an empty world."

The machine did nothing.

Sighing, he looked back out at the square.

"Like a chessboard."

He looked back at the machine.

"I once saw a mechanical Turk who could beat even the masters, but I suspect they had a dwarf hidden within its bowels. So, my soulless companion, could you play such a thing, a game perhaps, or at least whistle a steam-powered tune?''

A flicker of light caused him to turn with a start.

The empty square below was filled with forms. The first three rows of squares closest to him were now arrayed with geometric forms, the back line a mixture of pyramids, pentagons, hexagons topped with three-sided pyramids, and two octagons that tapered up to a point. Each form, nearly twice the size of a man, filled an entire square, yet they appeared to be translucent, the squares beneath ever so slightly visible. The second row was lined with tall narrow rectangles, the third row with short round cylinders. The far side of the square was matched with similar forms, white to his blue.

"A game?"

He looked back inquiringly at the machine.

The air between the emperor and the machine appeared to take on a solid form, a small representation of the board floating before him. With a speed too fast to comprehend, a white piece, a cylinder, moved forward three squares, a blue cylinder on the opposite side matching the move. Out on the plaza the corresponding pieces moved as well. A tall rectangle of the white slipped out through the gap created by the cylinder, moving in a diagonal line; a blue pentagon leaped over both lines and came down ten squares forward. Faster and faster they moved, and he struggled to follow, to gather it in, to understand the moves, the tactics, the goal to victory.

A blue rectangle disappeared with a flash; another move by white in the same turn then followed. A blue hexagon leaped forward and then turned, like a knight; a white hexagon crowned with a three-sided pyramid moved in what appeared to be an erratic pattern, a zigzag.

"Slower, I don't understand, damn it," Napoleon growled.

The pieces on the board floating before the machine disappeared. A single piece was now in the center. He watched its movement. It vanished, and a different-shaped piece took its place, moving differently. Pentagons, hexagons, pyramids, it was getting difficult to follow. He felt somehow as if his mind were being drawn outward.

"I don't like these pieces," Napoleon snapped. "Machine parts, a Greek philosopher's playthings."

The board disappeared, and the machine drew closer.

"Wait a minute," Napoleon growled, lapsing back into French, forcibly overriding the translator implant.

The silent machine stopped, hovered, and he felt as if somehow it were reaching inward, into himself.

A form appeared again, miniature, elegant, floating in the air, so real that he reached out to touch it, but his hand drifted through it.

"Yes," he whispered excitedly, "that is it."

The machine drew back slightly and the board reappeared, what he had just seen now floating as a playing piece. The piece moved.

"No, no, no. That one should be a fast-moving piece."

Napoleon held his hand up and pointed at the machine. "This, what I am thinking, this should be the slower one for straight lines. Yes, that's it. Now for the next one."

"Your majesty?"

Damn it all, he felt foolish calling for a man with the words "your majesty," but shouting out, "hey, Napoleon, where the hell are you?" seemed equally absurd. He did, however, make sure there was enough of a sarcastic tone in his cry to annoy the man.

Yaroslav, with Basak in tow for protection if it should be needed, heard a chortle of delight, turned, and started down the corridor. The others were still arguing, cajoling, and threatening Vush back down in the middle of the room. The Overseer had finally floated a dozen feet into the air, as if to escape them, and was simply turning in slow circles, as if trying to figure out where to go next.

The hell with the stupid bastard. If need be, he'd find the thing on his own. They had seen the First Traveler machine when they had first entered the building. Vush had tried to approach it, but the machine had turned away and disappeared up the ramp. And now Napoleon had disappeared as well. So he had to go look for them, and the thought of running as an errand boy looking for Napoleon was ever so slightly distasteful. At least it gave him a chance to explore a little bit rather than hang around at the edge of the argument.

As he wandered off, he realized that Napoleon had most likely thought the same thing and set out on his own initiative. The thought of that man finding something important ahead of him was troublesome.

"Napoleon?"

There was no reply.

"Damn Corsican," Yaroslav mumbled.

He turned down a side corridor, the floor lighting up dimly to guide his passage, the hallway ahead suffused with the outside light. He turned a final corner and came up short.

A master machine of the First Travelers, the same that he had met in the Ring and inside the base of the Skyhook tower, was ahead of him—and Napoleon was by its side laughing. Now, how the hell did that bastard find him first?

Yaroslav edged out quietly onto the platform.

"All right, you could call it the queen," Napoleon said, looking up at the machine. "Lower cut to the dress, Imperial style, make it 1806, breasts barely exposed. I rather liked that year."

Yaroslav edged around the machine and there, floating in front of Napoleon, was what appeared to be a miniature of a woman, dressed in a high-waisted gown, her exposed breasts spilling out of the top.

"Make them a bit larger," Yaroslav said quietly.

Napoleon looked over at him and smiled.

The woman's breasts swelled in size.

"Does that suit you?"

"Perfectly," Yaroslav replied with a lascivious grin.

The figure disappeared, and an instant later a heavy field piece floated in the air.

"Just what the hell is this?" Yaroslav asked.

"A game," Napoleon replied, as if stating the obvious.

Yaroslav went past him and looked out on the plaza.

Two armies of chess pieces were arrayed on the blue and white squares in the plaza.

"I think I have it now," Napoleon announced, and he turned away from the machine to look out at the square.

"It can read my thoughts," Napoleon said, looking over at Yaroslav. "I guess I should find that to be disconcerting, but for some reason it doesn't bother me. It's teaching me to play something like their version of chess."

From the far end of the playing field a front-rank piece, dressed in the uniform of a British Highlander regiment, moved forward three squares.

Napoleon, with a dramatic flourish, held up a finger and pointed. A front-rank piece, outfitted in the uniform of the old guard, moved in reply.

"No, not like that," Napoleon snapped.

The piece disappeared and rematerialized in its original square.

"More realistic, bayonet fixed and poised for attack. Smoothly now."

The piece, which was standing at attention, lowered its musket, bayonet glinting, and it marched forward three paces and snapped back to attention again.

"That's it."

Yaroslav settled back, fascinated.

The soft whine of a float chair crackled behind them and Yaroslav looked over his shoulder to see Hobbs floating out onto the porch.

"A game," Yaroslav announced, as if he were somehow refereeing it.

Hobbs surveyed the scene, watching intently as the machine moved a Prussian lancer out of the second rank, advancing at a gallop to the center of the field. Napoleon countered with a hussar leaping through the air over the two forward ranks, zigzagging down the field, and finishing by cutting down a Highlander in a realistic splatter of blood.

Frustrated, Napoleon suddenly looked over at the machine.

"I can't move twice? You did it, damn you!"

The board reappeared in miniature in front of Napoleon, who watched it intently for a moment, pieces moving and flashing in midair.

"Damn your soul, you cheated me, you didn't tell me that you only get an extra move with kills from the first two ranks."

He muttered darkly while an Austrian field piece moved forward and with a puff of smoke obliterated the hussar.

He took off his hat, slamming it down on the railing, and looked over at the machine, his eyes glinting.

Another guardsman advanced, a match made by the other side.

"I'll give you five-to-one on the machine," Hobbs said. "A hundred credits."

"Done," Yaroslav replied.

Napoleon looked over at Yaroslav and smiled.

"Just to make the game exciting, but I fully expect to lose my money on you."

Napoleon grinned.

"I didn't expect you to show any support for me."

Yaroslav shrugged his shoulders.

"It's worth it to say I bet on Napoleon and lost."

The game moved yet more rapidly, additional touches slowly being added in, explosions sounding when the guns were fired, hooves clattering when the hussars, chasseurs, lancers, and cuirassiers charged, bayonets flashing when the foot soldiers took another piece.

A marshal from the white side, dressed as a Prussian general, swept through Napoleon's left flank. He pulled a gun piece to counter, destroying the marshal. An alluring queen of the white then rushed forward, taking the tricolored flag in the middle. The plaza flashed with light as if fireworks were bursting in the air, "Rule Britannia" playing in the background. The pieces disappeared, and the machine tilted forward ever so slightly, as if bowing.

Napoleon looked around darkly at his companions, who watched him expectantly, a thin trace of a smile on Yaroslav's face.

Throwing his head back, Napoleon laughed.

"Well done, you trickster, well done indeed." He saluted the machine, then extending his hand Napoleon grabbed hold of one of the tentacle projections of the machine and shook it.

"Curious."

Yaroslav looked back to see Aldin standing behind them.

"I know. A game. Something of the First Travelers, like chess in a way. Napoleon here modified the pieces, though."

Napoleon leaned back against the railing and looked at those around him.

"Is this typical?"

"You mean a machine that plays games?" Aldin asked.

"Exactly. I knew I could not win; if it could create this, then it undoubtedly knew the rules far better than I. A chess master takes years to learn his craft." He hesitated for a second and then smiled. "That is why I never played one."

"I heard that you loved to cheat," Yaroslav interjected.

Napoleon looked over at the old man and wagged a finger at him.

"Your history books lie." He paused, and then broke into a grin again. "At least most of the time they lie. When they report my victories, that is the truth at least."

"Play it again," Hobbs asked.

Napoleon nodded, and turning, he beckoned to the plaza. The pieces reappeared, and within seconds the forms were moving again.

"Any luck so far?" Yaroslav asked, looking back at Aldin.

"Everyone's wandering about. It'll take months to search this one place, though, if we do it at random."

Yaroslav nodded.

"And we've got days at best."

"Besides, Vush can't even really remember what the hell it looks like."

"Well, he did say that there was a machine like this one next to it."

Aldin walked up to the machine and looked up at it.

"We're looking for a device that makes wormholes," he said.

The machine continued to face the plaza, intent on moving a hussar that destroyed an imperial guardsman.

"The Overseers Vush and Mupa came here and found part of it. Could you show us where that was? Could you show us other parts of that machine?"

Napoleon moved a battery out that blew a marshal apart.

"Damn your eyes," the machine whispered.

Napoleon laughed with delight.

"Could we hold this game for a second?" Aldin asked.

Napoleon looked over at him and then held his hand up to the machine.

"My friends here would like to talk to you."

The machine turned slightly.

Aldin posed the same question again.

The machine turned back slightly and then moved one of the queen pieces to the middle of the field.

Napoleon shrugged his shoulders in a typical Gallic gesture and, looking back, waved his hand. A guardsman leaped forward to bayonet the queen.

"Such a waste, she was radiant," Napoleon said quietly.

Yaroslav, watching intently, looked back at Aldin.

"It's obvious the damn thing has more important things to do."

Aldin thrust his hands into his tunic pockets and settled back to watch. The battle was played out swiftly, the machine's defense crumbling after losing one of its two most important pieces. Napoleon sliced in hard through the middle, sacrificing most of his front rank but thus gaining additional moves to bring up his rear. Just when victory seemed assured, a shimmer of light appeared above the entire plaza and an entire second playing level formed, floating translucent, several meters above the first. Above the second, a third level formed. The machine leaped its remaining queen upward and far to Napoleon's rear.

"Damn me, you scoundrel, you cheated again," Napoleon thundered.

"Another level of play," Yaroslav replied, while Hobbs cackled with delight.

Napoleon went up to the machine and half-playfully but half-seriously he shoved it, but it did not move. A miniature playing field again appeared in front of Napoleon, showing three levels and pieces moving up and down between them.

"You should have told me earlier," he snapped.

"You never asked," Yaroslav interjected.

The queen swooped down the following turn to kill a marshal. All of Napoleon's forces were far forward, the enemy in his rear. He moved a battery upward to threaten the machine's final defense, but it was too late, as his tricolor fell the following turn. The fireworks sparkled, "God Save the King" playing on what sounded like a full brass band.

"Bloody good show. Never did the English soldier fight so well as he did today," the machine whispered, its voice reverberating slightly as if projected from a dozen different sources. The figure of the marshal down on the playing field rode up to beneath the platform and with a flourish drew his sword. His horse reared back, and he saluted smartly, before vanishing into thin air.

Napoleon, his hands clasped behind his back, stalked around the machine.

"You stole my own quote. It should be, 'Never did the French soldier fight.' You're as perfidious as they are and just about as heartless as Wellington."

"I am Wellington," the machine whispered.

Hobbs could not help but break down into a quaking laugh, his entire float chair jostling back and forth as his rolls of fat quivered.

Napoleon looked up at the machine.

"I am Wellington," it said, its voice cold.

"All right then. We play again."

"Could I interrupt?" Aldin asked.

Napoleon wheeled about.

"Can't you see we are busy, this oil-stinking Wellington and I."

"We do have other business to attend to here," Aldin said soothingly, "just a little emergency involving a couple of hundred planets."

"Ah, yes, there are priorities," Yaroslav interjected.

"All right, then," Napoleon replied. "Wellington, do give your attention to my friend. Let the game wait for a minute."

The playing field was again arrayed with figures, the machine turning its back on Aldin.

"Gentleman from France, you may fire first," Wellington announced.

Napoleon looked over at Aldin.

"It seems our host has different priorities," Yaroslav said, unable to keep from laughing, filled with a secret delight that Napoleon was being suckered into another game that he would undoubtedly lose.

Aldin watched the game unfold for several minutes and then quietly turned away. Zergh was waiting for him in the shadow of the corridor, and the two went back into the pyramid.

"Curious," Zergh said softly. "We've encountered those machines twice before, but this is the first time one's ever interacted with any of us, or demonstrated even the slightest concern. Hell, the last time it stood by impassively while Yaroslav blew it apart along with the Skyhook."

"According to Vush it ignored him while he and his idiot companion were playing around with the wormhole machine," Aldin added in. "So why now, why Napoleon?"

They reached the corridor by which they had ascended into the pyramid.

"Vush and the others went up this way," Zergh said, and Aldin followed his lead as the causeway spiraled upward. A small machine rolled past them, going in the opposite direction, dragging yet a smaller device with several dozen arms flailing, a thin beeping protest echoing in the hallway. Seconds later half a dozen devices similar to the captive scooted past and turned the corner in pursuit. There was a clattering of metal, and a moment later the mob of machines returned, this time dragging back smashed parts of the captor, some of which were still twitching feebly.

"I think this place might be going amok," Aldin said.

Reaching another level, they paused for a moment while Zergh looked around to gain his bearings.

"Let's not get lost. There must be hundreds of levels to this thing."

"If it's even the right building," Zergh replied.

Distant voices echoed in the hallway, and the two followed the sound. A huge doorway, more than ten meters high and just as wide, opened to one side, and they ventured in.

"The junkyard of the gods," Aldin whispered in awe.

"So, you think then that Vush has revealed the secret of the Sphere?"

Mupa nodded sadly.

"He has obviously gone off with them," Mupa replied. "I always did have my doubts about him. He was not of the Select in all things. That is why I spent so much time with him—"

"Shut up," the Arch snapped, cutting Mupa off and reducing him to a quivering silence.

The Arch looked down coldly at the youthful Overseer of but twenty thousand years who had gotten them in all of this trouble. He had yet to find a sufficiently remote punishment planet where, alone, Mupa could double his life span in contemplation. It had to have the right combination of factors, freezing cold, or boiling hot, to start with, he wasn't quite sure which one he wanted yet; ideally there should be a desert world with both, and nothing in between. The problem with desert worlds was that they could make one wonderfully crazy from their stark beauty, and he would not give Mupa that opportunity.

"If they should find this thing, could they use it from there?" the Arch asked.

"They would have to bring it back," Mupa replied, "to where the runaway star is, or at least nearby."

The Arch nodded.

"Let Corbin chase him at the Sphere. If he should escape, we can meet him on his return and take care of things in the appropriate manner," the Arch announced.

Of course, it would mean eliminating Corbin as well once this was over, but he had gone this far—a little further in degree of eliminating was hardly troublesome to his soul at all at this point.

CHAPTER 10

EXHAUSTED, ALDIN LARICE COLLAPSED ON TOP OF A BROKEN-down, spindly machine that sagged beneath his weight.

"Careful, that could be it," Yaroslav said, even as he wiped off a thin patina of grease and dust from a multilegged machine that looked like some sort of cross between a Xsarn and a turbo jack for a Brusarian pleasure yacht, and plopped down beside Aldin.

The cavernous room seemed to stretch on forever, the insides of it a mad jumble of broken parts, twisted machinery, and what looked like remarkably advanced holo computers, some with lights still blinking. A slow but endless procession of other machines wandered in and out of the room, ignoring the presence of the intruders. Some of the machines entering were dragging other devices; occasionally their burdens were twitching and struggling. They would deposit their burdens and leave, and more often than not the "junk" would crawl back out of the room, or be rescued by similar devices and carried back out.

"If it wasn't so maddening, it'd almost be humorous to watch."

Aldin looked up to see Tia standing beside him, her face covered in grease and dirt.

"How's it going?"

"Oh, he's sure that this is the room. I think he's right. Apparently this is some sort of repository for broken machines. The only trouble is that it's been several thousand years since he and Mupa were here. Supposedly the room was damn near empty then except for one of the master machines.

"And now this," she sighed, pointing to the chaos around them.

A ratlike machine scurried past, followed seconds later by dozens more, and disappeared into the insides of what looked like a servobot, the crew reemerging a minute later with small pieces of holo crystal, memory units, and strips of wire.

There was a thin yet persistent cacophony of screeches, grindings, scrapings, and beepings echoing through the room, reminding Aldin of what some Gafs called deconstructionist music. He caught a momentary glimpse of Vush floating up, looking about, and then drifting off again.

"Oishi still with him?"

"I think quietly contemplating beheading," Tia sighed.

"This is obviously a junkyard," Zergh said, sticking his head up from behind a pile of bent pipes. "But most curious. It's inside to protect valuable machinery, what looks like workshops line the far wall, and tools are scattered all about. When Vush was here, the place was nearly empty; now it's packed to the gills."

"And everything working to cross purposes," Tia said. "I've seen things dragged in here, and then others come in of the same make and drag them back out again, even when they're obviously dead, if you could call a machine dead. It almost seems like a machine clan loyalty."

"An interesting philosophical consideration." Yaroslav yawned.

"Oh, spare me," Aldin snapped, realizing his temper was far too short.

Aldin stood up, stretched, and headed over to where he had last seen Vush.

The Overseer bobbed up again for a second and then drifted back down. Oishi, seeing Aldin's approach, gave him a grimace of frustration.

"Say, Vush, you got a moment?" Aldin asked.

Vush turned and looked down at him.

"It depends on the definition of a moment," Vush replied. "To some species it might be a mere nanosecond of an all too brief existence. To one such as me, a moment could stretch into one of your centuries."

"Just shut up and come down here to eye level."

Vush floated down to hover in front of Aldin.

"Making any progress?"

"Well by a process of elimination one could define it that way."

Aldin nodded.

"Do you know what you're looking for?"

Vush hesitated.

"Go on."

"Not really."

Aldin nodded, restraining himself from calling on Oishi to pull out the sword and start threatening.

"So what is it that you are doing?"

"Well, I'm just sort of floating around, figuring that sooner or later something will come up."

"I see."

"And how long might later be?" Oishi inquired.

Vush hesitated. "A thousand years, maybe more in an extreme case."

"By that time the entire cloud will have gone down the hole," Zergh snapped, coming up to join the group.

"Oh, that is most certainly an exaggeration. There are quite a few million stars; even at the rate of one a day it'd take several thousand years before even a sizable dent was made."

"Most reassuring," Oishi growled.

Aldin stepped closer, knowing that he was violating the ten

feet of personal space that Overseers felt was the closest they'd want another being to approach. Oishi, who was behind Vush, did not budge when the being backed into him. Aldin drew closer.

"Think of something else," Aldin whispered.

"Like what?"

"Well for instance, something other than prowling aimlessly through this junkyard."

"This is where we found the device to start with."

"Ah, excuse me," Tia interjected. "Just one question."

"And that is?" Vush asked, as if relieved to be able to turn away from Aldin and Zergh.

"It's obvious this was a place for broken machines. And yet you took the wormhole device out of here."

"You know Mupa and I debated that point for quite a few years. The First Traveler machine was here. At one point after a lot of prodding and poking it projected a holo image of how the thing supposedly worked. Now for myself I believed that this was an in-processing point, where things were brought for repair. Mupa argued that it was an out-processing, where things were placed once they had gone through the workstations. He took it without my even really knowing."

"Fifty-fifty," Aldin replied, "a nice safe bet when playing with wormholes."

"So what are you suggesting I do?" Vush asked, an actual note of exasperation in his voice.

"You could try and talk to the First Traveler machine for starters," Zergh said.

"We're not even sure it's the same one," Aldin replied, "and besides it's busy playing with Napoleon."

"How about accessing into some of the computer systems?" Tia said.

"How?" Vush replied.

"Well, damn it, think of something, anything!" Aldin snapped, and turning he stormed off, kicking another rat machine out of the way. The machine squealed and skidded across the narrow path that weaved in and out through the piles of junk and disappeared.

Cursing, Aldin made his way through the heaps of broken parts, and gaining an access corridor he went up it, glad to be away from Vush. The causeway did a sweeping spiral turn upward, curving out over the cavernous junk hall, which finally disappeared from view.

Aldin stopped and cursed.

Another room, acres in size, was before him, this one piled almost as high with junk as the one below. He turned away and strode up the next causeway. The room above was the same, and then the room above that one as well.

Just where the hell did they get all of this junk?

He felt a stab of pain, and hopping up on one leg he looked down at the ground. A tiny rat machine was at his feet, a pinching talon extended, holding in its claw a thin slice of his trousers. It scurried forward to pinch again, and leaping up he came down hard, nearly losing his balance, the machine scrunching underneath his heel.

Another one came around the corner, claws raised.

"Oh, shit."

Turning, he started back down the causeway, the tiny machine in pursuit. Zergh, who had followed him up, stopped for a moment and started to laugh, until the machine darted toward the Gaf while Aldin ran past. The Gaf leaped upward, the rat turning and retreating, triumphantly waving a torn piece of purple trouser.

"I think they're upset," Zergh snarled, hopping and cursing as the two ran back down the corridor.

Gaining the next level, they paused for a moment to look back. The corridor was empty.

"Damn place," Aldin sighed. "I think we're on a fool's errand. We couldn't get Korobachi, and chances are Corbin killed him. We come here without someone to tell us how the machine works, and we run into a junkyard. Vush doesn't know what the hell to get, and I've got a bad feeling about the whole damn thing. It was a nice dumb-ass altruistic idea that by saving the Core we'd get off the hook, but I think it's a washout.''

"Let's go back to the ship and get a drink," Zergh said, reaching down to rub his ankle, which was bleeding from the pinch.

Agreeing, Aldin followed him, shouting to Oishi, who was still with Vush, to join them when the Overseer finally decided to take a break.

Gaining the vast empty main floor, they stepped aside for a moment while a long line of machines rolled in, each of them bearing another machine, most of which were twisted and broken, some of them still sparking, others waving feebly.

Stepping out of the pyramid, Aldin came up short. The square seemed to be alive with forms—guardsmen, hussars, marshals, artillery pieces—moving back and forth.

"Well, at least the emperor is having a good time."

"Are you heading back to the ship?"

Aldin looked up to see Napoleon leaning over the balcony.

"Thinking about it," Zergh replied.

"Good. Get one of the servobots to bring out a bottle of brandy or a good wine. Also, something to eat."

"Beef Wellington perhaps for myself." Yaroslav was by Napoleon's side.

There was a low curse from above in French.

"Chicken Marengo will do," Napoleon shouted.

"What the hell is that?" Zergh asked.

He shouted down the ingredients as if passing an order to a waiter.

Zergh turned and walked away.

"Did you get that?" Aldin asked.

Zergh, obviously insulted, said nothing.

Munching on a chicken leg, Napoleon leaned over the balcony as the playing field was cleared after his twentieth defeat.

"It's not nice to lose, is it my emperor?" Yaroslav said, chuckling while pouring out two more brandies.

"It keeps advancing the rules," Napoleon replied.

The playing field was crosshatched with light. The sun above was down to the bottom of its variable phase, and the white squares of the field had in turn become illuminated to break the semitwilight.

Napoleon stretched and rubbed his hand over the stubble of beard.

"Aren't you tired?"

"No. Actually remarkably refreshed."

Yaroslav looked at him narrowly, wondering if the man was putting on an act of bravado. They had been at it for over half a standard day, and except for a brief pause to eat two meals and wandering inside to find a convenient spot to relieve himself, he still seemed almost as fresh as when he started.

Though he hated to admit it to himself, he found that he was actually admiring the man's stamina and ability to concentrate.

"Why don't we quit for a while?" Yaroslav finally suggested.

"Whatever for?"

"Well, for starters, I wouldn't mind a little rest."

"No one is stopping you," Napoleon replied, the faintest of contemptuous smiles on his face, as if this admission of fatigue was a victory in a contest of endurance.

"You're always competing, aren't you?"

"That's what life is. To see a challenge, to formulate your strategy, and then to win."

"But this is only a game," Yaroslav said.

"Is it?"

Yaroslav paused and looked closely at the man before him.

"Go on and explain," he finally said.

"Nine of us came here on a mission, a quest. It is obvious that none of you actually know what it is that you are looking for. Will you admit to that?"

Yaroslav nodded in agreement, though he hated to admit that even he was stumped this time.

"Have you ever seen anything like our friend here before?"

"I am Wellington," the machine said, its voice a whisper.

"Twice before. You know that."

"And from what I heard over these last days in talking with

Vush and with others, this machine and others like it are capable of thinking; they are some form of sentinel of the creations of the godlike First Travelers.''

Yaroslav nodded. "That's what we kind of assumed.''

"Assumed or knew? Be precise.''

"Is this an examination?'' Yaroslav snapped.

"Humor me,'' Napoleon replied, smiling in a disarming way and looking straight into Yaroslav's eyes.

Damn him, Yaroslav thought. He has the presence, the self-assuredness. His own image of Napoleon had never really been all that positive. Now Alexander, there was someone he had taken to immediately. After all, he was Alexander the Great. But Napoleon, that was a character of history he had never really cared for. Alexander had endured the march back from the Indus with his troops, had carried a full panoply of equipment on his back through the mountains of Bactria, had ridden in the vanguard in the charge at Gaugamela and at Granicus. Napoleon had always been pictured as abandoning his troops in the retreat from Moscow, riding away and issuing proclamations that the emperor was safe. The etchings of Goya came to mind, the cynical drafting of sixteen-year-olds to prop up his collapsing empire, the killing of the sick soldiers at Acre, the choked fields of dead at Borodino, Austerlitz, and a hundred other places.

This Napoleon didn't quite match it, though he sensed that such ruthlessness was indeed below the surface. Yet how had he done it? Yaroslav wondered. He could sense part of that answer as he looked at him. There was a Napoleon before the legend, a man of flesh and blood, who could imbue others with his dreams, and in the imbuing convince them that there was a higher ideal worth dying for. He had wrapped himself in the glorious dreams of the Revolution, lifting it out of the ugly squalor of the Terror and firing a generation with the dream of sweeping all of Europe into a new order of equality.

"You don't like me at all, do you?''

Yaroslav looked at him.

"Most of the time, I don't.''

"Because of what I did?"

"You and so many others like you," Yaroslav said, boosting himself up on the balcony to sit. "People like you might start out with a dream, but in the end millions die. Such madness is usually started by idealists."

Napoleon laughed softly, and refilling an empty tumbler he offered it over to Yaroslav, who took it with a nod of thanks. He looked over at Basak, but the Gaf was curled up in the corridor, fast asleep. Hobbs, however, was more than happy to join them in another drink and then settled back in his float chair to nurse the brandy and listen.

"This I find to be interesting. To meet my own historian, thousands of years after I supposedly died. And I hear in your voice that history was not kind to me."

"Oh, there are many who would disagree, but they forget the price of glory."

"Ah, yes, glory." Napoleon sighed. "And how would you define it?"

"A lie, a trick, a dupe to get others to die, a hunk of metal dangling from a piece of cloth in payment for a life. 'With baubles such as these I can lead armies.' "

"So they did remember that quote," Napoleon said with a sigh.

Yaroslav was silent.

"The medal is nothing but that, a bauble. Ah, but what it represents," Napoleon said, looking down, his hand brushing the Legion of Honor medal that rested on his left breast.

"But it is so much more. Certainly there are fools who see the medal and it becomes all, the way some would go to Notre Dame, when it was restored to the church, and grovel before a statue of marble and believe that the saint resided within. There are far too many such as they.

"But it is so much more. It is a dream, a vision, a belief, a goal. For what is man if he does not dream? I believed in the Revolution. I dreamed of the glory of it, a people raising their heads out of the dust and declaring themselves free. Even if the

Revolution had never existed, I would have dreamed it into being.''

"Yet you created your own nobility.''

"Yes, yes, I know. Yet who were my nobles? Ney, a cavalry sergeant, for one. A nobility of skill, of intellect. It is always that way. For some, the baubles of nobility gave a legitimacy of a higher ideal. Men will fight and will die if you offer them something to believe in. Even you, my cynical old friend, for I suspect that like most old cynics you were an idealist in your youth.''

Yaroslav shook his head.

"Xsarn food.''

"What is that?''

"Shit.''

"Oh, *merde*.'' He laughed.

"Tell me,'' Yaroslav said, unable to contain himself. "Is that what your guardsmen really said at Waterloo?''

"It's a good story, is it not?'' Napoleon said with a smile. "And that is precisely what I am saying to you. They were offered life, and yet their honor was more important, such that they could die with a crude jest. If they had not, would their memories be recalled now? If those men had lived quiet lives and died old in bed, who would sing their songs now? It is the spirit such as that that impells men to greatness. There are things that transcend life itself. It is that which I dreamed of, and that which gave a nation into my control, willing to shape that dream. We would have united Europe nearly two hundred years before it finally happened, from what I heard. And from what little I have learned of the years after my time, I doubt it would have been worse for the uniting, and most likely would have been spared much agony in the years to come. Is that so bad a thing?''

"Yet it is men like you who create the suffering.''

"There will always be men like me. There always were, there always will be. But I defend myself with the claim that at least I dreamed of a world of justice, freed from the old regimes of greed, spoiled nobility that starved its own people, and a society based upon birth rather than upon courage, intellect, and the spirit to reach beyond one's station.''

Yaroslav leaned forward, his face shadowed by the twilight.

"Do you honestly believe what you've just told me?''

Napoleon merely smiled.

"You've managed to divert things away,'' Napoleon finally said, breaking a long moment of silence. "There are more pressing issues than the fulfillment of your curiosity regarding myself.''

"Such as?''

"What have you learned by watching Wellington here and myself playing all these hours?''

"A look into your logic. A game of chess can reveal an awful lot about the type of person behind the board. You for one are impatient, aggressive almost to folly, yet terribly cunning.''

"Learning such about me is useless given what it is you came here for.''

Yaroslav smiled.

"Regarding our friend then?''

"The victory at Waterloo was won on the playing fields of Eton,'' Wellington said, and Yaroslav turned to look at the machine with surprise.

"He never said that, you know,'' Yaroslav said.

"I never heard it,'' Napoleon replied. "Sounds typically English though, pretentious and trite.''

"Curious,'' Yaroslav said, looking closely at the machine.

"Where did he get it then?'' Napoleon said.

The two were silent for a moment.

"It obviously can read my thoughts—a clairvoyant machine. The shapes and forms of the pieces were in my thoughts, and it made them for me. I assumed when it named itself Wellington, it took that from my mind, too. But that foolish quote.''

"I knew it, though,'' Yaroslav said.

Napoleon looked at the machine.

"Josephine,'' he whispered.

In a glimmer of pale yellow light, a holo image floated before him.

"A close enough proximity of her," Napoleon said with almost a wistful sigh, "at least when she was younger."

"Melinda," Yaroslav said.

Nothing happened.

"He obviously doesn't care much for your thoughts," Napoleon said, obviously pleased that the machine would do his bidding alone.

"Why, though?"

"Because I am Napoleon." There was a note of pride in his voice, as if the answer were all too obvious.

"Please spare me the false hubris. So, why?" Yaroslav said, ignoring the flash look of anger. "If it can actually read thoughts, it must know why we are here, what it is that we seek, the crisis we face."

"Because it simply doesn't care," Napoleon replied. "You attribute altruism to a steam-driven machine of cogs and wheels. If a man should come up and cut your arm off, he would be wrong, a criminal, and all would say that he is evil and must be punished. But if one of Watt's machines should catch you, and crush you in its gears, one would simply turn the machine off until you were free, and then turn it back on again to do its labors."

He paused and looked back at Wellington.

"Isn't that right, you haughty boiler?"

"Another game?"

Napoleon sighed.

"And you'll change the rules again."

"A progression, my emperor."

Napoleon looked over at Yaroslav.

"Do you think you'll actually find whatever it is this Vush is looking for?"

"I doubt it," Yaroslav replied. "I didn't expect much to start with, and even less now. It was a vain hope. A desperate last stand, if you will."

"Desperation can breed insight."

"The machine doesn't give a god damn about Vush, you saw that. It only wants you."

"It showed good sense, then."

"It isn't helping us."

"Oh, really?" Napoleon said with a smile.

"Go on and play it again."

"I'm bored with this game. Let's play something different if you like, something more challenging," Napoleon said, looking back over at Wellington.

A flash of light enveloped him, and for the briefest instant he inwardly cursed, believing that the machine had killed him. He felt a falling away, a terrible sense of disorientation, as if he had been turned and turned upon a spinning platform.

There was an open field before him; a low declining slope dropped away. Half a kilometer down an enclosed farmhouse was on his left, stout walls surrounding a small courtyard, home, outbuildings, and barn all joined together. A similar, though smaller structure was straight ahead on the road that ran past him and then continued on up the opposite slope. Fields of wheat, golden and thigh high, swayed in a gentle breeze. Several orchards dotted the landscape. He felt his heart start to race, and his knees felt loose, rubbery.

His senses reeled.

"Waterloo," he whispered. "Yaroslav?"

"I see it," the old man whispered. "Damn it all, I hate those jump beams. Didn't know the old machine had one in him."

Basak, who had been asleep, came to his feet, looking around, confused, and with a growl drew the double-headed ax out of its sheath.

"Shall we play?"

Napoleon looked over at Wellington, who floated beside him.

He looked overhead, as if to reassure himself. The pale sun was straight overhead, the vast sphere enclosing the sky.

"Mon Dieu," Napoleon gasped.

"How close is it?" Yaroslav inquired.

"Identical. Damn identical. There—" He pointed down the slope. "—Hougoumont, which held me up, the road to Brussels, the woods to the right, which hid the Prussian advance. All of it."

His hands shaking, he clasped them behind himself to hide the trembling and paced across the field, the high wheat swishing aside. He stamped the ground and then looked back at Wellington.

"It rained, you know."

The sun overhead went dark, and looking up he saw a small cloud hovering at the zenith that rapidly started to expand.

Napoleon nodded.

"Did you ever dream of doing something over again? A young lady lost by foolishness, a choice incorrectly made, a war lost?" he whispered, and looked back at Yaroslav.

The old man could not help but smile.

"Do you accept the challenge?" Wellington asked.

Napoleon smiled and nodded.

There was another glimmer of light, and a member of the old guard materialized, as if conjured up out of the dust.

The image saluted.

Basak stepped backward, growling, holding his ax up, ready to swing.

Yaroslav laughed and motioned for him to lower the blade.

"Come, come, my hairy friend. I think there's going to be a little war."

Basak grinned in anticipation.

"But there are risks," Wellington said.

Napoleon walked over to the guardsman, and, hand trembling, he reached out and touched him. His hand did not go through. He looked closely at the man.

"I remember you," Napoleon said, his voice trembling. "Jean Paul, you were with me from Egypt to Borodino."

"Where I died," the guardsman whispered, his voice sounding as if it were conjured from beyond the grave.

Napoleon stepped backward.

"It's just a transformation of matter, the clay of this sphere, into this," Yaroslav said, as if trying to reassure him. "A hell of a lot of energy to do that."

Napoleon passed his hands over his eyes and looked back at Jean.

"It is you?"

The guardsman looked at him with crinkled eyes.

"But of course, my emperor."

Napoleon looked back at Wellington.

"From my thoughts you took this?"

He hesitated, looking back at the guardsman.

"I had not thought of him in years, yet you pulled him from within my soul."

Another guardsman appeared, and yet another, until, within seconds, an entire company was formed. Wide-eyed, Napoleon gazed at them, whispering names, the forms smiling each in turn, coming to attention, saluting. He walked down the line, looking up at them.

"Pierre, I lost you at Wagram, and Claude, you died of typhus; O'Rourke, you were decorated at Austerlitz for taking that gun, and then you let a whore stab you in the back."

And they smiled, some saying a brief greeting back, a pledge of loyalty, an affectionate smile.

Tears in his eyes, Napoleon looked back at Wellington.

"Memories of the dead, your dead. He pulled them out of you," Yaroslav said, going up to the company, poking some of them, taking hold of a jacket to feel its weave.

"My dead," Napoleon said.

"Only a million, more or less," Yaroslav sniffed, looking over at Napoleon with a casual air.

Napoleon turned on the old philosopher.

"You know nothing of it," he snapped, "nothing. You write your histories and spin your lies. You know nothing of what is in here." And he thumped his chest.

Yaroslav said nothing, and going up to Jean he motioned for the form to hand over his musket. The guardsman, with cold lifeless eyes, looked over at Napoleon, who nodded an assertion.

Yaroslav took the musket and balanced it in his hands.

"I've always wanted to try one of these," he said. "Seen them on some of the more primitive worlds." He walked away from the line, and fumbling with the piece, he cocked the hammer. He turned back at a range of half a dozen paces and raised the musket. He pointed it at Jean.

Before Napoleon could shout out a protest, Yaroslav squeezed the trigger. An explosion snapped off. Jean, nearly lifted off his feet, crashed backward, knocking over the man behind him.

Yaroslav looked through the curling blue smoke, unable to hide a momentary astonishment at what he had just done, and looked back almost guiltily at Napoleon.

"You bastard," Napoleon shouted, going up to the company line, which remained motionless except for the one fallen guardsman.

The man was still, a neat hole in his chest, a pool of blood spilling out beneath him, staining the golden stalks of wheat. Napoleon knelt down by his side.

"He was just an illusion," Yaroslav said, though from the catch in his voice it was obvious that he was trying to reassure himself.

Napoleon looked up coldly at Yaroslav.

"It will be real," Wellington said quietly. "That is the risk."

Shaken, Napoleon came back up to his feet.

"I didn't really kill him," Yaroslav whispered. "Your Jean died over three thousand years ago. It was a creation of your memory."

Yaroslav hesitated.

"I'm sorry."

Napoleon nodded, looking back at the body.

"I needed to test something," Yaroslav said. "This is bloody insane. This thing—" he motioned toward the machine "—can actually transform things at will. We can do it, the jump beam is a form of it, but the energy involved, the sophistication of the programming that can take raw matter and change it to simulated flesh, wool, leather, iron, and powder, it's incredible. It even can kill its own creations, knowing just what a lead ball from a musket will do, all of it taken from your memory, or some store of knowledge."

He turned away, looking back at Wellington.

"Incredible."

"Absolutely," Wellington replied. "Now, gentlemen, I have picked my field and it is here."

"You mean a battle then, a replaying of Waterloo."

"In every detail. The Brown Bess musket, of .72 caliber, has an effective range of less than eighty meters, but can kill at three hundred. Everything is as it was."

"Why?" Yaroslav asked.

"Because," Wellington replied.

"Everything?" He looked around for a moment. Behind them a battery of nine-pound fieldpieces formed, first the guns, several seconds later the crews, then the caissons, the horses, and the guidons stirring in the breeze. The horses did not look quite right, the detail of muscles seemed flat somehow, the faces of the men indistinct, like the face on a coin that had worn down somewhat with time and usage.

A squadron of hussars came into sudden focus, another squadron behind it, the beginning of a regiment. Staff started to appear, sometimes the faces clear, others indistinct as if a blending of memories. A table came into existence, maps spread out upon it, log books, muster rolls, blank sheets ready for orders, a collapsed telescope with a set of worn gloves beside it. An ornate but battered field kit was on the ground, several bottles of wine inside, and a sudden scent of fresh bread and meat wafted up around them.

"Well, I think I'll find a safe spot somewhere back up there to watch the show," Yaroslav said, nodding toward the low hills to the rear.

"You are chief of staff," Napoleon announced.

"Ah, thanks, but I'll decline the honor."

"You are chief of staff. That was one of my mistakes last time. Soult was fine at the head of a division, even a corps, but here, today, he failed me. You know the historical battle, I want you by my side."

"Thanks but no thanks. I'll see you later."

Yaroslav, smiling wanly, turned to walk away. Napoleon looked over at Wellington.

Yaroslav suddenly turned back, his face wrinkled with a slight grimace of discomfort.

"Literally a pain in the ass," he hissed, rubbing his backside, a thin curl of smoke coming up behind him.

Napoleon could not help but laugh at the old man's discomfort.

"So much for desertion."

"I take it that there'll be a lot of lead and shot flying about," Yaroslav said, looking over at Wellington. "Will this stuff be real?"

"But of course."

"Oh, great."

He looked over at Napoleon, whose eyes were beaming with a sudden excitement.

"Again. To actually be able to do it again." He started to pace back and forth with nervous excitement.

"To victory," Wellington said, and he inclined himself forward as if bowing in salute.

"To the victor the spoils," Napoleon said quietly.

The machine did not reply.

"It takes two to play. To the victor the spoils? A free France, an empire, and I as its emperor?"

"Of course," Wellington said. "The play's the thing."

"And all the rules of war apply if we win?" Yaroslav asked.

"The rules of war? I'm a gentleman, of course the conventions will be observed," Wellington announced, its voice haughty as if it had been insulted.

Yaroslav nodded and smiled.

The machine turned and in an instant was moving at high speed down the slope. Within seconds it was past Hougoumont and curved back up the opposite slope to stop where the center of his line would be, barely visible in the twilight that was starting to shift back up toward full day, though still obscured by the gathering storm directly overhead.

"Aldin, something's up."

Tia shook him awake and he mumbled a curse, thinking at

first that it was Mari waking him up to complain that she had another one of her headaches and that he should fetch her medicine from the night table.

Grabbing a robe, he stumbled out of his cabin, cursing at the servobot that followed, Tia, Vush, the rat bite, everything.

Oishi, sleepy eyed, looked up from the main console.

"Tia noticed it first," Oishi said, fighting down a yawn.

"What is it?"

"A hell of an energy spike," she said. "It's like the disturbance from a jump-down beam, the initial energy pulse that creates the vacuum and moves all matter out of the way. The same signature, but it's thousands of times stronger."

"Somebody jumping in?" Aldin said, now suddenly full awake.

"What I'm thinking," Oishi said grimly. "We're getting one hell of a lot of company."

Aldin looked over at the holo screen and the stream of information running across it.

"Nobody's got a jump system like that," Tia said. "It'll move hundreds of men a second."

"Well somebody's doing it, and I think we better get ready to get the hell out of here quick," Aldin said.

"They're gone, just gone."

Aldin turned to see Hobbs, his float chair laboring on a nearly depleted battery, drift with a lurching motion into the room.

"Who?" Aldin asked, looking back at the agitated impresario.

"Yaroslav, Basak, and Napoleon. I was half asleep; they were talking about doing another game. Napoleon said something about being bored, and poof, they're gone."

"Damn it all," Oishi growled.

Hobbs, pulling out an embroidered handkerchief, wiped the sweat from his face.

"We're still getting the spike," Oishi said.

Aldin leaned over his shoulder to look at the screen.

"It's not directed from above," he said, suddenly confused. "It's surface-to-surface."

He punched up another screen and studied it intently for a moment.

"A couple of hundred kilometers from here."

"Think they might be there as well?" Tia asked hopefully.

"Well we can't leave them in the lurch." Aldin sighed. "We'll go in cautiously, check it out."

Within seconds the ship was secured, and turning it about, Oishi plotted a course to where the energy flux was located. Stirred awake by the movement of the rest of the crew stumbling about, Vush came into the room and nervously voiced a fear that perhaps his comrades had shown up and were coming down to the surface.

"Then why the hell two hundred kilometers away?" Zergh asked.

"Perhaps they aren't sure where to land."

"Just about as sure as you are then," Zergh snapped, and Vush fell silent, looking nervously over at the Gaf vasba.

The city behind them, they raced out across the open, gently rolling fields, the black mountain to their right, slowly moving upward and away. The land was undistinguished, open fields, groves of trees, meandering streams, sections of it very artificial looking and laid out in regular block patterns, as if imagination had somehow failed. A shimmer of light started to appear, flashing beneath a strangely isolated cloud that flashed with lightning, a shower cascading beneath it.

"Whatever's going on, is underneath that thunderstorm," Oishi said.

Aldin nodded, easing their speed back. The jump beam was cutting down from a distant source several tens of thousands of kilometers away, traveling inside the sphere, and thus coming across the surface at a very low angle. Aldin maneuvered to safely avoid the beam, since it could have a most unpleasant result.

He checked the monitor again. The power being generated was phenomenal. Moving just one or two people was a major drain on even a more powerful ship; this thing was pulsing at a remarkable rate, hundreds of times a second, each pulse carrying enough power to move several hundred kilos of mass.

"Enough energy being shot there to power a couple of hundred liners from one end of the Cloud to the other," Zergh said.

The beam shut down and Aldin waited, hovering low to the ground.

"Should we go in closer to look?" Tia asked.

"Whatever was doing that undoubtedly could detect our ship moving out here," Zergh said, "so what the hell, let's go take a look."

"Why don't we just hang back awhile longer," Oishi said.

"It's not like a planet here," Aldin replied. "Wherever you are, everything else curves above you. If someone wanted to fry us from further up, we're down here in the bottom of a bowl. We haven't been hurt, and I'm curious to go take a look."

He nudged the ship upward and started forward.

"Looks like a road," Tia said, standing up and going to the forward viewscreen, the landscape rolling by several hundred feet below.

Aldin stood up from behind his console, leaving Zergh to pilot the ship. Something was moving down there.

The road just suddenly appeared, starting out in the middle of an empty field that was barely covered with splotches of dirt; most of the surface was of the black sublayer of the Sphere. Gradually the terrain started to form into low, undulating hills, covered with the rich grass of late spring. Square fields appeared; the dirt road weaving through them. And then, suddenly, to his amazement, moving up the next low ridge line he saw a long column of blue, moving slowly, undulating like a long centipede, flashes of metal gleaming.

An infantry column.

"Zergh, get over here," Aldin whispered.

His vasba companion joined him and pulled on his facial hair, stroking his chin and watching with silent intent as the ship gained on the column and then whisked over it. The ridge cleared the long open road and turned off to the left, its entire length packed with troops.

"Infantry, Earth, musket period," Aldin whispered.

"Napoleonic," Zergh replied.

They crossed up over another low rise clad in a heavy forest, the column half a dozen kilometers behind. An open field whisked below them, blocklike formations of men drawn up, their uniforms black.

"Prussian, at least I think so," Aldin said, his voice edged with excitement.

"Definitely," Zergh interjected with the voice of authority of one who knew more about late ancient Earth warfare than his human companion.

"We're being scanned," Oishi announced. "A heavy spike of energy."

Aldin turned away from the viewport and went back to the controls.

The ship shuddered beneath them. For a second Aldin thought they had hit something. But no, they were still moving, but slower. It shuddered again, speed bleeding off.

"Almost like a force shielding."

Oishi brought the ship to a complete stop, and the energy dropped down to a barely perceptible scan. He nudged forward and the energy shot up again.

"Whatever it is, they don't want us flying into this," Oishi said.

"All right then," Aldin replied, sitting back in his chair.

"This terrain looks vaguely familiar," Zergh said, pulling up beside Aldin and punching in the access code to their old vasba gaming files.

"Take us up higher," Zergh said, and Aldin responded. There was no further resistance from whatever had wanted to slow them down, and within seconds he had them a kilometer above the surface.

"Sure," Zergh whispered, smiling as he overlaied a holo simulation map onto the radar sweep of below.

"We just crossed over the Prussian column moving out from Wavre. I bet if we angled over further, we'd go over Grouchy."

He stood up and went forward to look back out.

"And Waterloo is about five kilometers out there," he said, his voice edged with excitement.

Even as he spoke, the cloud that had been dropping a light but steady rain started to dissipate away, curling in upon itself. Within seconds the sky above them cleared.

"Look at it!" Zergh cried excitedly. "There, that must be the rear lines of Napoleon, the three guard infantry divisions, those buildings, that's Plancenoit!"

Aldin sprang out of his chair to join him.

"It's better than any holo sim we used to cook up for the Kohs," Zergh gasped.

"Because it's real," Aldin said with a sigh of envy. "That machine must have built it out here."

"Well, Napoleon said he was bored," Hobbs interjected.

"Now that we know where they are, I'm ready to continue my search," the Overseer announced.

"Not now," Aldin said, waving his hand behind his back as if to shoo an annoying companion away.

"Aldin!"

"Damn it all, Tia, it's Waterloo down there," Zergh said. "This isn't some damn holo, or dressing up a bunch of primitives, this is some sort of reenactment of it."

"We should be searching for the wormhole device," Tia insisted.

"What? You've got to be kidding," Hobbs said, pointing back at Vush. "That damn idiot doesn't know where to look for it. It's a fool's errand, and besides I want to watch this."

"If we don't find the wormhole machine, a hell of a lot of worlds are going to get cooked," Tia argued.

Aldin looked over at her as if she were a teacher who had broken up some guilty little game behind the school building. He looked over at Oishi, who he could see was bitten by the bug of curiosity as well, even though Waterloo meant nothing to this samurai who had lived a hundred years before the battle was even fought.

"We could search that building for years and stumble across

the damn machine and not even know it," Oishi finally said, coming up with a quick defense.

Aldin looked back at Vush.

"Ever see a battle before?"

He could almost sense that the Overseer was filled with curiosity.

"I don't think they're real," Aldin said. "Most likely simulationbots—artificial people—so there really isn't any blood being spilled."

"I'm relieved, even though this does seem like an evil thing to find amusement in."

"Come on," Aldin said, "be honest, do you even know what it is that you're looking for?"

Vush hesitated for a long moment.

"No. I barely remember even finding the first machine."

"There, the truth at last," Hobbs announced. "Now settle back and have a drink."

"But we should be looking."

Oishi stood up and went over to look out the window.

"If anyone or anything can guide us to it, it's that First Traveler machine," the samurai said while pouring himself a cup of sake.

He looked back over at Vush, motioning for him to take the drink. The Overseer took the cup and downed it, his multifaceted eyes flickering for a moment. Oishi poured another drink for himself.

"Something is broken on this world. We all saw that. Most likely when that mountain back there was made." He pointed to the black volcanolike peak still clearly visible.

"It hit near the control center and scrambled something up. Everything started to work at cross-purposes. Those First Traveler machines I suspect are the daimyos of this creation. It is no longer controlling, it is letting everything fall apart while it plays games.

"The game has become everything to it, and it picked Napoleon as its rival. There's nothing we can do now until it is willing to acknowledge that we even exist. You saw how it behaved, ignoring all of us. For some reason it found something in Napoleon, and I half suspect this game is a test.''

He downed his sake in one gulp, his eyes watering. A smile lit his features.

"So let us settle back and just wait for it to finish. Napoleon is down there, so is Yaroslav. When the battle's done we'll see what happened.''

He hesitated for a brief moment.

"Is that acceptable, my lord?'' he asked, looking over at Aldin as if he had momentarily forgotten himself.

Aldin smiled his thanks, as if he had been relieved from having to make a decision that he knew was futile and thus take them away from this spectacle.

"Power up the cameras,'' Aldin said. "Let's get some close-up views.''

"I'll bet one hundred thousand on Napoleon,'' Hobbs said happily, moving his chair up closer to the screen.

"There's an incredible energy flux down there, almost identical to a jump-down beam,'' Corbin said, looking up at Hassan, who stood beside him.

"What is that?''

"It means that something is moving matter, a lot of it, from one place to another.''

"How long to get there?''

"Twelve, thirteen hours. It's slow going inside this Sphere, there's too much junk and machines floating around inside here and it's way over on the other side,'' Corbin said cautiously, feeling a tickle of fear whenever he was now forced to say something that he knew Hassan would not want to hear.

"Make it faster,'' Hassan said, and all Corbin could do was lower his head and nod an agreement.

CHAPTER 11

"WHAT DO YOU THINK!"

Yaroslav looked around in stunned disbelief. For nearly an hour the formations had materialized, one after the other. Nearly a hundred guns of the Grand Battery appeared inside a prepared position, gunners, caissons, horses arrayed around the bronze guns. Blocks of men—regiments of the line, light infantry, and the vaunted Imperial Guard—were formed in columns, ready for the assault. The wide variety of cavalry units were last—light hussars in their splendid skintight trousers and dangling peacock-hued jackets; lancers, ulans, chaussers, and dragoons; and finally the heavy-assault horsemen, the cuirassiers with burnished breastplates and plumed helmets.

He had stood by watching in stunned silence, barely noticing that after the first few minutes Napoleon had gone over to the field table. As if conjured from his own will, a staff started to appear, the array of uniforms dazzling, some dressed in the skintight doeskin breeches and sky blue jackets of hussars, others in the resplendent finery of Imperial Guardsmen, high bearskin caps dripping with the light rain that came down from the clouds overhead, forming where clear blue sky had been only moments before.

The rain passed, the ground wet underfoot, the sun, building in its variable phase, becoming brighter by the moment. Several marshals were now present, along with a bevy of officers. The features of most were clear, distinct, and almost imbued with all the nuances of genuine life; others had that slightly vague look of not being fully formed, like indistinct extras standing in the background of a holo drama.

He kept thinking that this must be what it all was, a computer-generated holo drama. But no, it wasn't. A horseman, galloping off with a dispatch splattered him with mud, a marshal, shouldering his way past, actually pushed into him, almost knocking him on his back.

"Yaroslav!"

He looked up, and Napoleon was gazing straight at him.

"Stop gawking. You're supposed to be chief of staff, now get over here!"

Feeling self-conscious, the old philosopher and onetime historian went up to the table, realizing that the circle of men around Napoleon was looking straight at him. He suddenly felt decidedly underdressed for the occasion. He was wearing a loose-fitting tunic of silk in a design that could almost be Gaf, a pale yellow with red borders, his trousers red, offset by the latest craze of a broad sash of mauve-colored polyester, rather than a far more sensible belt.

The men about him were truly elegant, and he could see the sense to it, the decking out in finery for war; it lent it all a martial bearing, and he suddenly found himself wishing that he too could have a cocked hat and a broad-shouldered jacket with gold epaulets.

"You're familiar with the battle?" Napoleon asked.

Yaroslav nodded. "The history that's been handed down, that survived the destruction of Earth. Several good military histories of you are still around, written by the likes of Rothenberg, Chandler, and Schneid, which are considered to be the best."

Napoleon hesitated for a brief instant, a slightly aghast look on his features, but then he pushed the questions aside.

"And what did they say?"

Yaroslav looked around at the men who were waiting.

"Several mistakes were made. Jérôme should not have allowed himself to be drawn into Hougoumont, the battle on your left should have been a screening action to pin down the Alliance right, which was your original intent but not executed as you wished. Just threaten the right to make him use his best troops to cover the line of retreat to the coast. Hougoumont was a deathtrap that should have been avoided."

"Go on," Napoleon said, and he looked over meaningfully at a man who Yaroslav realized bore a resemblance to the emperor. The whole thing was now remarkably strange. He imagined that across a thousand nights Napoleon had, in the sleepless hour of midnight, replayed what had happened here and was now acting on it.

"But these aren't the real men," Yaroslav said softly.

"I know what they are!" Napoleon snapped. "But they are real to this moment, they need to understand, they will act as they really did. For the purpose of what is happening they are real. Now tell them!"

Yaroslav gulped hard, looking over at Jérôme, and could see that this man, or reproduction or whatever he was, was definitely not pleased to be told of a mistake in the presence of the emperor.

"Most importantly of all, though, you must take direct control of the battle," Yaroslav said sharply, looking first at Napoleon and then over at a red-haired marshal whom he suspected was Ney.

"You might have thought Wellington to be of small account, and thus Ney could handle him while you looked to your right flank, but Ney made too many mistakes."

"This is outrageous," the red-haired marshal snapped. "Who is this pajama-clad old goat?"

"He is my chief of staff for this battle," Napoleon said, his voice full now with a cold dark power.

"But . . ."

"No buts," Napoleon said, and he raised his gaze from the maps on the table.

"You might be Ney, you might not be Ney. But I suspect that you will act as my old comrade once did."

Napoleon came around from behind the table, and walking up to the marshal, he reached up and put his hand on the man's shoulder.

"We lost the last time. You were wrong, and I should have seen that. Now we do it again, and this time we do it right.

"I can assume—" He pointed out across the field, to where on the low distant ridge could be seen the deployed army of the British, Dutch, and Hanoverians. "—that the Wellington over there will do it different this time as well, attempting to anticipate my changes. And thus our own orders will be changed."

He smiled up at Ney.

"I should have put you in charge of the pursuit of Blücher and not Grouchy, he was always too slow. I need the Prussians stopped; you are the one to do it. I trust you enough to do that for me. Ney, I need you for this victory."

Ney's features softened.

"It is good to be with you again, my emperor."

Napoleon hesitated, looking back at Yaroslav.

"Is this real?" Napoleon finally asked. "All of this, it is too much, all too much."

"It is as real as it can be," Yaroslav replied, as confused by everything as Napoleon, but not willing to admit it at this moment when he sensed that the emperor above all else needed some reassurance in this strange world. There had to be a purpose behind this battle that could later be used to their advantage. He half suspected that the machine had clicked into an aberrant line of logic; if it was defeated, the defeat might shake it loose.

From the corner of his eye Yaroslav saw a puff of smoke. He turned to look, and from the direction of the enemy line, less than eight hundred meters away, another puff of smoke snapped out, and then all down the line. Seconds later a high moaning passed overhead, a plume of mud geysering up not fifty paces away. Within seconds sprays of mud and dirt were kicking up all around them. An orderly not a dozen feet away suddenly disappeared in a spray of blood, his decapitated body tumbling end over end.

"By the gods, this *is* real," Yaroslav screamed, his cry cut short when a twelve-pound solid shot hummed past, the concussion staggering him.

A howitzer shell burst overhead, fragments humming down; a mounted messenger started to scream, holding what remained of his left arm that had been severed at the elbow.

Replica, holo, or real, the arm lying on the ground sent a wave of nausea through Yaroslav.

"It certainly feels real," Napoleon said calmly, turning away to look back at the enemy line.

"So he decided to start things off instead," the emperor said, looking back at his staff.

"Ney, you have your orders, now ride like the devil. Skirt the south of the Paris woods and go cross-country; Grouchy will be south of Wavre. Take command of his corps, detach one division to pin the Prussian corps there, take the rest of your men and move west, and leave the artillery behind if need be to support the one division at Wavre. I want you back here with the rest of Grouchy's corps supporting my right at Plancenoit. They'll have to move twenty kilometers and be ready for action before the day is done. Do that, and the glory of this victory is yours!"

Ney, saluting, turned and called for his horse. A cluster of staff closed in around the marshal as he mounted.

"Sire, I'll see you at sundown on the field of victory!"

Rearing up his mount, he set off at a gallop, leaping his horse over a fieldpiece that had been upended by the British barrage.

"This time, by God, we're going to do it!" Napoleon shouted, looking back at the others.

Yaroslav could almost feel the electric charge of excitement gripping the men around Napoleon. He felt it as well, and for a moment he forgot the terror of the shelling they were experiencing.

Napoleon called Yaroslav over to the table and pointed at the map.

"Wellington's changed things already. I opened the barrage before; now he has done it instead. But he'd be a fool to try an assault. Less than a third of that army of his is reliable; a fair part of them were on my side only a year ago. They don't want this fight and will get out of it if we break the British."

A shell screamed past and burst directly behind the group, bowling over several more staff officers.

"And he's trying to kill us in the opening move," Yaroslav said. "Might I suggest we pull back a bit out of range."

Napoleon looked at him as if he were mad.

"And let the troops see their emperor run from a little rain?"

Yaroslav looked back up at the others, who were gazing at him disdainfully.

Basak growled at Yaroslav.

"First fun I've had in years," the berserker snarled. "When do we attack?"

Napoleon laughed, slapping the Gaf warrior on the back.

"Can you ride a horse?"

The Gaf growled as if insulted and nodded, even though it was the first time in his life that he had seen one.

"You can go in with the guard when the time comes. What time is it?" Napoleon asked.

"Ten-thirty, sire," an orderly replied.

"I started at eleven. It was too late, I realize now," he said. He looked down at his boots, which were caked in mud. "We can't move the artillery up closer yet."

He looked back at the British line.

"Tell the Grand Battery to open up and to concentrate to the left center of the British line."

An orderly galloped off, and several minutes later a deep-throated roar rolled across the field.

Napoleon stood impassive, while Yaroslav tried to avoid ducking whenever a shell or solid shot passed within fifty meters of their position.

"All right then," Napoleon finally said. "Jérôme, skirmish

on the left, one division, not a single man more. We want him to think that is where the main assault will hit, so act as if you are screening something bigger to come. Do you understand me?''

The slight man standing with a sulky expression nodded in reply.

"Do not get drawn into Hougoumont, but let them think that if they do not cover it well, we'll sweep past their right and threaten their communication to the sea.''

He turned away from his brother.

"D'Erlon, to you falls the hard task.''

"Whatever your command, sire.'' The portly marshal came up to salute.

"In one hour, at eleven forty-five, you are to go in there.'' He pointed across the field.

Yaroslav looked up and saw the emperor gesturing to the right of a small chateau that he assumed must be La Haie Sainte, a building that marked the center of the Alliance line and rested alongside the road to Brussels.

"You will advance in columns of battalions on a division front; you are to go straight in.''

D'Erlon nodded, looking across the field. "My support?''

"Milhaud, Jacquinot, their divisions of cavalry will be in support on your right flank.''

"And my left flank, sire?''

"In the air, but flanked by the Grand Battery.''

"They'll hit me there on my left; it's exposed,'' D'Erlon replied, unable to keep from ducking when a shot winged by so close that his cape billowed out.

"Exactly, let him. But you've got to hold. Bachelu's division will remain here on the crest and hold my center and left. At the same time, I want a second Grand Battery of guns to move forward toward Hougoumont; the ground should be drier by then. The battery is to suppress that chateau so it will not threaten our flank in the center, but it must not be done until he is moving to protect his left. Once he has committed his reserves against you, D'Erlon, Lobau and the entire sixth corps will advance by the oblique with you masking them. They will deploy to your right and we will have them flanked, while they have committed to your left!''

He looked over at Yaroslav.

''That will be the key moment. Lobau will swing into their left, Wellington will be shifting to counter, and then the Imperial Guard will sweep straight up the middle,'' he said excitedly, pointing out the movement on his map. ''The secondary battery will cover the guard's left, the main battery firing overhead to continue pounding their center. That will be the moment he breaks!''

Yaroslav looked out across the field and could not help but feel nervous.

''Looks a bit like Pickett's charge,'' Yaroslav said.

''What?''

''Oh, nothing, I guess you know best though.''

''Of course!''

A solid shot plowed in, striking the muddy ground just in front of the knot of officers, spraying Napoleon with mud.

''Now go!''

The men, with excited shouts, saluted and ran to their mounts, their staffs cheering as they wheeled and galloped off to their respective commands.

''Shall we inspect the line?'' Napoleon asked, and without waiting for Yaroslav's reply he went over to a horse, allowing himself to receive help to be boosted up into the saddle.

''I haven't ridden in years,'' Napoleon confessed, nervously edging the horse around as if to judge its temper. A howitzer shell exploded behind them, a second later an entire caisson going up with a thunderclap. The horse shied away, fidgeting, but he held in a tight rein till the animal calmed down.

Yaroslav looked up at Napoleon.

''Well, are you going to follow me on foot?''

''I can't ride,'' Yaroslav confessed, ashamed at the snickers that sounded behind his back.

Napoleon gave him a look of exasperation.

''Then someone can lead your mount. Now let's get going.''

Driven primarily by a desire to get away from the uncomfortable shelling, Yaroslav allowed himself to be boosted onto the back of a small mare, a hussar taking hold of the reins and falling in alongside Napoleon, who started down the slope to where the Grand Battery of nearly a hundred guns was methodically at work, bombarding the Alliance positions across the valley. The field was already choked with smoke, but through the billowing clouds he could clearly see the other ridge, the guns winking with a flash of light and a puff of smoke.

Everything was pandemonium, the whistling moan of shot winging by, the terrified screams of horses that had been hit, the cries of the wounded, the cheers of the men as Napoleon rode past, the units drawn up in battle-line formation, taking off their caps, waving, calling out the emperor's name.

Napoleon's eyes were ablaze. He reined up in front of a formation, stopping by the regimental colors, and leaning out grabbed hold of the stained silken folds of a French tricolor.

"Men of the Thirty-second, I remember you!" he shouted.

Yaroslav looked closely at the unit. Almost all the faces had that hazy indistinctness to start, but as Napoleon looked out upon them, more and yet more of them suddenly started to take on a sharper form, as if the First Traveler machine were still reaching into his memories, and with a light stroke of an imagined brush, now painted in the fine details.

"You gave me victory on half a dozen fields; I am certain you will do so again today."

The men cheered as he kissed the folds of the flag, and he then continued on to stop at the next regiment down the line and grabbed hold of their flag.

"Men of the glorious Twenty-eighth, you were with me at Austerlitz, you were among the first to break their line. Will you add a new legend to your crown of glory today?"

The men roared their approval, several of them breaking ranks to come up to his mount, reaching out almost reverently to touch his horse or his mud-caked boot.

He looked out at the men, and Yaroslav could see the tears in his eyes as he let the flag drop from his hand and rode on.

Yaroslav looked back to see a heavy shot plow into the ranks where they had been only a moment before. The round cut a bloody swath through the line, a loud scream cutting the air, but Napoleon did not look back.

Yaroslav felt his senses reeling. What was real anymore? His sense of logic, of reality, told him that somehow this was not real. The real Waterloo had been fought on a world long since dead, a legendary home where legends had lived.

Yet now he was riding with a legend, the cheers echoing across the fields. And what was the reality of all this? How was it to be interpreted? Was this a game? What was happening to the men around him, was that an illusion? Could he be killed in this madness? He felt another shot flutter past. He didn't want to test that question out, suddenly wondering if the machine was tapping into his thoughts. If I wish my own death, would that now happen? he wondered with an almost superstitious fear.

And yet why was this happening? Was the machine insane, was this entire world insane and this was now a manifestation of it?

"You're wondering just what in hell is going on," Napoleon said, looking over at Yaroslav.

"You could say that," Yaroslav replied, shouting to be heard above the thunder of the Grand Battery.

Napoleon paused for a moment and breathed in deeply. The field stank with a rotten-egg smell, but Napoleon seemed to breathe it in as if it were a fine perfume.

"This was my world," he shouted, gesturing with his hand to all that was around them. "I don't know why he did this for me, but by God, I'll give him a fight he won't forget."

Napoleon looked over at Yaroslav, smiling.

"And you get to try it one more time."

A flash of a pained look crossed the emperor's features, and he drew closer.

"I know it is not real," he whispered, and then he paused.

"But then again," he finally said, a smile crossing his features once more, "who is to say what is real, and what is illusion. I'll leave that one to the philosophers like you."

Yaroslav looked past Napoleon to where an entire division stood in formation, flags floating on the breeze, shells bursting overhead. The sight was magnificent. It was becoming increasingly difficult to keep a sense of abandon from taking hold.

"It's a machine you're fighting against," Yaroslav said, as if trying to reassert some type of inner detachment from the incredible display around him. "It can calculate every aspect of this battle down to the final probability. It will know every odd, everything to the twentieth decimal point. It will be nearly impossible to defeat."

Napoleon looked over at Yaroslav and smiled.

"But this—" He pointed to the serried ranks of D'Erlon's corps. "—this is a different reality from pieces moving on a chessboard. This is the ultimate game, a game of timing, of knowing the precise moment to strike. In that he faces a grand master, and I shall beat him at it."

A thunderclap showered them with mud and a hot gust of wind.

"I do think our Wellington is aiming directly at me," Napoleon said. "Most unsporting of him."

Napoleon urged his horse forward, and Yaroslav followed.

"For that matter," Yaroslav said, "it can read our thoughts, we know that. It could thus already know everything you plan and act accordingly."

"A gentleman wouldn't do that," Napoleon replied, "and Wellington, damn him, is above all else one of those damn haughty English gentlemen.

"And besides, if it could, then what purpose would there be? There would be no challenge, no spirit, no game. He has made illusion into reality and must live by the spirit of that reality."

He looked over at Yaroslav.

"I think that is the key to all of this. It quite simply is bored. It has the power to make a universe." He swept his arm out with a dramatic flair. Yaroslav looked about as if almost to remind himself that he was inside the Sphere.

"It wanted something different, a challenge, and I shall give it to him."

He paused, looking over at Yaroslav.

"And then you shall write the peace as you need it to be written, that is what I shall give to you and your friends for returning this to me."

A shot hummed past in front of them, striking into a column of men, several of them going down in a bloody heap. Napoleon barely looked.

He paused for a second and then turned back to Yaroslav.

"You thought me heartless," he said, his voice sharp with a sudden anger. "A general who loves his men too much will not win battles.

"And," he continued, his voice dropping, "he will also go mad. At least this time I will not have that thought to bother me when I watch them die."

Even though he believed it not to be real, it nevertheless did look all too real as he gazed at an infantryman, holding the body of a comrade, and though its face was that hazy indistinctness, it nevertheless had a look of anguish to it as it gazed upon the stilled body cradled in its arms.

Reaching the top of a low rise, Napoleon called for a telescope, and uncapping it he quickly scanned the enemy lines.

"They're moving some of their units to the reverse slope. Just as he did last time. Good, very good, it means they're getting hit hard. Another half hour should do it. By then the ground will have dried out a bit more."

Yaroslav suddenly realized that he was starting to feel warm, and he looked up to see that the sun was shining brightly straight overhead. He noticed as well that their ship was hovering more than a kilometer above them.

It must be quite a show from up there, he thought, remembering how so many years ago he would have been in the ship, having a drink with Aldin while monitoring some primitive conflict on a backworld for the pleasure of the Kohs. Well now he was in the middle of it.

He looked up, and unable to contain himself, he waved a crude but unmistakable gesture, at the sight of which Basak, who had been trailing behind them on foot, gave out a barking shout of approval.

Aldin sat back in his chair and roared with delight.

"Well, the old devil is certainly having the time of his life," Hobbs announced, waving a salute at the screen as if Yaroslav could somehow see him.

"I'd give anything to be down there with him," Zergh said, shaking his head with envy.

"It looks like real cannon shot flying around down there," Aldin said.

"The hell with it. I'm old, it'd almost be worth it to be able to say I rode with Napoleon at Waterloo."

"A deadly simulation of Waterloo," Oishi interjected.

The samurai got up from his chair and went to the forward viewport to look straight down at the action a kilometer below.

"Impressive though, damn impressive," the samurai said almost wistfully. "We hadn't seen armies like that in Japan since Tokugawa. My grandfather, my mother's father, was with him during the Civil Wars. I always dreamed of leading a division of mounted samurai in a charge."

"Well, it's Yaroslav that got lucky," Zergh sniffed, "and we're stuck up here."

"The Prussians are definitely on the move," Aldin said, motioning to a side monitor that was tracking events on the right flank.

"He'll be outnumbered two-to-one by the end of the day. I don't see how he can do it," Hobbs said.

"He's Napoleon," Zergh replied defensively, as if a personal insult had been leveled.

Aldin ordered up a light lunch, and the servobot returned from the galley loaded down with a tray of sandwiches and cold drinks. The shifting of several Alliance regiments down to Hougoumont, and the withdrawal to the reverse slope of most of the infantry, elicited a flurry of comments and a number of small side bets as to intentions and results. Zergh, with a brief play on the computer, brought up an old holo sim of the actual battle and projected it into the center of the room, with an overlay of the situation below so that comparisons could be made.

"I think something is stirring," Oishi said, and motioned to a monitor.

Aldin looked up, catching a worried tone in Oishi's voice.

"What is it?"

"There's something moving on the far side of the sun. It's been tracking straight toward us for half an hour, weaving through the junk out there."

Aldin went over to look at the screen. It was still more than two million kilometers away, but looking at the tracking it was obvious that whatever it was, the object was coming straight toward them.

"A ship?"

"I think so," Oishi said.

"Who then?"

"It wouldn't be Bukha, he'd have contacted us. That only leaves the Overseers."

"Or Corbin."

"Damn it," Aldin hissed, turning away from the screen. "How long before they get here?"

"Hard to say," Oishi replied. "They keep changing their speed. Maybe eight hours, perhaps nine. If they go much beyond two hundred thousand k an hour they're bound to run into something, it's such a mess out here."

"Can we go down and get those fools out of there?"

"I wouldn't try it," Zergh said. "You saw the energy field that blocked it off. It might fry our systems, and stupid as it sounds, a twelve-pound shot could actually do us a lot of damage."

"There they go!" Hobbs shouted excitedly, pointing to the forward viewport, barely noticing the other crisis that was looming.

Aldin stepped away from the scanning monitor and went up to join Hobbs and the others who were pushing around the port to get a better view. Even from a kilometer straight up the sound was almost deafening. The batteries on both sides were in full play. An entire corps from Napoleon's line was advancing forward, the deep rumble of the drums, the bugles, and cheers counterpointing the deeper bass of the artillery. The large block formations moved forward with a stately grace, like an inexorable wave, the men moving in a steady cadence, a cloud of skirmishers sweeping ahead of the line, swarming out in an arc several hundred meters forward of the advance.

"Starting his move out the same way as last time," Zergh announced. "That's D'Erlon's corps hitting the left center of the British line."

A flurry of activity started on the Alliance side. Two block formations of cavalry mounted up and started to move to the opposite flanks of the French advance. On the reverse side of the low hill, other block formations of infantry started to deploy out into lines, while from the center a brigade of infantry started to move at a right angle to the advance, to position itself where the main blow would fall.

The main column continued its advance, reaching the bottom of the valley and starting up the opposite slope. The skirmishers were by now heavily engaged, driving back a thin red line of British skirmishers who suddenly broke and ran straight up the slope. Hobbs, who by now was betting a significant portion of his remaining fortune on the battle, let out a groan until he realized that they were clearing the field for the artillery to open up.

The charge now moved to a quick step, and at almost the same moment half a dozen batteries opened up, the front of the advance crumpling. From the right flank of the advancing column several regiments of French cavalry deployed out and started in at a trot. On the far left of the British line their cavalry started to deploy out to counter the advance of the French horses.

"He's still tracking in on us," Oishi announced.

"Well, we've still got plenty of time left," Aldin said, unable to turn away from the viewport.

"I bet Yaroslav's having the time of his life," Zergh said jealously.

* * *

"Damn it!" Yaroslav screamed, ducking low as a lazy shot, which had skipped into the ground fifty meters ahead, bounded up over his head with an ugly hiss and then continued on.

The battle ahead looked like complete chaos. The head of the column continued up the slope, the front ranks going down from the artillery blasts.

"Another hundred paces, that's all," Napoleon snapped, nervously slapping his hand against his thigh.

He looked over at Yaroslav.

"A bit too soon; another half hour of artillery from the Grand Battery would have shaken them up enough; just a bit too soon. It's timing, it's always a question of timing."

The left flank of the advancing column started to crumple in, while the right flank battalions appeared to gain momentum. The distant roll of the *pas de charge* echoed even as the column broke into a double-quick time, fifteen thousand voices shouting. The charge swept up over the crest of the hill, swarming two of the batteries under.

"Now comes the counterstrike," Napoleon said, and he pointed to the devastated left flank of D'Erlon's column.

From over the crest of the opposite ridge an advancing column of British cavalry appeared, coming in hard.

"Scots Greys?" Yaroslav asked.

"The same," Napoleon replied, scanning their advance with his telescope. "They're the best troops, and the worst led in all of Europe."

The charge came on over the slope, and the Grand Battery, firing over D'Erlon's column, started to place its shot in among them. The charge swept around La Haie Sainte and pressed in.

"Tell Roussel to move his cavalry up to support!" Napoleon shouted and another courier galloped off.

The fighting on the right flank of the advance continued to press in, but the left continued to waver; a scattering of men, turning into a steadily increasing torrent, were breaking away and streaming toward the rear.

"It's not looking good," he said quietly.

A high clarion call sounded, and to his left Yaroslav saw

Roussel's cavalry division move out. Beyond the division and to the left flank, however, there was another sight that caught him by surprise: several British regiments were moving out on the far side of Hougoumont and actually advancing toward the main French line.

Napoleon noticed it at the same time and studied the advance intently for a moment.

"A smart one, that Wellington. He knows Jérôme is on my left; he's trying to draw him into a fight, to weaken my center. Courier!"

Another staff officer moved up.

"Tell my brother not to be drawn in—to hold position."

The officer saluted and galloped off.

Roussel's cavalry moved past, heading down into the valley where the entire left of D'Erlon's corps had given way, the center of the corps starting to waver as well, some units continuing to advance into the assault while others attempted to pivot. Two of the regiments were already going into square formation, thus halting the advance of regiments further back in the line of assault.

"He's got to hold," Napoleon snapped, and turned to look back at the main part of the assault. It was impossible to distinguish anything now. A steady stream of messengers started coming back from the front, calling for reinforcements to bolster the left of D'Erlon.

Napoleon waved them off impatiently, watching as an entire division broke and was routed, the enemy cavalry wading in among them.

"Tell Kellermann to get ready and for Lobau's corps to move out now!" Napoleon shouted.

Excited couriers galloped back over the ridge, and a moment later Yaroslav found that he could almost feel the rumble of fifteen thousand men of the sixth corps starting out, masked by the ridge and moving to the right.

Napoleon continued to wait, and the first refugees of the defeat of D'Erlon's left started to stream past his headquarters, rushing to get past staff officers who attempted to re-form the broken units. Yaroslav suddenly started to feel as if the battle was getting out of control. Napoleon seemed to be caught in a paralysis of inaction, unable to respond to what looked like a disaster.

From the opposite crest there were occasional flashes of French standards, the division of Durutte having taken the château of Papelotte, thus anchoring the advance of the extreme right; beyond the chateau a swirling cavalry action was still in progress, Jacquinot's cavalry engaged in a freewheeling brawl with that of the Alliance.

And then from the right, spilling over the crest, came the advancing wave of Lobau's corps, moving fast to the right; a solid block of men, in columns of battalions on a division-wide front, started down the slope, trumpets and the *pas de charge* rumbling. Yaroslav felt his heart going into his throat at the sight of it, a cold sweat of excitement giving him a strange chill sense.

Directly ahead, Roussel's cavalry finally brought some relief to D'Erlon's battered left, but the center of the valley was still a mass of confusion.

On the far left, the secondary battery was moving forward to bring Hougoumont into close range; however, the British regiments deployed forward were putting up a spirited fight, and it was apparent that Jérôme was gradually being sucked in.

"They're shifting," Napoleon said, offering his telescope over, and Yaroslav brought the instrument up to look. It was hard to see the opposite ridge until the smoke parted for a moment. There seemed to be a cloud of dust rising up and occasional flashes of musket barrels and blocks of men moving just beyond the ridge, barely visible. They were moving hard to their own left. He was right. Wellington, seeing Lobau, was moving to counter the blow, while demonstrating on his own right. The Alliance army was on the move, and he knew enough of Napoleonic warfare to know that it would take long minutes to change deployments once orders had been given. Even a computer enemy could not alter that.

"Now for the guard, move it all now!" Napoleon suddenly shouted.

The group broke, riding off to their respective commands.

Roussel's division of cavalry continued its move against the British cavalry that had harried D'Erlon's retreating troops, but D'Erlon's right was still holding the ridge, Lobau's corps moving rapidly to push alongside of him.

He thought a rattle of drums was sounding from behind; it grew in volume, a thunder that set his teeth on edge. Up the road from the rear came the guard cavalry with several batteries of guns, their drivers lashing the mounts. The heavy cavalry plunged up over the ridge, past where Napoleon was.

"Vive l'empereur!"

The charge swept down the hill. A flourish of bugle calls sounded in the valley, and Roussel's command, having completed its task of screening, pulled aside. The British cavalry, seeing the fresh onslaught, turned and started into a retreat.

Behind them Yaroslav saw all the Imperial Guard start to move out, moving straight up either side of the Brussels road, deployed out into columns of battalions, their front a quarter mile across, fifteen thousand men moving as one. Forward, the Grand Battery redoubled its effort, plunging a concentrated bombardment into La Haie Sainte, covering for the guard batteries that galloped up to within seventy-five meters of the chateau before turning to unlimber. Smoke cloaked the field.

Yaroslav looked to where Napoleon was pointing off to the right. Lobau's corps was moving up the slope, the men advancing at the double-quick, the forward battalions shaking out into a linear front to enhance firepower. A sheet of smoke snapped out from the British side, and long seconds later the first volley rolled across the valley and everything was lost to view.

"He's putting everything there!" Napoleon shouted. "Everything!"

The advancing column of the guard was now several hundred meters past the inn of La Belle Alliance, the column coming up over the top of the ridge.

"See, see!" Napoleon shouted, pointing to the center. "He went for it. D'Erlon breaks, and he thought he was drawing me in to support the right. He must have sent Uxbridge in with Lambert, perhaps even Picton, to block Lobau! Now he must rebalance or in fifteen minutes the guard will cut right through the middle!''

The center of the French army was shifting to the right flank behind the chaos of D'Erlon's assault, while the guard reserve advanced straight up through for the killing blow.

A courier came riding up from the east and reined in.

"Sire, the Prussians, they are moving into the woods.''

Napoleon nodded and waved the man off.

"They'll be on your flank soon,'' Yaroslav said.

"And if I wait for them, I'll be caught like last time. I must finish off Wellington now, then turn on Blücher. I must do it now!''

He looked over at another courier.

"Tell D'Erlon he's done all he can. Have him pull back and re-form on the Grand Battery, then prepare to shift front to the east to face the Prussians.''

The valley was chaos, but Yaroslav let himself be swept away with the grandeur of it all. Behind him the guard was continuing to move at a quick pace, a mounted band playing "The Victory March of Marengo.''

Napoleon looked over at them as the front of the column moved past and, unable to contain himself, tears streaked down his mud-splattered face.

"It is as it was,'' he said.

As if on impulse he turned his horse about and did a slow gallop across the field, moving to the front of the advancing guard. Yaroslav turned to follow him, grabbing hold of his own reins and clumsily kicking the horse to move. Basak, pulling out his great battle-ax, let out a triumphant roar and started to run alongside.

"Soldiers of the guard, your emperor fights alongside you today!'' Napoleon shouted, riding up alongside the column, taking his hat off and waving it.

A bone-chilling growl went up from the ranks, the men waving their muskets, some calling for him to go to the rear, others chanting his name. With a dramatic flourish he came up to the head of the great column, and taking up the battle-scarred standard of the guard, he held it aloft, and a triumphal shout of joy went up.

"It's worth dying right now!" Napoleon shouted. "He gave it back to me for a moment, and it's worth dying now!"

"We just might do that after all," Yaroslav said. "Don't you think your job's at the rear, in command?"

"This is the moment. If we do not break him now, before two o'clock, we stand no chance of turning in time to face the Prussians. It must be now!"

He stood up in his stirrups and raised his voice to a shout.

"I go in with the guard!"

Yaroslav found that there was no face-saving way in which he could turn aside. And besides, he realized, there was a fair part of him that did not want to turn away.

It'd be a hell of a story if I make it, he realized, and a hell of a story even if I don't.

The advance moved forward at a steady hundred and fifty meters a minute. From what he could see down in the valley, D'Erlon's corps was smashed except for a handful of regiments that still held the right of the line atop the crest. The ground finally started to flatten out and then gradually started to rise back up again, and directly ahead Yaroslav could now see the farmhouse of La Haie Sainte, ringed in fire, showers of rock and building timbers going up from the pounding delivered by the guard artillery that had drawn up before it.

To his left, the secondary battery was heavily engaged against Hougoumont, but several guns in the enclosed area were firing into the flank of the guard, tearing bloody furrows through the ranks. The ground ahead was chaos: dead and dying men and horses covered the field, the wheat trampled into mud. The guard cavalry, which was now forward, was nearly up to the crest of the hill, driving the British gunners back, the artillery fire slacking off at last.

Napoleon handed the standard to a waiting captain and motioned for the column to start forward at the quickstep. It was still several hundred meters out, but Yaroslav knew that timing was everything; they were now being unmasked from the smoke and confusion as they advanced straight up the slope, the *pas de charge* keeping a steady beat.

An advance line of skirmishers, moving in front of the main column, started to run, advancing toward the chateau less than two hundred meters ahead to join the guns. A musket volley snapped out, and the men charged. Moments later, from the far side of the chateau, a stream of men came pouring out, Keller-mann's cavalry sweeping in to cut off their retreat.

Yaroslav realized that this was the classic combination, all three armies advancing together, each in support of the other. On the ridge beyond, there was still heavy skirmishing between the few units of D'Erlon's that were still hanging on to their position and the British and Dutch units deployed to meet them. The guns that had been pounding the chateau started to limber up again to continue the advance.

The front of the guard columns swept past the battery posi-tion, the guns moving out only seconds before their arrival. The timing of it all awed Yaroslav, who turned and nodded to Na-poleon with admiration.

"Shouldn't we pull out of the charge now?" he shouted. "It's going to get awful hot once we crest that hill!"

Napoleon ignored him.

Damn, he was going all the way in, and Yaroslav found that there was nothing he could do but to follow, while Basak, wav-ing his ax, chanted a death song.

All were crowded about the viewport or the close-up moni-tors. Whatever it was that was approaching them was still a good five hours out, and Aldin could only hope that things below would be finished by then.

The formations below moved with a slow, majestic grandeur. The guard units were heading straight into the English lines, forward elements shaking out from column into line formation for increased firepower. On the far right the battle was at a crescendo. Lobau's sixth corps was over the crest of the ridge, smashing straight into nearly twenty thousand of Wellington's troops. Several more British columns were moving that way, though one in the middle seemed to be breaking down, part of it turning rapidly to face the advancing guard. The front of the British division still rushed to meet Lobau, the men in the middle stopping and milling about in confusion. Several of the units in the center were in square formation, engaged against French cavalry; others were attempting to shake back out into line formation in anticipation of the infantry assault.

The cavalry sweep to the far right was swinging into what looked like open air, the few Alliance elements there breaking and running. The trouble spot Aldin could see was the center. D'Erlon was having difficulty rallying his men, and a close-up camera revealed that the corps commander was in fact already dead in the confusion.

Several English brigades were firmly wedged into the battered corps, one of them nearly up to the French Grand Battery, which could not fire, so great was the confusion in front of them. Aldin caught a brief glimpse of "Wellington," who was at that moment moving to his own center, staff galloping alongside, several infantry regiments being pulled in to join him in a mad dash to face the main attack coming straight in. The sight looked bizarre in the extreme, a First Traveler machine surrounded by men on horseback, decked out in their resplendent finery. He wished that somehow the machine were wearing a cocked hat to make the absurdity of it complete.

The real trouble though was obvious. Several miles to the right of Kellermann's flanking attack, the Prussians were advancing through the Paris Woods. Already there was light cavalry skirmishing. Within a couple of hours the Prussians would be arriving.

"They're moving somewhat faster than the historical scenario," Zergh said.

"Well, maybe he's cheating," Aldin countered. He kept trying to remind himself that, after all, this was some sort of elaborate game, but he couldn't quite get it out of his mind that this whole thing was far more important than any of them quite realized.

Then there was the mysterious other ship closing in. Just who the hell were they? he wondered.

He had to stay, at least for the moment, but if the battle was still going on, and the interloper was Corbin, he'd have to leave Yaroslav, Basak, and Napoleon behind and hope for the best.

"There they go!" Oishi shouted, caught up in the excitement of the battle below.

The advance regiments of the old guard, screaming with a near maniacal fury, went into the charge, bayonets leveled, sweeping up the slope past La Haie Sainte, which was now wreathed in smoke and flames. Napoleon moved directly alongside the lead battalions, shouting, pointing for the advance to press in.

Basak leaped forward, battle-ax raised high, running with a long-legged stride, pushing his way through to be at the front.

They crested the hill, and for a brief instant Yaroslav felt as if they had charged straight into an empty field. And then, without warning, a solid, long rank of red stood up out of the high grass. For a brief instant he thought he saw Wellington on the far side of the field, and then everything disappeared in smoke.

Several things seemed to happen to him at once. He saw Basak stagger and go down, while beside him Napoleon's mount reared and turned, the emperor leaning forward, his features gone ashen. Yaroslav felt something pluck at his left arm, and then a numbness.

A whisper of an inner voice told him he had just been shot, but strangely there was no feeling.

The charge was staggered by the blow.

"The emperor, the emperor's been shot!"

Yaroslav looked over at Napoleon. He could see the streak of blood on the tan trousers, the ragged hole. Yaroslav edged up to him.

"You're hurt!"

Napoleon looked around wide-eyed and saw that he was now on center stage, the guardsman about them standing as if riveted, while another volley ripped out from the British side.

Yaroslav, balancing unsteadily on his stirrups, stood up.

"Soldiers of France, your emperor lives. Now charge!"

Napoleon, as if recovering his senses with Yaroslav's cry, looked about and held his hand up for all to see.

It was as if an explosion were unleashed. Up forward came a wild cry, the death song of a Gaf berserker, and it made Yaroslav feel like someone was driving a corkscrew down his spine.

The army surged forward, pulling Yaroslav and Napoleon along with it. They crested up over the top of the ridge, smashing into the enemy line, bowling it underfoot, and continued on forward. The next line held for a moment, another volley slashing out, and then it, too, disappeared, and within seconds Yaroslav felt as if he were caught in a mad race.

A staff officer came up to him, grabbing hold of his reins to pull him out of the advance, and Yaroslav swore at him, wanting to continue on in, madly envious of Basak, whom he could still hear, the death song replaced with one of joy, the battle-ax rising and falling.

The old guard pushed forward, the middle guard turning to the left oblique, the division of the young guard moving to fill the gap where D'Erlon's divisions had been torn apart, cutting in behind the British units that had been impetuous enough to advance down into the valley.

Yaroslav suddenly saw Napoleon again, off his horse amid a knot of men, and following the staff officer, he came up and slid down from his own mount, grimacing with the first shock of pain from his dangling useless arm.

"How bad is it?" Yaroslav cried, feeling a genuine concern.

"Bleeding a bit."

Yaroslav knelt down to take a look. There was no arterial bleeding, that would have been trouble. The musket ball had gone clean through his upper thigh, leaving a ragged hole that was slowly but steadily oozing blood.

An orderly had already removed his own sash, and tearing up a towel, he packed the wound under Yaroslav's directions and bound it tightly.

"That should take care of it for right now; we'll get you back aboard ship and patch it up once this is over."

"There's still a battle to be won," Napoleon said almost cheerfully. "You're hurt yourself," he said, and Yaroslav was touched that the emperor had noticed.

"A bit of a scratch."

"It's broken," Napoleon said. "You'll lose your arm."

"Not likely," Yaroslav growled. "Just splint it for me."

He stifled a groan while a rough splint was fashioned from a broken board and his arm was bound to his chest.

Napoleon, favoring his injured leg, stood back up and looked over at Yaroslav.

"You are hereby appointed major general with the Legion of Honor for what you did here."

Yaroslav could not help but beam with pride.

From the low rise he looked back out over the field. The entire left of the British line was giving way, streaming to the rear, Lobau's reserve division moving out in pursuit. Straight ahead, the old guard was pushing up toward the village of Waterloo. The guard cavalry that had pulled aside to let the main assault go in was now charging, hell-for-leather, against the English right, artillery in support. Infectious panic raced ahead of it, and the formations started to break up, streaming toward the rear. Red-coated infantry came pouring out of Hougoumont, which was now threatened with envelopment from all four sides. The Alliance army was in a rout, catching the infectious panic spreading from their own left.

Hobbling, Napoleon looked around the field, breathing deeply, his eyes damp.

"This is how it should have been!" he shouted, arms extended.

The staff around him was exuberant, shouting its congratulations as the spectacle of Wellington's army collapsing and streaming to the rear was played out before them.

Basak came hobbling back, his face streaming blood, more pouring from a bullet crease to his leg, and his ax dripping red.

"By the gods, these men know how to fight!" he roared, and

Napoleon went up to him, slapping the Gaf on the shoulder and looking around proudly.

A courier, pressing his way through the crush of the young guard, which was streaming past and advancing to the oblique behind the middle, maneuvered his way up to Napoleon.

"Sire, Prussian infantry are clearing the woods on the right!"

Stunned, Napoleon turned about, calling for a telescope. An aide brought the battered instrument up and stood before Napoleon so that he could balance it on the man's shoulder.

He scanned the field to the east, and as the smoke from the battle to take the ridge drifted away, Yaroslav felt his stomach knot up. Coming out of the woods two miles away was a solid black column of men.

"What is the time?" Napoleon shouted.

"A quarter after two, sire," an aide replied, holding up a glittering pocket watch.

"Too fast, far too fast," he grumbled. "Did that Wellington cheat somehow?"

"He changed things as you did," Yaroslav said. "He somehow put the spur on Blücher to move faster."

"It can't be all of his men, it can't be," Napoleon snapped, as if trying to reassure himself. "A division, two at most. They must be strung out on the road from a forced march. We should have at least had another hour."

"We don't," Yaroslav replied, and pointed down to the southeast where more and more units were emerging from the forest, extending the Prussian line southward.

"They'll be across my line of communication; if Plancenoit falls, they'll cut in from behind."

He turned away and looked back to the north, and Yaroslav sensed that the general was running a rapid calculation, weighing the odds, sensing out what needed to be done.

He looked back at his staff.

"Order the guard to halt their advance and to retire back to Plancenoit; they will be the reserve. Lobau is to press the British, drive them, don't stop. Push them back to Brussels and the sea. Kellermann's divisions of cavalry are to press in, but they're not to close the sack. Let them run, they're out of the war anyhow after this. Those damned Dutchmen and Hanoverians will be on our side anyhow within the month. D'Erlon is to rally at La Belle Alliance. Jérôme, Foy, and Bachelu are to turn to the east and form the center. Piré and L'Heretier's divisions of cavalry will screen our left and push the English back. Now all of you, ride!''

Napoleon hobbled back to his horse and grimaced with pain while a hussar gently eased him up into the saddle.

"Half a day's work done, my friends,'' he said. "Now let us finish the business.''

"By the gods, I've never seen forty thousand men run a footrace like this before,'' Zergh announced, holding up his glass as if in salute to the emperor.

"All right, they've won, now let's get them out of there,'' Aldin said nervously, looking over to the tracking monitor, which was showing that their company was coming in at an ever-increasing speed.

"How?'' Oishi asked.

"Try and get us down there,'' Aldin said.

Nodding in agreement, the samurai edged the controls forward and started to drop the ship down. The first hundred meters of descent the ship seemed to handle normally, and then it shuddered to a stop. Oishi eased the thrust up, they dropped a bit more, and then he was finally up to full power, but they remained stationary.

"You better shut it down,'' Hobbs said nervously. "If that mechanical monster should decide to suddenly shut his end off, we'll dig one hell of a crater down there and blow half the battlefield apart.''

Oishi snapped the throttle off.

"Jump-down beam?''

"Through that shielding?'' Zergh said. "They'll come up here looking like beef stew.''

"How much time before company arrives?''

"Four hours, maybe less.''

"Damn it," Aldin hissed.

"Should we leave them?" Vush asked nervously.

Aldin looked over at him coldly.

"He saved my life down on the Hole, I'll be damned if I leave him, let alone Napoleon and Basak."

"That berserker's having the time of his life down there anyhow," Hobbs interjected. "I think he'd kill you with his bare hands if you interfered in things right now. Besides, the battle isn't over yet."

Aldin looked back up at the side-mounted projection system. A full corps of Prussian troops was coming out of the woods, a second corps deploying out behind them. Further to the south, swirling columns of dust and the distortion created by the force field laid out over the battle zone obscured the view, but it looked like at least another corps was moving in.

"So what do we do?"

"I still haven't lost my bet," Hobbs said. "Let's see it out, perhaps Napoleon will get finished up by Blücher and we can get out of here before our visitors come in."

"They're hurt down there, all three of them," Tia said angrily, annoyed that the others had not even considered that fact.

"Part of the game," Vush said absently, to the surprise of everyone.

"They're going in," Hobbs suddenly cried, pointing to the monitor that was focused on a regiment of Prussian cavalry that was moving out toward Plancenoit, advancing down the road from Wavre.

"Just what the hell is he doing?" Zergh growled, and Aldin looked up to where his friend was pointing. It was evident that the new crisis was on the right. The guard divisions were already moving back in good order, having disentangled themselves from the fracas. They were in column, with flags held high, deploying back toward Plancenoit, moving through the carnage of where D'Erlon's corps had been so badly chewed up. The guns of the Grand Battery were being repositioned to face eastward as well, and the battered remnants of the dead Count D'Erlon's corps were forming. But Napoleon's left flank, which should have been moving in to cover the center and act as a fresh reserve, was advancing off in the opposite direction, the entire formation moving forward in pursuit of the retreating British.

"One corps can handle the pursuit. He's sending in two. Is he crazy?" Hobbs asked.

"That's his brother on the left; I think the other one was Foy—both under Reille. He's most likely run off on his own just like the last time."

"Well, he's going to have a hell of a hole and no reserve," Hobbs announced with a satisfied air. "I still might win this bet after all."

Yaroslav, his throat burning with a thirst he had not imagined possible, gratefully took the canteen from a guardsman. Tilting his head back, he let the water run down his throat. He tried to still his guilt with the thought that these men were not truly real. But from the corner of his eye he could see the man watching him intently, as if measuring out each precious drop that was disappearing. He stopped drinking, recapped the wooden flask, and handed it back down.

"*Merci.*"

"An honor, sir," the guardsman said, and turning away he continued to limp toward the rear.

"What time is it?" Napoleon shouted, trying to be heard above the steady roar of musketry that was volleying out barely a hundred meters away.

"Five o'clock," an aide replied.

Yaroslav looked over at the boy, who swayed unsteadily in the saddle, a trickle of blood coursing down his face from a saber cut to the forehead.

A regiment of Prussian cavalry had cleaved right through the line only minutes before, and they had all sought safety in a square of guards. The square had actually been cracked open at one point, until a charge of guard cavalry had driven them off. It seemed as if the Prussians had realized that Napoleon was sheltered within the unit, and they nearly all died trying to cut a way in. The hole in the line had been cobbled back together with a makeshift unit patched together from half a dozen different battalions.

From La Haie Sainte down to Plancenoit, the Prussians were exerting a steady and ever-increasing pressure. Yaroslav could easily imagine that as more units came in from Wavre they were immediately deployed and thrown in. The last of Napoleon's reserves had been used long ago. He was grimly holding with what was left, riding up and down the line, urging the men on, shouting encouragement until his voice was barely a whisper, his features drawn and ashen, the wound in his leg still trickling blood.

A report had come back from the north that elements of the British had rallied several miles beyond Waterloo and that the sixth corps was battering them, coming to a near standstill, the only good news being that Kellermann's cavalry was pushing around the flank and driving what was left. As for Reille, he had simply disappeared to the north, pursuing the Alliance troops up the road toward Braine-L'Alleud.

The mere mention of Reille or Jérôme would cause Napoleon to explode in a towering rage that would take minutes for him to recover from.

His army, outnumbered two-to-one, had smashed half of the enemy, but now an equal number, all of them fresh, were closing in, and he now had but barely thirty thousand exhausted men to face their sixty to seventy thousand.

Yaroslav found that with the increasing exhaustion he had become almost oblivious to the danger that was humming all about him. The steady thunder of battle had deadened his senses, except for the throbbing ache of the bullet-shattered arm, which was now jolting him every time the horse took even a single step.

"Bring me night or bring me Ney," Napoleon gasped, pulling up beside Yaroslav.

"I don't think we can count on nightfall around here," he said, looking up at the sun, which still glowed brightly directly overhead. The ship was still there, and he cursed them. Damn it all, couldn't they see he was hurt? But at the same time he felt a strange sort of pride for still hanging on, and not simply falling down, faking a convulsion of some sort to prompt them into using a jump beam. But then again, he wondered, if they could jump, Zergh would not have missed this for anything. Wellington must have put some sort of block on that.

"Sire!"

Napoleon looked up as a blood-smeared orderly, his horse limping, came up and saluted.

"They're forming up again. It looks like a fresh division at Plancenoit."

Napoleon nodded.

"Artillery is almost depleted. If they hit again we'll break."

He nudged his horse around and started southward, Yaroslav cursing, falling in beside him. To his amazement, Basak was still following them about, patting his ax, talking to it, chanting songs, exulting over the Legion of Merit that Napoleon had borrowed from one of his generals and pinned to the berserker's padded jacket.

A distant call of trumpets echoed, and a thundering volley of guns rolled out across the field. Napoleon reined up at the rear ranks of his guard divisions. The thin ranks waited while across the field the heavy block formations of the enemy came relentlessly forward, flanked to the north with regiments of cuirassiers and several batteries of mounted artillery. The guns pushed forward, deploying out a bare two hundred meters away.

Napoleon cursed angrily, turning to an orderly, screaming to him to find some guns, and the man galloped off.

The cuirassiers moved in closer.

"Should we form square?" Yaroslav asked.

Napoleon shook his head.

"Either way we're lost. Form square and the guns will pound us apart and their infantry will close in. Don't form square and the cavalry will crash through us.

"We stand here and if need be die. I allowed myself to leave my guard last time. I will not do so again."

The guns opened up, ranks of men going down from the

sprays of canister. To the right flank of the guns the cuirassiers started forward, slowly gaining speed.

A brigade commander came up to Napoleon, looking for orders.

"Hold the line, hold the line!" Napoleon shouted, his voice coming out a hoarse whisper.

The thunder of the hooves grew louder, the ranks of the enemy spreading out, sweeping forward. The trumpets rang out, sounding the charge, and with flashing swords, an inexorable wave a quarter mile across came in, the artillery to their flank cutting holes in the French line.

The disciplined ranks of the guard waited, first rank going down on one knee, bracing musket butts into the ground, bayonet points poised upward. The second rank stood behind them, muskets pointed straight forward. The third rank raised weapons up, waiting for the command, the few squadrons of cavalry still in any order forming up behind the line, ready to seal any breech.

The charge thundered in, sounding to Yaroslav like a tidal wave rolling forward to engulf them. He had an almost childlike desire to cover his ears to block out the sound of death, to close his eyes, hunch down, and look away. If this was a game, he had forgotten it long ago. It was deadly real, the carpet of bodies around him bleeding, screaming, crawling to escape, or torn and still looking up with blank eyes.

The cuirassiers were at a hundred meters, then seventy-five.

Yaroslav knew that so much of this was a deadly game of morale, of group psychology. Unless Wellington had programmed the horses to be totally insentient, they would react like any rational creature and refuse to be impaled upon the wall of bayonets, swerving aside at the last possible second. The cavalry was counting however on the simple terror that their approach would create. Yaroslav could see all so clearly just how terrifying that was. The ground shook beneath him, the air was filled with their thunder, and wild hoarse screams, sabers waving and flashing. Each man looked to be ten feet tall, and as they rode in stirrup to stirrup, it seemed as if they had become a single living machine, unstoppable. He wanted to turn to start to run. He could not imagine how any man in the line would not do likewise. Yet he knew as well that all of them, if disciplined enough, and if their courage still held after the hours of horrific pounding, had to realize that as long as they stood united they might possibly live. But if they broke, they would be a mob and cut to ribbons as the cuirassiers waded through them.

And as he thought these things, he barely heard the shouted commands for the rear rank to fire.

A plume of smoke roiled out, and all along the line horses and riders tumbled over, high animal shrieks now sounding clear above the thunder. For several seconds it looked as if the charge had been broken, and he wanted to raise a triumphant shout, but then through the smoke he saw them still coming on, sections of the enemy line moving in. Where shots had hit the line had buckled, but the weight of the second and third line pushed around and through the tangle. The charge closed in.

He could feel the line wavering, as if a collective will were coming to a decision, the decision between an inexorable mass moving forward, and a thin wall of steel deployed to stop it.

Here and there individuals turned, looking back, the entire line seeming to be pushed rearward by several feet, but not a single man broke and ran—they were, after all, the old guard. The charge closed in and then started to slide to a halt.

There was a clatter of steel, more shrilled screams of the horses, and a rising shout of thousands driven by terror, rage, and mad exultation. Here and there a mount, either already dying and blind or driven by madness, plunged into the bayonets, kicking and shrieking, the line beneath it buckling. At several points the wall was broken clean through, and the rear ranks of the Prussian cavalry surged forward into the gaps, like water pushing against a dam and springing through wherever a hole had been breeched.

Most of the line held, and the horsemen turned, slashing out with sabers, guardsmen thrusting upward, parrying the blows and then trying to stab rider or mount. Some of the horsemen let their sabers drop, leaving them dangling by their cinch cords to their wrists, and drew out pistols that popped off with low staccato bursts, while the rear rank of the guard worked feverishly to reload, discharging their muskets at point-blank range. Even the horses fought, turning, kicking, or reaching out to bite, one of them grabbing a guardsman directly in front of Yaroslav by the throat and pulling him up, snapping the man's neck before the horse was accidentally shot in the head by its own rider and both went down in a heap.

Most of the holes in the line were quickly sealed off, but one gap, to the south, started to broaden, Prussian cuirassiers breaking clean through into the open field behind the line. Napoleon looked over at the break in the line fifty meters to their right. A squadron of his guard chaussures galloped off to try to contain them. Forward, the battle raged on, while to the flanks of the advancing Prussians the artillery fire continued to pour in, striking so close that some of the shots plowed through their own men. To the other side of the artillery, a heavy column of infantry started to angle in, to strike the break at an oblique.

"The crisis is at hand," Napoleon announced sharply. He looked around, as if hoping somehow to conjure additional troops out of the ground, but none were to be had. To the north, what was left of D'Erlon's men were grimly hanging on. As to the pursuit of Wellington's men, Reille's corps had finally acknowledged the recall command but were still far off beyond Hougoumont.

The Prussian infantry closed in at double time, not bothering to deploy from column.

"If I had a dozen guns right now, I could blow them to hell," Napoleon snapped, and Yaroslav could not help but think of Richard's lament from Shakespeare.

The Prussian infantry forged in, striking just to the south of where their mounted comrades had started the breech. The entire line staggered, the volume of noise redoubling.

"Sire, the battle is lost!" an officer shouted, coming back from the line.

Napoleon looked around at his staff.

"Why are you staring like frightened children?" he roared, somehow regaining his voice.

He turned his horse about to face the widening breech.

"I lost the battle of Marengo at five o'clock," he cried, "and I won it back again at seven!"

He started forward.

Yaroslav came up alongside him.

"You'll get killed," he shouted.

Napoleon looked over at him.

"Go to the rear!"

"It's only a game, damn it!" Yaroslav cried. "It's only a goddamn game."

"Not for me. Not this time. I'll not lose this one again. It's better to die!" he cried, his voice carrying across the field.

A knot of guardsmen, falling back from the onslaught, turned to look at him.

"My emperor, save yourself," one of them shouted.

"I die here," Napoleon cried out in reply. A staff officer came up to grab his reins, and he reached out and with an angry jerk pulled the reins back so that the horse shied away.

"Soldiers of France!" Napoleon shouted, his voice high and clear. "Who of you will today turn your back on your emperor?"

The men around him stopped as if stricken.

"Then die with me for the glory of France," he shouted, urging his mount forward.

A drummer boy standing at the edge of the group picked up the *pas de charge*. Yaroslav watched in amazement as a thin line of stragglers, of broken and wounded men, fell in around Napoleon and surged forward, mingling in with the chaussures who struggled to contain the breech. On the far side of the break the line seemed to be melting away, but as if by strength of Napoleon's will alone the line to the north of the breech held firm.

Napoleon moved up to the very front, and at the sight of him the Prussian cavalry stormed forward, cursing and screaming, eager for the kill. Unflinching, he waited, guardsmen pushed forward around him, shouting their defiance, flinging themselves bodily in front of their emperor. Yaroslav, unable to contain himself, pulled up a lance stuck in the ground and moved up beside Napoleon, weakly thrusting it out, stunned when it caught a black-clad officer in the leg, sending the man backward. Basak was up on the other side, ax rising and falling as if his knotted arms were made of coiled steel.

The mad melee continued, and in spite of the indomitable will that seemed to radiate a resolve into those around him, Yaroslav realized that they were being swarmed under.

And then, as if from far off, he heard a roll of drums, the steady, bone-shaking roll of the *pas de charge*, a distant shout welling up to the heavens. A roaring volley cracked out.

Yaroslav, confused, looked around.

A growing cheer sounded, echoing louder and louder.

"Vive l'empereur, vive l'empereur!"

It came on louder and yet louder. And then another cheer sounded, rolling up from the south. Through the swirling confusion he could see that on the far side of the break the guard units, which but moments before were breaking apart, were now coming about, some with bayonets leveled, to charge back into the fray. Others, too exhausted to move, held their shakos aloft, waving and shouting.

"Ney, Ney!"

From out of the smoke a blue wall seemed to be advancing in, catching the Prussian columns full on the flank.

The attack before them started to break apart. A final surge of Prussian cavalry, unwilling to retreat, so close were they not only to victory but to the death of their foe, surged in, with one last desperate bid to snatch victory. Basak stood in front of Napoleon's horse cutting in low, crippling a cuirassier's mount and then with an uphanded swing cutting the cavalryman's arm off as he raised a sword up to strike Napoleon.

The charge broke apart, as Ney's troops and the remaining guard pushed in from behind.

The battle melted away.

A swarm of French infantry passed in front of the battered guard line at the double, their faces indistinct and yet neverthe-

less marked with exhaustion after a forced march of fifteen kilometers and a running assault at the end, accomplished in less
than five hours' time.

At the fore of the advance, Yaroslav saw Ney, hat gone, red
hair streaming, sword pointed forward, shouting with triumph,
urging the attack in.

Weakly standing in his stirrups, he watched as the first division of Ney's assault stormed past, pouring out of the south end
of the Paris Woods. It was obvious that the commands were
jumbled together. Yaroslav could sense that these men must have
been the strongest of Grouchy's troops, driven relentlessly, the
weakest falling by the wayside during the forced march to the
sound of the guns, the ranks mixing together and then surging
in. But the taste of victory drove them forward. Down the entire
length of the Prussian line the assault started to waver, and then
as if guided by a single hand the Prussian army started to break
off, turned, and retreated to the northeast. The few Prussian
cavalry to the front tried to slash their way out, one of them
turning and leveling a pistol. The gun went off, and an instant
later the man went down and disappeared.

Napoleon visibly slumped in the saddle and seemed to reel.
Yaroslav came up to his side to support him.

"A near run thing, a very near run thing," Napoleon said.
He was trembling with nervous exhaustion, but there was a
beaming look of triumph in his eyes.

"Should I get Ney?"

"Let him have his chase, he was always best at those things.
Most of those Prussians are *Landwehr*, second-rate troops. Once
broken, they'll run straight back to the Rhine."

All up and down the line cheers of exaltation sounded.

"Tell Ney to push them, to push them east."

He paused and looked about.

"I've dreamed this moment for five years. Thank you," he
whispered.

He leaned back with a sigh, and for the first time Yaroslav
realized that Napoleon had been hit again, an ugly stain spreading out from his chest.

"The emperor's been hit," Yaroslav cried.

Guardsmen pushed around, and reaching up they helped to lower him to the ground, the men gathering around, their looks of joy replaced in an instant with fear and anguish.

Yaroslav dismounted, groaning and nearly losing his footing. He pushed his way through to kneel by Napoleon's side.

"It's been a good day," Napoleon whispered.

Yaroslav found that he could not speak, his throat tight with emotion.

"It was an honor to serve you."

Napoleon smiled.

"I knew I'd win you over, Marshal Yaroslav."

The old man nodded.

Napoleon looked up at a guardsman.

"André, is that you?"

"I am here, my general."

"But I lost you, it was at Arcola."

The guardsman smiled.

"I am here nevertheless, my general."

He looked around wide-eyed.

"Pierre, you fell at Rivoli. Vincent, you died at Leipzig trying to save the regimental flag. And Guillaume, how I missed you."

The cluster of men knelt around the emperor. Yaroslav looked from one to the other. All of them were silent, most weeping quiet tears that streaked their powder-stained faces, dampening their drooping mustaches.

"My old grumblers. How I killed you all. Forgive me, my children."

"We died for France, for you, my emperor," one of them whispered, his voice choked, as if comforting a child who was at the edge of the darkness.

"Emperor Napoleon."

Yaroslav looked up. It was Wellington, floating at the edge of the circle.

Napoleon looked up, squinting, as if barely able to see.

"Emperor Napoleon, I offer my surrender," the machine said. "You have won the battle of Waterloo. I am your prisoner."

Napoleon raised a hand and weakly pointed to Yaroslav.

"Marshal Yaroslav will arrange the terms."

Napoleon smiled weakly and closed his eyes.

"I die happy," he whispered.

Yaroslav leaned over him, placing a hand on his chest.

"He's going into cardiac arrest," the old man shouted. "Damn it! Do something!"

The machine looked down in silence.

"We'll have target lock in a couple of minutes," Corbin announced.

"Just don't miss," Hassan said, looking at the full magnification view of Aldin's ship, the strange confusion of the battle spread out below them.

"Miss? With these First Traveler missiles?" Corbin replied haughtily, as if the six weapons were of his own design. "Hardly likely."

Across the Cloud, the wormhole had finished its meal of a class M star, the last light of it winking out. Within seconds the several small planets that had been orbiting, but now were streaking straight out into the darkness, were captured by the wormhole and devoured.

The seething mass at the other end of the hole seemed to pulse and shudder, thinly balanced between the outward pressure of the thermonuclear furnace within its core and the ever-increasing burden of its own monumental mass, which was almost ready to start the mad rush in that would lead either to the creation of a black hole or the cataclysm of a supernova explosion.

The open end of the wormhole wavered for a brief instant, tracing out the waves of gravity that flowed about it. Locking onto the strongest of them, it leaped outward at translight speed, streaking in toward the Core Cluster as if eager to feed upon the hundreds of stars within.

The few residents still on Yarmu, a Gaf vacation world, looked up at the sun above them. A thin line appeared like an arrow driving into the light. A coiling column of fire shot out from the sun and streaked off into space.

There was a mad clamor for the last ships, their masters having counted on this event and now realizing that the cancellation of all bookings and then the reselling of tickets at a 10,000 percent markup was proving to be a most profitable venture. Several of the more suicidal patrons of the planet, who belonged to one of the more unusual Gaf cults, settled back to watch the show, not even aware that their leader was already aboard the last ship out, with plans for future investments.

An errant spin of the wormhole caught the ship, however, and the cult leader made it to eternity long before his worshipful followers.

The wormhole continued on with its deadly work, oblivious to the panic setting in across the Cloud.

CHAPTER 12

"JUMP HIM UP, JUMP HIM UP NOW!" ALDIN SCREAMED. "THE FIELD'S just shut off!''

Zergh was out of the room, pushing to get into the small master control room for the jump down. It'd take a minute to build up the power load necessary, and he swore vehemently while he watched the slow upward curve of power on the console.

A shimmer of light filled the room, and he felt the outrush of air. There was an audible pop, and he looked up to see Yaroslav straddling Napoleon's chest, leaning in rhythmically with his one good arm to try to keep the heart going, Basak standing protectively over them, and the First Traveler machine floating alongside.

Zergh found himself actually looking back at his console, as if somehow the machine had initiated the jump without a command, while at the same time realizing that the First Traveler device had done it.

"Get us into the medical bay!" Yaroslav shouted.

Zergh felt a moment of panic, not sure what to do, wondering if he should interrupt Yaroslav. Tia was in the doorway carrying a med portapack, a servobot behind her. She knelt down, shouldering Yaroslav aside, and slapped the pack onto the emperor's chest. The portapack computer took over, jolting a charge in, injecting medication straight into the heart. A float bed was pulled in, and the emperor was lifted up onto it, the servobot punching an artificial blood unit into his arm, while with another tentacle hooking a respiration unit in.

"How long?" Zergh asked, his voice choked.

"Maybe a minute, a minute and a half," Yaroslav said.

"Didn't we put a new heart in when we did the make-over on him?" Aldin asked.

Tia nodded and looked over at the portapack screen.

"Heart's not been hit, but one lung's got a hole in it the size of a small fist. It might be too much damage. He most likely lost way too much blood from the first wound. The second hit the pulmonary vein in the lung, and that did it."

Aldin looked over as the bed floated into the medical bay. A medbot inserted a drainage tube into the entry wound, and the tube pulsed with bright red fluid.

The float bed went into the medical bay, the servobot following, clicking with a nearly Human sound of anxiety, and the door slid shut.

Yaroslav slumped against the wall, eyes hollow with exhaustion and shock, waving Tia away when she came up to look at his arm, and then motioning for Hobbs to fetch a drink instead. Basak looked around at the group, his emotions torn between exaltation from the thrill of combat and despair over the emperor.

"Incredible," Yaroslav whispered, finally looking up at the stunned group. "He was incredible. I can see why they said his presence on the field was worth forty thousand men."

"Not like him, though," Zergh replied. "He only really exposed himself once, at Arcola; he was reckless to the point of madness this time."

"He had a chance to do it one more time," Aldin replied. "He couldn't live with himself if he had lost it again. He must have wished he had died in that fight every night of his exile when he was alone. A warrior's death to cement the legend in blood, that must have been his nightly dream.''

''Aldin.''

The vasba looked over to see Oishi in the doorway to the forward control and recreation room.

''We've got to get out of here now. I can still pilot us through the opening, but in another two or three minutes they'll be in position to block our escape.''

Aldin nodded and looked over at the First Traveler machine and felt a cold anger. Because of this damn machine, any hope of solving their problem had been blown.

''You most likely killed him,'' he snapped angrily, ''and for what?''

''He won. I fought it fairly, he had his inner wish.''

''Well if that's the price, I'll forget my inner wishes,'' Hobbs interjected.

''I am Wellington. I am his prisoner for the rest of the day, that is the game.''

Yaroslav looked up.

''You are the prisoner of the emperor,'' Yaroslav said, ''and he assigned me to arrange the terms.''

''I expect to be treated with the consideration worthy of my rank as a duke, as a general, and as a gentleman.''

''Fine,'' Yaroslav replied. ''I am a marshal of the empire, appointed by the emperor, and am now in command. I accept your surrender in the name of the emperor.''

The machine nodded toward Yaroslav.

''I would enjoy sharing a bottle of claret with you,'' Yaroslav said, ''but first might I ask you a question?''

''Within reason.''

''But of course, my lord.''

''Then ask.''

''Do you know what a wormhole is?''

''A biportal material-transformation transporter, capable of creating a field distortion to fold space and to activate—''

''Yeah, that's the one,'' Aldin snapped, cutting it off.

''I know of it.''

"Do you know him?" Yaroslav asked, and he pointed over at Vush, who floated in the far corner, his pale features even paler as he continued to stare at the trail of blood leading out of the jump-beam room and down the hall into the med unit.

"That entity has been in my presence."

"Aldin, we've got to move now!" Oishi shouted.

He held his hand up and looked over at Yaroslav.

"Do you remember the machine that Vush and his companion took, a device to create wormholes?"

The machine floated before them.

"It is recalled."

"All right," Yaroslav said, nodding a grateful thanks to Hobbs, who drifted back into the room bearing a glass of wine. Yaroslav downed half the glass in a single gulp and sighed.

"It is believed that they took only half the machine, that there is another part that was left behind."

"That is true, element 2371881773 second unit was not taken."

"Why the hell didn't you tell us, you bastard," Vush snapped angrily.

The machine turned slightly, as if to face Vush.

"You did not accept the offer to play, you did not defeat me, you did not unlock the proper security sequence in order to elicit the necessary response. And most of all you told me to leave you alone when I attempted to warn you of the danger of the machine you and your friend were playing with."

The machine paused.

"You are scum, sir. I like my officers turned out smartly, and your dress is abominable."

Aldin could not help but smile. A friendly game of chess or whatever. It was all so simple, reminding him of an old classic story where the sign to enter a door had simply said "speak friend and enter," and all puzzled over the proper word, until finally someone had simply said "friend."

"Would you fetch the other half of the element? Such an action is within acceptable protocol of surrender, the equivalent of surrendering your sword."

"If it is wished, I am Wellington, prisoner till the end of the day and the next game."

"The machine, is it functional?" Tia interjected.

"It is functional."

"Aldin, now!" Oishi shouted. "We've got to move now!"

"Find the other half and bring it back!" Yaroslav said, his voice taking on the tone of command.

A shimmer of light flooded the corridor. The machine barely dematerialized and then it was already back, a box not much bigger than a small book resting on the floor before it.

All looked down at it in astonishment. It was jet black, no instruments visible, no controls, simply a jet-black cube that held such a dark color that it almost appeared as if space itself were floating within its confines.

"He's launched some trackers," Oishi shouted.

"At that range," Zergh laughed, "it'll take ten minutes to get to us."

"Under two minutes," Oishi replied. "They're different, already up to .002 light-speed and accelerating. Whatever it is, it's coming in fast. It's got a lock on us!"

"Get us out of here!" Aldin shouted, breaking away from the group and running into the forward control room. He pulled up beside Oishi and looked at the screen.

"Oh, shit." He sighed. The incoming vessel was still a hundred thousand kilometers away and closing fast. Spreading out from the vessel, however, were half a dozen small blips. One of them suddenly winked out with a flash, undoubtedly running into some sort of debris. The signal on the others became faint, almost disappearing, then reappearing for an instant, several thousand kilometers closer, then winking out again.

Whatever Corbin had thrown at them, it was capable of masking. It was remarkable, the blips were closing straight in, able to see them in spite of all the clutter created by the mass of the Sphere below.

"Let's go!" he shouted.

Yaroslav, still looking up at the First Traveler machine, felt the ship surge beneath him.

"Can you move this ship?" he shouted, trying to be heard above the roar of the thrust systems kicking in while the outside ports were not yet fully closed.

"Too much mass in one unit," the machine replied. "Where are you taking me? Am I to be exchanged?"

"You're the prisoner of the emperor for the rest of the day. Can't you do anything about the ship approaching toward us, the weapons they've fired?"

"Another game? Most interesting, not part of our agreement. I like to watch."

The ship bucked beneath Yaroslav, nearly knocking him over. He could feel the grating of the shattered bone in his arm, and he groaned with pain. He realized he must be in shock as well. The stress of the battle had kept him focused on other things, but now that it was over, it was all getting to be a bit too much. The machine now seemed to be far away, as if floating at the end of a distant tunnel that was now hovering straight overhead. He slid down to the floor, out cold, the others not even noticing, except for Basak, who had sat down by the door into the medical bay, cradling his blood-soaked ax in his lap and talking to it gently. The berserker slid over to sit by Yaroslav.

"It was a good day, a joyful day," Basak said.

Aldin looked back out from the control room and saw Yaroslav slide down to the floor in a dead faint and shouted for Hobbs to go look after him.

"A lot of good it'll do," Hobbs cried. "We're all going to get cooked in about ten seconds!"

"Run for the opening we came through," Aldin shouted.

"We can't, one of the incomings has tracked over that way. It's turning toward us now!"

"Sit back and hang on," Oishi shouted.

The *Gamemaster II* was already up to a dozen kilometers a second, the ground below getting ripped up by the shock wave of its passage, the smoke-clad battlefield of Waterloo behind them. He pushed the throttle up to the limit and started to climb.

"What the hell are you climbing for!" Zergh shouted. "Try and hide in the clutter; get in a gully, behind a hill."

"They're coming down, a lot of good it'll do," Oishi replied.

He pulled up to a dozen kilometers, the atmosphere thinning out, the drag dropping off, and the ship accelerated rapidly. Waterloo was now a hundred kilometers astern. He pulled a sharp turn and pointed straight at the black mountain on the edge of the city, adding another kilometer of height.

"Ten seconds!" Aldin cried, watching mesmerized as one of the incomings did a spiraling turn away from the lock it must have achieved when they were over Waterloo. The missile disappeared momentarily and then appeared again, sending out an incredible burst of a radar signal and a snap of laser light as if looking to designate them. It locked on, following their track for a second, and then completely disappeared.

It was a brilliant piece of machinery, Aldin realized, unlike anything available. It would mask to avoid having anything sent back against it, appearing only long enough to get a fix, and then masking again before a counterstrike could be locked onto it and track it for a kill. There was no beating it.

It reappeared less than ten thousand kilometers away, locked, and then disappeared. One, maybe two more. Aldin tried to point the ship's one laser gun against it, but a firing solution could not be calculated quickly enough in the fraction of a second that the device revealed itself.

He looked forward again. The mountain was straight ahead, rushing up as if they were going to smash straight into it.

"Hang on," Oishi cried, even as he slammed a full reverse on.

The inertial damping system almost made a perfect response, but Aldin felt as if his eyes were about to pop out of his head nevertheless.

"What the hell are you doing?" Zergh screamed, reaching over as if to grab the controls from Oishi.

Oishi slammed them to a complete stop directly over the top of the mountain, while rotating the ship to point straight down.

"Holy shit!" Aldin screamed, wanting to stop him. Hobbs's

high-pitched screams could be heard in the doorway. The entire forward screen was black as they looked straight down into the hole punched clean through the Sphere. Aldin felt his last three meals coming back up.

Oishi slammed the throttle forward, and the ship shot straight down, going into the mountain, buffeting with the turbulence of the atmosphere that was sucked through the hole.

The universe straight ahead was darkness. An instant later a blinding snap of light washed about them.

"Impact!" Zergh screamed.

Their ship shot out of the Sphere, and Oishi rotated it yet again as they cleared the hole. They turned, skimming along the outside shell of the Sphere. Behind them a column of nuclear fire blew outward, a tongue of radioactive exhaust from the impact of the missile atop the mountain. The tongue of fire pulsed, began to dissipate, and then renewed itself, flaring up an instant later as if redoubling.

"The other's impacting," Oishi said, leaning back in his chair and wiping his brow with the sleeve of his robe.

"Did we get cooked?" Tia asked nervously.

Aldin looked over at the monitor, which was flickering from the EMP, and then unscrambled.

"Not much, shielding cut it down to a couple of rem, but a second earlier and we would have been inside the oven."

Zergh got up without a word and went over to help a servobot right itself, ignoring Hobbs, who was floating upside down in the corner, his float chair completely scrambled by the roller coaster ride. Pulling the servobot up, he punched the sake dispenser, poured out a cup, and came back over to Oishi. He drained half the cup and then offered it over, and suddenly his hands began to shake.

"You're chief pilot now," he said, his voice shaking almost as much as his hands.

Oishi looked over and nodded his thanks.

"We kept hanging around, waiting for the battle to clear. I kept trying to think of an escape, and that was the last alternative."

"Suppose there'd been debris in there?" Zergh asked.

"We'd be history," Oishi replied dryly.

"Speaking of history," Aldin said, and he unbuckled himself from the chair and got up, his knees feeling like jelly. "Get us to the nearest jump gate and let's head for home."

He went across the room, first grabbing hold of Hobbs's chair and flipping him back upright, laughing wanly when he saw that his friend had made as much of a mess of himself as he had. The corridor was a mess as well, pictures torn off the walls, their frames shattered. Basak rested in the corner, with Yaroslav pulled in tightly to his chest. The old man's eyes were open.

"You trying to kill us?" he asked weakly, grimacing from the berserker's embrace.

"Almost."

The First Traveler machine still floated in the corridor, Vush stretched out cold beside him.

"What happened to him?" Aldin asked.

"Struck its head against the ceiling and sleeps now," the machine replied. "Where are you taking me? I am a prisoner only to the end of the day. I must return home."

Damn, he had forgotten about the machine in all the confusion.

"Part of the game is a signing of conventions, an armistice before prisoners are all exchanged," Aldin said quickly. "The emperor alone can do that—as soon as he is fully recovered. Is that acceptable?"

The machine actually seemed to hesitate.

"Acceptable," it finally replied.

He went up to the medical bay door and punched it open. He expected far worse. Several containers were on the floor, but the medbot had secured the float bed to an anchor point before the chaos had started. It was working attentively on the emperor.

Aldin went up nervously and looked over at the monitor, expecting the worst.

"A steady pulse, thank God."

He looked back and saw Yaroslav standing weakly behind him.

"First time I've ever heard you thank a deity," Aldin replied.

The bot, with needlelike fingers, was working inside the emperor's body, reattaching shattered vessels, stitching fragments of lung back together, analyzing the genetic code of individual cells, replicating them and patching in where too much tissue had been torn apart. It was slowly working its way outward, from the deepest injury back up, repairing on a microscopic level as it went. An auxiliary arm was working simultaneously on the bullet wound to the leg, spinning out a fabric of muscles, vessels, nerves, and flesh to close the injury back up.

"Leave some sort of scar on the wounds," Yaroslav said to the bot. "It'll please his vanity."

His color was already back, the grayish blue hue replaced with a near-healthy pink. A tray to one side held a misshapen piece of lead.

"Pistol shot, lucky it wasn't a musket ball or canister, or he'd really be dead," Yaroslav said quietly.

"We should get you attended to, and Basak as well."

"We can wait. He's more important at the moment."

"Sounds like you're getting sentimental about him."

"Who, me?" Yaroslav sniffed.

"Well, he did save us," Aldin replied. "Never expected it. I think on a gut level he knew the machine was playing the game out for a reason. When that hole got slammed into the Sphere, it must have scrambled some fundamental programming for the entire Sphere. That'd explain the chaos that was going on."

"He did insist on the prisoner agreement before he'd play."

Yaroslav looked down at the emperor and smiled.

"He did almost as good as I would have."

"Now that is an admission."

Yaroslav shrugged his shoulders.

"He'd better recover. He owes me a marshal's baton. And I want a painting done, in the style of David. *Marshal Yaroslav and the Emperor Leading the Guard at Waterloo.*"

"The Emperor and Marshal Yaroslav Leading the Guard."

Napoleon, his eyes barely open, looked up at them and smiled.

Aldin, reaching out, patted Napoleon lightly on the shoulder.

"Go to sleep, let the machine fix you."

"You will have your baton, Marshal Yaroslav, you earned it - this day," Napoleon whispered, his voice slurring as the bot, working with a mild paralytic anesthesia, continued its repairs.

Aldin, forcing a smile, turned away.

Now the only question was how the hell to get back.

"I tell you we got him," Corbin said. "The trackers the Overseers gave us couldn't miss."

He turned a monitor around to show the top of the still-glowing mountain where five of the warheads had hit. The storm boiled and rolled, spreading outward.

"He must have been mad to go in there," Corbin said. "There was no hiding from those trackers."

"Go in closer for a look," Hassan snapped.

"What for?"

"Go in closer. There must have been a reason for him to go there, rather than turn and run."

Corbin, cursing silently, swung the ship down and approached the mountain.

"I thought an explosion would burst outward," Hassan finally said, watching as the cloud of radioactive debris, which in the beginning of the explosion had pulsed outward, now appeared to be contracting in upon itself.

Corbin felt suddenly nervous.

"There's a hole there," he finally said, figuring it was best to announce the fact rather than let Hassan find out for himself.

"A hole?"

"The explosion tore the top off the mountain, punching through to the underside of the Sphere. The atmosphere is getting sucked into the vacuum of space on the other side."

He was afraid to admit the other scenario that was already forming.

"Could the hole have been there before?" Hassan finally asked.

Corbin hesitated.

"It's unlikely. Why would they have a hole that could drain out their own atmosphere?"

"Could it have been there?"

"It's possible," Corbin finally admitted.

Hassan stood in silence, looking at the screen.

"Take us through it. That is what they did."

"They might have been caught in the burst anyhow."

" 'Might have been' is not good enough."

Hassan looked down at the smoldering explosion.

"Take us through it."

"It's deadly down there," Corbin said. "We'd have to slow to a near stop as we went through. We'd be cooked by the radiation. It'll be an hour or more before it's safe, and even then there might be so much twisted wreckage that it will be impossible to get through."

He was surprised by his own self-assertiveness and looked up defiantly at Hassan. At least the barbarian didn't understand a whit about space travel.

"Then we wait," Hassan said, his voice deceptively calm. "I trust that if they did pass through you'll be able to detect them on the outside of this ball."

"There'll be some traces of an exhaust trail. If they survived, they'll either wait to come back in to finish their search or they will run for a transfer gate back into the Cloud."

"You realize what will happen if they successfully escape."

Corbin did not reply.

"What was that?"

The Arch looked up, startled and still disoriented from the transfer jump that they had completed only seconds before.

"Something going past us in the opposite direction," Mupa replied lamely, looking over at the Xsarn pilot who nodded a confirmation. They were continuing straight in toward the Sphere even while the holo camera loop was replayed. With a combined closing speed of nearly 20 percent light-speed, it was almost impossible to distinguish anything beyond a blur. But whatever it was, it had passed less than a kilometer away to port and jumped through the gate at nearly the same instant they had emerged. The near miss reminded the Arch of all the myriad reasons of why he hated to travel. To survive for so long, only to be winked out of this plane of existence by an overeager barbarian pilot, left him with a simmering rage.

"It was them," Mupa said, his voice weak and shaky with fear from the near miss.

"Who is them?"

"The ship, *Gamemaster II*. It was them."

The Arch was silent for a moment. Couldn't Gablona do anything right? He had the information to trace them down, the weapons to destroy them—what more did the fool need?

"Turn us around," the Arch shouted.

"But I thought we were going to look for the machine," Mupa said weakly.

"Turn us around and get after them, they've already got it!" the Arch shouted. "And I want a coded message sent out at once."

Zola settled back in his chair and nodded for the others to leave the room.

This would be a tough one to call. He was tempted to pour out a quick drink to help sooth his nerves, but not this time, maybe afterward.

In the last score of days he had managed to make a huge killing, recouping a major portion of the assets lost in the lottery and futures fiasco of the Shiga game. Transport space aboard his fleet of junk cargo ships that were going into the threatened region was making 1,000 percent more than the day before the wormhole started. There was such a shortage of shipping throughout the Cloud that even in safe regions transportation had gone up 500 percent. With his own fleet of vessels, he could keep internal shipping between his own factories and worlds at the usual cost and thus make an even bigger killing against the mad upward spiral of prices.

Real estate was going beautifully as well. A third-rate pleasure world of marginal climate and a fierce indigenous population of carnivores and insects was now a hot new development site, since it was at the far end of the Cluster. Salesmen were already hawking lots at three times the old asking price, as everyone started to come to the conclusion that life in the Core Cluster was becoming decidedly unhealthy.

The question was, should he allow it to end?

He looked at the memo on his desk, hand delivered for the sake of security. There was a slight bit of sentimental attachment that welled up for a moment. A lot of good games in the past, some of them quite profitable indeed. Beyond sentiment, there was another concern. A fair part of the Core Cluster would be rather uninhabitable if the runaway star received any more mass and detonated into a supernova.

He tried to imagine that scenario. He tried to allow himself the humanitarian viewpoint, as if by so doing he could later talk down any sense of lingering guilt. Chances were that no one would really die, even though a billion beings were in the danger zone. Every ship could evacuate most all of them in that time, he'd already checked on that one. There might be a small shortfall, but that could be easily solved—he'd skip evacuating the lawyer's planet and everyone would thank him for it.

He sat back and spun out the calculations. The insurance companies would be intact; after all, every policy ever written had included the proviso that exploding stars and impacting bodies from space were not covered. They could sue the Overseers if they wanted, and that thought made him chuckle. Give them a dose of their own morality for a change.

All those people paying passage—it was boggling to contemplate. There wouldn't be any whining about service and food aboard ship, basic emergency rations and fares 1,000 percent of normal with operational costs cut in half. And the new real estate to be sold, the construction to be done.

I'll be the richest Koh inside of a year, he thought.

He looked over at the projection charts of which worlds would be hit. And only three had major assets of his on them, all the rest were either the old territory of Corbin, the acquisitions of

Bukha and Aldin, or one of the banking, legal, or administrative worlds, and who the hell needed them anyhow?

He leaned back in his chair and sighed. Friendship was friendship but a good profit line was, in the end, the bottom line.

If it had been aware, it would have known that mass had already exceeded the level whereby a supernova was all but inevitable. All that was keeping it from blowing was the central core of oxygen, superheated to half a billion degrees and thus fueling a nuclear reaction that was keeping the center burning with such intense forces that the outer shell of the star was thus prevented from collapsing in.

The sun that the cultists had been watching was gone, swallowed up, the gravitational force that had kept the planet in its elliptical orbit gone as well, so that it was now heading straight out into space. There were a lot of *oohs* and *ahs* coming from the crowd, though the event was taking six minutes to reach them visually, and thus from their perspective the star still appeared to be collapsing in and dimming out.

Most of them were thus able to actually let out a shout of surprise when it appeared as if the show was still going on and then also suddenly stopped. The wormhole, detached from where the sun had been, first hit a gas giant further out, consuming it in half a dozen minutes, and then came back in to the small planet. There was a second of confusion and disappointment; after all, their leader had said they'd see the sky go completely dark and thus gain at that instant total knowledge of nothingness and liberation. Instead, there was still some light in the sky when from the opposite direction the wormhole bored straight into the heart of the planet from behind and within the first second caused it to start to collapse in upon itself.

Several of them had just enough time to sense that somehow things were not quite going according to plan, and were considering quitting the cult and getting a refund, when suddenly they stretched out into a long thin stream of matter and disappeared.

The planet was gone, and there was a momentary searching

for the next gravitational wave to chase down. Another class M star almost won, but an ever so slightly greater presence was sensed, a burned-out black dwarf, a solid sphere of compressed iron with a mass of hundreds of trillions of tons.

The wormhole transfer gate leaped across space, actually moving in somewhat closer to its point of origin, and in less than half a minute locked onto the dark star, actually encountering some resistance as it bored into its heart before starting to pump the compressed iron out and shooting it back up to the pulsing giant.

The iron hit the thermonuclear center. Anything below iron in the order of elements would have continued to drive the reaction; iron was one element that could not. Chunks of it had been fed in before, especially when a solid planet was consumed. It would cause a confused swirling reaction in the heart of the star, actually triggering a momentary collapse of the sun's outer layers until some other element finally emerged and reignited the nuclear pile.

But this was iron, nothing but supercompressed iron pouring in at tens of billions of tons per second, instantly acting like a jet of ice water shot into a cylinder of superheated steam. The nuclear heart of the sun started to shut down, and the surface began ever so gradually to fall in upon itself. The final, inevitable supernova had begun.

CHAPTER 13

"I TELL YOU, WE'LL BE OUT OF FUEL AND IN THE MIDDLE OF NO-where," Zergh said wearily. "We've jumped all the way down to the Milky Way, back up to the Sphere, and now halfway back into the Cloud. It's simple math, either turn off at a Xsarn world at this next gate or we sputter out when we get to our destination."

Aldin, rubbing his eyes, looked at the ceiling.

"Great, one more jump, a couple of hours of running, and now you're telling me we can't make it?"

"If you stop, Corbin will be ahead of us," Oishi said sharply. "He was less than a half hour behind us at the last gate. He'll close it the rest of the way at this one."

Aldin looked around at the group. They were all looking the worse for wear. Water had to be rationed, food was almost gone, and there was a decidedly gamy smell in the air, especially from Basak and Hobbs, who seemed to revel in an excuse for not bathing.

Aldin looked over at Napoleon.

"A tough pursuit. Do not hesitate with victory in your grasp."

Aldin nodded in agreement. If they stopped at the small Xsarn world, they'd be pinned on the ground in a matter of minutes.

There was only one alternative, to run till the fuel ran out and hope they reached their goal.

"All right, we push through then."

The next transition jump point was strangely quiet. Usually there was some traffic moving back and forth, exiting out of one point and maneuvering to go into the next. He expected some form of resistance by this point. A coded Overseer message had been sent from near the Sphere, but so far no reaction, most likely due in part to a couple of turns through seldom-used jump lines, thus evading any blockades that might have been laid out. But it was coming down to the end now. There was only one way in toward Beta Zul from this direction, and they had to take it and hope for the best.

Boosting power up to the maximum, Oishi moved them across the small barren system, which was composed of a red dwarf and several dead planets, noted only for the small supplies of titanium that had been found there centuries ago and thus had resulted in this back path being laid out.

Oishi, letting the computer do the navigation, watched intently as they moved at maximum speed, doing the transit in under half an hour.

"Funny, Corbin should have come through by now," Oishi said. "He's been gaining on every transit by a couple of minutes."

"Maybe he had fuel problems as well," Tia said hopefully.

"Or he took another route," Zergh said.

"We checked that, there were no others."

"At least none that we knew of," Aldin replied. "He might have free-jumped. It was the straighter line in."

"Corbin free jump?" Hobbs said, shaking with laughter. "He's like me, too much of a coward to do something that crazy."

"Well, you've been floating around with us haven't you?" Yaroslav said.

Aldin looked over at his friend sitting in the corner with Napoleon, the two of them deeply immersed in some arcane point of tactics, both of them alternating with raised voices.

The medbots had worked their usual wonder, something he was grateful for the investment in. The units had been installed to alter replicants for the old days of gaming when substitutes had to be changed to match up with the individuals they were replacing. The system had cost millions. It had restored Napoleon when first brought aboard and had, after this latest injury, put him back on his feet in two days, Yaroslav beside him, sporting a neat circular scar on his arm, which was exposed more than once to hammer home a point when arguing with the emperor.

Wellington hovered to one side and would occasionally chime in with a comment. It conceded that Lobau's assault to the right of D'Erlon had thrown it off, since it expected Napoleon to keep the guard in reserve in anticipation of Blücher's early arrival on the field and thus assumed that Lobau was the main blow. Napoleon never confessed that he had no knowledge of the early Prussian advance until already committed to the assault in the center.

"A near run thing," the machine was now fond of saying.

There had been a formal surrender signing in the medical bay, the document drawn up by Yaroslav. The interpreting of the key point had been crucial, Wellington arguing that it was against the conventions of war for gentlemen prisoners to be used for labor. Yaroslav had countered that since the wormhole transfer gate was a substitute for Wellington's sword, all it meant was that he was being asked to give a demonstration of its use, nothing more. The agreement was finally signed when Yaroslav added the provision that all prisoners were to be exchanged back home once the "demonstration" was completed.

The latest debate between the three fell silent as they stopped to watch the final run in.

"Let's jump it," Zergh announced, and Aldin settled back for the transition.

His stomach did the usual flip over as they pulled the instantaneous leap to translight speed, and at nearly the same instant the alarms went off.

"There's something in the line!" Zergh shouted.

An explosion rocked through the ship, airtight integrity disappearing for a brief instant till the access door into the forward chamber slammed shut.

"What the hell?" Aldin and Vush screamed at nearly the same instant.

"We hit something. Something was in the line ahead of us."

Oishi scanned the monitors and looked back up at his companions, his features pale.

"We should have been dead. Our shielding never could have stopped an impact. As it is, a fair section of port side, including the medical bay, is gone.

"We never should have . . ." Oishi's voice trailed off, and he looked over at the First Traveler machine.

"According to the convention agreement, I am to aid in the delivery of what you call the device. The unshielded impact of this vessel would have destroyed it, thus preventing delivery."

"Well, nice going," Yaroslav said, almost matter-of-factly, running a hand through his hair to straighten it out after the tornado of a temporary decompression.

"Could you have done the same thing back in the Sphere?" Yaroslav asked.

"The convention of terms had yet to be signed."

"Well, what else can you do for us?" Aldin asked.

"Energy has been dissipated," the machine replied.

"In other words, not much."

"Not much."

Aldin nodded.

"Well, somebody just tried to kill us; let's just hope there isn't a reception committee waiting on the other side."

"Corbin's ship has just come through," Mupa announced, and then turned away to look nervously back at the star that filled the entire forward screen.

The cataclysmic collapse had begun, the outer edge of the star accelerating inward. A sensitive enough eye could have by this stage detected a slight Doppler shift in color, a dropping off into a deeper red. A rapidly increasing burst of radiation was pulsing outward.

The star was going into supernova.

The wormhole line was glowing hotly, the great mass of the black dwarf pumping into the heart of the developing explosion.

The Arch watched the show intently. He knew he should be feeling some moral revulsion with all that was happening. He had supplied weapons to Corbin and the mad assassins aboard his ship to track Larice down, knowing that it would kill one of his brothers if successful. He had revealed an unknown jump point to Corbin, allowing both of them to get ahead of Aldin. He had allowed information to leak to one of the Human Kohs, who had, against all custom and tradition, scattered wreckage in a jump line with the intent of stopping Aldin after his escape from the Sphere. He was participating in the destruction of a sun that would render a not unsizeable portion of the Cloud uninhabitable.

The Arch clicked off these sins and felt no remorse.

He already had his next plan firmly laid out, giving yet more weapons to Corbin to allow him to wage war and thus plunge the rest of the Cloud into chaos. By his projections, within twenty years, the civilization, if it could be called that, of the three species would have totally collapsed and they would revert, trapped on their own worlds. Then there would be peace again, and solitude, and contemplation.

Contemplation of my own sins? he wondered. Perhaps, but there could be endless millennia to work that out, to expiate the stain and to find tranquility, something now impossible with a universe full of brawling barbarians.

"Full detonation in less than ten minutes," Mupa announced.

The Arch settled back in his chair to watch the show.

"We've got the Overseer ship on track," Hassan said, smiling and looking up at the screen.

Corbin could only nod dumbly in reply.

"If he somehow evaded the debris, we'll be waiting."

"And then what?" Corbin Gablona said coldly.

"We finish him."

"And then?"

Hassan looked over at the fat old man who sat glumly before him. He was filled with a sense of loathing for his former master, the mere thought of being subservient to him filling him with yet more rage.

I'll have you spaced, destroy the Overseers, and take over, he wanted to shout at him. But no. He would still need this one as a figurehead, a puppet to dance before the multitudes while he ruled the strings from above.

Behind Hassan, the disk of the sun continued to collapse.

Zola sat quietly watching his private monitor. It had been a tough job to sabotage the one ship that was to carry the pool of newscasters out to the rogue sun. There was to be no one there. For one thing, he had already arranged a monopoly on the holo film from Mupa, worth a small fortune in itself. And secondly, if there was any last-minute unpleasantness, it'd be bad for business to see the effort to stop the explosion being prevented in turn by the Overseers and Corbin.

He poured a drink and settled back to wait it out.

"Jump-transition point in five seconds," Zergh announced nervously.

Aldin nervously clutched at the arms of his chair. The light shift hit, and an instant later the angry glow of the collapsing sun was before him.

"We've got barely enough to make a straight in pass," Oishi announced.

"Company's here!" Zergh cried, jamming the throttle up to maximum.

The ship was bracketed with a burst of light.

"Corbin," Zergh snapped, jinking the ship to avoid the initial shots.

They dove in toward the sun, Gablona's ship moving up to match the speed they were still running with as they came out of the gate.

To one side, the Overseer ship snapped past, and within seconds was a hundred thousand kilometers astern, but Corbin was still behind them and gaining.

Aldin looked forward and found himself fascinated by the sight. Though they were approaching the sun at a high rate of speed, the disk was actually getting smaller.

It was remarkable, beautiful, radiating an unimaginable power.

"Fuel's out," Oishi cried. "We're losing control!"

Aldin looked over at the samurai and smiled sadly. There was nothing more to be done. The sequence of explosions had already started, and they were falling straight into it. He felt the gravity on the ship go with the power, his stomach lifting up inside. Too bad, he thought, I wish I could have had another drink before going.

What scared him most of all, though, was the fact that he wasn't even sure if he really cared anymore. He looked over and saw Tia and Oishi, their hands clasped. For them, he wanted something, but for himself? There was really nothing anymore. No dreams, no goals to reach. He was far too tired of the struggle that no longer seemed to matter.

He strapped himself into his chair and waited for the show to end and the lights to come up.

Several hundred trillion tons of highly compressed iron had been pumped into the heart of the storm, shutting down the reaction. The inward rush was generating at the same time a pressure increase of a full magnitude, and then another magnitude in less than a second.

A giant that had been nearly a hundred million kilometers across was now down to a million, and in that final second the iron made a final instantaneous transition to every other possible element in existence, a billion tons of mass compressing into an area the size of a thimble. Gravity had held it in upon itself. If the mass had been less, it would have simply continued to compress until finally winking out of this particular universe, disappearing down the long event horizon into another realm.

But the inward rush of so much mass created temperatures in that last instant far in excess of a billion degrees. Not even gravity could withhold this final onslaught of outward pressure.

There was only one place left to go, and that was out.

The star exploded into supernova.

The vision stirred within the First Traveler. For it was indeed just that, what others called a First Traveler, the master builder of the universe, far exceeding the powers of its long-dead creators.

It could sense what was ahead, a vision that would take several minutes to reach those around him as they tumbled in toward the explosion, their ship powerless—but contracts and surrenders were indeed binding.

"The forward monitor indicates supernova detonation," Mupa shouted.

The image was replayed on the screen, showing the last second of the inward rush, the holo relayed from the edge of the star as it started its final death throes. All that could be seen was the final incandescent snap, and the monitor disappeared, the signal dead.

The Arch looked up at the main screen, which showed the view from fifty million kilometers out.

"We better get out of here. The radiation burst will hit in less than three minutes," Mupa announced, and all in the room could detect the shocking reality of exaltation on the part of Arch of the Overseers.

Bukha Taug looked away from the screen and, lowering his face, he covered his eyes.

A lousy five minutes, that would have been all the difference. Maddeningly, the Xsarn shipping guild had suddenly announced a strike, with all pilots refusing to fly. He suspected Zola's hand in it all, bribing the guild officials to shut everything down. The plan had been so well laid out. It had been an insane scramble, a full day of waste to finally dig up a crew willing to lose their guild licenses to prepare a ship for departure.

Coming in from the Yalla jump line, he had been able to see Aldin's mad plunge straight in toward the star and intercept the holo relay of the event that must have been sent up to the Overseer ship.

It was simple enough, he had thought. Bring in a news crew not controlled by the Overseers and grounded by Zola's maneuver. Let them witness Aldin defuse the sun, and in the exultation of having saved the Core Cluster the frame-up of the war would be forgotten.

The news crew was excited to be sure, gasps of astonishment greeting the intercepted signal of detonation, the long-distance filming of Aldin's plunge in forgotten.

"Shock wave approaching. I'm pulling us back out of here in ninety seconds," the Xsarn Prime said, his voice filled with disgust.

"There goes Aldin's ship," Mari said, and Bukha felt as if he could actually pick up a note of regret in her voice, even as she snaked an arm around one of the Gaf berserkers as if seeking solace.

Bukha looked back up. The *Gamemaster II*, out of fuel and now tumbling out of control, continued a death plunge straight in toward the sun, which from this distance of nearly eighty million kilometers still appeared to be in existence.

"He's millions of kilometers further in," the Xsarn replied. "Shock wave will hit him any second."

"Corbin's coming around, the bastard's getting away," one of the minor Xsarn Kohs announced.

"What's happening?" Hassan screamed.

Corbin Gablona looked up, his stomach still in knots, a distant memory telling him just how much he hated jump-down beams.

This was wrong. The room around him was all wrong. Where was his float couch, the fine teak paneling, the plush two inches of carpet?

Where was his ship?

The battered interior of the *Gamemaster II*, that's what this was. There was another instant of memory, which was about all that time was now allowing. This was the old game ship of Aldin's, built to go to Earth to fetch Alexander—or was it Kubar Taug? Why am I here?

Hassan and the other assassins were crowded in the room with him. Gravity was gone, the ship must have lost power. He could feel the weightlessness. He was floating. Damn, how I hate weightlessness, he thought.

Hassan, holding on to a railing, was looking back at him, wide-eyed. And behind him the sun, growing impossibly small, getting dark.

Why would it get dark?

The last second before supernova, matter rushing in at nearly light-speed before the detonation, that's why it would be dark, he realized.

"We're on the wrong ship!" Hassan screamed. "We've been jumped to their ship!"

It was a joke, a wonderful, incredible joke.

A box floated before him. It was curious, beautiful, as if space itself were contained within it, and he reached out with chubby hands to grab hold of it, pulling it in to his chest.

Corbin Gablona threw back his head and laughed.

The viewport before him flashed with a billion degrees of heat, and at the same instant a micro-servo clicked within the box. Space itself opened up within the box, a doorway swinging open into another dimension, another universe, and a very different time.

Caught between fire and night, Corbin Gablona plunged through the gate, the first Human to travel to another dimension, Hassan, the assassins, the *Gamemaster II*, the supernova, all rushing to join him.

"Hell of a nice ship," Aldin said, exhaling slowly.

Forcing a wan smile, he looked around the room. They were all here, including the First Traveler machine.

"Talk about a deus ex machina intervention," Yaroslav

quipped, standing up with wobbling legs to go over to the side-
board to look for a drink.

"Has the convention of surrender been fulfilled?" Wellington
asked, looking over at Napoleon. "Perceiving that you were
about to crash, I exchanged your existence aboard your ship with
those aboard the one in pursuit and then activated the device.
As a friendly gesture I brought your friends and staff along as
well."

Napoleon looked over at Aldin and grinned.

"A final custom is to escort an exchanged prisoner back to
his border with full military honors," Napoleon finally said.
"Yes, you have done your duty well."

"That is sufficient, then."

Aldin looked up at the screen. It was hard to tell what was
happening. They were pulling away from the sun, and from this
distance it still appeared to be in the final seconds of presuper-
nova. It would be a close race to get out of the way of the shock
wave.

A drone shot past in the opposite direction from the ship he
assumed must be Bukha's.

Aldin punched up the commlink.

"Bukha Taug?"

"Larice?"

"Who else?" Aldin replied.

He could hear whoops of delight from the other end and then
shouts of disgust.

"The Xsarn must have been a little too happy," Tia said,
shaking her head.

A shouted argument broke out in the background, the news
crew fighting to gain the commlink for an interview, not at all
understanding just what was going on.

The drone continued to plunge in and then halted and started
to back outward.

But there was no shock wave.

Curious, Aldin looked up at the monitor, which was locked
onto the holo camera of the drone.

Finally there was a flash, a mild burst of radiation, and the system disappeared.

"It was late," the Xsarn shouted. "The shock wave should have hit the drone some three seconds before it did. It's slowing down."

"You activated the device?" Yaroslav asked, looking over at the First Traveler.

"As intended."

"It'll be a hell of a show if we can ever record it," Yaroslav said, "but I still advise we get out of here for right now. The system went supernova, and then he opened the other half of the wormhole, an exit point. The entire damn thing is getting sucked into another universe, and if we're still loitering here we might get sucked in as well before the other half of the machine gets pulled through and disappears."

The enormity of what they had actually pulled off finally started to settle in on Aldin, and he motioned for Yaroslav to bring a drink over.

"You heard it here first," Aldin said, knowing that within seconds it would be getting broadcast throughout the Cloud. "The crisis is over. Now let's get the hell out of here."

He shut the link off, and with Oishi pushing them up to the transit jump they followed Bukha out of the system.

Yaroslav turned and looked back at Napoleon and then at Wellington, who floated in the middle of the room.

"A near run thing," Wellington said dryly. "Upon my soul, a very near run thing, indeed."

CHAPTER 14

"SO I GUESS THIS IS GOOD-BYE, FOR NOW," ALDIN SAID, UNABLE to keep a slight tremble of emotion out of his voice.

Napoleon looked at him and smiled.

"What place is there for me in your worlds?" he replied.

"Your administrative talents, they're legendary. We could use you."

Napoleon laughed softly.

"In your worlds, not mine," he said with a mock-haughty tone. "Though I hate that race, their poet Milton had summed such things up well enough."

Aldin nodded sadly. The slow, leisurely cruise back to the Sphere had been fascinating. Napoleon had held forth throughout the trip, recounting his adventures, discussing his campaigns and dreams.

Aldin looked over at Yaroslav, who was decked out in the regalia of a marshal, baton in hand, Legion of Honor dangling from his chest.

"Take good care of the painting," he said, and nodded to the gilt-framed oil that dominated one wall of the cabin. The argument between Napoleon and him had gone nonstop for hours after the unveiling of the creation of one of the servobots, until Tia had finally settled it by calling it *The Heroes of Waterloo*. It was indeed done in the style of David, showing Napoleon, Yaroslav, and Basak, all looking magnified and imbued with martial valor, holding the line in the final moments of the battle against the Prussians.

"Come by in a couple of months and check on me. We might hate each other by then and I'll want to go home," Yaroslav said.

"We've still got to fight out the campaign after our victory at Waterloo," Napoleon interjected. "Wellington insisted upon it. The Russians and Austrians still need to be dealt with. It'll be more than a couple of months, and you're still chief of staff."

"As long as there's fighting, I'll stay," Basak chimed in, looking somewhat absurd in the uniform of a general of the Imperial Guard, the bearskin hat towering him to over ten feet in height.

"Just keep it a bit safer this time," Tia said.

"We've got the medical bay transferred down there," Yaroslav replied. "Wellington knows the rules about getting us into it if we're hurt."

"A decapitation from a cannonball is a bit hard to repair," Oishi said.

"Well, there's always a little risk, but that's what will make it exciting," the old philosopher replied. "Besides, if it was totally safe it wouldn't be real."

Aldin nodded and then punched the door open. The scent of fresh air wafted in, suddenly clouded with the sulfur stink of gunsmoke from a battery firing off a twenty-one-gun salute, the concussion causing Aldin to flinch.

As the last gun thundered, a band struck up "The Victory March of Marengo," and Napoleon stepped out of the ship. The vast pavilion, all the way to the pyramid, was lined with the serried ranks of the Imperial Guard, the men standing at attention.

"What glory still to be won," Napoleon said with a happy sigh, and looked back at Aldin.

"Maybe it is an illusion, my friend. But isn't that life, after all? I was dying, dreaming that I could somehow change my past. You know what I mean, you dream so hard it almost becomes real, but then there is always the tragedy of awaking at dawn. Well, it is dawn, and this looks real enough. And who is to say that those out there, my children, are not real as well? We can build an empire here in this new world. I will fight my wars, and perhaps there will be slightly less of a sin upon my soul if they die. We will build a new empire here and have it grow. Come back someday and you will see the truth of what I dreamed, but what the world was not yet ready for. I hope you will someday find such contentment as well.''

Aldin looked at him closely and smiled, unable to answer.

He wanted to shake the man's hand, but knew that somehow that would be inappropriate with an emperor. All he could do was smile and fumble a clumsy salute.

''Ah, if you ever want a command, just come here and you will know the thrill of victory.''

He stepped over to Tia. Taking her hand, he kissed it lightly, and then reached up and tugged her gently on the ear. He looked over at Oishi and flashed a smile.

''I hope you find peace, warrior, but never boredom. But with her I would truly doubt that.''

Putting his hands behind his back, he turned and walked down the entry plank and out onto the plaza.

''Well, can you blame me? The guy is kind of hard to resist,'' Yaroslav said almost apologetically. ''Stay out of trouble now, you won't have Yaroslav around to bail you out at the last second anymore.''

He put his hand up to rest on Basak's shoulder, and the two went down the plank after the emperor and then paused to look back.

''Don't forget to check back in. I think he might drive me crazy after all.''

They followed Napoleon out onto the square.

''Well, now what do we do?'' Bukha said, coming up to stand by Aldin.

He looked around at his companions, Tia and Oishi. They were happy as long as they were together, wherever that might be. He could go back to the Core for a while. After all, he was something of hero there now. The quiet negotiations with the Overseers, spiced with a good deal of blackmail of the Arch, had worked wonders. He had come to realize that they still needed the Overseers, and the story had finally been settled upon that in the end it was they who had stopped the supernova and that he and Corbin had wandered into the scene almost by accident. Of course, the entire war was blamed on Corbin.

The fact that Vush had been set up to be the Arch and that the old Arch was sitting out a long and lonely exile of contemplation had helped to settle things a bit as well, when the other Overseers had risen up in rebellion against their leader. The right documents were found in the end to exonerate Aldin and his companions and in fact set him up as something of a hero for helping Vush to find the device.

There was a status quo returning to the Cloud. Zola, as usual, had come out on the losing end. He had, of course, pleaded innocence with the little incident of the debris, but a complete bankruptcy from overinvesting in hundreds of now-worthless planets was punishment enough, Aldin realized. Zola was the laughingstock of the Cloud, owner of swamp and ice worlds purchased from Bukha at ten times their worth, while Bukha and Xsarn Prime, using the information gained from Xsarn Tertiary, had in turn made massive investments on the threatened worlds and picked up entire systems at a fraction of their worth. The richest Kohs had come out even richer.

Aldin looked back into the ship. It was pleasantly quiet. Mari had most of his assets and had taken off with one of the Gaf berserkers. It had hurt a bit, but the quiet was worth it. If it'd make her happy, which he doubted, then that was fine enough. Even Hobbs had come out ahead, since with Corbin gone, there were some family assets floating around with which he could rebuild his amusement emporium.

The music died away, and Napoleon stopped in front of the colors of the guard. He hesitated and then stepped up, taking the silken folds and embracing them.

"Soldiers, my children. Your emperor has returned!"

A thundering shout rose up to the heavens, and the ranks broke, the men pressing in around him, and he was lost to view.

Aldin looked over at Zergh, who was wiping tears from his eyes.

"Come on, let's get out of here."

"To do what?"

"I don't know," Aldin replied glumly. "We could retire, or maybe be vasbas again."

"You're still worth billions," Bukha interjected.

Aldin laughed sadly.

"So what."

Zergh stood silent, looking out across the field of celebration, and Aldin could see the longing in his eyes to join them. He knew that his oldest friend had no intention of leaving if he could avoid it.

From around the corner of the ship, Wellington appeared.

So this was the First Traveler after all, Aldin thought, somehow guessing the truth at last. Its programming was scrambled to be sure. He looked over at the mountain, the top of which had been blown off by the missile strikes, the outrush of air now double in volume.

The entire Sphere was winding down, though it'd be thousands, maybe tens of thousands of years before things got out of hand. And only this one surviving machine, a bit of a mad machine at that, to somehow keep it together. Someone would have to do something about it sooner or later if this magnificence was to be saved.

"The game's the thing," Wellington said, "reality an illusion, and the illusion reality."

Wellington tilted over as if to gaze into Aldin's eyes—and soul.

"Tell me, Aldin Larice, what do you dream for?" Wellington asked. "What worlds are there still for you to conquer or save?"

Suddenly, Aldin Larice smiled, finally discovering at last what he had been looking for all along.

About the Author

William R. Forstchen and his wife, Sharon, reside in West Lafayette, Indiana. He is currently finishing up a Ph.D. in American Military History at Purdue University.